A Flight of Green Parrots

"A great empire and little minds go ill together"
Edmund Burke
Eighteenth-century English statesman

BookSurge, LLC
North Charleston, South Carolina
Library of Congress Control Number: 2004113363

To order additional copies, please contact us.
BookSurge, LLC
www.booksurge.com
1-866-308-6235
orders@booksurge.com

A Flight of Green Parrots

Dipak Basu

2004

In loving memory of Shanti and SNA

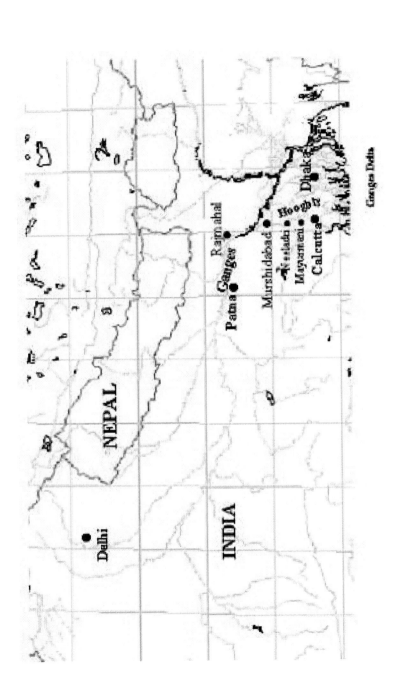

Ganges Delta

Delhi

NEPAL

INDIA

Patna
Ganges
Rajmahal
Murshidabad
Kasiadsi
Hooghly
Mayurneni
Dhaka
Calcutta

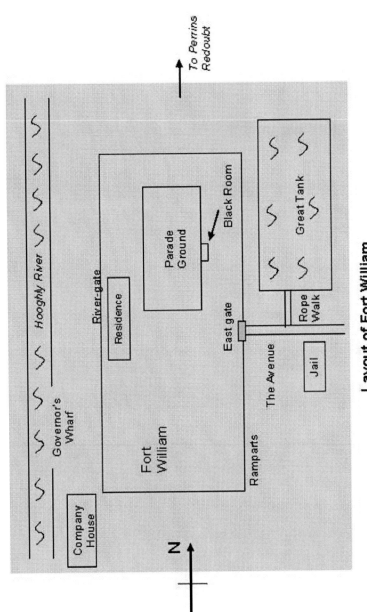

Layout of Fort William

Principal Characters

Frederick Wainwright	Naval captain
Pauline Wainwright	Wife of Frederick
Richard Armstrong	Governor of Fort William
Clarence Clarkson	Magistrate of Fort William
Col. Peter Linnington	Commander of Fort William
Angus McIver	Shipping Councilor
Dicky Glynnis	Army Lieutenant
Benjamin Morley	Trade Councilor
Ajoy Sena	Prince of Rajmahal
Maggie Clarkson	Wife of Clarence
The Jagat Seth	Banker of Bengal
Shiraj Doula	King of Bengal
Harihar Mullick	Headman of Mayurmani Village
Rahamat Khan	Commander of the Bengal Army
Badri Narayan	Minister at the King's Court
Bessie Armstrong	Daughter of Richard
Ashraf	Odd-job boy
Raja Ranjit Rai	Ruler of Neeladri
Aruna	Princess of Neeladri
Mujtaba	Palace Guard
Shipling	Army Ensign
Bracken	Master-gunner

The Black Hole

It was just after daybreak on June 20th 1756.

Under dark clouds in a lowering sky with the threat of monsoon rain, a palace guard of the Bengal Army was trying to push open the iron door to a makeshift prison cell inside a battle-scarred fortress.

Devastation of war lay all around him.

The guard was surprised at the effort it was taking him to get the door open, for he was unaware of the bodies massed behind it.

With the help of hastily summoned colleagues, the guard at last got the door open and stood back aghast as twenty-two men and one woman staggered out or were helped from the cell, only to be overwhelmed by the abundant morning air and collapse on debris-strewn grass of the fort's parade-ground.

The released prisoners left one hundred and twenty-three dead behind.

Chapter 1

It had been snowing heavily in the east of England on a January afternoon of that same year when Captain Frederick Wainwright of the Royal Navy and Viscount of Ipswich, returned unexpectedly from the Russian War and made a startling announcement.

"Pauline," said the captain. "We are going to India."

His wife went rigid with shock and stared at him in horror.

They had been married for just over a year and seen little of each other during that time. Pauline, pretty, golden-haired and only sixteen, expecting news of the front and of her husband's voyage from Murmansk, was staggered by the unexpectedness and finality of his statement.

"*Where?*" she exclaimed in confusion. "To *India?* What on earth for? I don't want to go to India, Freddie."

Captain Wainwright was twice her age and had been fighting Russians in the Arctic for a long time. When the handsome officer with his craggy face and glittering decorations first appeared at their home and asked her father for her hand, young Pauline had been completely swept away. His finely tailored uniform, his serious aristocratic good looks, and his well-known naval achievements cast him as a fairy-tale suitor to the uncomplicated and impressionable girl. Not knowing then that she was part of a financial package that involved Father's land and long-standing debt, Pauline had readily said yes. To her dismay Freddie had left almost immediately after the wedding to be in the Arctic with his men – until his return today. Freddie's parents were both dead and Pauline had whiled away the months in the company of a deaf aunt in cold and drafty Wainwright Manor.

"Listen to me now," Freddie said as though to a child. "I have left the Navy and I have accepted a Master's commission on the merchant gunboat, *Europa.* Do you understand? The East India Company has assigned this ship to Calcutta and to Canton. Since it is a permanent peacetime posting, you *will* accompany me. Uncle William will arrive shortly from Canterbury to manage the estate. It is all decided."

Pauline was speechless.

She had not even got over the shock of Freddie's sudden return. And here he was asking her to go to…to India. *India!* What else had he said? Calcutta? Canton? The unfamiliar place names meant nothing to her. She vaguely remembered hearing of Calcutta as a disease-ridden swamp where black heathens performed pagan rites and Canton as a teeming city where all manner of creatures were eaten. Those places were at the other end of the earth. Why was this happening to her?

Then a thought struck her.

"Freddie, why have you left the Navy?"

The captain was silent and looked out at the falling snow. The winter wind whistled among the eaves while Pauline tried to recoup her scattered senses. Then Freddie replied in his resonant upper-class voice, weighing each word carefully.

"Pauline, my health no longer warrants the turmoil of battle. I have had a few turns. Moments of severe strain. Commercial shipping is more amenable, although East Indiamen have their own complement of guns. And anyway, *Europa* sails in a month."

Freddie continued to talk but Pauline did not hear the rest of his explanation and after a while he left her.

The farewell parties at Wainwright Manor passed in a blur. Pauline had a vague recollection of packing her clothes and of the subsequent coach trip south to Portsmouth harbor to embark on the long voyage.

***

During the weeks at sea aboard their ship, *Europa,* Freddie and Pauline rarely exchanged words. Every night after desultory supper conversation with officers and passengers, they retired to the master's cabin in the ship's sterncastle. Pauline would lie wide-eyed in the lamplight while Freddie sat at his desk and studied reports and charts. Around midnight Freddie went out on deck to check the watch and have a last smoke. When he came back Pauline would be asleep. Freddie would turn the lamp to a glimmer and lie on the other side of the bed, not touching her – a million miles away. The pattern repeated every night as first one month, and then another, slid by. During the early part of the journey, northerly winter gales lashed the ship and continuous seasickness assailed Pauline. It grew warm as they entered tropical latitudes and sailed south with the antipodal summer along the west coast of Africa. They rounded the Cape of Good Hope and met heavy seas of the Indian Ocean and still Pauline suffered from nausea abetted by sultry heat and continuous pitch and roll of the ship. She managed to keep her sanity only by thinking that one day this trial would end, and whatever waited in store for her, even in India, had to be better than the emptiness of the sea and the proximity of her husband.

The voyage continued.

Chapter 2

A pitiless March sun blazed down on a large and unhealthy town that was to be journey's end for Pauline.

Mid-eighteenth-century Calcutta was a burgeoning market community in eastern India. Since its founding fifty years ago out of three adjacent villages separated by a marshy swamp, Calcutta had rapidly become the apex of England's trade in the Orient. In spite of its adverse climate, Calcutta's commerce had attracted large numbers of Europeans from England, France, Portugal and Holland, as well as Arabs, Persians, Armenians, Afghans and Chinese.

On Calcutta's western edge a large fortress raised its ramparts above a sluggish mud-brown river. This was Fort William, a garrison that sheltered several hundred British men and women and a multitude of camp-followers.

The river was the Hooghly.

In the darkened Residence of the fort a fat harried man sat perspiring at his desk and stared moodily at a scroll of wilting parchment.

Richard Armstrong lived his life believing that his role as Governor of Fort William, the English East India Company's most important outpost in the Orient, was a vitally important one. This was true to a large extent. Key decisions on execution and expansion of trade were his to make. A world away in London, the East India Company's Court of Directors was influenced in its thinking by his flowery reports.

Armstrong was a short man in his early forties. He was overweight, balding and forever suffering from heat and dust. He had been employed for over twenty-five years in the Company's service and his elevation two years ago to the post of acting Governor, was due more to seniority than to any brilliance on his part. However, for reasons nobody could understand, his appointment had never been confirmed. As a result, Armstrong went to extreme lengths to instill his authority. Consequently, his subordinates disliked him immensely.

Drops of perspiration from Armstrong's forehead dripped onto the scroll in front of him. The message it contained was written in triangular Bengali script which he did not comprehend. But the ornate flourishes and flamboyant colors and seals left no doubt about the origin of the communiqué. The scroll had been delivered to the Governor personally by the ambassador of the new King of Bengal.

The twenty-year-old ruler of the enormous province of Bengal held the royal Persian title of *Nawab*. He had ascended the throne a few months ago, having emerged as the unexpected victor of palace intrigue and infighting caused by the death of his grandfather. His full name was *Shiraj-ud-doula*, which literally translated meant 'Lamp of the World'. Shiraj's personality was always described in extreme and conflicting terms: cruel, pious, despotic, brilliant, egotistic, charismatic and insane. Thus it was no wonder that the Nawab was a complete enigma to the Englishmen of the fort.

Next to the scroll on Armstrong's desk lay a sheet of paper on which his Armenian interpreter, George Hartunian, had prepared a translation. The Governor studied the tortured composition and tried to decide on a course of action.

The translation read:

Allah is Great
[Royal Seal of the Nawab of Bengal]

To the Most Honorable Governor
The English East India Company
Fort William, Calcutta

Your Illustrious Excellency,
May the grace of Allah, the all-merciful, keep yourself, your family, your colleagues, and your glorious King in good health and prosperity until the very end of time.

It is the Nawab's most unfortunate duty to inform Your Excellency that the English traders of Calcutta, while they have been bequeathed land upon the benevolence of my wise and all-seeing grandfather, the late great Alivardi Khan Sahib, they have nevertheless built and are now fortifying defenses all around the town.

What need is there of the English for fortified defenses when royal troops of the Bengal Army remain ever vigilant for their protection?

Now therefore, it would please the Nawab much and prove seemly an attitude for a foreign trading company, if such defenses were immediately and completely demolished and the Royal Ambassador invited to certify the same.

It would further please the Nawab if the English acquiescence to this edict was returned by the messenger who carried it to your Excellency.

It is needless to add that this request is reasonable and delay in the execution of this edict will cause the Nawab's greatest displeasure.

Shah-en-shah Nawab Shiraj-ud-Doula
Moghul Overlord of Bengal, Bihar and Orissa

Later that evening, when the heat had marginally abated,

the Executive Council of Fort William met to review the Nawab's edict and formulate an appropriate response.

The Council was composed of nine men. They were Governor Armstrong; Magistrate Clarence Clarkson; Colonel Peter Linnington, commander of the garrison; Angus McIver, supervisor of shipping; Benjamin Morley, supervisor of trade; John Wolfe, warehouse keeper; Captain Muldoon, supervisor of the armory; Matthew Broderick, paymaster; and Stanislaus Kyle, engineer.

McIver, Morley and Wolfe held titles of Councilor, a rank below Governor. McIver was seniormost of the three.

At today's meeting there were two members absent. Morley was hunting big game. Wolfe could not be found.

The Council went through stages of horror, disbelief and outrage regarding the Nawab's intentions—and then dissolved into its normal mode of operation: endless controversy over real and hypothetical issues.

Angus McIver demanded a peremptory strike on the Nawab – to teach him a lesson. The Colonel impatiently enquired how this could be achieved by their miniscule force against thousands of the Nawab's soldiers. They argued this for an hour. Then Armstrong asked for status of the defenses that Shiraj wanted destroyed. Engineer Kyle explained that the fortification in question, known as the Maratha Ditch, was a 25-mile-long trench that formed a rough semi-circle around Calcutta, encompassed the fort, and ended at the Hooghly River at both its northern and southern ends. It had been dug a decade ago as a barrier against marauding Maratha bandits from the west. Kyle informed the Council that the trench had never been completed and was nowhere more than six feet deep. Since it was not actually connected to the river, it did not act as the moat it was designed to be. Over the years it had degenerated into a public dump for refuse and excreta.

A debate developed about the efficacy of the Maratha Ditch.

The grandfatherly magistrate—the hand on which his cheek rested beginning to ache—woke up after another hour. Clarence Clarkson despised these pointless discussions and had become adept at dozing off when they raged around him.

"Why the devil don't we tell the Nabob the ditch's not a defense and all go for supper?" he asked peevishly.

"Ah yes, the Nabob," remembered Armstrong. "Got to reply to the Nabob. Y'know gentlemen, he's got cheek, the fellow, issuing an 'edict'. Hah!"

"You tell him, Guv'nor!" McIver breathed Scottish fire. "Got to keep them natives in line."

Angus McIver was always irascible. Clarkson tried to placate him.

"We have enough troubles with the Nabob's taxes and river tolls, Mac. Why antagonize the fellow more?"

"Nonsense!" interjected Captain Muldoon, a self-confessed alcoholic. "Can't have petty despots dictating to us. Got to teach them a thing or two. Right, Guv'nor?"

Armstrong smiled and nodded. He liked to teach people a thing or two. Fresh in his memory was the tongue-lashing he had had received from the youthful Nawab during his recent ascension ceremony in the capital city of Murshidabad. Richard Armstrong hated the man profoundly.

***

Two hours later the Nawab's ambassador was handed a sealed letter. It read:

His Highness Shiraj Doula
Nabob of Bengal
Murshidabad

Written on this tenth day of March of the Sixteenth year of the Reign of our Sovereign Lord George the Second, by the Grace of God King of Great Britain, ye Anno Dom 1756.

Your Highness,

The Executive Council of Fort William is honored to have received your epistle.

This Council has deliberated extensively upon the actions of which you are desirous. It would be most gratifying if this Council were able to comply with your esteemed edict. However it humbly begs pardon of your Highness for its inability to so comply.

This Council respectfully puts forth its reasoning. The two Crowns of England and France have lately been at War among themselves. Quite contrary to the neutrality promised by the Great Moghul in Delhi, the French Nation has in the past attacked and taken the Towne of Madras to the south. The Crowns are thus imminent of another War between them in the land of India.

This Council is apprehensive of the French, who reside but a few miles upstream, attacking our position in Calcutta on the account of such War. In our desire to prevent Calcutta succumbing to the French enemy, we wish to repair and strengthen the guns of Fort William on the water-side. Your leave to such will oblige greatly.

Your most obedient servant,
Richard Armstrong,
Governor.

***

Richard Armstrong, who comforted himself with the thought that he was an important person in England's premier trading company, would never know how monumental an impact his petulant letter to the King of Bengal would have on the history of the world.

Chapter 3

On the fateful night at the end of the second month of the voyage, it was especially humid and still. *Europa's* limp sails drooped on yardarms while the ship lay in dead calm just above the equator and south of the island of Ceylon.

Pauline found it stifling in the cabin.

Despite the absence of motion, the ever-present butterflies in her stomach threatened to come to the surface. When Freddie went out for his customary midnight cheroot, Pauline, unable to suffer any longer, decided to go up for air herself. She pulled a thin shawl over her shoulders, emerged through the sterncastle opening and stood for a moment, gratefully breathing in the salty turgid tropical air. The feeling of seasickness lessened. She relaxed and walked across the deck and looked out over the gunwale.

There was no moon. A few stars appeared between clouds and faintly lightened the gloom. Pauline knew land was near but invisible in the murk. Below her, in the blackness that was the sea, puffs of emerald phosphorescence gleamed eerily.

Pauline looked around the ship. There was no one near. Far away in the direction of the bows she made out a red glimmer that had to be the tip of a glowing cigar. That must be Freddie. She looked back at the inky water and wondered what it would be like to end it all by throwing herself into it. What had happened to her marriage? To her life? Was she being punished by God for the happiness of the first fifteen years that she cherished? Would she have fun again? She had forgotten what fun was. Fun was a lifetime ago. Now she was married. Married right and proper as her ex-beau, Robert, had pointed out with chilling innocence. How she missed Robert now, the sweet-natured baker's son, who had once thought the world of her and promised to be there for her always. But that was before Freddie arrived in his shiny carriage. Where was Robert at this moment? Was he still...

Without warning there was a shuffling sound from close at hand.

Pauline swung around and stared at a large dark mass beside the gunwale about thirty feet away from her. From daylight she knew it to be a shrouded whaleboat. The sound was coming from its direction. And as she watched, the cover of the whaleboat shook and from under it, as if by magic, rose a ghostly figure. It vaulted unsteadily onto the deck and began to walk toward her. Stifling a scream, Pauline instinctively sank down to her haunches and became invisible against the gunwale. The figure came closer. In spite of the darkness she realized from its gait and height that it was her husband.

What in Heaven's name was Freddie doing inside a whaleboat in the middle of the night?

Suddenly her attention was diverted by another sound and the cover of the whaleboat shook again and a second shadowy figure forced its way over the edge.

Pauline's mouth went dry.

At once she knew the answer to the question that had beleaguered her for months – why Freddie had ignored her. It was a woman! A *kept* woman. So that was it. Strangely, she felt no outrage. She knew after a year that Freddie had no interest in her and had married her for her father's land. She disliked him so completely that another outrage made no difference.

Whoever his harlot was could have him. She felt unclean and an unwilling participant in a cheap drama. But she also felt an overwhelming desire to find out who the woman was. There were only four other females on board, all passengers, and only Millicent Rae was young and unmarried.

Did Freddie know Millicent before leaving England? Did he have a long-standing affair with her?

Freddie came closer, unaware of her proximity, and passed on toward the bows, lighting a cigar with a match that he struck against a barrel. Luckily, he was past her when the match flared and did not see her. Pauline looked back at the whaleboat. Freddie's woman still stood against it, hanging on to its side as though for support. Pauline felt dizzy. An awful vision came to her of her husband and Millicent Rae thrashing about in stifling darkness among the thwarts of the whaleboat.

Pauline stayed crouched as she was, turned to stone.

At last the woman started to walk slowly toward her. She was dressed like a sailor. She staggered once and Pauline thought she might collapse onto the deck. But she recovered and continued walking.

The figure came closer. The smell of rum wafted in advance of it. Her nose wrinkling, Pauline looked closely from her hiding place. And then the hair on her arms and neck rose and a cold chill traveled down her spine.

It was not Millicent Rae.

It was not any of the other women aboard the ship.

It was not the figure of a woman at all.

It was the figure of a man.

Pauline crouched frozen as the drunken sailor reeled away toward a hatch cover and went below. Then she jumped to her feet and hung over the gunwale retching uncontrollably into the black waters of the Indian Ocean.

Chapter 4

25th March 1756 was a landmark day for at Fort William.

A batch of new additions to the growing English community in Bengal had just arrived. More importantly, the legendary Governor of Fort St. George, Colonel Robert Clive, was in temporary residence at the fort.

Richard Armstrong had ordered all stops be pulled out in his effort to impress his famous visitor. Tonight's reception would be the most opulent in the drab social fabric of Fort William. To mark the occasion the Company's staff and invitees appeared resplendent in their most formal attire. For those arrived after their long voyage on *Europa,* it was their initiation into the community.

Armstrong beamed like a happy gnome as he surveyed the festive transformation of the normally prosaic Residence. Lamplight from Venetian chandeliers and Tudor candelabra lit up the large hall and the freshly polished dance floor. A jaunty Welsh lieutenant, Dicky Glynnis, was singing. Clarence Clarkson, the Company's bespectacled and silver-haired magistrate, accompanied Dicky on a Queen Anne piano that had been lovingly preserved during its sea voyage from Winchester. Three ships' fiddlers and a cymbalist kept them company.

Luxurious fashions were the rage of the times. On the dance floor, men were dressed in fine velvet frock coats and breeches, augmented by silk stockings, ruffled shirts and neck cloths. Many wore waistcoats with gold brocade and had stone buckles on their boots. The men and women who danced were all European. Some of the younger soldiers and junior employees of the Company had brought Indian women to the reception. These women did not dance and gazed spellbound at those who did. And no wonder! Armstrong's reception offered the ladies of Fort William a rare opportunity to display their latest and best, and the most audacious riveted attention with sleeveless, strapless and backless gowns that against all laws of nature still managed to conceal. An abundance of neck, shoulder and bosom was on display, with the rest of feminine anatomy encased in flowing Mantua or mohair silk, Scottish plaid, Geneva velvet or Norwich crepe.

Armstrong had commanded his taproom to release generous quantities of whisky for the men and gin for the women. This, coupled with welcome reduction in heat due to an afternoon storm, enlivened the party. Couples on the dance-floor whirled and bobbed in abandon.

Dicky had a fine tenor voice and was weighing into Boswell's latest craze, *A Matrimonial Thought,* set to music by Garrick. With piano, violin and cymbals in spirited support, Dicky sang:

> *"In the blithe days of honeymoon,*
> *With Kate's allurements smitten,*
> *I lov'd her late, I loved her soon,*
> *And call'd her dearest kitten.*
>
> *But now my kitten's grown a cat,*
> *And cross like other wives,*
> *O! by my soul, my honest Mat,*
> *I fear she has nine lives."*

Dicky ended with a flourish and the crowd applauded enthusiastically. Drinks were replenished. The hum of conversation was punctuated with bursts of laughter.

Armstrong, with Clive at his side, looked around with a benign smile. His smile vanished as two newcomers appeared at the entrance and were announced into the ballroom.

Benjamin Morley was clad in quiet elegance that bespoke his English nobility. A merchant by choice and an explorer by passion was the way Benjamin liked to describe himself. He was also an aristocrat, second in line to the earldom of Ashford in the English county of Kent. He was a tall, blond, strongly-muscled man, twenty-three years old, deeply browned by the relentless Indian sun. Those who knew him said he was a hopeless idealist and a conspicuous exception amid the commercialization and corruption that plagued the Company. And if they were of the opposite sex they might add that Benjamin was one of the most eligible English bachelors in the East.

At Benjamin's side Armstrong saw the Indian prince, Ajoy Sena of Rajmahal, a tall dark man in his late twenties, dressed in a magnificent robe of creamy silk that was offset by a pink cummerbund and a cream turban with a glittering diamond set in its center. Armstrong, his Yorkshire origins humble, involuntarily looked for a sword at the prince's side but found none.

The arrival of the two handsome men caused a silence and then a flutter of talk, especially among the women.

Armstrong's frown deepened.

He did not like his Trade Councilor, but he had to grudgingly admit that the young fellow was remarkably efficient. His knowledge of local politics, languages and customs and his network of contacts among the disparate power *blocs* of the region, made him an invaluable asset to the Company. Unfortunately, he was so straitlaced and idealistic that it made him a nuisance during discussions of the many private profiteering schemes that the members of the Executive Council had underway. But Morley's father was an earl and a senior director of the Company to boot, all of which did not leave even the Governor of Bengal latitude in dealing with him.

Armstrong transferred his attention to the native prince and shuddered. He had met the man recently and immediately disliked him with a vengeance. Armstrong was convinced that as an Indian, albeit a royal one, Sena was given far too much attention and importance by Morley. The man's flamboyance, his unnatural way of talking, his politicking and his habitual criticism of the King of Bengal, irritated and confused Armstrong. He was not a man given to strategic thinking and his personal dislike prevented him from appreciating the prince's potential as a counterweight to the Nawab's mounting threat.

Benjamin caught sight of Armstrong across the crowded floor and the Governor of Fort William had to switch his smile back on and nod affably to his deputy and his unwelcome guest as they strolled across. Turning to Clive he said, "Your Excellency, may I present our Trade Councilor, the Honorable Benjamin Morley of Ashford, a rising member of one of England's most illustrious families?"

Colonel Clive shook Benjamin's hand.

"How are you, Morley? Glad to meet you. I know your father."

Robert Clive's voice was strong and decisive. Benjamin carefully studied the great man whom he admired but had never met. The Governor of Fort St. George, near Madras in Southern India, was a portly and commanding personage who looked much older than his twenty-eight years. He had a mature and composed face that was accentuated by an aquiline nose and strangely penetrating eyes. He was dressed in refined style in maroon velvet frock coat, fawn-colored breeches and a waistcoat from which emerged the ruffles of his neck and sleeves. From humble beginnings in Shropshire where, as one of thirteen siblings, he had been packed off to clerk in India, Clive had progressed incredibly fast up the Company's ranks in twelve years in his adopted land. His primary claim to fame was the 1752 Siege of Arcot, when heavily outnumbered, British forces had refused to capitulate, first defying and then driving off their French and Indian assailants in contravention of all the laws of war. During that engagement, Clive, a lowly clerk, leading a small band of native soldiers, displayed superhuman stamina, an ability to think on his feet, and to maintain a principle of audacity at all times. From that moment of glory Clive had never looked back and unlike most successful expatriate merchants, he had not returned to the Home Office, but stayed on in the East.

His scrutiny complete, Benjamin bowed and said, "I am quite well, sir. I have heard so much about you. It is a great honor to meet you at last. I do hope you will stay awhile." He felt Ajoy stir and hastened to introduce his companion. "Sir, I would like permission to introduce my good friend, His Highness Ajoy Sena, Prince of Rajmahal, whose ancestors ruled Eastern India from the north bank of the Hooghly until the Moghuls came to power."

Clive thoughtfully studied the Indian prince. He seemed to like what he saw and said with diplomatic aplomb, "Your Highness, I hear you were dispossessed by the Moghuls. When was it that your family ruled Bengal?"

Prince Ajoy Sena was the stormy petrel of Indian politics. An avowed adversary of the Moghul Nawabs, he was frequently accused of treason. Only taxes from his rich domain and the support of several local warlords kept him from imprisonment and execution during Shiraj Doula's grandfather, Alivardi Khan's reign. With the emergence of Shiraj as King of Bengal his sands had run out and he became a hunted fugitive under protection of the British. Ajoy's English language skills were very uncertain, but were compensated by his natural brilliance as an orator. Coincidentally, Clive's question had broached his favorite subject. So with a glitter in his eye and a ring in his voice, Ajoy launched into a narrative of bygone Sena wars of the 12th and 13th centuries.

Benjamin, who had heard it all before, looked across at the assembled guests who were now gravitating to tables covered with sailcloth and laid with Wedgwood china. Liveried and turbaned waiters were filing in with tureens of soup. Benjamin had learned that among the arrivals on *Europa,* was its captain, Freddie Wainwright, a friend of his elder brother, Christopher. Old Chris's letter that had also arrived on *Europa,* said that Wainwright was an ex-naval officer who had risen rapidly during the war with Russia and taken early discharge on account of health problems. He had then accepted a commission in the less demanding world of commercial shipping and had been appointed master of the East Indiaman, *Europa.* Arriving in Calcutta with Wainwright, Chris wrote, would be his wife, Pauline.

Among the packed crowd of uniformed men, Benjamin tried unsuccessfully to make out which one was Wainwright, so he began the always pleasant task of appraising the women. Of the fifty or so present tonight, only five were Indian and wore voluminous gold-threaded *saris* draped around themselves. Benjamin studied them closely for a moment. He knew two to be wives of English clerks, who were disparagingly referred to as having 'gone native'. Junior merchants had invited the others from among the flotsam that formed concentric social classes around the English community. Not one of the handful of invited Indian dignitaries had brought their wives. Benjamin knew this was to be expected. High-class Hindus and Muslims alike dictated their women be shielded from eyes of foreigners.

Benjamin's attention returned to the European ladies. They were predominantly young wives or sisters of Company merchants and soldiers who had had made the difficult decision to leave the security and comforts of Britain to make a home for their men in a distant land with an uncertain future. There were a few unattached women who had come east on missionary zeal or to snare a husband. They knew Benjamin and boldly returned his scrutiny. One pretty thing actually fluttered her lashes at him. Benjamin, always susceptible to feminine charm, smiled back. Sipping his whisky, he had begun to assess the night's possibilities when he became aware the visiting dignitary was speaking to him.

"...the whole country is rife with your exploits..."

With an inward sigh Benjamin switched his mind back. Now what had Armstrong told Clive?

Clive gave him his cue.

"Morley, I hear you matched the nabob's tax increase for silk with a price increase for our wool. Good man! Shows courage. Trouble with taxes rears its ugly head once again, eh?" Seeing Benjamin's rueful expression he added, "It's the same old story the world over."

Discussing the obstacles to profitable trade on account of local payoffs, the four men moved in the direction of the table of honor. Armstrong's solemn wife, Martha, joined them on the way. Those already assembled at the table, and who had not sat down in deference to the guest of honor, were a strange combination.

A very thin and exotic-looking man, dressed in the garb of a devout Muslim, was moodily studying the silverware. His name was Hazrat Sayyid Naseer. He was the ambassador of Nawab Shiraj Doula in Calcutta.

A roly-poly Indian, the fabulously rich banker of Bengal, known only by his title, the Jagat Seth, was smiling ingratiatingly. He wore a flowing and rose-scented starchy-white costume and displayed teeth that were discolored by betel juice.

Standing beside him were the Company magistrate, Clarence Clarkson, and his motherly wife, Maggie.

On the opposite side of the table a pallid Colonel Linnington waited with his sultry Latin wife, Leonora.

And in a far corner, looking awed, were the newly-arrived Captain and Mrs. Wainwright.

Richard Armstrong introduced the Wainwrights. Benjamin hurried over and warmly shook hands with his brother's friend and was impressed by his dashing appearance. He noted the captain's erect frame, the high collar and ruffled shirt under the master's jacket, the line of brass buttons down the sides of his breeches and the shining buckles on his boots. A craggy and weather-beaten face reinforced by a supercilious nose added to his commanding mien. He did not look ill as his brother's letter had suggested. Benjamin briefly wondered what had made him take discharge from the Navy.

Then he turned to greet the captain's wife and involuntarily sucked in his breath. *Good God!* he almost said aloud. *She's gorgeous!*

Benjamin, who could usually control his emotions, gaped in open admiration at the stunning young woman. Her golden hair was piled under a delicate hat and innumerable little ringlets framed her oval face and perfectly etched features. Her riveting eyes were cornflower blue with dark pupils that were unnaturally dilated. Then, without knowing it, he was looking down her slender silk-encased form. His eyes, with a complete will of their own, moved over the wide expanse of soft white skin above the low neckline and the impudent mounds below, and on down the narrow waist. His mind whirled and he felt a stirring in his veins. Then he looked up and their eyes met and Benjamin found himself drawn into limpid pools that were at once tempestuous yet filled with a haunting sadness.

Oh hell! he thought. *What* is *this?*

As he touched her limp fingers and let them go he had the feeling there was something profoundly unnerving and unbalanced in the personality of this striking woman.

Armstrong, the jovial host, came to his rescue.

"Well, well, well! Let's sit down. Let's sit down. Soup's getting cold."

Benjamin sat between Martha Armstrong and the Indian banker. He looked across once more at Mrs. Wainwright, still overcome by the powerful influence she had had on him. But she was not looking at him and was answering a question from Colonel Linnington. With difficulty Benjamin concentrated on breaking the crease in his napkin and tried to bring his mind back to affairs of state. He looked slowly around the table and took in the diners one by one.

At Benjamin's insistence, Armstrong had departed from long-standing policy and invited native dignitaries to an official British reception. As everyone settled and Armstrong dominated the first round of conversation, Benjamin gave rein to his habit of thumbnail-sketching people.

What forces are at play here tonight, he told himself, *what adversaries! What studies in contrast!*

...Wainwright seems a strong and capable fellow, but is his extraordinary wife sending a distress signal?

...Old Armstrong wishes me perdition because I audit his books and limit his personal gain, yet I help him through decisions over which he would otherwise stew forever. I'll bet my boots his term of duty is almost over. Now which one of us will fill his boots?

...All of us in the Company abhor the Nawab's practice of taxing us to death and forcing us to go to this fat banker who exchanges our Spanish dollars for Moghul mohars at cutthroat rates.

...Ambassador Naseer and Prince Ajoy, deadliest of enemies! The Nabob will hear of Ajoy's presence at Fort William by tomorrow and there will be hell to pay. There's a revolution brewing. Should we side with the Senas? What if they lose? How will the Nawab react?...

...Colonel Linnington and Governor Armstrong, our warring behemoths! The soldier and the trader. Jockeying to demonstrate who's king of the hill. The garrison's Punch and Judy show!

...Magistrate Clarkson and dear old Maggie. Bless them. May he always play the piano and advise us on finances while she bakes her crumpets and lends a sympathetic ear.

...Here we all are, blood foes at the waterhole, sipping long drinks, exchanging pleasantries without a care in the world!

***

Benjamin tuned back to the conversation.

"...Your Excellency," Clive was saying. "Would you be so kind as to tell us about your ruler?"

Hazrat Sayyid Naseer was a dark and emaciated man— almost a skeleton. His hair and regulation four-finger beard were a curious mixture of iron-gray and orange. He was dressed in a flowing emerald tunic known as a *sherwani*. Over it he wore a black waistcoat and under it tight black trousers. His orange hair was surmounted by a tasseled yellow fez. All through the preliminaries he had been completely silent. At Clive's question and to everyone's astonishment, he sat up straight and began speaking in a deep rumbling voice—*in Persian!*

No one understood.

Naseer continued for a few moments before he seemed to realize this and stopped. He looked around disdainfully at his audience that was ignorant of the language of the royal Moghul courts and abruptly switched to rapid and flowery Bengali. Benjamin had a rudimentary grasp of the language but his capabilities quickly fell behind. It was the banker who saved the day.

"Nawabzada Shiraj Doula, gloriously omnipotent ruler of the great domains of Bengal, Bihar and Orissa, representative of the illustrious Sultanate in Delhi, sends you heartfelt greetings," translated the Jagat Seth. "He waxes confident that the English, French and Dutch traders in his kingdom will engage in commerce in continued harmony in this, our corner of paradise."

The others gazed at the two Indians, one thin as a rake, the other round as a ball. Trained in practical affairs of seafaring and commerce, unfamiliar with lofty verbiage, they listened spellbound while diplomat and capitalist continued the drum roll of hyperbole.

Meanwhile, dinner was served with care to satisfy the variety of preferences. To Prince Ajoy, a Hindu, beef was sacrilege. To Sayyid Naseer, a Muslim, pork was the product of an unclean animal. To the Jagat Seth, a Jain, all animals were God's inviolate creatures. Linnington, recovering from an attack of dysentery, was able to eat only the blandest of foods.

As they ate, Ambassador Naseer painted a lustrous canvas of mutually cooperative international enterprise under the benevolent tutelage of the Nawab. Benjamin and Ajoy, striving to read between the lines, found veiled threats, satirical jibes and attempts to play the foreign communities against one another. As the ambassador wound down, the men impatiently waited for the opportunity to debate. But Maggie Clarkson, perceptive as always and sensing tempers rising, forestalled and diverted the talk to less dangerous waters. The conversation moved to quality and variety of silk in the markets of Patna and Canton. Maggie and Leonora Linnington, now in their element, held the table together by encouraging small talk until the end of dinner. Martha Armstrong remained characteristically silent. The Wainwrights, new to the environment, said nothing, but Benjamin was surprised to see Pauline listen with attention to the ambassador's diatribe, and actually nod in agreement during parts of the wretched man's speech. How fascinating! He examined her surreptitiously and discovered to his surprise that she was a good deal younger than he had first thought. Why, she must be just seventeen or eighteen!

After dishes were cleared, Richard Armstrong delivered a speech welcoming Colonel Clive to Calcutta. Clive responded graciously. Then they toasted by turn the King in London, the Sultan in Delhi and the Nawab in Murshidabad with superb Madeira that was rumored to be the spoils of a sea-battle with the Portuguese off the Mozambique coast. Afterwards, Clarkson took his customary seat at the piano and dancing resumed.

***

Later that evening, Richard Armstrong experienced a nasty encounter with the Nawab's ambassador.

In the mail packet that had arrived on *Europa*, Armstrong had received a strongly-worded letter from the Court of Directors informing him that, because of mechanical improvements in the mills of Manchester, profitability of textiles made with Indian cotton had dropped to abysmal levels. In the letter, the honorable directors had ordered him to immediately negotiate a lower cotton price in Bengal. And so, while the dancing got underway, Armstrong maneuvered the ambassador into a quiet corner and signaled to his Armenian translator, Jorge Hartunian.

"Your Excellency," Armstrong began. "Could I talk to you about our cotton trade terms?"

After his flowery speech at the dinner table, Sayyid Naseer had returned to his silent sphinx-like self. At Armstrong's question he looked pained, assumed a posture as though he was elsewhere, and said nothing.

"Your Excellency," Armstrong tried once more. "I am aware your Nabob is disinterested in mundane commercial matters. But still, could we discuss a very important issue?"

Naseer studied the intertwined dancers, compressed his lips in disapproval, and still said nothing.

After one more unsuccessful gambit Armstrong lost his temper. Resorting to native Yorkshire directness, he fired a broadside.

"The Government of Bengal *must* give us better concessions."

Hartunian translated and this time evoked a response.

"Keno?" demanded Naseer. Why?

"Why?" Armstrong exclaimed. "Ye ask why? I'll tell ye why! After we pay your exorbitant rates, and follow with duties to your collectors at fifteen river check posts between the Nabob's capital and our loading docks, not to mention the many rounds of *baksheesh* to move things along, our profits are non-existent. This is especially so after the fall in the price of cloth in Europe due to increased mechanization in Manchester."

When Hartunian finished translating this, a furious Naseer brought his long hooked nose close to Armstrong's pudgy one. His temper matched the Governor's and his voice took on a deep growling timbre.

"That, sir, is *not* the Nawab's problem! The Nawab is not forcing you to buy his cloth. Why should the Nawab be concerned with what happens in your foreign cities? *Manchester! Pah!* Is your King concerned with what happens in Patna or in Dhaka?"

Armstrong felt the remnants of his control slip away. Why did these damned self-righteous native officials make things so maddeningly difficult? *Pompous ass!* He wished the English could simply go in and do things the way they did it in the American colonies. He looked around angrily. Where was the bloody idiot, Morley? Finally, controlling himself with great difficulty, he turned back to the ambassador and tried to reason with the man.

"Mr. Naseer, your Nabob is forcing us *not* to buy his cotton. Without better trade concessions, we will be forced to end commerce in Bengal. Ye know, the Nabob should carefully think of what could happen as a result."

This was a serious mistake.

Naseer's orange-tinted beard bristled wrathfully. The floodgates of his invective broke and Jorge Hartunian's translations became rapid-fire.

"The Nawab of Bengal and the Sultan in Delhi have been Allah's chosen rulers in India for centuries. And you? You foreigners have only just arrived as strangers to our land. You have been received courteously. You have been allowed to acquire land. You have been made free to trade. And yet you dare dictate terms to the Nawab? You dare to threaten the great Nawab? Do you believe Nawabzada Shiraj Doula will suffer even a moment's loss of tranquility at the thought of ending commerce with your arrogant country?"

Hazrat Sayyid Naseer paused for breath. His thin frame shook with outrage and his pointed beard trembled with fury. Attracted by the commotion, the Jagat Seth hurried over and made soothing noises. But the angry ambassador would not be deterred.

"This is *not* your country!" he thundered at Armstrong. *"It is ours!* You English, allowed at the Nawab's pleasure, into this land. You English, allowed at the Nawab's pleasure to build your trading post and your fort. You English, allowed at the Nawab's pleasure to travel where you wish. You English have surpassed yourselves in thanklessness and deceit. After the Nawab has expressly forbidden it, you have continued to erect defenses around your fort. Against whom? The weak French or the even weaker Dutch? Have not the western bandits been defeated? Had not the late Alivardi Khan Sahib promised security under his wing to all foreign traders? *Conspiracy!* While the Nawab has granted you concessional duty rates for movement of your Company's purchases, you have continued to transport your merchants' personal goods under that guise. *Deceit!*" Hazrat Sayyid Naseer took two steps back and flailed his arms in the air. "Sir, I have held my peace as a guest in your house for as long as humanly possible. Yet I shall be remiss in my duty if I do not speak out in answer to English arrogance. Having done so, it is impossible for me to remain. *Khuda Hafeez!*"

Naseer fired the Persian farewell and stalked away. His assistants formed up and marched behind him up the steps and through the main entrance. The dancers and musicians stopped and watched the angry entourage depart.

A buzz of animated conversation broke out.

Armstrong realized he had handled this badly and was at a loss about what to do next. He desperately wanted Morley. Where, for God's sake, was the bloody fool? Then he noticed that the banker was still with him and was looking at him quizzically. Now what deviltry was this fellow up to? He was in the Nawab's camp, and should have stormed out after the puffed-up ambassador. Or wasn't he in the Nawab's camp? Impatiently he ordered Hartunian to fetch Benjamin.

The words *"jagat seth"*, translated from Bengali, mean "Banker of the World". Just as the line of Nawabs were not of Bengal, but from Afghanistan, the Jagat Seths were mercantile immigrants from Rajputana in Western India. The first Jagat Seth had provided cash for battles that ultimately led to the very first Nawab's ascension to the throne of Bengal a century ago. Since that time the dynastic Jagat Seths dictated and financed commerce and even war and politics of Eastern India.

The present incumbent, whose real name no one remembered, was an elderly, rotund, balding and mustachioed individual. He always dressed in starched white clothes that were liberally sprinkled with essence of rose. He was immeasurably wealthy and had a very shrewd political mind. Like his predecessors, he could accurately judge and align himself with shifts in the local balance of power. He spoke basic but understandable English and whenever he smiled, which was often, he displayed teeth that were stained crimson by the betel leaves he habitually chewed.

As Benjamin and Hartunian hurried to Armstrong's side, they were joined by Prince Ajoy.

The music and dancing resumed.

Making no attempt to hide his contempt for Naseer, the Governor told Benjamin what had happened. Benjamin tried to point out the folly of Armstrong's heavy-handed approach at which his superior's temper showed signs of flaring again.

At this point the Jagat Seth took command. First, with a look he indicated Hartunian was superfluous and the swarthy Armenian withdrew. Then the banker turned to the Governor and spoke with quiet conviction.

"You realize of course, your Excellency, that Hazrat Sayyid was perfectly justified."

"*What!*"

Armstrong's face turned deep red. He was about to give

the banker a dose of Yorkshire artillery when Benjamin gently intervened.

"Sir, it might be better to hear him out."

Armstrong fumed but contrived to curb his hair-trigger temper. The Jagat Seth smiled his thanks and continued.

"Your Excellency, I understand your situation. You are under great stress..." Armstrong grunted rudely but the banker seemed not to hear. "...you are in the difficult position of being squeezed by both buying and selling markets. However, the Nawab will not be brow-beaten."

"Oh, is that so? What can he do to us?"

The banker regarded Armstrong with his usual suave smile.

"I am sure, your Excellency, you do not wish to find out. You are merchants, not soldiers." He paused delicately then said, "Or am I mistaken?"

A silence ensued.

This was a sensitive subject over which there was heated controversy not only in the Council chamber at Fort William, but even in the East India Company's offices in London's Leadenhall Street. Taking advantage of the lull, the banker took snuff. Benjamin watched Armstrong and thought vindictively, *let's see you get out of this one, you insensitive moron!*

"Your Excellency?"

A new voice unexpectedly entered the discussion and they all turned to face Prince Ajoy Sena.

"Your Excellency, I have lived most of my life in Rajmahal, a two-day journey from the Nawab's capital in Murshidabad. Even though the Senas and the Moghuls have been declared enemies for generations, I know what motivates Shiraj Doula."

Ajoy had a remarkable way of speaking. The pitch of his voice rose and fell dramatically with his emotions as he talked. "Shiraj Doula is charismatic," ...*melodramatic pause...* "he is self-centered" ...*pause...* "power-hungry," ...*pause...* "and greedy. Shiraj loves to win..."

"Yes, and so?" Armstrong interrupted impatiently. Ajoy's histrionics jarred on him.

"Throw him bones, your Excellency! Pay him vacant compliments. And…" *expectant seconds building up suspense,* "…when the Nawab is steeped in self-gratitude…" *pause and in a rush,* "…extract what you want from him."

"*Wah, wah!*" applauded the Jagat Seth. "When did Prince Ajoy, the warrior, learn to barter like a fruit merchant? The prince is absolutely correct, your Excellency. Throw the Nawab some bones. But be careful he does not bite, for he is vicious! I can remember clearly when Arakan invaders came from the east…"

"Seth-*ji,* interrupted Benjamin. "What is it that we can offer the Nawab?"

They thought about this for a long time and the solution, when it came, was from the most unexpected quarter.

"The Nabob wants us to take down the bloody fortifications, doesn't he?" asked Armstrong. "In his letter he was rather insistent, ye know."

Chapter 5

"Oh! Look at the pretty birds, Maggie!"

Pauline watched entranced as a flight of green parrots, calling to each other in shrill tones, swept past like a cascade of darts.

It was three days after the Governor's reception.

As she settled into the new environment of Calcutta with Freddie preoccupied with restocking his ship for the onward voyage to Canton, Pauline's depression from her shipboard days had lifted. The debilitating effect of the ship's constant motion was almost gone. Her naturally curious, buoyant and fun-loving temperament responded to stimulating colors and sights all around her and to the fascinating people she was encountering every day. Following the reception, Pauline had explored her new surroundings filled with the excitement of a child. In truth, being only seventeen, she was little more than a child.

The Wainwrights were billeted at the Company House, a large brick building situated by the river, just south of the fort. At daybreak when the air was fresh and invigorating, Maggie Clarkson had come to collect her as pre-arranged.

Pauline impetuously took the motherly woman's arm as they walked out. The broad green vista immediately in front of the fort was simply called The Park. Senior merchants such as the Clarksons had homes that bordered three sides of The Park, while the eastern wall of Fort William formed the fourth. In its center was a large man-made pond called the Great Tank. The two women stopped at its edge and looked down at the dark water. At once large shiny-scaled fish rose and agitated its surface.

"They're looking at me!" exclaimed Pauline.

"Food, lass," said Maggie. "That's what they want. They're fed regularly and are actually quite tame. And no wonder! They form a staple at the Armstrongs' table."

Pauline bent and picked up a big silver-green beetle from the dew-wet grass and dropped it into the water. There was a great splash as several fish jumped for it. The beetle disappeared. As they watched the water settle, Maggie supplied Pauline with information.

"The path at the end of the Great Tank, by that big tree, is called Rope Walk."

"Why, Maggie?"

"Would you like to guess?"

"Guess? Hmmm, let me think. How about this? Since Europeans frequent this walkway, native peddlers display their wares on both sides of the path. A peddler did a rope trick for a sahib one day and he called it the Rope Walk. And, presto, the name stuck."

Maggie sighed.

"I wish it were as innocent as that, my dear. In truth, the reason for the name *Rope Walk* is that while Muslim rulers, even though they have their gruesome punishments, do not hang their criminals, we British do. And this was where the hangman's rope was once wielded."

Sobered by the image, they walked along by the Great Tank and before long joined a wide dusty road that swept up to the east gate of the fort, now on their left.

"These are the Cross Roads," said Maggie. "If we went through Cross Roads for a mile we would arrive at the crammed Black Town where all the natives live. It's not a place for ladies so we'll just turn left here and walk down to the river. And to complete the picture, dear, that big road going away east across the Cross Roads is called The Avenue, and the part of Calcutta where we live is called White Town."

"What *awful* names!" Pauline cried. "It's as though a giant has made a town for black and white people and given it names for his children to play with." Pauline tightened her hold on Maggie's arm, came close and made a conspiratorial face. "Can you hear the little giants singing, Maggie? Hark! There they go:

> *Great Tank, White Town,*
> *Rope Walk, Black Town,*
> *Cross Roads by The Avenue,*
> *I'm in The Park and where are you?"*

Maggie stared in astonishment as the young girl sang the words to the tune of a popular nursery rhyme. Why, she thought, this one was going to be a hit in Calcutta! No question. Lucky Captain Wainwright.

They walked companionably along The Avenue. Pauline was filled with wonder by the riotous red-and-gold tops of lofty spreading flame-of-the-forest trees that lined the way, each one adorned with masses of yellow-bordered crimson flowers. Behind the trees there were a line of two-story high-ceilinged brick houses set in gated low-walled gardens, their balconies brilliant with many-hued bougainvillea.

Maggie kept up a stream of chatter about the society of Fort William. The Armstrongs lived in the Residence inside the fort. The Clarksons, Linningtons and other senior staff had their own houses. Most of the clerks and junior employees, called 'writers', shared rooms in a big terra-cotta mess-house inside the fort, again inelegantly called Writers' Building.

Glad to be out in the open after months of confinement

aboard *Europa,* Pauline walked along happily beside her new friend. She scuffed the dust with her shoes and raised little clouds. She was reminded of Burnham when a large black sow with thick bristles on a mud-covered snout led a brood of nine piglets across the road, all strung out in single file behind their mother and running as fast as they could. How cute! She forgot the pigs and hurriedly retreated behind Maggie when an enormous orange bull looked up from a pile of rubbish and shook its massive head.

"Don't be frightened," Maggie reassured her. "He only *looks* ferocious. Bulls here are actually placid as cows. Except of course, when they've a territorial disagreement. Then what a din! You can hear them belling and roaring for miles. The Avenue was blocked for hours by a bullfight between this brute and an intruder. Did you know his name was Lali?"

"Whose? The bull's? He has a name? What does it mean? Does he belong to someone?" Pauline marveled at sight of the huge beast which had now stuck its head back into the garbage. She watched its long tasseled tail flick flies off its hindquarters.

"Lali means 'Red'. Nobody owns Lali. He's free as a bird and loved and fed by everyone. Did you know that Shiva, the Hindu destroyer god, the one who wears a tiger-skin and carries a trident, rides on a bull? No wonder Hindus consider bulls sacred."

"Oh? I thought cows were sacred in India!"

"So they are too, so they are. Pauline dear, you will soon find other myths corrected as you get to know this country. I do wish Richard Armstrong would take more interest in India though. It would do him good. He might as well be in England for all he cares."

"How do you know so much yourself?" asked Pauline as they moved on, leaving the bull behind. Seeing a movement she looked up at a guava tree where a big yellow bird with a black head sat on a branch with its long, forked tail hanging down. "What a pretty bird. What is it?"

"It's an oriole, child. You should hear it sing. How do I know about the country? Benjamin Morley…do you remember the nice young fellow at the do?"

Pauline nodded enthusiastically. She had liked Benjamin from the moment they had met, and the honest hungry way in which he had looked at her, and the way his eyes had filled with concern as he seemed to sense her sadness.

Maggie continued.

"He knows the local people and their ways. The English girls adore him, and I don't mean just the unmarried ones. And him an eligible aristocrat!" Maggie rolled her eyes. "Give the boy a couple of glasses and flutter your lashes and you'll hear stories you'd never believe!"

Pauline resolved to do just that. Her delight became more pronounced and she looked expectantly at Maggie, who smiled and continued.

"I know his stories are true. He never lies to me. Why, only a week ago, cross my heart, he went and sat all night in a tree in the middle of a jungle, and along came a tiger and tried to pull him down. Of course, he shot it in the end."

"Goodness! Tigers! Here?"

Pauline shied as an animal came out of a side street. But it was only a stray dog.

"No, child. Tigers keep to the jungles and the marshes on the other side of Black Town, but leopards and wolves *have* entered our gardens at night. So remember to keep your captain close when you go out after dark."

Pauline abruptly turned away. The expression on her face lost its warmth and the childish sparkle left her eyes. Maggie noticed, frowned, but said nothing.

The Avenue took them between the Great Tank and a big church. The church steeple was lying on its side next to the main entrance.

"What happened to the steeple?" Pauline asked.

"Oh, it's quite a story. About fifteen years ago, there was a terrible cyclone and a strong earthquake at the same time.

The level of the river rose by twenty-five feet or more. Twenty-five feet! Fancy that! This place we're on must have been under deep water. The church steeple fell during that storm and the earthquake and hasn't been repaired. Clarence has tried to get Richard to sanction the funds, but hasn't succeeded. It's a *church,* for mercy's sake!"

Her kindly face clouded over at the thought of the Governor's perfidy, but cleared as she continued her story.

"Anyway, there was a French ship that was blown miles inland by the storm and ended up on its side. When the owners tried to unload the wrecked ship's hold through a gaping hole on its side, the natives who went in didn't come out."

She stopped and looked at Pauline theatrically. Pauline danced with impatience.

"Why, why?"

"Well, after the third man went in and didn't come out, the overseer and his men took torches and carefully entered. And what did they see?"

She paused again, enjoying the suspense she had created.

"Mag-*gie!* What *did* they see?"

"An absolutely enormous crocodile crouching inside the hold and waiting for its next victim."

"Oooooh! How horrible!" Pauline pictured the torchlight reflected in the reptile's eyes and bits of its victims hanging from its jaws. "But of course, it's not true."

"It *is* true, dear. The story appeared in *Gentleman's Magazine* of that year. It even said that many tigers and several rhinoceros drowned near the fort."

This remarkable picture occupied Pauline as they walked past the east gate and along the warehouses on the southern side of the fort. The road sloped down to the wide sun-drenched river. The ramparts of the fort rose behind them, set with massive columns. The thick walls had little openings for cannon to fire on the river. Small boats, poled by dark-skinned men with springy hair, ferried bales and chests between the high-masted ships and river barges. A herd of water buffaloes waded in the shallows, with only their heads and curved horns above water. On the back of one sat their herder, a boy wearing only a straw hat. His feet trailed in the water.

Maggie talked on about India and its people and places, embellishing her descriptions with exciting anecdotes. As she listened, Pauline was attracted to a sweet-smelling jasmine bush and, beside it, a tree bearing vermilion hibiscus blooms. Without taking her attention off her companion, she made up a bouquet adding soft green leaves and little white wildflowers.

The sun became hotter and the two women started to walk back. Perceptive and motherly, Maggie sensed in Pauline an uninhibited spirit and an avid interest in life. At the same time she perceived a strange melancholy and thought to herself, poor thing, so young and pretty and such a dashing husband. Something's wrong. Perhaps we can help.

The Clarksons' house on The Avenue came into view. At the gate Maggie said, "We're very informal here. Clarence and I would be delighted if you and the captain dropped in whenever you liked. Do say you will!"

"I'd love to, Maggie dear."

Like everyone else, Pauline had fallen under her spell.

"Wonderful!" smiled Maggie. "Shall I see you to the Company House?"

"Oh, no! I wouldn't think of it. It's just a bit further, Maggie. Good bye."

***

Lali the bull had moved on.

His vagabond spirit took him wherever he wished. Whenever he was hungry Lali put his enormous head and wet black nose over someone's wall. With patient liquid black eyes, he would watch as children rushed to find banana peels and discarded vegetable leaves, and then clamor to be lifted up for the privilege of feeding him and caressing his soft neck.

Now Lali ambled along The Avenue for a while. He passed an uninteresting house and looked down a side alley. He spied a big rolled-up object that appeared promising and entered the alley. But this wasn't his day. The lump turned out to be a tangle of coconut hemp that smelt nastily of tar. Lali was not fussy, but even he drew the line at eating tar. Breathing disgustedly through his wide nostrils, Lali turned and came back to The Avenue just as Pauline started to cross the alley.

Normally Lali would not have noticed the woman, but her piercing scream made him stop and turn. She was only ten feet away with her mouth wide open. But Lali did not look at her mouth, but at the juicy leaves and flowers she held out for him to eat.

Frightened out of her wits by the sudden appearance of the bull, whose nearness filled her whole view, Pauline held the bouquet defensively and screamed and screamed. And when the monster came rapidly toward her she dropped the flowers and turned and ran. She raced blindly back the way she had come, breathing in big gasps, her ankle-length dress impeding her progress. She ran past the Clarksons' house without even seeing it. She expected at any moment to feel the stubby horns of the bull lift her high in the air and the ground rush up to meet her as she fell.

The morning was quite advanced and there were other people now on The Avenue. They heard Pauline's screams and rushed in her direction. Then they stopped and stared blankly at the foreign woman who was running and stumbling along the path and shouting frantically for no apparent reason. No one paid any attention to a big orange-colored bull that was contentedly eating a bunch of leaves and flowers.

Chapter 6

Meanwhile, in Murshidabad, the stately northern capital of Bengal, the English delegation to the Nawab's court was having its own moment of truth.

Inside the decorated audience hall of magnificent Hazarduari Palace – palace of a thousand doors – the ruler of Bengal wanted to shout in frustration. Simultaneously he felt an uncontrollable urge to clap the fat uncouth foreigner before him in chains. Uncharacteristically, he did neither. The young king leaned forward on his throne and glared balefully at the broad back of his negotiator, the Jagat Seth, who stood below his dais. The banker, aware of his monarch's eyes drilling into him like points of heated swords, folded his arms tightly across his ample stomach and concealed a shiver.

During all this Richard Armstrong stupidly watched the wool-and-velvet fan that was being waved over the Nawab's head. He could not for the life of him remember what he was supposed to say to this…this king. Irrationally, he thought that a real king should wear a crown on his head, not a ridiculous tasseled fez! He regretted his decision to come to Murshidabad. He should have let Morley take the heat as the young idiot had wanted.

Before setting off on their hundred-mile journey up the river, Armstrong had agonized over the decision to visit Murshidabad. Should an English Governor travel to a Moorish court to meet the king or should he send a representative? Morley, the Trade Councilor, was the natural choice to lead the delegation on a trade-related issue. But Armstrong feared that if the project succeeded, his junior would corner a great deal of credit in London. Perhaps he should go himself? The discussion on this topic had gone on interminably in council, when an exhausted Linnington urged him not to go – which naturally made Armstrong decide on going! Before they left Calcutta the Jagat Seth had spent several hours with Armstrong and Benjamin, discussing the alternative offers to persuade the Nawab to reduce taxes, the infinite ways in which the unpredictable monarch could react, and the possible ways of handling him. The banker knew he was playing an exceptionally dangerous game. He was riding two horses at once: he was acting as a local advisor for betterment of trade terms for the East India Company, and, more perilous, he was carrying the confidence of the Nawab in ensuring that he, the Nawab, came out of the bargain feeling that the foreigners had been squeezed the utmost.

Now Shiraj Doula, haughty and disdainful, abruptly adjusted the lapels of his silken green-and-pink robe. One of his moccasined feet began to tap the floor.

"Answer the Jagat Seth!"

The high-pitched bullet-like command in Bengali made Armstrong flinch as though struck. There was no translation required. Benjamin, standing by the side of his superior officer, realized that the situation was rapidly unraveling. Armstrong was completely overwhelmed by the state of affairs he had got himself into. The array of armed soldiers that had lined both sides of the road to the palace gates, the plumed horses and liveried elephants and the imposing Katra Mosque by the riverside, had all served to intimidate the Governor upon their arrival. The arrogance and contempt with which he normally held the natives of India had been completely overpowered by the crystal, mirrors, tapestry, carpets and lacquer that combined to dazzle the visitors to the Nawabs' *Durbar.*

Benjamin decided it was time he took control.

Making sure he did not look at the Nawab directly, as befitted his own subordinate rank, he spoke carefully in his best Bengali.

"We are guilty, Seth-*ji,* of not making our proposal clear to the Nawabzada. Please let me restate simply. We are offering to stop fortification of the Maratha Ditch." He repeated the sentence as, out of the corner of his eye, he noticed the Nawab's foot stop its tapping. Had he captured the Nawab's interest? Or was the Nawab simply surprised he could speak the local language? "In recognition of our concession," he plowed on, "we humbly request a reduction of thirty percent on duties on silk that we buy..." The foot started to tap again. "...which will be more than offset by increase in our overall volume of trade. We believe this is to be an extremely munificent conclusion for both parties."

Benjamin stopped and the Jagat Seth took up the story and tried to impress on Shiraj the economics of volume discounts. But the Nawab was tiring.

"*You!* Councilor-sahib! How did you learn Bengali?"

Shiraj Doula interrupted the banker in full flow.

All eyes at once turned on Benjamin. There were ministers, scribes, lesser officials, bodyguards, servants, and other functionaries scattered around the large hall. The other Englishmen, Armstrong, Muldoon and five soldiers, had not understood any of the preceding conversation and were watching nervously.

Now that he had been directly addressed, Benjamin raised his eyes and looked at the Nawab. What he saw made his heart sink.

Pitiless light-gray eyes bored into him from above a hooked nose and a wispy beard, all set in a thin wasted face. It was a face aged beyond its years by alcohol and debauchery. At the same time Shiraj's expression and body language displayed intense nervous energy. Impatience danced in constant movements of his eyes, fingers and feet. And antipathy—no it was stronger than antipathy, it was hostility, perhaps even hatred—of his foreign visitors, was evident in every gesture.

Benjamin shivered.

Here was a very dangerous man. A man whose mind was rumored to be deranged, and who was known to pathologically despise foreigners. He had heard that Shiraj's cruelty toward his prisoners bordered on madness. But his schizophrenic nature was such that his subjects and his army viewed him as a charismatic leader and were extremely loyal. A time would come, and soon, when the English would need to come to terms with this man, otherwise...

Hastily Benjamin put the train of thought away.

"My Lord," he began, using the Persian term for royalty, *jahan-pana,* and weighing each word meticulously, "I have learnt Bengali from your people. I believe it is important that we to do so. We cannot trade in your country without knowing your language."

"Oh, is that so? How noble! Councilor-sahib probably picks up more news thus than do the other hatmen."

The Nawab looked angrily at Armstrong who did not understand any of this and had dropped his eyes in confusion. *Hatmen* was the local derogatory term for white foreigners. It referred to the khaki helmets they wore as protection against the sun and which the locals found ludicrous.

"Why do you harbor the traitor, Sena?"

Shiraj's manner of suddenly firing questions in his shrill voice was very unnerving. Before anyone could reply, the Nawab shot another blast at Armstrong.

"Release the traitor before you talk of trade!"

No one replied.

The pitch of the Nawab's voice rose even higher, almost to a scream. "What? Why are you silent?" He suddenly stamped both his feet at once startling everyone. "The Nawab *shall* be answered!"

"Morley? What?" Armstrong stammered. His face and jacket were bathed in perspiration.

"He wants the prince," Benjamin whispered over his shoulder.

Then he looked at the Nawab once again. Would he be able to carry out the falsehood to save his new friend?

"My Lord," he said quietly. "Prince Ajoy is no longer under our sanctuary."

"What? Lies! Where is he? The Nawab *shall* have him here. *Now!*"

By now Benjamin was used to Shiraj referring to himself in the third person.

"Prince Ajoy has decided on his own accord to leave Fort William, my Lord. We have no knowledge of his whereabouts."

"Lies! All lies! *Laat-sahib!*"

Armstrong, who knew the Indian word for governor, snapped to attention.

"Yes, your Excellency!"

The Governor was fortunate that the Nawab, not knowing English, could not differentiate *excellency* from *highness*.

"Where is the traitor, Sena?"

There was no need to translate for Armstrong. Benjamin, sure that the Governor would wilt if he tried to lie to the livid monarch, pre-empted his reply.

"Prince Ajoy left Fort William after the *Laat-sahib's* banquet. He did not tell us where he was going."

"Why did he leave? Was he alone?"

"We do not know why, my Lord. I understand he took his servants with him."

Shiraj Doula glared at him venomously. Suspiciously. Benjamin was expecting another harangue or worse when the Nawab swung around abruptly and called out *"Sipah-sala!"*

"My Lord?"

An impressive and well-built man stepped forward. He wore leather armor and a heavy sword hung from his side. Benjamin studied the man with interest. This must be the celebrated Afghan, Rahamat Khan, the Nawab's new *sipah-sala* or general, the one who had distinguished himself in campaigns against the Marathas.

"*Sipah-sala!*" Shiraj fumed at his general. "A search shall be started instantly. Instantly! The swine *shall* be in chains tonight. He shall be bound and paraded down the streets of Murshidabad on donkey-back and stoned to death in the morning in public view. Is that clear?" He voice rose to a shriek drowning Rahamat Khan's reply. "And if the hatmen are lying I shall not wait to put Calcutta to the sword!"

He stood abruptly and arranged his robes.

"Enough of this. Honorable Jagat Seth!"

"My Lord?"

"Let the terms of the deal be fixed and the foreigners removed from my palace at once. *At once!* Accursed prevaricators!"

Shiraj Doula swept out.

***

The negotiations went on in earnest and it was decided that the English would immediately stop fortifying the town and digging the ditch, and, over the next two months, dismantle all barricades. In return, a twenty-two percent duty reduction on silk purchases would be made available to them.

While the Jagat Seth and the Nawab's Minister conferred on a separate topic, Benjamin left his countrymen and slowly walked down to the river's edge, leaving behind the curved colonnade and regal façade of Hazarduari Palace. A squad of the Nawab's soldiers sauntered along behind him. He stopped before the high-domed Katra Mosque which contains remains of the great Murshid Quli Khan, Shiraj's forebear, the warlike founder of the ruling dynasty of Bengal and of the city itself. Filled with disquiet, Benjamin looked across the wide Ganges River and mused on the present Nawab's antagonistic demeanor. His rabid animosity and uncontrolled paroxysms of rage were disquieting in the extreme.

Benjamin sensed serious trouble. Something Shiraj Doula had said struck him sharply: "If the hatmen are lying I shall not wait to put Calcutta to the sword!"

`Shall not wait...'

Was it a manner of speech? Or was there something sinister already brewing? For the sake of safety of the fort he must secrete Ajoy elsewhere. Should the Company secretly start an insurrection against the Nawab with Ajoy's help?

Put Calcutta to the sword!

What a horrifying thought. Should they really tear down their fortifications and be completely at the mercy of an insane king?

Chapter 7

Prince Ajoy Sena, unaware of the dramatic events in Murshidabad, was woken early by the raucous cries of peddlers from outside the window of his chamber in Fort William. Stimulated by what he had heard at the English Governor's reception, he had spent the past three days thinking of ways to unite the fragmented province of Bengal under his own leadership and to bring down Shiraj Doula. With Moghul power waning all over India, and with the English on his side, the time might never be better.

He had finished a cup of tea and had started to pace his room when, through the open window, he noticed the two English ladies walking back from the river.

A few minutes later he heard Pauline's cries.

Fresh in Ajoy's mind was the anguished wail of his sister, Aruna, who upon learning the news of her husband's death, had fainted into his arms. And so, while other passersby stared in surprise at the spectacle of the foreign woman screaming and running for no visible cause, Ajoy reacted at once and rushed out of the east gate and into The Avenue.

After fleeing panic-stricken for three hundred yards in her high boots, petticoats and weakened condition, Pauline was completely spent. Her breath came in big gasps. Hearing a noise behind her, she tremulously listened for pounding hooves but instead perceived someone jogging along by her side and saying something to her. Pauline came to a stop, breathing in a ragged wheeze, and looked around.

There was no mad bull.

She saw a crowd beginning to gather around her. Dark-skinned boys with big brown eyes ran up and gazed at her wonderingly. Men carrying tools of their trade - brooms, shovels, baskets of vegetables, barbers' razors - all gaped at her. A palanquin came to a halt on the other side of the road while its bearers stared and someone peeped through its parted curtains.

Pauline heard an urgent voice speaking in her ear and turned to see a tall distinguished-looking Indian by her side. He said something unfamiliar again. Pauline pulled herself together and tried to understand what the man was saying.

For Ajoy, the situation was becoming acutely embarrassing and also dangerous. From his window, Ajoy had recognized Maggie and Pauline, having sat with them at Armstrong's dinner, and had rushed out to help because he thought they were in danger. He was a known figure to the people of Calcutta. The predicament of being seen in the streets with an unescorted hysterical foreign woman was certain to cause gossip. Even worse, spies in the crowd could carry news of his presence in Fort William to Shiraj Doula. As Pauline appeared to be unhurt, he now wanted desperately to remove himself and the crazy woman from public view. At this, however, he was at a disadvantage, having never, in all his twenty-seven years, dealt with a foreign woman.

He tried once again, speaking as clearly as he could.

"Come inside the fort, Wainwright-memsahib. The gate is here." He pointed at the wide gateway of the fort.

Pauline understood at last.

In her few days in Calcutta, she had learned that she was a memsahib, a white woman. She now realized that the man was saying "Wainwright", even though his strong accent and his unfamiliarity with the letter 'w' made it sound as "Bhen-rah-it". She took stock of her situation and discovered that her 'escape' had brought her back near the river. She looked again at the growing crowd of inquisitive faces staring at her and a comprehension of her situation began to dawn. She suddenly wanted desperately to get away from this place.

"Yes. Oh yes, let's go. Quickly, please."

They walked briskly toward the east gate and the crowd parted to let them through. Pauline rearranged her dress and patted her hair back as they passed curious Indian sentries at the massive iron doors and entered the tunnel-like passage through the fortress wall. They emerged into a big sunlit courtyard with the reassuring sight of English soldiers on parade. At last everything seemed familiar and safe after her trauma.

Pauline heaved a sigh of relief and looked once more at the person who had 'saved' her.

"Who are you..." she asked, a little breathlessly, and then added, "...sir?"

The man looked at her with an unsmiling face and replied, "I am Ajoy Sena. From Rajmahal. At the reception I sat at the *Laat-sahib's* table. Why did you shout, Memsahib? Why did you run? Did someone attack you?"

Pauline concentrated and tried to understand Ajoy's sing-song diction. The word 'attack' brought back the vision of the bull's inflamed eyes and out-thrust open mouth inches from her face. Her eyes widened and she staggered. Ajoy automatically put a steadying hand on her elbow. Pauline shook her head to clear the vision and blurted out, "A bull! A big red bull! It chased me!"

"A bull!"

Ajoy came to a stop as he realized how frightened the woman must have been. And so soon after her arrival in India!

They were standing on the grass at the edge of the parade ground. Still holding her arm, Ajoy said reassuringly, "The bull has gone, memsahib. You are quite safe inside the fort now."

Pauline closed her eyes tightly - 'clenched her eyes', as she used to tell her father when she was a child - took a deep breath and pushed the scary picture out of her mind. Her eyes flew open and she looked at Ajoy with a valiant little smile.

Watching her, Ajoy was fascinated by the play of emotion on her face. He noticed the determined shift from fear to courage. He looked carefully at her for the first time and, like Benjamin earlier, revised her age downwards. She was very young and—even though Ajoy had never before thought of beauty in white people—extremely pretty. *And* she had been frightened and alone. *And* he had 'saved' her!

Ajoy felt a warmth inside and protectively tightened his grip as they negotiated a slushy spot.

"Come, Memsahib," he said, and they started to walk across the main grassy courtyard of the fort.

Suddenly Ajoy remembered that this woman was married to the big Captain-sahib and hurriedly released her.

While they walked, Pauline, who had been confronted by a sea of unfamiliar native and European faces on the night of the party, dug into her memory.

"You do seem familiar, sir," she said. "But…something, something is different."

"Yes, Memsahib, there is something different. I wore my proper attire that night. And my turban. I did not speak much at the dinner table as the ambassador mostly talked." He smiled. "Then memsahibs spoke of silk."

Pauline was taken in by the smile. She watched as his face crinkled, his eyes twinkled, and his expression underwent a remarkable transformation from taciturn to gentle and friendly. She looked at the tall, strong, confident person by her side. Oh yes, she remembered him now. This was Mr. Morley's friend, the one with the diamond in the turban— the prince.

Goodness!

A prince!

Her hands went cold.

"Thank you for helping me, your...your Highness!" Pauline managed to stammer. She wondered what Father would say if he saw her walking with a Hindu prince? He *was* Hindu, wasn't he? And how big and straight and resourceful. She studied Ajoy out of the corner of her eye as they reached the opposite side of the parade-ground. He had fine dark chiseled features and an aquiline nose. His eyes were strange and striking. They were large and black, intense and at the same time strangely feminine. But they were kind and soft when he smiled. His curly jet-black hair hung to his shoulders. Today he wore a sky-blue knee-length shirt, a white *dhoti* and a pair of well-made sandals. The material of his clothes, she noticed, was expensive silk. He was the first Indian she had met who looked at ease in an English setting—servants, peddlers, merchants had been deferential and submissive—except of course that funny-looking tough-as-nails ambassador. Pauline had been in the crowd that watched Armstrong being roundly berated by Hazrat Sayeed Naseer.

A flash of anxiety hit Pauline.

Where was he taking her?

As though he read her thoughts, Ajoy said, "we are here, Memsahib. This is the guest quarter of the fort where I am staying." They had arrived at a building very like the ones on The Avenue and entered through a large open doorway. "Please wait in the drawing room while I send word to the *Laat-sahib*." Then he disappeared into the interior of the building.

Pauline obediently entered the simply furnished room and sat down on a straight-backed velvet-covered sofa, luxuriating in the peace and quiet that descended on her. After a while got up and went to a mirror that hung on the far wall. A hot dusty face with disarrayed hair looked back at her. She stood a while thus, staring at herself, trying to fix her hair, while her mind ran through the events of the morning. Presently she heard a cough and in the mirror she saw a wizened servant holding a tray. She turned and nodded at him and the old man set the tray on a table and, after inclining his head and giving her a funny little bow, he left. The tray held a brass tumbler of water, an earthenware cup of tea and a brass dish of different sweets. Suddenly Pauline realized her throat was parched and leathery. She thirstily drank the water and had started on the tea when Ajoy came back.

"Ah, Memsahib. You are feeling better. The boy will pull the *punkha*."

Pauline looked blank.

Ajoy gestured upwards and she looked up. A thick cloth strip, several feet wide and weighted along the bottom, hung lengthwise from a pole in the ceiling. As she looked it began to sway back and forth.

"The boy is outside," Ajoy explained. "Pulling on the rope."

The air in the room began to circulate and cool Pauline's perspiring face. She sat on the sofa while Ajoy took a chair across from her.

"I have sent word to the *Laat-sahib* to come as soon as possible. But I do not know where you stay and could not send for Captain-sahib. Shall I do so now?"

"Send for Freddie? Oh, no thanks. I shall be fine when Mr. Armstrong arrives."

Ajoy did not miss the lack of enthusiasm.

"Are you sure you are not hurt, Memsahib? Did the bull touch you?"

"No, but it came very close. Maggie and I saw it before, as we set out. She said he was harmless and his name was Lali. Then why did the bull come after me?"

"I do not know, Memsahib. Bulls do not usually attack people. I am sorry your first experience in my country was so unpleasant."

Pauline relaxed and sat back with a sigh. She thought,

what a polite and hospitable person! And he a prince and she a commoner. It required quite an effort to understand his words, but how different from what they had told her about Indians back in England. How could anyone describe this cultured and considerate man as a boorish heathen savage?

"Perhaps the bull was stung by a hornet," she said but he did not understand. "Oh, let's forget the bull. Let us talk of other things." She saw him waiting and went on, "Oh, like your kingdom, your Highness? Where is it? Is it big?"

With this Pauline touched Ajoy's favorite subject. He immediately forgot his self-consciousness about being alone with a foreign woman. He called the servant to bring fresh tea for them and began to recount the history of the famous Senas. Pauline listened, impressed by the dramatic manner of speech that brought alive his narrative. She had difficulty following his words and missed most of the names of people and places, but her innate curiosity for the exotic and his exuberant style kept her engrossed. Ajoy had just started to describe the confrontation between Laxman Sena, the last great indigenous king of Bengal, and the Afghan invader, Muhammed-bin-Khalji, in the ancient city of Nadia, when the Governor's wife burst into the room.

Ajoy jumped to his feet.

"Mrs. Wainwright! There you are!" Martha Armstrong cried ignoring him. "Oh, you're sitting up. Did it hurt you badly? They'll shoot the brute. They've gone to find Richard and the captain."

Martha fussed over Pauline and looked pointedly at Ajoy who withdrew. The messenger had clearly let his imagination run away and it took a few minutes for Martha to realize that Pauline was not harmed. She looked around the room warily and with obvious distaste.

"Why did you come here?" Martha lowered her voice. "You should have requested one of the Englishmen to help you."

"How could I? There weren't any when the bull attacked me."

"No, Mrs. Wainwright, I meant you should have asked one of the Englishman for shelter and to send for Captain Wainwright and for us."

"But…," began Pauline and then understood what Martha was saying.

Well, she thought, one doesn't need to be in Ipswich to find narrow-mindedness. It's right here. The prince had done exactly what Mrs. Armstrong wanted, yet she refused to recognize it. Pauline sighed. She was learning.

"At least," said the older woman, "you are safe now."

Martha Armstrong as a rule spoke little. When Pauline did not reply, she pursed her lips and stood silently near the window, disdaining the sofa. Pauline folded her hands in her lap and let her mind wander to the battlefield scene long ago where Muhammed-bin-Khalji and Laxman Sena faced each other on decorated war-elephants.

Presently carriage wheels crunched on gravel and Richard Armstrong hurriedly entered the room. The misinformed scene of horror and outrage was repeated. Armstrong's words and demeanor made it clear he found the situation highly irritating as he bustled the two women out and handed them into his carriage.

"I will remain to straighten things with this fellow," he told Pauline stiffly.

The horse shook its head and jingled its harness. The carriage rolled toward the east gate. Pauline looked back through the little opening in the rear. The prince had come out onto the portico and was standing behind the Governor. Just before the coach turned a corner, she saw him raise a hand. From the distance she could not be sure if it was to brush something away or to salute her in farewell.

***

After Martha Armstrong returned with her to the Company House it took a fair amount of persuasion for Pauline to rid herself of the finicky cheerless woman. Freddie was probably on his ship or at the docks. Colonel Clive, the other temporary resident, was also absent. The big house was a quiet haven after the excitement of the morning. Pauline asked her maid, a jittery Eurasian woman, to run a bath.

Luxuriating in the cool water, she recounted her experiences of the day. The courteous, dignified and even chivalrous treatment she had received from the Indian prince made her feel happy and wanted; in striking contrast to the way Freddie had abused her.

Pauline lay back and began to reflect on the people she had met after arriving in India and began a classification. On the good side, Prince Ajoy headed the list, with Mr. Morley a close second and tied with Maggie Clarkson. Her husband led the rogues' gallery with Martha hot on his heels. She thought about the Indian ambassador whose tirade against Armstrong she had overheard. She knew the Englishmen considered the nabob an enemy. But weren't they in *his* country? How would King George feel if that ginger-gray ambassador came to London and threw his weight about like Armstrong?

She notched Hazrat Sayyid Naseer in her 'good' category.

She changed into a light frock having decided against putting on her corsets. Since coming to India the whalebone hoops were becoming impossibly tight and uncomfortable. Suddenly she felt terribly tired. Waves of nausea passed over her. She controlled herself with difficulty and realized she had had nothing to eat or drink today except what the prince had given her. No wonder she was so exhausted. She called the bearer, and asked for breakfast which was ready in the high-ceilinged dining room in minutes. Pauline ate a mango and then dug into potato curry with little balloons of fried flour dough called *loochis*. She felt better but still tired. After toying with a book she decided to take a nap. She slept through the fiery afternoon and into the coolness of the evening.

When she awoke, feeling very groggy, it was with a premonition that all was not well.

She turned over and found Freddie standing by the bed and somberly looking down at her.

Pauline shrank back against the wall with a little scream.

"Pauline!" Freddie said unmoved. "I have been waiting for hours. Are you ill?"

Pauline stared back, her mind full of conflicting emotions. Disgust, fear, anger, mixed with frustration and helplessness. She wanted desperately to run past him. *Away*. Anywhere but away. But his big frame blocked the door so she stayed where she was.

"Dress yourself," Freddie said. "We must talk."

He left the room.

Feeling like a prisoner Pauline put on her crinoline, petticoats and frock. Then she hesitantly entered the drawing room of the Company House and was surprised at the lateness of the hour. Several wall sconces had oil lamps burning in them. Sofas, tables and chairs were arranged in groups on the stone floor. English river scenes vied for space on the walls with hunting trophies. Tiger, leopard and deer heads regarded her solemnly with flickering lights reflected in their glass eyes.

Captain Wainwright sat erect in a high-backed leather couch.

"Sit down," said Freddie as she stood uncertainly in the middle of the large room.

Pauline remained standing.

"Sit down!"

Freddie's voice became edged with anger and Pauline wearily sank down on a wooden chair.

"You are aware this cannot continue?"

Pauline, her mind dulled by apprehension and misery, said nothing.

"What on earth is the matter, woman? People notice your behavior."

When there was no response and Freddie's voice rose an octave.

"You have to stop it."

"Stop what?" Pauline finally said.

"We are married and must appear so."

Pauline felt drained of energy. The enormity of the injustice and the charade he was asking for were quite plain. But she had no will to fight. If only he would go away. When she replied it was in a small voice.

"Yes, Freddie."

The captain looked at her indecisively, surprised by the absence of resistance.

"My duties aboard *Europa* have lessened and I may remain ashore nights. We have a few more days in Calcutta...

A shock wave passed through Pauline.

"We?" she croaked. "A few more days?"

"Yes, a few more days. A week at most. Then *Europa* sails for Canton with us aboard."

Slowly Pauline's face crumpled and she fell back against her chair. Sail with him on that awful ship again in that dreadful cabin?

There came a peremptory knocking on the front door and the uniformed house bearer hurried to unlock it. A plump smiling Clive strode into the room.

"Good evening, good evening!" he said heartily to the Wainwrights. "Nice to have you among us landlubbers, Captain. Good evening, Mrs... *Oh!*"

Clive broke off in astonishment and nimbly stepped aside as, with a sobbing whimper Pauline rushed past and closed her bedroom door with a crash.

Chapter 8

That night she dreamt of Robert.

She saw him from a distance as she rode in the cart that was taking her to Ipswich for the departure to India. She saw him standing at the door of the baker's shop, looking at her gravely, twisting his cloth cap in his hands. She wanted to call out to him but the words would not come.

And when the cart turned onto Ipswich High Road and the bakery was lost from view, it was the last time she saw Robert.

***

Nine months after their wedding while Freddie was still fighting Russians in the Arctic, Pauline had been drawn out of her lassitude in Wainwright Manor by a mild winter's day. She decided to go for a walk along a sunny Ipswich lane.

Two miles from Wainwright Manor she saw him.

Robert was coming toward her, pushing a wheelbarrow loaded with loaves of bread. The bells on the barrow's axle jingled merrily. He looked exactly as she remembered him, chubby, ruddy-cheeked, wearing an oft-darned shirt, dusty breeches, and the familiar cloth cap. His hair stuck out in places from under his cap in the same endearing way. He would have passed on had she not called his name.

Robert stopped and lowered the barrow. The silencing of the bells caused a hush. He stood up straight and touched his forehead with a knuckle.

"Yes'm?" he inquired politely.

"Robert! Look, it's me!"

Robert peered at the well-dressed lady under the summer bonnet and his eyes widened in astonishment.

"Lord luvaduck! It's our Pauly!"

He took a step forward and then caught himself and looked down at the ground.

"G...g'd morrow Mum," he said in confusion.

Pauline's old verve came back.

"Oh Robert!" she exclaimed. "Don't be a stuff-arse! 'Good morrow Mum' indeed! Who *do* you think you're talking to?" She came close and took his arm and shook it. "Aren't you glad to see me?"

"Yes'm! 'Course I am." He squirmed and tried to free himself but Pauline held him tightly. Finally he said in a petulant voice, "Let me loose, Pauly. Yer a married lady, ain'tcha? Wedded to the cap'n right and proper are ye."

"What's the difference? I'm the same person, aren't I?"

He looked at her critically and his disbelief was apparent.

"By gum, no, ye ain't the same and that's the truth. Pauly, girl, a body wouldn-a reco'nized ye. And, y'see I dinna? What's the cap'n gone and done to ye? Ye look proper sick, Pauly. Ain'tcha happy?"

"Oh, Robert!"

The last question unbound the months of misery. Pauline burst into tears and threw herself at him.

"I've been sad. *So, so* sad! And we had such fun together, Robert. Didn't we? I've been such a fool."

Robert staggered under her weight and tried to push her off, but she clung to him tenaciously as if releasing him would bring back the terrible loneliness. After a while he relaxed and his arms went round her and he made soothing sounds to make her stop crying. He took her by the hand into the depths of a glade out of view of the path and lowered her to the ground that was covered by fallen leaves. Then he went back and brought his barrow, making sure it too was invisible.

They settled down comfortably just like the old times. Pauline dried her tears and holding a blackberry scone in one hand and linking the fingers of the other with Robert's, told him her story. He listened, nodding sympathetically, now angry, now bewildered, shocked that someone could reduce his magnificent beauty to such a sorry state.

"But why, Pauly, girl? Why? Why don't the cap'n like ye? Yer so pretty, I could die!"

This made Pauline sob brokenly once more.

"I don't know, Robert! I've done nothing to him. There's nothing wrong with me, is there? Look at me. You used to like me, didn't you?"

"Oh lor', *did I!*" said Robert. The old helpless look was back in his expression. "But now yer good and married to the cap'n an'...an' I will be horsewhipped if they done catch me with ye."

Pauline threw the scone away.

"Kiss me!"

"*What?*"

"Come here Robert, and kiss me."

"Shan't! Are ye daft, girl? I'll be killed dead! *Proper dead!*"

"Oh, you!"

She pulled his face to hers and fiercely kissed him. Her bonnet fell off. Robert tried to fend her away, but Pauline held on firmly, her long pent-up passion giving her a panther-like strength. She wanted to devour him. When he struggled deliciously in her grip she thrust her tongue into his mouth and he froze. Then he groaned and relaxed, shivering. Slowly he drew her to himself and returned her kiss with growing feeling. Pauline laughed throatily. This was more like it! They kissed for a long time with their eyes closed, losing themselves in each other, the sensation of their bodies touching filling them with growing ardor. Pauline felt his hardness through the soft cloth of his breeches. His masculine smell and the feel of his fluttering eyelashes on her cheek had started an excited throbbing in her loins. She took his hand and guided it to her breast and felt her nipple tauten at once at his touch. She wanted him. He moaned softly. She had always wanted him. She wanted him desperately. Now. She realized she had wanted him from the first. Now she wanted to give herself to him completely.

Abruptly she broke the embrace and sat back. She held his eyes and very deliberately took off her coat and then her blouse. He gasped and his eyes grew large. He licked his dry lips as she undid the bodice of her skirt and her breasts sprang free. She saw him sway as though the effect was too much. Quickly, she took both his hands and placed them on her breasts and immediately a powerful shock ran through her. She drew his head down to her bosom. Robert whimpered, completely helpless under her spell. Then he hesitantly, caressingly, kissed her breasts, first one, and then the other, his lips dry and warm. Each time he did so, an ecstatic thrill passed through her and she wanted him to continue forever.

"Oh, Pauly!" she heard him say in a strangled voice.

They kissed again, more urgently this time, and his hard work-worn hands played on her body and under her petticoats driving her wild with anticipation. She frantically undid the buttons of his shirt and he shrugged it off. The touch of her nipples on his bare chest drove her into frenzy.

"Now," she whispered urgently. "Quickly!"

They tore off the rest of their clothing. A wild passion engulfed her as she saw his strong body and his arousal. She lay back and held out her arms and he came into them. They kissed, intensely aware of every point where their bodies touched. The sensations grew as they held tightly to each other. Their bodies moved together and then Robert thrust forward convulsively. Pauline felt an obstruction, then a sharp stab of pain, replaced immediately by a feeling of elation that was like heaven. She squealed his name in joy and tried to pull him even closer inside her, deep inside her.

"I love you!" she cried, "Robert, I love you. Yes. No. Don't stop!"

"Oh, Pauly!"

They stayed in each other's arms for a long time after it was over, not saying anything, their minds closed to everything except each other as they relived each moment.

The sounds of a group of people walking along the path came through the trees. Robert sat up and put on his shirt. He looked down at the glorious figure spread before him and gulped.

"Oh, Pauly!" Yer more lovely'n before."

"It was your first time wasn't it?"

Robert nodded shyly.

"Mine too," she said happily and sat up. "And I'm glad you were my first."

They stayed as they were for a while longer. Then Pauline shivered as a breeze dried her perspiration. Robert covered her with one of her petticoats.

"What's to happen now?" he asked finally.

"Nothing, silly. Aren't you happy?"

"Ne'er been so happy in me whole life! But we've gone and done wrong."

Pauline held out her arms and when he came into them she kissed him tenderly.

"We've done no wrong, Robert dear. You're the one I want and that's all that matters. Let's run away."

Robert rocked back and stared at her.

"Run away? Where?

"What does it matter where? Let's just run away together."

"Oh, Pauly!"

The weather stayed unusually warm that year. They met

three more times in their secret glade and made love on each occasion, resolving to run away each time. But it was simpler to come back and make love than to run away. And after their fourth clandestine meeting the weather broke and Frederick came back unannounced in the middle of a January snowstorm.

After Freddie gave her the shattering news about going to India Pauline's first thought was to run to Robert at once. But she had to wait three agonizing days before the storm subsided and she could send word to him to meet in their glade. They met. They argued. They raged at the injustice of it all. They cried at the futility of it all. Where could they run away? The stark reality was that they would starve or freeze wherever they fled. And then, in the deep snowdrift, heedless of the cold, they made love—passionately, madly, blindly, urgently—for they knew in their hearts this would be the last.

She saw Robert for a final time when she rode through Burnham with her father and brother Giles in the cart that was taking her to Ipswich for the departure to India. She saw him standing at the door of the baker's shop, looking gravely at her, twisting his cloth cap in his hands. She wanted to call out to him but the words would not come. Then the cart turned onto Ipswich High Road and the bakery was lost from view.

Chapter 9

In his palace of a thousand doors, Nawab Shiraj Doula danced in rage.

"Traitors!" raved the Nawab. "Usurpers! How dare they? They *shall* be driven out. Minister! Minister! *Sipah-sala!*"

Footmen rushed from the chamber to call the officials and within minutes Minister Badri Narayan and General Rahamat Khan hastened into their monarch's presence. They found that their king more enraged than he had ever been before.

Shiraj Doula shook a scroll in their faces.

"Do you see this?" he screamed. "How dare they? In *my* land? Our allies, the French, have just sent word the English hatmen are at work not demolishing but strengthening – *strengthening!*—their defenses around Calcutta. They have defied the royal edict after promising to obey. *How dare they! How dare they question my ability to protect them? Who are they afraid of? The spineless French? The miniscule Dutch? The spent force of the Marathas?"

Minister Badri Narayan was a stooping, middle-aged and long-serving functionary who had weathered many a crisis in Moghul politics. Now he watched helplessly as the Nawab worked himself into greater and greater paroxysms of rage.

Any attempt to soothe him would very likely bring the force of the king's wrath on himself. And it would be suicidal to inform the Nawab that the hatmen were perhaps afraid of the Nawab himself!

"Loathsome *feringhis!* They shall be destroyed. I want blood! *Blood!* Do you understand, *Sipah-sala?*"

"Yes, my Lord?"

"Hear me carefully then. We shall march. Prepare the army, *Sipah-sala.* Letter-writer! *Letter-writer!*"

A gaunt man wearing a check sarong and collarless shirt came out of the shadows. He exhibited scholarly status with a traditional four-finger-length beard and prayer cap.

"My Lord?"

"Letter-writer! Compose a message immediately and send it by fastest courier to Hazrat Sayyid in Calcutta. Tell the honorable ambassador that the English fortifications that have been preserved against my express command shall be destroyed by the Bengal Army. This has our highest priority and the Nawab himself shall march on Calcutta at the head of his army. Hazrat Sayyid is hereby commanded to notify the *Laat-Sahib* that the time for talk is past. He has been given the chance to make amends and he has impudently...*impudently,* do you hear me, letter-writer?...impudently tried to deceive the Nawab by speaking of attacks by the French. The French have assured us they have no hostile intentions. So what are the English doing? Traitors! Tell the English Governor that even if he begs at my feet, I shall have no mercy. The Nawab has made his resolve."

The letter-writer wrote as fast as he could. His quill furiously scratched and blotched the paper. But he was not fast enough.

"Give it to me, fool!"

Shiraj Doula snatched the paper from the trembling scribe. He took up the quill and wrote across the bottom half in big Bengali characters:

'*The Nawab hereby swears in the name of Allah and the Prophet Mohammed that unless the English consent to fill their ditch and raze their fortifications, they shall be totally expelled from his country.*'

Chapter 10

Lieutenant Dicky Glynnis was extraordinarily happy.

Always a popular person, it took little to make the young Welshman content. Four years ago when only fifteen, he had walked away from Denbigh-on-Clwyd, his tiny highland birthplace, to seek his fortune. By all indications he was well on his way to finding it. In Cardiff, despite his youth, he had secured a commission in the Bengal Lancers and come to India. Only three months ago he had been promoted to lieutenant. And he was a full member of the Fort William syndicate that bought and sold ivory in quantities moderate enough to avoid scrutiny, but rich enough to build a new stone house and mill for Ma, Pa, Daffyd and Meg Glynnis back in Denbigh-on-Clwyd. And, Dicky often chuckled to himself, wouldn't his adventures make old Ma and sister Meg cross themselves several times over! To cap it all, just two nights ago, while grumpy Armstrong and his gloomy wife were away, Dicky managed to get past the governess, into the bedroom and into the arms of their daughter, Bessie. Aching for each other after many interrupted trysts, Bessie and Dicky had shyly explored their healthy young bodies. She had cried on his shoulder later and clung to his shirt when carriage wheels sounded in the darkness outside her window. Dicky managed to jump over the balcony railings in the nick of time. All the way to the mess house he had lustily sung *'O signorina, wilt thou fly with me?'* indifferent to indignant barking of several dogs.

Now Dicky was standing at the prow of the Company cutter, his red hair ruffled by the stiff breeze. Ahead, he could make out a woman filling her pitcher at the river's edge. As they came closer, Dicky saw that she was young and very pretty and stared at her in delight. The girl's long black hair was wound into a thick plait that hung down her back and below her hips. She had shining dark-brown skin. Her only covering, a white red-bordered *sari*, revealed her legs below the knees, her back and her midriff, and snaked across her breasts. Dicky's world overflowed with happiness as he drank in her beauty and thought of Bessie. As always on such occasions, he burst into song. All on board turned from what they were doing and watched as Dicky sang to the village girl with verve and mime.

> *Of all the girls that are so smart,*
> *There's none like pretty Sally;*
> *She is the darling of my heart,*
> *And she lives in our alley.*
> *There is no lady in our land*
> *Is half so sweet as Sally;*
> *She is the darling of my heart,*
> *And she lives in our alley.*

Benjamin Morley and Clarence Clarkson tapped the gunwale in time to the tune. Three English deckhands bounced a jig on the deck and waved to the girl who was now directly broadside and only twenty yards away. She was standing erect now with the pitcher on her hip and was staring at the boat, her eyes wide in amazement. The ferns of the riverbank and a cluster of mud huts formed a gentle backdrop for the idyllic scene.

The two Indian lascars were unperturbed. They were used to the strange ways of Englishmen. Maggie Clarkson smiled indulgently. Martha Armstrong, had she been there, would have been shocked by Englishmen making eyes at a native girl. But Maggie knew her husband of thirty-five years well and also knew the effect the shortage of eligible women had on young men living far from home. Standing beside her, Pauline looked on enviously at the Indian girl falling astern. She wished men would sing and dance for *her* with such gusto...

***

They were sailing north on the Hooghly River.

In an effort to relieve the daily tensions and the Nawab's threats, Maggie Clarkson had decided a break from the pressure of business would be good for the officers of the fort. She and her husband had organized this little outing up the river and invited Benjamin, the Wainwrights, the Linningtons and Dicky to come with them. Armstrong was known never to leave the fort except on urgent business and wasn't even asked. Colonel Linnington, still weak from dysentery, had declined. Benjamin was glad Dicky was coming. The high-spirited army officer was always the life of a party and Benjamin had shared several escapades with him.

After his return from Murshidabad, Benjamin had spent a fair amount of time in the company of Ajoy. He had first offered the Indian prince sanctuary in Fort William on a hunch that Ajoy could be an important factor in the growing need to dethrone the Nawab. Later he was pleasantly surprised to find that they had many things in common, not the least of which was a passion for big-game hunting. For this reason, and to see how he interacted with Englishmen, Benjamin had persuaded Clarkson to invite Ajoy.

As soon as the cutter cast off from Fort William, Maggie had declared a moratorium on business talk.

They left at daybreak and had sailed with the tide for five

hours. A camaraderie settled. Freddie even tolerated Ajoy's accentuated theatrical speech, especially after he surprised them with his breadth of knowledge of Indian geography and history. As they sailed north Ajoy made time pass by vividly describing events that led to establishment of the great empire of the Moghuls and the others that preceded it. He told them of a fabulously wealthy young man named Siddharta Gautama who, tired of the pleasures of life, strove for and found divine enlightenment on a riverbank close to where they were, and came to be known as the Buddha. He told them of fierce Arakan invaders of Burma who periodically laid waste to the coastal plains of eastern Bengal. He told them of hardy travelers from a distant mountain kingdom called Nepal who crossed and re-crossed the lofty spine of the Himalayas into a mystical land called Tibet.

Standing at the cutter's rail Benjamin sensed Ajoy come up beside him.

"Hallo!" he said cheerfully. "And what do you think of Sally of the Alley?"

Ajoy shook his dark head in perplexity. Dicky was still reeling off stanzas of Henry Carey's song even though the object of his attention had long disappeared astern. The boat rocked and the crowd on the deck whooped as Dicky launched into Carey's last verse.

> My masters and the neighbors all
> Make game of me and Sally,
> And but for her I'd better be
> A slave, and row a galley;
> But when my seven long years are out,
> O, then we'll wed, and then we'll bed,
> But never in our alley!

Dicky ended with a flourish and everybody applauded. Freddie joined Benjamin and Ajoy.

"A tiger shoot, eh, Morley?"

"Yes, Captain."

"Isn't that a touch dangerous?"

"Oh, we will take the necessary precautions, but I'd be untruthful if I said it wasn't dangerous. But it's exciting and, mark my words, you'll enjoy it."

"Well, it does break the monotony."

"Cap'n, did you know Prince Ajoy here is a veteran *shikari?* A big game hunter. He's bagged several tigers and many leopards and bears."

"Has he now? The only game I've bagged are Russians. This is going to be quite an experience. I still marvel at this warm breeze, the wet air and the brown water. Those northern seas were *cold!*" Freddie shivered in reminiscence and added, "Bears, eh? I've seen big white bears near Murmansk."

"White bears?" Ajoy exclaimed. "There are no white bears."

Freddie tensed in annoyance but when Benjamin gestured *peace*, he relaxed. Ajoy continued.

"As a matter of fact, bears are rarely found hereabouts. In the hills north of my Rajmahal, there is a black bear, which, when it stands on two legs, is taller than a man. It displays white stripes on its chest like your English letter *V*.

"How do you shoot these animals? Do they come when called?"

Ajoy missed or ignored Freddie's sarcasm and Benjamin answered.

"In a way, Captain, that's exactly what happens. I was going to detail my plans over lunch." He looked around. "As a matter of fact the ladies are digging into baskets, so we might as well get started."

When they had settled with a plate of food each, Benjamin outlined what was to happen.

"In another two hours, we shall come to a small village. Its name is Mayurmani. My man, Murali, went there yesterday to make arrangements for our visit, and I happen to know the headman of this village. The jungle which, by the way, has already begun on the left bank, borders Mayurmani's rice fields. I've ordered a buffalo be tied under a tree in a jungle clearing. When it gets dark, the buffalo will get anxious and bellow to come home. Meanwhile we shall be sitting on hidden platforms built on trees above the buffalo and shoot predators that are attracted by its calls."

Pauline thought this was rather hard on the poor buffalo but decided to say nothing. She was overjoyed to be free of the intolerable environment of the Company House and Fort William and out in the open air in the company of, mostly, friends. She looked out across the muddy water at the thick tangled mass of trees and creepers which had taken the place of fields. The jungle appeared impenetrable and forbidding. Birds called in varying tones and pitches. A flock of yellow teals swept by, flying just inches above the surface of the water.

"Your brother didn't tell me you were up to this sort of thing," remarked Freddie. "How long have you been at it?"

Benjamin finished the last of his fish preparation and sat back with a satisfied sigh.

"The first thing I shot was a large crocodile that was dragging off a worker while we were clearing the jungle for the Garden Reach docks three years ago. After that I've shot leopard and wild pig within the bounds of Calcutta. Then I suppose word got around that I was good at shooting big animals. The idea of tying out live bait and sitting over it came to me when some villagers wanted me to rid them of a tiger that was killing their livestock. It's been a success almost every time. I used to hunt with Conrad Hugh-Smith, our last Governor."

"Hugh-Smith died of snakebite!" exclaimed Clarkson.

"Well yes, but that was in Calcutta itself."

The Clarksons and Wainwrights looked doubtfully at the jungle.

"Hmmm... Let's be clear," said Freddie. "Just what animals are you taking us to?"

"Captain-sahib," Ajoy joined in. "These jungles contain deer of many types. And leopard, tiger, elephant, wild pig, wolf and...and...*gondar.*"

"Cor! What on earth be a *gondar?*" Dicky asked. "It sounds right nasty."

"I do not know the English word."

Benjamin said with a deadpan face, "It's a great gray beast that weighs a ton."

"Bigger than a bull?" asked Pauline, her eyes wide with apprehension.

"Much bigger than a bull."

"Bigger than a buffalo?"

"Oh, much bigger!"

Pauline nervously pointed at the jungle.

"And it's in *there?*"

"True, madam."

Maggie rounded angrily on Benjamin.

"You insufferable twerp! Stop frightening the poor child. What *is* it?"

"Rhinoceros, Mrs. Clarkson." Benjamin replied meekly but his eyes were dancing. He found that he enjoyed teasing the impressionable Pauline. "They're big, but don't worry, they're quite harmless. They live in swampy areas which we'll avoid and they retreat when they see humans."

He felt a thrill pass through him as Pauline gave him a look of playful wrath. As a result he did not hear Maggie as she asked him, "And what about snakes?" so that Ajoy replied injudiciously on his behalf, "Yes, Memsahib, there are many kinds of snakes."

"Well, that settles it. Clarence, you are not going in there. By the way, laddie, who *are* you expecting to join your jaunt tonight? This wasn't part of our planning."

"Mrs. Clarkson, I thought this would be a nice diversion for the men. Here is my plan. While all of you rest during the afternoon, I shall take Murali with me and check the arrangements in the jungle clearing. Then around five o'clock we men will enter the jungle and sit through the night on the platforms in the trees and return at dawn. You, ladies, will sleep inside the cabin on the boat. Murali, the deckhands and the village headman, Mullick, will stay here in case you need anything."

"How shall we see them animals in the dark, sir?" Dicky asked.

"Glynnis! What a question from the likes of you. Don't tell me you haven't noticed how bright the tropical moonlight can be on your night forays?" Dicky grinned back unabashed and Benjamin continued. "The moon will be full tonight and will rise soon after sunset. An ideal night for *shikar.*"

A thought struck Maggie.

"Just a moment, Benjamin! Suppose a...a tiger, finds you out and attacks? Looky now, I don't approve of this one bit."

Benjamin felt his control of the situation slipping.

"Mrs. Clarkson, there's really no need to be afraid. I've studied the habits of these cats. Tigers, and all other Indian wild animals for that matter, do not attack humans unless they're disturbed while eating or sleeping. We'll be safely on our high branches while the sun's still up. Prince Ajoy here will corroborate this. No animal will harm you if you follow my instructions in the forest. But whoever wishes to remain aboard the cutter may certainly do so."

"I'll come too."

"*What?*"

Everyone else stared at Pauline in astonishment.

"You will do absolutely no such thing!" Benjamin said emphatically. "The jungle is no place for a woman."

"And why not?"

"Because..."

Pauline smiled sweetly as Benjamin stopped in confusion. He was about to hold forth on the dangers of the forest when he realized he had just finished discounting them. He realized he had been neatly checkmated! Smarting at her audacity, he wondered why on earth she wanted to come on the shoot, especially after her encounter with the bull. But what a daredevil for a girl! He looked at her eager face and shining eyes and his heart skipped a beat and he knew he would give in. He loved the forests and wildlife himself and admired her nerve. This popsy, he told himself, was a treat!

"Pauline!" said Freddie irritably from the background. "You can't possibly go into the forest."

"Oh, I'm not afraid of forests," Pauline rejoined without looking at him. "We had forests near Burnham," she told the others, "with wolves in them. My brother, Giles, and I've even seen wolves hunting stags. And there was a fox den deep in the forest where I used to go by myself to watch the little red cubs."

"Foxes and wolves are a far cry from tigers," Maggie tried to dissuade her.

While the argument raged, the crew brought the cutter close-in to land. Soon the pier at Mayurmani appeared around the trees. Benjamin made out the expectant Murali and the headman waiting on the stone steps. Behind them a crowd of curious faces strained eagerly to see their visitors and to look upon the very first white women that had ever come to their village.

***

The sun was still bright when they set off in single file along a footpath in a direction away from the village. They were five, Benjamin, Pauline, Freddie, Dicky and Ajoy. Benjamin, Ajoy and Freddie each carried a loaded musket and powder. Dicky carried his own musket and two spare ones. Pauline was unarmed. The Clarksons had remained behind. To reassure them, Benjamin had enquired and found that no animal attacks had occurred at Mayurmani in recent memory.

It had all seemed quite safe while he planned the 'adventure' in Calcutta. But as they were about to leave the dry open rice fields and enter the jungle, doubts began to assail Benjamin. At the expense of a thrill, was he exposing the others to unnecessary danger? And quite unexpectedly, he had the safety of a woman on his hands. But all of them, even Freddie, who must have seen enough action and blood, seemed quite unafraid and cheerful.

Benjamin was acutely conscious of Pauline who followed close behind him. Of all the reasons they had put forth in the boat for her not to join them, the one that was most convincing was when Prince Ajoy pointed out that her wide hooped skirts would catch on thorns and twigs and impede their progress. But Pauline had been equal to the challenge. She abruptly disappeared inside the cabin. When she reappeared her corset and layers of petticoats were gone and her skirts seductively followed the contours of her body instead of billowing around her. Everyone had stared at her open-mouthed. And then, with everyone watching she solved the problem of the excess length of the skirt tripping her, by tearing away the cloth below her calves. Benjamin had drunk in the sensuous gypsy-like figure with seductive curves. Ajoy remembered her warmth and softness when he had guided her across the parade-ground. But when Pauline turned around, looked him square in the eyes and asked, "Your Highness, do you still object to my dress?" Ajoy felt hot and foolish and could only shake his head.

Now walking along between the rice fields, Benjamin put Pauline out of his mind with an effort and concentrated on the tasks ahead. The clearing was situated two miles inside the jungle and was approached by a narrow but well-defined forest path. The path was used by the village folk to collect fruit and honey and to graze cattle, and by travelers to and from Mayurmani. At night it was a game trail. Embedded in the dust Benjamin saw hoof and paw marks of many sizes and shapes.

All at once the trees closed in and Benjamin stopped to check their armaments. The muskets were loaded and primed. They went on. Their only possible danger lay in disturbing a large sleeping animal or a mother with cubs.

The very remote possibility of a tiger attack, if it happened, would be directed against the first or the last person in the group, which were the accomplished hunters, Benjamin and Ajoy. Benjamin studied the bushes and rocks by the path with utmost care as they proceeded slowly. He had instructed his followers not to panic if anything unexpected happened. If an animal appeared, Ajoy or he would deal with it. They were to keep complete silence and watch where they were going. Benjamin had demonstrated the few hand signals they would need.

***

Pauline walked along dreamily behind Benjamin.

She had already decided that she loved her new country. This expedition really brought home to her that India was finer than anything she had ever imagined. The boat ride had been thoroughly enjoyable. The river breeze had filled the big sail and blown through her hair. The water scintillated in the sunshine and they passed little sailboats, herds of water buffalo, flocks of egrets, and miles and miles of harvested rice fields. The incident of the village girl was somehow terribly stimulating. As she watched the dusky nymph-like form, she had felt clumpy and over-dressed herself. She wondered how one draped a *sari*—not in the skimpy way of the village maiden, now wouldn't *that* be a scream!—but in the genteel manner of women of Calcutta. "Thank you for arranging this excursion!" she had told Maggie and given her an enthusiastic hug. How had the men stared when she had taken off her corset and petticoats! Even young Dicky had ogled her. This made her think of Dicky and Bessie's exciting romance. Dicky had confided in her about his devotion for the Governor's daughter. Delighted to be involved in their escapade, Pauline promised to get them together whenever she could, and after that Dicky followed her around like a puppy.

Pauline picked her way along the path. The shortness of dress and absence of corset gave her a wonderful feeling of comfort and freedom. She made up her mind she would never wear the hateful whalebone corset again. In her happiness she had succeeded in momentarily pushing away the impending voyage to China from her mind. The sun was still quite hot. Little beads of perspiration formed on her upper lip. The fields were dusty and a dry warm raspy odor rose from them. She heard a continuous whirring undertone on all sides, which Benjamin said came from insects on the move. Looking closely at the undergrowth, where there was nothing before, she saw gaudy dragonflies poised on reeds, strikingly patterned moths, metallic beetles, ladybugs, and ants of many sizes and hues.

Abruptly their world changed.

They had entered the jungle. A profusion of foliage descended. The surroundings changed from dry brown to lush green. It became dark under the canopy of trees. As they went deeper, Pauline's senses were assailed by the dank smell of overripe vegetation. The path wound through thick undergrowth and thorny bushes. Trees had broad leaves and many had roots which spread away from their trunks and threatened to trip the intruders. The forest floor was dappled with mosaics of light and shade. It became cooler. Pauline looked around enthralled. Every visual, aural and sensory perception was new and overwhelming.

After a while they gained their bearings and the blur of images began to take shape. Pauline made out thick coils of a maroon creeper that wound round the branches of a big tree and was slowly strangling it. Bird calls began to differentiate themselves. She recognized the high-pitched *miao-ow* of peacocks, warbling of mynahs, rasping of crows, shrieking of parrots, and the ever-present chirp of sparrows. Bevies of quail rose up on whirring wings at their approach. From almost under her feet, a jungle cock crowed stridently like a farm fowl and made her jump. They walked slowly trying to be as silent as possible. Benjamin pointed out roots and twigs to Pauline who stepped over them and pointed them out to Freddie behind her, and so on down the line. While they avoided snapping twigs or falling over roots, the velvet carpet of fallen leaves rustled and crunched underfoot. They went deeper. After half a mile or so, they entered a section of the forest where bamboo grew in clumps and their world changed once more. Hard spear-like bamboo shoots towered above their heads. Soft sickle-shaped leaves cushioned their steps and their progress became soundless.

Abruptly the bushes ten yards ahead and to their right swayed and a big horned head magically appeared. The next moment a large and lovely animal stepped onto the path and turned to face them. The deer's big eyes were delicately soft. Its many-tined antlers spread back over its body. Its color was a deep bronze. To Pauline it appeared rather shaggy and big for a deer, larger even than an English stag. They stopped and the animal continued to stare at them. Pauline thought it was looking right at her. How adorable! She wanted to go forward and touch its silky head and wet nose.

"*Sambar,*" announced Benjamin in a whisper.

That was enough to break the spell. The animal lifted its head and barked a deep *'dhonk'* of alarm and crashed away.

They proceeded along the path and flushed various other animals including a herd of smaller spotted dear that loped away, stopping periodically to look back over their shoulders. Pauline thought their long erect ears and golden-brown coats speckled with white spots made them look absolutely darling. They appeared quite plentiful in the area. The bucks had impressive antlers while the does and fawns had none. Benjamin tactfully did not mention that a profusion of deer implied the presence of a proportionately large number of predators.

On they went.

After a while Benjamin stopped, pressed a finger to his lips and pointed straight ahead. Pauline looked in the direction, but could not make out anything. Then there was a snuffling wheezing noise. Following the sound, she discerned, in a small clearing beside the path about fifteen yards away, a very dark and hairy man bent double over a tree stump. She wondered what he was doing and why he was making those peculiar noises. The man continued his labors quite unaware of them. Then Benjamin cleared his throat, startling them. The man immediately turned, stood up straight and faced them and Pauline got the shock of her life. It wasn't a man at all! It was a bear with an unusually long and pointed snout that was smeared with a sticky liquid. It had long claws that curved inward. The bear waved its head around short-sightedly as it tried to make out the source of the sound. Benjamin clapped his hands. At once the bear dropped on all fours with a grunt, spun around and, finally focusing, saw them. Then it shuffled away into the forest, grumbling irritably.

Pauline wanted to laugh out loud at its cross behavior.

"Sloth bear," Benjamin informed her shortly.

As they passed the hollow tree trunk she heard a loud humming and saw that the bear had ripped the bark with its claws in his efforts to get at honey from a hive that bees had build into the trunk.

Behind her, Freddie directed a nasty look at Ajoy.

"`No bears hereabouts!'" he muttered.

Ajoy smiled blandly and refused to be intimidated.

Pauline was delighted. All these sights. All these animals. All putting on a show just for her. Not one had been threatening. Who was it that had warned her in England that India was full of dense forests and dangerous beasts?

As if on cue, Benjamin suddenly stopped dead and once again put a finger to his lips. His demeanor was much more taut this time. Apprehensively Pauline looked past him and strained her ears. A long moment passed during which she heard no sound other than the ever-present birds. The she heard a low rumbling sound from the bamboo thicket. What could it be? It didn't sound like an animal growl, and reminded her of distant thunder. But the sky was bright and clear. There was a minute or two when the sound stopped.

They stood in a line, absolutely still. Then the sound came again. A continuous rumble. Louder and nearer.

All of a sudden there was a loud tearing crashing noise to their right front. On one spring they whirled to face it. Simultaneously Ajoy pushed past Pauline and stood beside Benjamin.

The tearing noise was repeated from even closer. It sounded as though a monster was approaching. There was another minute of silence and then a bamboo clump shook violently and the slate-gray bulk of a monstrous creature emerged from the thicket into sunlight just fifty feet ahead.

An elephant!

To Pauline it appeared absolutely gigantic. It was facing away and had not seen them and was walking away slowly while chewing on a bamboo shoot that protruded on either side from under the base of its trunk.

Pauline's throat went dry. The elephant was immense and towered above the surrounding spear-grass and bamboo. It was bigger than anything she had ever seen. Its proximity made it seem like the side of a cliff. As it walked it swayed ponderously from side to side on its pillar-like feet. The little whippy tail looked ridiculous on its large creased hindquarters.

What would it do if it turned and saw them?

And at exactly that moment the muskets that Dicky carried shifted and knocked against each other with a loud rattle.

The elephant dropped the bamboo shoot and spun around in a flash. It was unbelievably fast for its size. Peering between the two men in front of her, Pauline fearfully watched its small piggy eyes. They were unfocussed and very mean. The sharp points of its long dirty-white forward-curving tusks gleamed wickedly in the sun. The great beast swayed back and forth, back and forth, and waved its trunk in the air.

Clearly it was trying to catch their scent.

They stood still and quiet as mice. Pauline was petrified. The presence of the huge animal, so close, was more frightening than anything she had ever experienced in her whole life.

A breeze rustled the bamboo fronds and at once the elephant's trunk went up high and coiled back against its head and the monster took on a more menacing posture.

It had caught their scent!

Pauline wanted to run for her life but found she could not move a muscle.

"Hrrrrr-ooooon-eeeeeeeeeeen!"

The utterly spine-chilling sound at such short range turned Pauline's legs to jelly. The elephant trumpeted again and took a few short steps, stopped, went back a step, angrily shook its ears, and trumpeted once more. Then it came forward with short quick strides, rapidly reducing the distance between them.

In one motion Ajoy and Benjamin raised and leveled their muskets and the elephant stopped dead. It lifted its trunk and blew air at them in noisy gusts.

The world stood still.

In the next instant the elephant swung around and crashed into the bamboo thicket and vanished from sight. The noise of its passage grew fainter and then died.

Absolute total silence reigned. Even the birds stopped calling.

Slowly, very slowly, Pauline's legs began to crumple. Sensing this Benjamin turned and caught her just in time and lowered her to the ground. Ajoy, his musket still level, stayed where he was and intently watched the place where the elephant had disappeared.

Freddie moved off the path and sat down heavily. Then he doubled over and vomited.

Dicky laid down the muskets with a sigh and wiped his brow. He was the first to speak. In the stillness his voice sounded unnaturally loud.

"By all the saints, Mr. Morley, sir! That there screaming

was the last peal of doom. I'd a-thought the beast'd be all over us. Perhaps there be others?"

"*Oh!*"

Pauline's limp body tensed on hearing this, but Benjamin held her tightly. Dicky looked down worriedly first at her and then at Freddie.

"Ye all right, Mum?" he asked. When Pauline nodded, he said, "I'll see to the Cap'n," and walked across to Freddie.

During all this Benjamin was studying her anxiously, hating himself. The suddenness and closeness of the encounter had been totally unexpected. But Pauline hadn't fainted. In another moment she sat up, her face chalky-white.

"Will it return?" she asked. "Are there more?"

"It's gone, Mrs. Wainwright," said a relieved Benjamin. "It was a lone tusker. And if you can still believe me, it never meant to attack us. I heard the rumble of its stomach before it actually appeared, but didn't want to make a noise in case a herd was present. With all those short rushes and screaming, it was only trying to frighten us away. When we raised our guns it decided it was time to go. Terribly sorry you had such a turn. How do you feel?"

"I'm better."

She struggled to get on her feet. Ajoy lowered his musket at last and came to help. Pauline looked up at the troubled faces of the two big men, one dark and one fair. Touched by their concern and courage, her heart stopped its thumping, and she smiled to allay their distress. At once she saw a strange look came into their expressions. Relief? Admiration? She was proud of herself for being brave and suddenly felt a secret camaraderie with them and fought an urge to fall into their arms.

Pauline stood up straight and tried to arrange her hair.

"Mark two adventures for me," she said in a breathless voice as color began to return to her cheeks. "I thought that bull was big, but, crikey, *was* I wrong!" Feeling quite free of inhibition, she gave Ajoy a roguish grin. "Your Highness, do you have anything bigger in your country to threaten me with? A *gondar* perhaps?" Her smile disappeared. "Oh my God, look at Freddie!"

Captain Wainwright was certainly in a bad way. Supported by Dicky, he was now sprawled on his back while his eyes stared wildly. Saliva dripped down the sides of his mouth. Hesitating for only a moment, Pauline went over and wiped his brow and his face with her handkerchief and loosened his collar. Freddie's breathing came in painful gasps. It took a while before he could sit up and even then he was obviously in no shape to go on. Benjamin immediately decided to call off the *shikar* and get the captain back to the boat and to Calcutta as quickly as possible. But could he walk?

They sat on the ground close to Freddie, giving him time to recover. The shadows lengthened. With the trumpeting challenge of the bull elephant still ringing in her ears, Pauline found it quite incongruous when sparrows resumed their chitter and a troupe of athletic long-tailed silver-gray black-faced monkeys arrived in the branches above them. One of the *langurs* caught sight of the silent group of humans below and raised a frantic whooping alarm. The troupe scattered with loud outraged whoops. Then a big porcupine crossed the path shaking its long black quills noisily. The descending tranquility slowly calmed her nerves. Pauline sighed and relaxed and began to breathe in the sights and smells of the forest once more. Peace returned where pandemonium had raged. After a while, Benjamin, sitting beside her, gently touched her arm. Turning, she followed his gaze and a beautiful tableau formed before her. Three pairs of long ears trembled over erect heads and quivering noses barely fifteen feet away. The red glow of a waning sun burnished tawny coats of the deer and highlighted their myriad white spots. It was a lovely sight. Then a bird or a rodent rustled the bamboo leaves. In a flash, the deer were gone.

***

Several hours later Maggie Clarkson lay back worriedly on a makeshift mattress on the deck of the boat. Next to her Pauline sat propped on pillows. The two women were to have slept inside the covered area of the cutter, but after Freddie staggered in supported by Dicky and Benjamin, they had given it up to him. The captain was now sunk in exhausted slumber under mosquito netting.

Maggie was very concerned. She suspected that the battle-scarred naval officer had suffered more than just a bad scare. While they cleaned up and settled Freddie into the covered portion of the boat, she had placed her hand on his heart and had felt it fluttering uncontrollably. He should be examined by the garrison surgeon at once. She wished they could have got underway right then. But the perilous bends and sandbanks in the river precluded night travel.

Freddie was now sleeping like a dead man. To Maggie's relief, his heart rate had steadied.

Little had been said while deck hands and Murali served the ever-present fish curry with ship's biscuit and boiled spinach. They ate sparingly, overcome by reaction to the elephant incident, to the arduous walk back with the dysfunctional captain in gathering darkness, and to the anticlimax of the aborted adventure. Clarkson had given them all, including the women, a strong shot of rum with their tea. Maggie made a few attempts at conversation but soon gave up. They ate the meal in silence, looking out over the water, lost in their own thoughts.

Hidden in the darkness, Benjamin, Ajoy and Dicky were talking in low tones at the prow of the cutter. Clarkson's glowing pipe, a dim lantern set on a thwart, and flashing fireflies were the only points of light in the blackness. The boatmen, the English hands and Murali were sleep on the pier, wrapped up in sheets like corpses.

The night was warm and clear. Something, a fish perhaps, splashed beside the boat. The water lapped gently on the river bank. A steady drone of cicadas counter pointed the continual swish of moving water. Bullfrogs croaked their mating songs. Fireflies in their thousands blinked in brilliant pinpoints.

And then, in tremendous glory, an immense full moon arose majestically. It cleared the trees in minutes and turned the river into a lake of glittering gold.

Pauline could not breathe.

She had never imagined anything could be so dramatically beautiful. The pristine setting, the menacing jungle, the shining river and the brilliant moonlight painted a vision of heaven into her sensitive and impetuous heart.

Maggie felt her stir.

"Pretty, isn't it, child?"

"Oh, Maggie, it's lovely." Pauline's voice came low and broken. "It's *so...so* lovely that I can't bear it. It makes me sad."

"My, how strange. I don't understand how that can happen."

"You don't have to, Maggie dear. I say silly things. Ever since I've come to India, everything has been so...so *extreme!* So much kindness, so much danger, so much beauty, excitement, so much...so much color. So much history! It's like something I've been looking for all my life but didn't know. And to think I hated the idea of coming to India. Do you love this country, Maggie? I do. I do."

Maggie smiled.

Pauline's mood changed.

"I do hope Freddie's all right. He's had such a turn. On the way back he said the elephant sounded like the screaming of a Russian boarding army that killed half his crew in the war. It was so *big,* that elephant!"

Maggie listened sympathetically while Pauline went on.

"Poor Mr. Morley. He had planned this thing in such detail. And, oh, the poor buffalo! It's still there tied up. What a shame if it's killed by a tiger now." She changed the subject again. "I did so look forward to the night in the jungle."

Maggie sighed.

"You're a wild one, aren't you? I wouldn't go ashore there in the daytime let alone in the dark."

Pauline sat up.

"Oh, I say! What a marvelous idea. Really, Maggie, could I go for a walk? Just a bit? Please? The moon. It's calling me. It's so exquisite."

Pauline began to adjust her dress, determined to immediately turn thought to action. Maggie sat up aghast. Involuntarily she looked toward the cabin. Pauline saw this and said, "Don't worry, Freddie won't mind. I was a wild one when he married me. He knows I can take care of myself."

Maggie shuddered.

"You mean you'll go out there by yourself? With those animals? Those snakes? What if another elephant comes?"

What was she going to *do* with this girl? And she had thought she had seen everything when Pauline appeared before the men without her underpinnings and ripped the hem off her dress in public view.

Pauline stood up.

"I'm going, Maggie. Don't worry. I'll keep the boat in sight. I'll be all right."

"Sweet Jesus, girl! You bloody well are *not* going. Clarence!" Maggie struggled up in consternation. "Have some sense in your head. At least take Dicky with you, or Benjamin. Ask them to take a gun."

Pauline walked across to the men.

"Anything the problem, Mrs. Wainwright?" Clarkson was looking in their direction having heard his wife call. "Is the captain sleeping?"

"Yes, Mr. Clarkson, thank you. Freddie's sound asleep. I can't sleep myself though, and a walk would be nice. It's bright as day."

"*What?*"

The men gaped at her and Pauline, now thoroughly enjoying herself, smiled back impishly. From her mattress,

Maggie listened to the ensuing argument. It was an exact repetition of the afternoon. This time Pauline settled the issue by lifting her skirts and vaulting over the gunwale and onto the pier. Benjamin and Dicky got in each others' way trying to follow her off the boat. Dicky was first off and by her side. The sleepers on the pier sat up to see what the disturbance was. Clarkson looked down uneasily from the deck.

"We must go with the Memsahib," Ajoy said firmly from the deck. "She cannot go into the fields without protection."

"Protection from what?" Pauline wanted to know.

"From what, Memsahib? From everything! Elephant herds come to feed at night. Snakes wait for mice. Leopards hunt village goats and dogs. Wild boar dig in the fields. Wolf packs roam."

Pauline was enjoying the attention and, knowing her men, she was certain half the dangers were being made up to impress her. If all the prince said was true, Mayurmani village must be a regular zoo in the night.

"But," she objected innocently, "if all of you come with me, who will protect the people on the boat from all those fearsome animals?"

There was a sudden silence as the men looked at each other. Quite unexpectedly, it was Ajoy who broke it.

"Only Morley-sahib and I have knowledge of animal shooting." His accent did not in away disguise the complete conviction in his voice. "One of us must accompany this memsahib and the other must remain with the rest of the party. Because of the Captain's condition, Morley-sahib must remain on board."

Benjamin, about to put in his bid, was completely disarmed. *He* wanted to be alone with this turbulent woman and was about to turn on Ajoy in furious contradiction, when he stopped himself. Gentlemen did not brawl before ladies.

Dicky Glynnis spoke at last.

"I'll come with me musket, Mum. Be careful, won'tcha?"

***

Pauline followed Ajoy as he walked up the path to the village without speaking. Dicky stayed a few yards behind, his eyes darting to left and right.

The moon had climbed higher and had turned into a brilliant beacon in the night sky. It bathed the rows of sleeping huts in bright silvery tones. Every object stood etched in sharp relief. Pauline felt she was walking through a silver wonderland with her prince leading the way. All she needed now was a dragon to appear and her prince to slay it. The fact that close to a dense jungle such a thing could actually happen, made her laugh ring out gaily in the silent night.

Ajoy, his musket balanced on his shoulder, turned around and looked at her inquiringly. Hoping he would not see her blushing, Pauline told him the story of St. George and the dragon, and why she found the analogy humorous. She had to explain the meaning of the unfamiliar word, chivalry. And as he concentrated Ajoy's grave face softened into a smile.

Dicky listened to all this with interest. They all relaxed and the tensions of the day eased.

"Do you have many instances of this chivalry in your country, Memsahib?" Ajoy asked over his shoulder after they had walked some more.

"In England? Oh, yes. Lots."

Ajoy slowed his pace and let her catch up with him.

"There was once a king called Arthur. A long time ago. One of his knights was called Sir Galahad. He was famous for chivalrous deeds. Another knight, Sir Lancelot, tipped the balance the other way though. He went and fell in love with King Arthur's queen! In more recent times, another knight, Sir Walter Raleigh, spread his cape across a pool of water so that his lady could keep her feet dry. Are there such stories in India?"

"Of chivalry, Memsahib? Or of falling in love with another's wife?"

She looked up at him in surprise and their eyes met. Bright points of moonlight reflected in his dark pupils teased her. All at once formality fell away and she joined in his spirit and replied without hesitating.

"Oh, it doesn't matter! Stories of men and women and their loves?"

"Of course, Memsahib. Legends of Lord Krishna are full of such stories. Once, when village girls bathed in a pool, Krishna hid their clothes. And hundreds of songs through the length of my country pay homage to Krishna's devotion to his beloved Radha."

They strolled on and Ajoy talked to her of poetry and song just as he had expounded on Indian history on the boat. He spoke of Tansen, the immortal musician in Emperor Akbar's court; of the great poet Chandidas; of the child Krishna who broke milkmaids' pitchers for their butter.

Pauline walked by his side and drank in the picturesque anecdotes. Suddenly she was struck by the incongruity of her situation. Here she was, an English woman in a remote Indian village, walking unconcerned through a thick jungle full of fierce wild animals of which she'd had a savage taste only a few hours ago; walking in bright moonlight dressed like a gypsy; talking of love and poetry and of men hiding women's clothes; walking by the side of a native prince.

Did he feel anything, she wondered.

With Dicky following, they cleared the last house of the village. The fields stood out in stark relief, molten and bewitching. Pauline wanted to treasure every moment.

"You must think I am incorrigible."

When he did not understand she explained.

"Incorrigible means bad. It means someone who gets into trouble all the time. Someone who cannot be controlled. I fit all those descriptions."

"No, Memsahib," Ajoy replied without a moment's hesitation. "You do not fit those descriptions. You are not bad. You are good. You are the bravest and most wonderful woman I have ever known."

Pauline stopped dead.

Me? asked her astounded expression.

"Yes, you, Memsahib," Ajoy had gauged her feeling perfectly. "The world, my world, is filled with deception. Filled with men and women who are strong only in a crowd. Dull colorless people. I hope you never change."

Pauline stared at him incredulously. He was making fun of her of course. He must be. The first time he had seen her she had been running from a non-existent bull. On the next occasion she had torn up her clothes before of a throng of men. Then she had collapsed in terror in the jungle.

Brave? Strong? She?

Then she saw he was absolutely serious. In their two brief encounters she had learned enough of his ways, so different from those of reserved and distant Englishmen, to know that he was forthright and sincere. Her heart beat faster and again she found it difficult to breathe. Something made her accept his compliment without simpering.

Dicky was a forgotten presence.

After a while Pauline found herself saying, "Your Highness, wait, please wait. I have something to tell *you*. I love your country very much. I love the stories of your ancestors. I am sure you will win in your quest to rule your country. And you will make a wonderful king. And then, because I love your country I shall stay here when you *do* rule. I shall become your loyal subject."

As she said all this Ajoy stared at her with a somber fixed expression. Pauline's hand went to her throat in fear that she had said something wrong.

During all his adult life, Ajoy's consuming dream had been to return the Senas to the throne of Bengal and to see his elder brother, Prince Bikram Sena, installed as the Maharaja of Bengal. But the Moghuls had consolidated their hold on the land and had thwarted his every move. The death through malaria three years ago of his far-thinking brother and hero had been a severe blow. Ajoy's pride and self-confidence had gradually eroded until Benjamin's suggestion of starting an insurrection re-ignited visions of himself as the ruler of Bengal. And now this woman, this foreign woman, this girl, was telling him he would prevail. *Could* he prevail? Could he *really* prevail and reinstate the rights of his forefathers?

Ajoy looked down at the soft upturned anxious face framed with ringlets of golden hair. Her complete belief in him was engraved on her lovely face by the light of the moon. He felt an emotion come over him that he had never experienced before. His severe countenance yielded into a gentleness that reached out and enfolded her. He sighed deeply and his whole frame shook as though something horrid had just passed him by. Before her eyes he grew straighter and she knew she had done something good for him, important for him, and felt a fulfilling sense of happiness and achievement. At the same time she felt a strange power over him, 'her' prince.

For a long time they remained as they were, looking into each other's eyes, their thoughts and feelings bridged over the immense gulf that separated their far-flung worlds. They perceived instinctively that words would shatter the grandeur of the moment. Surreal moonlight and the song of crickets sealed the magic into perpetuity. They would have stood there all night had not a worried Welsh lieutenant begun to say things like, "It's late, Mum," and "Them be fussing, Mum."

Still bemused by their wondrous experience, Ajoy and Pauline allowed Dicky to lead them back to the boat while the silvery moon sailed serenely through fleecy clouds in the night sky.

Chapter 11

Two days remained before *Europa's* departure for China.

Pauline alighted from a horse-drawn carriage and stood bemusedly on the wide stone of a Garden Reach wharf and held tightly to Maggie's arm.

Wearing a broad smile, a junior officer came over and introduced himself as Midshipman Nathaniel Roberts. Pauline nodded to him vacantly. Roberts instructed a detail of sailors to take charge of Pauline's sea-chests.

Maggie looked worriedly at the girl beside her. At Fort William, with a strange feeling of foreboding, Maggie had helped Pauline pack, and then insisted on accompanying her on the hour-long journey to the wharf.

A week had passed since the memorable hunting expedition. During this time Maggie observed a steady decline in Pauline's attitude. The uninhibited exuberant demeanor of the outbound journey to Mayurmani had collapsed into dejection on the return trip. During the week Maggie had hinted more than once that she was prepared to lend a sympathetic ear to Pauline's problems, but the young woman would say nothing. Maggie's heart grew heavier as the day of *Europa's* sailing drew near and Pauline became bowed down increasingly with the weight of woe. On today's carriage-ride Pauline was a lamb being led to slaughter.

Soon the two women were sitting on thwarts of a flat-bottomed boat and facing into the wind. Two Indians with long poles walked back and forth in rhythm along the boat's gunwales, pushing them into midstream. The single large sail was not hoisted and the boat floated swiftly with the current and under control of the rudder toward the tall East Indiaman that dominated all shipping offshore.

As they approached the side of *Europa* a net was lowered from a winch on her side. Maggie eyed the net with trepidation. She had a fear of heights and the thought of being lifted bodily fifty feet in a net and landed like a large fish made her feel acutely sick.

Their boat came alongside and was made fast. Midshipman Roberts jumped nimbly and swarmed up netting affixed to the ship's side. The other deckhands followed with Pauline's luggage until the two women and the Indian boatmen were the only ones left. Pauline turned from the ship and her eyes filled with concern when she saw the greenish hue in her elderly friend's face.

"Maggie, dear," she said. "Go back to shore. There really is no need to come aboard. I shall be quite all right and back in the Company House before supper. Thank you kindly for coming."

When Maggie demurred Pauline hugged the motherly woman and then sat her down firmly on a thwart. Then she turned and jumped into the suspended net and held on with both hands. "Hoist away!" someone called from above and with a piercing squeal from the winch, the net with Pauline in it rose above the boat. Maggie looked on unhappily. In minutes Pauline was at the top and willing hands helped her to the deck. She looked down and waved to Maggie who waved back half-heartedly as her boat headed back to the wharf.

Pauline turned and came face to face with Freddie. Immediately she walked around him to the odious passage that led to her old cabin. Seamen followed with her belongings. The captain made an attempt to go after her but was distracted by a call from the quarterdeck and changed direction.

The confrontation took place as the sun was sinking behind serried coconut palms on the west bank of the river and pouring light through the big window.

As she waited in the hot cabin a transformation came over Pauline. It began with a monstrous idea which at first seemed impossible. Then, as she sat still as a statue, thinking, it gathered conviction. Finally it lit a spark of anger that fanned a flame of determination. She remained grimly staring out of the window and awaiting the critical moment. When the sound of heavy boots heralded her husband's arrival she knew that moment had come and welcomed it.

Freddie came in.

For a long moment neither spoke.

The Wainwrights, husband and wife, faced each other from opposite corners of the small sterncastle cabin. Ever since the incident with the drunken sailor in the whaleboat Pauline had not been able to look her husband in the eye. Now she lifted her chin and looked straight at him. Freddie's pallor still bore testimony to the trauma he had undergone in Mayurmani forest. But if there was any residual weakness in him it was submerged in the set of his expression that showed equal parts of malice and disdain. He was the first to speak.

"Pauline, I want to make it quite clear. Your behavior has been atrocious. It has to stop. Now."

Pauline said nothing and let Freddie continue.

"The crew is watching. My authority cannot be undermined under any circumstances..." then like a whiplash, "...*any circumstances!* Do you hear? This has gone far enough."

A muscle twitched on his forehead.

Pauline had never seen her husband so uncontrollably angry. Before today the spectacle would have terrified her. She flinched slightly at his tone, but her gaze remained steady and unafraid.

"We sail tomorrow," said Freddie. "I shall *not* tolerate further nonsense."

"I am not going to China."

It was said in a most matter-of-fact way but Freddie took a step back in surprise.

"What?"

"I am not going to China, Freddie. And you can go to hell."

Captain Wainwright's jaw dropped at the total unexpectedness and finality of the words, so highlighted by her flat tone. It was the first time that his wife was not demure, submissive or despondent. It took him several moments to recover.

Then a muscle in his forehead spasmed and his eyes narrowed in anger.

"What in blazes do you mean by that extraordinary statement? Of course, you are going to China."

"No."

It was said softly but with complete conviction. Freddie scowled and replied with equal firmness.

"Yes. And you don't have a choice. You are not getting off this ship until we reach Canton. And if you don't behave it'll be the worse for you."

Golden sunbeams withered on the dark blue counterpane while husband and wife glowered at each other.

Suddenly the walls of the cabin closed in on Pauline and she could not stay inside another moment. She made to go around but Freddie shot out a hand and grabbed her arm tightly.

"Did you understand what I said?"

Pauline gritted her teeth to keep from showing the pain where he held her and controlled her voice.

"Let me go, Freddie. I am leaving your ship now."

Abruptly Freddie grabbed her other arm and shook her violently. So violently that her teeth clicked together and her head flopped like a rag doll's.

"*Will you behave?*"

For a instant Pauline drooped weakly against the captain. Then the mist cleared and with a surge of savage loathing she jerked her arms free and staggered away to the opposite end of the cabin.

A dead calm descended on her.

"Freddie, let me leave or you will regret it all your life."

She said it with such assurance that Freddie, his chest heaving in anger, looked at her curiously. He had not missed the change in her attitude since the time they rounded the island of Ceylon and had wondered about it. But his pride had prevented him from asking the reason.

With a wary eye Pauline walked toward the door with measured steps. Suddenly Freddie made a movement toward her.

"*Freddie!*" Pauline screamed. "I'll tell the Guv'nor…"

Freddie brought the back of his hand across her face in a stinging blow. Pauline reeled but managed to keep herself from falling. Her hand went to her mouth and she felt the blood. Stars danced behind her eyes and a monumental anger welled up inside her.

"*Captain Wainwright!*" she cried through bleeding lips. "*I shall tell your secret.*"

Freddie froze.

"I shall tell the world you lie with men."

The last sunbeam died.

Freddie, his face white with shock, stared at the change in his wife. The flat steadfastness was gone. Pauline was absolutely raging. Her face was contorted with aversion, her breast heaved, and her eyes poured out hate. When she spoke it was with virulent authority.

"Let me off the ship, you gutless bastard, or your name'll be mud."

Freddie recoiled at the profanity, but only for a moment. He recovered and searched her face. Also, he did not unblock the doorway.

Pauline stamped her foot.

"You fucking worm! Get out of my way!"

"Pauline!"

She took another step toward him.

"Move away! *Now!*"

"You're bluffing."

Pauline's fury boiled over. Her hands went to her hips and her voice rang out.

"You *bastard!* You greedy, malicious, spineless, perverted bastard. You wanted my father's land and you married me, didn't you? That was the only reason, wasn't it? You didn't care that you've ruined my life, did you? *I hate you!* I hate everything about you. I shall tell Mr. Clive and Mr. Armstrong and Mr. Morley about your whaleboat meetings. And that'll be your end. Now let me go!"

Freddie stared at her incredulously and asked in a chastened voice, "You know?"

Pauline made a sound that was a contemptuous snort.

But Freddie wasn't beaten. A crafty look came into his rugged visage.

"It was that night near Ceylon, wasn't it?" When Pauline said nothing he went on. "All right, you can go…"

Pauline relaxed visibly and at once Freddie fixed her with a wicked look.

"…but old Solomon goes off my land."

"What…?" Pauline spluttered, thrown completely off guard. "Father? But Father's done nothing!"

"Listen you ungrateful harlot. And listen carefully. You behave the wife you're supposed to be or your precious father starves. All I have to do is send a message to Ipswich by any westbound ship and he will be run out of the county so fast that…"

Without finishing Freddie turned and left the cabin.

Defeated, Pauline sat down heavily on the bed and with a sob covered her face. She had never suspected her husband capable of such cruelty. But before the tears came, the ever-lingering nausea grew with a vengeance and she rushed to a corner and vomited into the washbowl. The heaving of her body slowed but the tears would not be held back and she wept brokenly for several minutes. Then the sobbing stopped and utter desolation swept through her as she began to think about what he had done. One by one he had destroyed everything in her life. And now she was bonded as his captive because he held sway over Father. At his age Father could not start anew. She thought about Robert, dear simple Robert, aristocratic Benjamin, the mercurial Indian prince. They were all good men who liked her and understood her. But there was nothing they could do for her. Their personalities receded under the hulking shadow of the captain. Once more she remembered Robert's declaration, now oh so painfully prophetic: Wedded to the Cap'n right and proper!

The steward came in with a lamp, saw her slumped form and withdrew.

Evening turned to night.

Life stretched away uselessly. Colorlessly. Eternally.

After a very long time she dimly heard footsteps in the corridor and recognized the sound of those boots and could not bear to see him again, bear to be near him again, bear to think of him again. But she had to because he had nailed her into a coffin she could not escape from. She had to get away, she had to get away, she had to, she had to. With a stricken cry Pauline dashed out of the door, pushed Freddie roughly aside, tore blindly into the darkness of the deck and without stopping leaped at the gunwale and the next moment was falling through space.

Freddie followed her out of the sterncastle and watched with horror as she jumped overboard. He was about to rush to the side and raise an alarm when a thought struck him and he stopped.

After a minute Captain Wainwright turned on his heels and rapidly walked back to his cabin.

Chapter 12

For the first time that year great charcoal-colored clouds scudded up from the south, customary harbingers of the end of summer and the onset of monsoon rains. The countryside lay cracked and parched. A gritty wind created dust-devils and blew dust and leaves in blinding gusts. A brassy sun fought the clouds and filled the earth with an overpowering humidity that could be touched. The thirsty earth waited eagerly for the annual downpour that was its lifeline.

But the rains did not come.

Away from the depredations of nawabs, captains and governors, a fugitive sat cross-legged on the porch of a tiny thatched hut in a forest-encircled village. The upper half of his body was bare and ran with perspiration. Beside him a servant sat and waved an ineffectual bamboo fan.

Prince Ajoy Sena, who had stayed behind at Mayurmani when the English visitors had left, was oblivious of discomfort and absorbed in a letter. The runner who had just brought the letter from Murshidabad lay exhausted in the shade of a tree.

Ajoy read the Bengali text again:

"Submission with ten thousand salutations!

Respected Sir,
It is my unhappy duty to send news of grave consequence.
We have again underestimated the faculties of the Nawab.
Our plans are undone.
It appears the French Laat-sahib *has spread lies about the*
English. Are they lies? They have said the English are even now
building fortifications around Calcutta and are preparing to
attack their own outpost, and even Murshidabad. They have
cited the recent arrival of a big English battleship to drive home
their point. The Nawab is convinced the English have violated
their solemn promise to demolish the fortifications.
His armies will be ready to move in two weeks and he will
reach Calcutta in two weeks beyond that.
We must act now.
We must pre-empt the Nawab's move. If he prevails over the
hatmen our cause is lost.
I respectfully await your bidding."

The letter was neither addressed nor signed because the
writer did not want the letter to be damning evidence should
his messenger be apprehended. But there was no doubt the
writer was the Nawab's Minister, Badri Narayan, Ajoy's secret
ally.

This was a crushing blow to the embryonic revolution that
Ajoy was in process of launching from his jungle hideout.
He looked out with unseeing eyes at the distant trees that
marked the jungle. For three weeks after the English party
returned to Fort William he had eaten irregularly, ignored
his appearance and paced his little courtyard and the path
that led to the jungle. The heat, the planning and the
tension made his features more austere than ever, almost
haggard. He had sent messages and received emissaries from
sympathetic leaders who were spread across a region of more
than ten thousand square miles. In addition to the British his

allies included Jaidev Tolpadi, local emissary of the faraway Maratha Kings with whom Shiraj's grandfather had signed an armistice; Wazir Ali, uncle to Shiraj, who had been defeated in the succession struggle and licked his wounds and bided his time in Orissa under protection of the Marathas; the prominent Raja Mathura with his sizeable following in Bihar; and finally the Nawab's own Minister Badri Narayan, a vital participant in the revolt

Ajoy started to consider ways beyond the new situation but he stopped as he remembered the courier who had run the gauntlet of the Nawab's spies to bring him the warning.

"Ananta!"

"*Huzoor?*"

"Ananta, see that the messenger is given water and is fed. He has come a long way without rest. Let him sleep the afternoon on the inside dais. He has had a dangerous journey. And he will begin another tonight."

Ananta went across to the prostrate runner and the two men passed through the door into the interior of the hut.

Ajoy returned to his problem.

He had two reasons to take rapid action. First and most pressing was Badri Narayan's suggestion to pre-empt the Nawab's move. The second was his, Ajoy's, constant worry that the longer they waited, the greater was the chance of a leak in their planning or, worse, treachery. It was now confirmed that the French were on the Nawab's side and would oppose the rebellion. The French were not as powerful as the English but they were disciplined and had modern firepower, two attributes that would complement the limitations of the Nawab's large ragtag army.

Ajoy looked uneasily at the gray sky. The southwest monsoon was almost upon them and could undo everything. Suddenly an idea came to him.

Shiraj's move on Calcutta would require all his troops. This would leave Murshidabad unguarded.

Ajoy sat up straight.

They could strike right at the Nawab's base.

A once-in-a-lifetime chance!

To be able to achieve this timing was vital. Ajoy *had* to find out at once the exact details of the Nawab's plans for marching south. How could he do this? *The Minister!* He had to meet Badri Narayan right away. Where could they meet? Ajoy thought rapidly. Going to Murshidabad would be fastest but he could not very well walk into Shiraj's arms. Should he ask Badri Narayan to come to Mayurmani? No, that would involve a delay of at least six days. Was there an intermediate place? Ajoy thought furiously and another idea formed.

He began to write a letter for the messenger to take back.

Chapter 13

A ship about to depart for the high seas resembles a hive surrounded by busy bees. Innumerable boats ferry and unload provisions for the journey. As in a beehive, with the approach of dusk comings and goings grow to a frenzy and then slow. Finally all activity ceases for the night. But wait! Sometimes a lost dilatory insect hopefully hums around the dark nest in the hope of finding a way to deliver the day's last honey.

It was dark around *Europa* and a dilatory little peddler was clinging to the side of the ship. He was a small boy and he was urging his indolent master to hand up sacks of salted fish from a boat below. The fat bare-chested man in the boat had a problem. He was suffering the after-effects of opium he had smoked while his diminutive eleven-year-old helper had rowed them from the Garden Reach docks. They were several hours late with their load and, even though Master was beyond caring, the boy Ashraf knew that the fortune Master had paid for the fish would ruin him if they could not deliver and receive payment. And this would rob Ashraf of his meager but desperately needed income.

"Master! Oh Master, be careful!" wailed Ashraf as his boss staggered with several sacks in his arms and almost capsized the boat before sitting down heavily on a thwart. Ashraf looked up the netting on *Europa's* side to the railing and was wondering whether he should bring up sacks one at a time himself when he heard a loud splash. He twisted round fully expecting to see Master overboard. But no, Master was still in the boat and trying once more to lift sacks to his shoulder.

"What was the sound, Master?" Ashraf called down. "Did a sack fall in the river?"

Master grunted more from effort than in reply. Certain that a precious sack had fallen into the river, Ashraf squinted into the small semi-circle lit by the turned-up lantern in the boat's prow. At first he saw nothing and was about to direct his attention back to Master when he noticed a movement in the water.

"Master! Crocodile! Crocodile!" yelled Ashraf, giving his boss a nasty fright.

"You stupid little godforsaken idiot!" stormed Master. "There are no crocodiles in midstream. Now shut up and take this sack."

But Ashraf could see it was a bundle of white cloth that had fallen into the water from the ship. It was coming closer as the current floated it downstream. Then the bundle struggled and a faint cry came to his ears.

"Master! A man! A man!"

Ashraf pointed excitedly.

Master, his senses dulled by opium, ignored him and concentrated on balancing sacks of fish on his shoulder. Meanwhile the bundle of white had come abreast of the boat and was clearly visible in the lantern's glow. It would pass them in another few seconds.

"Catch him! Catch him!" shrieked Ashraf. "Master, there he goes."

"Who's there?" intruded an English voice from above.

Ashraf craned his neck and made out the pale face and broad hat of the watch looking down at them.

"Hotha, Sahib, *hotha!"* Ashraf shouted up at the watch and

pointed to the spot where he had seen the floating human form.

But the white bundle was gone, out of range of their feeble lantern. In desperation Ashraf forgot the sahib and swarmed down the netting and jumped into the boat. Master raised a hand and was about to clout him when he sat down heavily with a wild oath as Ashraf pushed the boat away from the ship with a jerk.

"You son of a pig," bawled Master. "Go back to the ship at once!"

"Master! Master! A man fell overboard, Master." Ashraf shouted and pulled as hard as he could in the direction of the bundle. The little boat skipped forward with the current.

"We have to save him, Master."

The fact they were pursuing a human being was finally registering on Master when, by sheer luck, in the middle of the wide Hooghly, the white bundle hove back into the lamplight. And, to his amazement, Ashraf saw that it was a woman who was in the water. Her eyes were closed and her hair was plastered to her face and her arms were thrashing feebly. But it was a woman. Then to his greatest astonishment Ashraf recognized it as a *white* woman.

"Master! It's a memsahib. Master! *Hotha*, Master!"

This was by far the most exciting thing that had ever happened in Ashraf's young life.

All the ferment and the boat's violent motion was making Master sick, but even he could now see that a rescue was required. In another minute they caught up with Pauline. It was not easy, but after two unsuccessful attempts they lifted her unresisting into the boat.

Master, completely spent with the effort and the effect of the drug, sat back gasping on his sacks of fish.

Ashraf looked with interest at the remarkable object they had plucked out of the river. Her face was ghastly white and her eyes were closed. But in her lacy and sodden dress and even with her strange yellow hair she looked exactly like a *jolpori,* a water fairy, whose story Ashraf had heard from his mother.

He had been studying her thus for perhaps ten minutes when Ashraf realized that no one was guiding the boat. It was floating downstream by itself. Master was sunk in the stupor of an addict. The woman was still unconscious. Ashraf knew *he* had to do something or they would end up floating all the way down the river to the sea. But he was still fascinated by the *jolpori* and his attention kept returning to her. Who was she? She had obviously fallen off the ship. Should they take her back to it? He looked around in the pitch blackness. Where *was* the ship? Not a light showed in the blackness. He was trying to decide what to do when there was a coughing sound behind him. He swung around to the *jolpori* and saw that her eyes were open and that she was gagging and struggling to sit up. Hesitantly Ahsraf put out a hand and touched her arm. When nothing happened he stood and helped her to a sitting position.

Pauline coughed, spat out water and stared around blankly. In the light of the lantern she saw a small brown boy wearing a torn sarong who was gazing at her with avid interest.

The boat rocked on a broadside wave and Ashraf once again remembered it needed to be guided. Hurriedly he pushed past her to the bow and grabbed the oars, dug the right one in the water to turn the prow in the direction he thought was the east bank and pulled in the direction of shore. Pauline meanwhile, none the worse for her submersion in the Hooghly, was examining her surroundings. She found that she was in a boat that smelt vilely of fish. A fat man was snoring at the stern.

She tried vainly to reconstruct the events. The last thing she remembered was hearing Freddie's footsteps in the corridor outside her cabin. Had she fainted? Why were her clothes wet? How had she got on this boat? Had he put her in it to send her back to Fort William? The dirty vessel did not look like Company transport. And who was the gross man sleeping in his filthy sarong? And who was the boy who seemed to be in charge?

"Who are you?" she asked Ashraf.

Sitting opposite her Ashraf smiled sweetly in incomprehension. He liked the sound of her voice. Realizing he did not understand, Pauline decided to let matters go the way they would. An unexpected sense of relief came over her and she realized it was because she was away from Freddie. She smiled back at the boy. She looked past him and as she did the light of the lantern fell on the edge of the river about twenty yards away where the bank sloped up steeply.

"*Stop!*" she cried and Ashraf smartly brought them around so they followed the bank, but upstream now.

Where was he taking her?

She asked him this and again he smiled winningly. Pauline shrugged her shoulders and nodded at the bank. She first thought that he understood and then to her horror he shrugged back!

Ten minutes later Pauline was debating in her mind whether to wake the fat man when a small stone pier with boats tied to it hove into the lantern light. Ashraf's piping voice woke several boatmen who had them fast in a flash. Pauline found herself facing a fascinated crowd of boatmen all wearing sarongs, beards and prayer caps.

***

The first light of dawn was brightening the sky and a sleepy crow squawked from the branches of a *neem* tree when the Clarksons' old bearer Khurshid, taking delivery of the morning consignment of milk, heard the shrill cry of a child. He looked up and his eyes opened wide. The earthen pitcher slipped from his nerveless fingers and smashed into pieces. The milk splashed on his feet.

"*Memsahib!*"

The staid Indian butler threw dignity to the winds and ran back to the front door.

"Memsahib, open the door! Come, Memsahib, come!"

Then Khurshid turned to watch the extraordinary pair stumble wearily up the walkway. The door behind him opened and Pauline collapsed into the arms of an astounded Maggie Clarkson.

A small tired boy sank down on the stone floor at their feet.

***

That afternoon, after hours of sleep had revived her tiredness and Ashraf had been dispatched home to Black Town with money and gifts for his mother and sister to make up for his loss in wages, Pauline described her adventures to the Clarksons and Benjamin. Even though she left out her confrontation with Freddie, the listeners understood the gravity of the situation. From Ashraf they had already learned that the woman had been rescued from the river. How had she fallen in? Try as she might Pauline could not recollect and the others made surmises but no one ventured to accuse the captain. She told them of the boat trip in the darkness and the unexpected landing in the riverside village, whose name she had been told was Falta. From Falta a boatman had guided them through the night along the ten miles to Fort William.

After she finished they stared at her for several speechless moments.

At last, with absolute clarity, Pauline said, "Maggie, Mr. Morley, I shall not go to China. I shall not remain with him. I shall remain in Calcutta when he leaves. It is over."

There was another very long silence. Finally Benjamin spoke with his eyes on the floor.

"Mrs. Wainwright, I am deeply sorry for your troubles and I can assure you that you will *not* go to China." When Pauline's eyes opened wide he held up his hand. "There is more. Last night the Executive Council took a major decision. The Council is directing *Europa* and her crew to remain in Calcutta for the foreseeable future. If Captain Wainwright demurs, Mr. Armstrong will invoke executive powers since *Europa* is in service of the Company."

"Oh dear God," gasped Maggie. "Freddie will stay then? But why?"

Another pause before Benjamin continued, still not looking at Pauline.

"We have received a letter from the Nawab that now makes it clear he has definite warlike intentions. The situation is extremely serious. *Europa's* firepower is needed as a deterrent and possibly, only possibly mind you, for protection."

He looked up and saw Pauline's enormous blue eyes filling slowly with tears and her face crumpling into abject despair.

"He won't go to China?" she asked in a small voice.

"Three hundred British lives require preservation, Mrs. Wainwright."

"Where can I go?"

I was a simple question, but it was asked with such desolation that every protective fiber in Benjamin's body was aroused and he felt painfully powerless and miserable.

Then reality set in.

"Where *can* you go, Mrs. Wainwright?" he said. "Fort William is our home and our castle. For all its exoticness India is a dangerous, sickness-ridden and foreign world. We have had a foothold in Bengal for only fifty years. We have lost hundreds of men through malaria and cholera and worse, just to keep that foothold. English women have come to India for less than twenty years and have remained in the confines of this fort. It can be a beautiful place but India is no fairy-tale land."

But Pauline had not heard. In the same small voice she said, "Isn't there somewhere, anywhere, I can go? Away from here? Where there are people, Indians, with whom I can talk and learn their ways? I like this country and I can't stand Fort William and its awful stuck-up people. With the exception of you three of course. Oh! Oh! Now that Freddie isn't going away, if I don't stay with him, everyone will talk. I can't bear that." Suddenly her face cleared. "Can I stay in Black Town, Mr. Morley? Maggie told me about it."

Benjamin sat back in shock while Maggie exclaimed, "No, of course you can't stay in Black Town. The very thought of it! Yes, I *told* you about the vile place, dear, and didn't I mention it teems with disease and sin?"

"We're afraid of visiting Black Town ourselves," Benjamin added.

"What can I do?" said Pauline plaintively.

A silence followed during which Benjamin tried to get his frazzled mind to work. She wanted to go away. He didn't blame her. He wanted to go away too! She wanted to go away to a place where there were Indians – fancy that!—who would look after her. Black Town was quite obviously out. What about Mayurmani? The old headman was a trustworthy fellow. And Prince Ajoy was staying there and could be looked upon to protect her. Then he rejected the idea. Mayurmani was too primitive for a western woman.

"Wait!" he exclaimed.

Pauline's clouded face cleared. She stared at him with her eyes large with anticipation.

"Aruna!" said Benjamin.

"What Mr. Morley? Ruin her? Who? What did you say?"

"No, Aruna. *Just a minute!* Let me think for a second, can't you? Hmmm... Yes, we may have something here. Aruna is Prince Ajoy's sister, recently widowed, and she lives in Neeladri with her old father-in-law, the Rai Raja. But it will take a few days to arrange."

Pauline's eyes lit up like stars and she spoke in a rush.

"That's right! That's right! Prince Ajoy has told me about his sister and how her poor husband was killed by a tiger and how much her husband did for his people and how much they all like you. I'll manage a few days somehow. Anything to get out of here. Oh, what a breath of fresh air!"

Benjamin, overcome by Pauline's kaleidoscopic mood changes, was wondering resentfully whether his own existence counted for anything when she jumped up, ran forward and threw her arms around his neck and hugged him tightly. Benjamin's big exploration-hardened heart lost its moorings with a lurch. Then Pauline was gone and he found himself looking at Maggie Clarkson who was shaking her head of gray hair sorrowfully.

"What are we to *do* with that girl?"

Chapter 14

A welter of fuss and bother swept Fort William.

Freddie Wainwright and Richard Armstrong had just had a mammoth confrontation. The captain's interpretation of his commission was to police the waters between Calcutta and Canton and keep shipping lanes clear. Armstrong pointed out that this implied safety of the Company's men and *materiel* in the area and that *Europa* must remain in Calcutta to deter the belligerent Bengal Army. It was a hostile stalemate until Robert Clive sided with Armstrong and directed *Europa* on behalf of the Company's Court of Directors to remain in Calcutta. Very reluctantly Freddie agreed. Benjamin made the angry captain sign an acceptance document in the presence of the two Governors because Clive was leaving for Madras shortly.

Later Benjamin flatly informed Captain Wainwright that his wife had decided to stay with the Clarksons—and closely watched the captain's reaction. Freddie controlled himself but Benjamin did not miss the fleeting expression of relief. Was it because Pauline was safe he wondered. Was it because they could be separate? Was it because he was absolved of abetting her suicide attempt? Her attempted murder? Or was it something else? He could not ask but he was sure it included all of the above reasons.

Another tumult greeted Pauline's announcement of her decision to go to Neeladri. Richard Armstrong had another fit. How *could* anyone, he said, not want to stay in Fort William? The women, Martha Armstrong, Catherine McIver, Leonora Linnington and others, were outraged and considered Pauline's intention a personal insult. *Which it is!* Pauline thought maliciously. But Benjamin, Clive and the Clarksons supported her, and, after another hostile confrontation, Freddie gave his consent.

A week later Clive set sail for Madras to a fond and tearful farewell from his new friends in Calcutta. Pauline stood once again on the Garden Reach pier and waved mechanically as *Isle of Skye* raised anchor, hoisted topsail and moved downstream. Her mind was on her imminent departure for Neeladri. A wave of conflicting emotions assailed her. Like the ship getting smaller in the wide river she was about to sail away from her old existence. What lay ahead? What was to be the next chapter in her life? To her surprise she found she was not afraid. She did not feel lonely. As *Skye* disappeared around a bend a warm and completely irrational excitement seeped through her heart like a bird opening its wings to the early morning sun. She could do as she pleased. No ties. No regrets. A new beginning. A new land. A storybook land. Storybook people. Comrades. An intrepid explorer to lean on. A handsome sensitive prince who battled an evil king...

Then followed one more long boat ride up the same mud-brown Hooghly with the faithful Dicky by her side.

Pauline managed to keep the seasickness under control while the familiar scenery of fields, palms and jungle passed by on either bank. Upon docking at Neeladri her small party waited at the pier while Murali went ashore with a letter from his master Benjamin to herald her arrival. Pauline wondered who would come to receive her. The Raja? Aruna? She had heard that Indian men did not talk to or even look at strange women, especially foreign ones. A bout of uncertainty assailed her. She desperately hoped that the Raja's household would not resent her precipitating herself on them.

In spite of her preoccupation and the midday heat, she could not help admiring the countryside. Willows, ferns and palm fronds drooped from the riverbank. Cattle grazed in harvested fields or lay in the shade. High in the branches a cuckoo sang its summer song. *Cooo-ooo,* it went. *Cooo-ooo! Cooo-ooo!* Then a friendly mother goat came down to water's edge and accepted a reed from her hand while its timid offspring stood on the bank and bleated piteously. The river lapped quietly by her side. A group of nut-brown boys came toward the pier. They caught sight of the foreigners and stopped and stared. Pauline wondered whether she was keeping them from their bath. It was an extremely hot day. What would it be like to bathe in the river? She put a hand in and found the water warm and inviting.

As she straightened up she saw a group of people approaching along the river-path in her direction and her heart started to beat fast. She saw Murali among them. The elderly person hurrying along at their head must be the Raja. She could see that he was walking as fast as his limp and walking stick would allow. This was the moment she had dreaded ever since the day Benjamin had offered her the possibility of going to Neeladri. Would the Raja dislike her intrusion and demand she return at once to Fort William?

But she need not have worried. Raja Ranjit Rai could not have welcomed her more profusely.

"*Namaskar,* Memsahib, *namaskar!*" he called as he came down the steps. "Welcome to my humble home!"

The Raja spoke very broken English but his intention was quite evident. Pauline stepped out of the boat and joined her palms to her forehead as was customary. The Raja returned the gesture and then frightened her by saying, "Memsahib! Why are you here?" Before a taken-aback Pauline could reply, he continued excitedly, "Why did you not come to the house instead of waiting in the boat in discomfort? These horrible flies!" He flailed at a gnat with his stick almost jabbing Murali in the face. "We are so glad you have decided to visit us."

"Oh, thank you, sir."

Pauline was quite overcome by the Raja's genuineness and spontaneity. She liked the distinguished old man immediately. He reminded her of her own father. Even after all that Benjamin had told her, Pauline had half-expected the Raja to look like one of those English kings whose grim portraits hang in museums, all brocade and velvet and drooping moustache. The Raja wore a rust-colored shirt that reached his knees and a white *dhoti*. Both were of immaculately starched cotton. He had gold studs for shirt buttons and wore leather slip-on shoes. He did have a moustache though. But it was the clipped salt-and-pepper variety which together with his iron-gray hair gave the Raja an air of command.

The men with him were dressed more simply. They all beamed their welcome.

"I hope I am not intruding, sir" said Pauline as she climbed the high steps of the pier.

"No, Memsahib, no! What things you say! It will be so good for Mother to have a young English friend as a guest."

While the Raja went on speaking, stumbling to find the right words, Pauline wondered who Mother might be. She had been told that the Raja's wife had died a long time ago. It couldn't be *his* mother, could it? She would have to be a hundred years old!

"Morley-sahib has always been our honored guest. He has written that you wish to learn our ways while your husband is busy with his ship. I know nothing of ships. You must tell me about ships. We shall do our best to make you comfortable. Of course we will. *Oh, Niamat...!*"

He turned to direct the unloading.

Dicky came up to Pauline.

"The Guv'nor said to leave Corporal Wellman behind with you, Mum. Come to think of it, I'd like to stay a day or two meself. See the lay of the land, y'know. Them coveys look proper peaceable but ye never know."

"No Dicky, and thank you for asking." Pauline smiled at him. "You've been such a dear. And take Wellman back with you. I'll be all right and back soon. Benjamin has told Murali to stay in case I need anything. And don't forget," she arched her eyebrows, "someone has to make sure Bessie's all right."

Soon they were walking along the river-path past harvested rice fields and across open ground with gnarled trees and a faint smell of burnt wood in the air. Someone told her it was a cremation ground complete with ghosts that lived in the tree branches. Then more fields, dry and dusty, and finally in the distance she saw an imposing lilac building with dark-green shuttered windows. It had no perimeter walls but was ringed by trees and looked cool and comfortable.

While they walked, the Raja asked about her family, her husband, her voyage and her life in Fort William. Pauline chattered brightly and told him about her encounter with Lali.

The horrified Raja stopped dead and brought the procession to a halt.

"*Shiva! Shiva!*" he cried. "A bull chased you the day after you arrived in India! And you have still come to the countryside? You are very brave, Memsahib."

Pauline glowed with pride.

"Oh, I got over it quite quickly, sir. Actually, it was only because of Lali that I met Prince Ajoy and that is part of the reason I am here."

She told him how Ajoy had 'rescued' her.

"Ajoy!" the Raja harrumphed. "The boy is a firebrand!"

Pauline was surprised by his vehement use of the word. Firebrand? Where in the world had he learned it? He certainly had a different view of the prince. To Pauline, Ajoy had a brooding, smoldering, quixotic quality. But she had not seen any explosive dynamism that would mark him as a firebrand. Well, the Raja had known Ajoy long before

Benjamin brought him to Calcutta. Had his confinement in Fort William changed Ajoy, she wondered.

"...made it his life's mission is to dethrone Shiraj Doula," the Raja was saying. "Remove the Nawab! Is that possible? Do you know how old Ajoy is, Memsahib? Almost thirty! And not married because of his craze for power. I hear Ajoy has left Fort William and is hiding again. I worry about the boy. So does Mother."

Pauline almost said, *so do I!* She did not mention the elephant encounter to the Raja. That, and the enchanted night, were secrets of 'her' prince and herself.

Even before they reached the mansion, Pauline knew she was coming home. By then she had managed to convince the Raja to stop addressing her as 'Memsahib' and he had agreed to call her 'Miss Pauline'. To the Raja's hearty announcement of "Welcome to *Rai Bari*...uh...Rai Mansion, Miss Pauline," they entered the building through studded front doors and went into a high-ceilinged room lined with glass-fronted cupboards full of books. In the center of the room was a large round marble-topped table on which were piled more old books and papers. Several deep armchairs stood beside the table. This was clearly the Raja's study. Sleepy sunlight filtered in through shuttered windows and high brick walls made the room pleasantly cool after the arid heat outside. All around her was a pleasing aroma of leather, tobacco, paper, old furniture and knowledge.

Pauline sat down on the edge of one of the armchairs while the Raja fussed over her and Niamat, who seemed to be the Raja's chief retainer, brought frosted glasses of beaten yogurt—sweet and deliciously cold.

Then a striking woman appeared through an inside door.

Pauline jumped to her feet. Was this Aruna?

Uncertain of what to expect, she saw a cold and forbidding lady whose natural stateliness was accented by delicate, almost transparent skin. Her extreme thinness was accentuated rather than disguised by her voluminous white *sari* which in turn made her appear even more remote. But the plain traditional widow's attire widow could not mask her elegant bearing.

Pauline, in a panic, felt clumsy and common. Then Aruna smiled. With a shock Pauline recognized in the smile the same remarkable trait shared by brother and sister. The severity and haughtiness of the face in repose and its warmth and sincerity when animated. Must be a Sena characteristic, she concluded. But whereas Ajoy was dark and had long wavy hair, Aruna was fair. Pauline tried to see what Aruna's hair was like and got her second shock when she realized that under the fold of the *sari* that covered her head, Aruna's hair was shorn.

"Mother, look who has come!" Raja Ranjit spoke to his daughter-in-law in Bengali. "Miss Pauline is English. She will stay with us. Morley-sahib has sent word she wants to learn our customs and traditions." He changed to English, still addressing his daughter-in-law. "You will again have a chance to speak English." Then he turned to Pauline. "I hope you and Mother become good friends."

So *this* was Mother!

Aruna came forward and spoke in Bengali.

"How are you, Memsahib? We are happy you have come."

Pauline did not any have trouble following this, or when Aruna added, "You are very beautiful!" and came close and took both her hands in hers. When she spoke she looked directly at Pauline, who blushed in embarrassment, overcome by the older woman's directness and sincerity. How strong and forthright brother and sister were! She had no option but to like this remarkable person. It must be quite an effort to react pleasantly to the sudden intrusion by a visitor from another world. But how natural was her welcome! Was it the intrinsic hospitality of Indians? Or was it due to Benjamin's stature here? Or had Ajoy told them something of herself? She realized she had to say something. They were all looking at her. She could sort all this out later.

"Thank you so much," she said slowly so that they would understand. "I am Pauline. Please call me Pauline. I am only seventeen years old." She counted them out on her fingers. "Ten and seven, see? I am so happy I can stay with you. I am sure I will be no trouble. I want to know *so* much about India. We cannot do that in Calcutta."

The Raja beamed. Pauline was sure the only reason he did not clap her on the back was because she was a girl. Then she bent down and opened her carpet bag.

"I have brought some presents."

Over their protests she gave the Raja a horse made of Bohemian crystal and Aruna a musical jewel box.

"These are my own. I did not bring any gifts when I left England. I hope you like them. Aruna...may I call you Aruna? Please? If you turn this key, the jewel box plays an English song."

Aruna opened her box and admired the soft velvet interior. "Thank you, Memsahib," she said, finding the English words one by one. "It is very good." Her eyes were warm for an instant. Then she seemed to recede. "But, but I have no jewels," she ended in Bengali. Strangely, Pauline understood the words.

"Just think of it as a memory of my visit," she replied. "You must listen to the music."

Aruna nodded and turned the key. The jewel-box tinkled. Pauline sang with the tune:

> *Hark, hark, the dogs do bark,*
> *Beggars are coming to town,*
> *Some in rags and some in bags,*
> *And some in velvet gowns!*

Unexpectedly Aruna laughed out loud. It was a very pretty sound, like the ringing of a bright little bell. Pauline remembered that Benjamin had twice described to her the way Aruna laughed. On the second occasion, Pauline had looked at him sharply wondering if there was more than just sympathy in his feelings. Now she realized how pleasant and full of happiness the sound of Aruna's laugh was. Then she remembered the transformation in Ajoy Sena in Mayurmani forest when he was really happy. These people, she decided, are extremely focused in their emotions.

"How surprising!" said Aruna in Bengali – and again Pauline understood. "It is a song we all know. Would you like to hear it?"

Pauline nodded enthusiastically.

As Aruna hummed to herself for a moment, the Raja quietly explained that this was a lullaby from the days of bandit attacks and persecution by avaricious kings.

To the tune of the music box and in a clear musical voice Aruna sang:

> *"Khoka ghumolo*
> *Para jurolo*
> *Borgi elo deshe,*
> *Bulbulitey dhaan kheyeche*
> *Khajna debo kishey?"*

Later Aruna and Pauline would translate the words:

> *My little one sleeps,*
> *The neighborhood stills,*
> *Robbers have come to town.*
> *Birds have eaten all my grain,*
> *With what shall I pay the Crown?*

The Raja sighed and wiped a tear from his eye.

"See, Miss Pauline? Now you have actually made Mother sing. Thank you for coming."

***

A week later Pauline was standing on the wide second-story

verandah of Rai Mansion. A flock of black jays with startling red underbellies were squabbling on the thick spreading fruit-laden branches of a mango tree that shaded her from the sun. Pauline wore a light cotton dress and had abandoned her restrictive whalebone corsets forever. Immersed in her new surroundings she was thinking about how much the men and women of Fort William were missing because of their inability to absorb their host country, when the sudden sound of many voices disturbed her. She walked across to the brick balustrade and looked down.

A pretty tableau was forming below.

The ever-present brown Hooghly flowed tranquilly in the background. Closer, a swath of green lawn, bordered by multi-colored flower beds, lay speckled in light-and-shade of large and noble trees. From the front portico of her palace-with-no-walls, a gravel pathway led away and met the dusty road that connected the little town of Neeladri to its pier. Halfway down this path, Niamat, the Raja's elderly valet was arguing with a group of young boys and girls. Niamat's deep voice and the children's penetrating tones blended pleasantly. The children were pointing at the overripe green-and-yellow mangoes that hung from the trees around the mansion and it was evident that they wanted the fruit while the old retainer was determined to shoo them away.

Pauline, engrossed in the scene, silently cheered on the children. She spun around startled as a hand was laid on her arm. Seeing who it was, she relaxed and smiled.

"Oh, Didi, it's you! How quietly you tread! How on earth do you walk barefoot on this stone? My feet burn even through my slippers!"

Aruna smiled and shook her head slightly as though such discomfort was not worth even discussion. In her white *sari*, she looked cool and collected as befitted a *didi* or elder sister.

"Are the children bothering you?" she asked.

It was Pauline's turn to shake her head.

"Oh no. I have just realized what is the most important

thing missing in Fort William." She looked down at the noisy debate below. "Children's voices. Very few families I met there have young children. Children's voices are the happiest sounds in the world!"

Suddenly she gasped and turned quickly to look at Aruna.

"I'm *so* sorry, Didi. I say *such* silly things. I didn't mean to hurt you."

Impulsively she embraced the older woman. After a few moments Aruna gently disengaged herself and stepped back to study her friend. She saw bright tears in Pauline's blue eyes. With a sigh she took the edge of her cotton *sari* and wiped them away.

"You too would like children, wouldn't you?"

"Very, very much."

Pauline loved children and knew that Aruna's husband, Prince Mohendra, had died before they had children of their own. Aruna would never have children because a Hindu widow could not remarry. As for herself...a lump formed in her throat at the injustice of it all. Linked in sadness, the two women stood in silence and watched the drama below.

The clamor grew louder. The childish voices became more insistent and the tumult increased. Niamat put a finger to his lips and pointed toward the house. But it was too late.

Tap! Tap! Tap!

The measured tapping sound was accompanied by a deep cough and Raja Ranjit Rai emerged from the interior of the house. From above the women had a clear view of his thinning iron-gray hair as he approached the mob. The Raja used a walking-stick and favored his arthritic right leg. As usual he wore a long white starched shirt and *dhoti*. In spite of his limp, he carried himself with authority and caused an immediate hush among the children. The children gaped at their overlord, poised to flee. Niamat hastened to apologize and in the same breath berated the children. The Raja silenced him with a raised hand. Pauline did not make out the ensuing words but their enactment made their meaning obvious. The children came to life and shouted in unison and pointed at the fruit on the tree above Pauline and Aruna. The Raja put his stick under his arm and covered his ears. Then he looked up at the tree and, in so doing, noticed the women and smiled conspiratorially. Aruna immediately covered her head with the end of her *sari*, an instinctive female gesture in the presence of an in-law. Pauline smiled back, her sadness forgotten for the moment.

The children clamored for attention and the Raja turned back to them. He said something to Niamat and the children's increased uproar indicated their victory. Niamat stood sulky and rebellious. Then the Raja took him aside and spoke in his ear. The old man's face brightened and he nodded vigorously. Having settled the issue, the Raja smiled up at the women again and went inside the house.

After a quick parley one of the children, a boy of about thirteen, armed with a long bamboo pole with a cross-piece at its top, reached up, secured and shook a branch of the tree. Several mangoes fell with loud thuds and the youngsters ran to pick them up.

The tree was shaken violently again. A few mangoes landed on the verandah. Pauline bent and picked up one in each hand. They were large and plump and were colored light green and dark maroon. A sticky juice oozed from the stems. They smelt delicious.

All of a sudden, disjointed memories of her carefree childhood wafted through Pauline's mind like gossamer-winged dragonflies that she could reach for but never touch.

***

Pauline felt very much at home at Rai Mansion. Eight unhurried days had passed since she arrived and the Raja's prophecy that she and Aruna would be friends had come true.

Every day Pauline awoke to the pleasant clatter of pots and pans being scrubbed in the open courtyard outside her bedroom window. Mindful of the heat she dressed lightly and loosely as did everyone else around her. She now found the tight-fitting dresses of England uncomfortable to the extreme. A plump widowed maid, who went by the interesting name of Dilip's Mother, brought her tea. While she drank Dilip's Mother stood and stared at her. Pauline had become used to this. To the Raja's household staff her white skin was a novelty and her blond hair and blue eyes were totally fascinating. She wondered how she was being described in the town. At first she had felt like a circus attraction but later rationalized that an Indian woman, Dilip's Mother for example, would draw equal attention in Burnham or Ipswich. And she got used to the attention. She studied Dilip's Mother and tried to communicate with her which proved rather difficult. The moment she was addressed Dilip's Mother would become acutely embarrassed. She would chew the end of her *sari* in consternation and scuttle away giggling uncontrollably.

Aruna would spend the mornings in prayers which would culminate with the watering of a *tulsi* sapling in the center of the palace courtyard. She would then serve her father-in-law his morning meal in a wide brass plate containing several brass bowls of preparations. As he ate she would sit opposite him waving a hand-fan. Then the two women would eat a simple repast of rice, spicy lentils, vegetable curry and sweetened yogurt. Sometimes Pauline would be given a fish preparation, which Didi would not eat. She enjoyed the meals and found them tasty and wholesome. It appeared that she had got back her appetite and at last was putting on some weight. She wished Aruna would not pick at her food but did not remonstrate. And then they would talk.

On summer afternoons sitting at opposite ends of the high four-postered bed in Pauline's room, they would talk of politics: of England under Hanoverian king, George II; of India under the crumbling Moghuls; of Shiraj Doula and his many-faceted character; of the lives of the rich and the poor in their respective countries, their customs and mannerisms; of marriage and raising of children; of the pros and cons of *purdah,* which banished women from outside affairs; of the future of Bengal and Calcutta and Fort William and Murshidabad and London and Neeladri and Rajmahal and Ipswich and Burnham. They found that they could communicate quite well in a mixture of simple English and Bengali, a language Pauline was rapidly learning. The countryside would blaze with dry heat while the monsoon dallied. But the high-ceilinged room with watered-down jute matting in its windows stayed cool. A servant would doze outside as he mechanically pulled an overhead *punkha.*

And then, hesitantly at first, they began to tell each other about themselves. Pauline spoke wistfully of her old father and of her dead mother, whose loving face she still remembered, and of her childhood.

Aruna described her early life with Ajoy at Rajmahal Palace under the watchful eye of Ananta, their adopted servant-uncle, and of growing up surrounded by imagery of past grandeur when Senas ruled the land. Her marriage to Prince Mohendra Rai was the event of the decade. Pauline listened enthralled while Aruna told her of the pomp and ceremony of the wedding. With eyes wet she held her hand when Aruna described the intelligence and altruism of her dead husband. Didi described how the talk in the Rai household dwelt on administrative betterment instead of Senaesque militancy characteristic of her own home. Aruna had been married to Mohendra for four years. The two outspoken princes, Mohendra and Ajoy, had had titanic arguments in this house. On occasion Aruna was required to intervene to prevent them from coming to blows. Mohendra had first met Benjamin on a trip to Fort William to call on the earlier Governor, and had liked Morley-sahib immediately and invited him to Neeladri, never realizing that the then-senior-writer would take the invitation seriously. But Benjamin had come, and come four times to Neeladri. On two of those occasions, Aruna had hesitantly joined them, thus taking the enormously symbolic step from the interior to the exterior of the household. She had admired the remarkable Englishman for his knowledge and his unfeigned interest in India. Her husband and Benjamin shared many ideals. They were both determined to take their respective countries into a prosperous and enlightened future.

Pauline decided to move the subject to herself and, omitting only the story of Freddie and the drunken sailor, told Aruna about her own marriage to Captain Wainwright and the unhappy years with him.

Hearing this Aruna sat back in consternation.

"Little Sister, your husband is your lord and your master, for better or for worse, and for all time."

"*He is not!*" Pauline rejoined hotly. "Not Freddie! Why should he be?"

Aruna was horrified.

"How else can it be?" she asked as though Pauline was five years old. When Pauline glared back at her mutinously, she continued, "Little Sister, listen. Every woman has three men in her life: her father when she is a child, her husband when she is of marriageable age, and her son when she is old and widowed. If any of them is absent when she needs them, a woman is lost." Aruna sighed deeply and the sound twisted Pauline's heartstrings. "I have none of the three. And I never shall. I love and respect my dear father-in-law and as long as he is alive I shall serve him. After he is gone? God will decide."

There was a long silence.

Finally Aruna said, "How can you, who are married, have a life without your husband?"

"I don't know, Didi. I do wish I had your patience and... and...your serenity! I am too hot-headed. I feel a prisoner with Freddie."

"Now look, Little Sister. You are very young. You are full of life. Restless. Looking for things to fall into place quickly. Life is not so simple. You are luckier than most, Little Sister.

You are beautiful. You have a rich and powerful husband. You have land. You will have children. Your discontent will mellow with age and experience. What alternative is there?"

Pauline stared out of the window and past the matting that hung there. The dry fields and the dull sky shimmered in heat waves. Indeed, what alternative was there? The dreadful picture that haunted her nightmares materialized once more. A whaleboat cover shook. An unsteady figure emerged. It staggered toward her. She physically smelt the reek of rum. And then came the awful awareness that the figure was of a man. That Freddie was in carnal contact with a man. Freddie! Her husband. The one she had once long ago thought would love her and make love to her. She shuddered at the recollection. Where could she go? What could she do? In spite of the fact that she knew the answer, for the thousandth time she asked, *Why? Why did you marry me, Freddie? Why?* She knew why. He had married her for the Leavenworth lands and for the resulting title of Viscount. *I hate him! I wish he were dead! I wish I was dead!*

"Oh, Little Sister, what is the matter?" Aruna cried out. "Don't weep. Don't weep. Tell me what is the matter."

Pauline's eyes had turned dark and were flashing in anger and simultaneously tears poured down her cheeks. Quickly Aruna gathered her into her arms and held her tightly.

Into Pauline's nostrils from long long ago came the forgotten lavender perfume of her dead mother.

"Mummy!" Pauline sobbed on Aruna's shoulder. "Mummy, I hate him! I hate him!"

Aruna felt Pauline's heart beating wildly and her body wracked by huge sobs while tears dampened her *sari*. She wondered what it could be that her husband had done. And then it began to dawn on Aruna that immense though her own tragedy was, here was someone who may have suffered even more grievously. As she comforted the English girl Aruna marveled at the cheerfulness with which she bore her sorrow.

Slowly Pauline's sobs quieted and she lay back on the bed completely drained, her eyes shut, her face ravaged by tears. Aruna held one of her hands tightly. Presently Pauline's breathing grew regular. Her muscles twitched and finally relaxed. Aruna continued to sit protectively beside the sleeping girl, holding her hand, her own eyes unseeing.

It grew dark. The sound of voices came through the open windows as members of the household ventured into the evening coolness. Later still came the strident wail of a conch shell blown in farewell to the departing day. Dilip's Mother came to the door and looked curiously at the two women in the dark. Getting no response, she went away.

***

Several hours passed before Pauline awoke with a start and sat up. In the steady flame of a small kerosene lamp she saw Didi was asleep, sitting propped against the headboard. At her movement Aruna's eyes opened and, without preamble, Pauline began to speak. The bottled-up misery of her situation, the nights of frustration and anger at Freddie's perfidy and the harrowing sick feeling of desolation that would not go away, all of this streamed out in an intense suppressed monotone. Aruna listened without a word or movement. Only her luminous eyes mirrored her compassion for her tortured friend. She began to share Pauline's abhorrence of her husband as Pauline told her everything about the captain avoiding only the homosexual episode of which she simply could not bring herself to speak. Presently Aruna's mind began to focus on the recurring theme of Pauline's nausea and her aversion to confining corsets. She stole a wary glance at the young woman's waistline. And then Pauline was telling her about the elephant encounter at Mayurmani and the depth of her feeling for Ajoy. Aruna listened spellbound. She was awed by the strength of Pauline's belief in her brother and her admiration. Was it really the same irresponsible hotheaded brother she was describing? Was it hero worship?

Or was it more than that? Pauline told her about the walk in the moonlit night and the legends of Krishna and her unshakable belief that Ajoy would overcome and Aruna knew it was more than hero worship. As she listened it was clear that several incredible things were happening to this innocent foreign girl which she wasn't aware of herself!

At last Pauline stopped and lay back with her eyes closed. Aruna pressed the fevered girl's forehead and wondered what she could do to help. She got up thinking furiously and came back with a tumbler of water and a bunch of bananas. While Pauline sipped from the heavy glass she decided to tackle the most tangible of the items.

"Little Sister, when was your last flow of the moon?"

Pauline lowered the glass and looked at her blankly. The Bengali words made no sense and it took several exchanges before she realized that Aruna, for some strange reason, was asking about her menstrual cycle. Submerged in her troubles Pauline had not kept track. Why was it important, she wanted to ask, but decided it was too delicate a matter. These Indians! They talked easily about things that would make an Englishwoman's face scarlet. Then she saw Aruna was waiting. With a touch of embarrassment she marshaled her thoughts and tried to recall a recent 'flow'. She could not remember one after she came to India. Or on the ship. There had been one back amid the snows of winter when Freddie had unexpectedly returned. That must have been the last one. How long ago had it been? How long ago had been that ill-omened day in Ipswich. It seemed like years...

Aruna, tense with suspense, watched her calculate.

"Three months, Didi," said Pauline finally. "Maybe a little more. It has been never so long before. Why has it been so long...?"

Pauline stopped when she saw Aruna staring at her with a peculiar expression. Suddenly she pulled her into a close embrace.

"Your life is about to change, Little Sister. Praise Lord Narayan!"

But even though Pauline asked her many times, Aruna would say no more. "In good time, Little Sister," was all she would say.

At last Pauline gave up and fell asleep. But Aruna stayed awake, her mind working.

Chapter 15

Wrapped in early morning mist Ajoy, Ananta and Harihar Mullick landed at the pier at Neeladri. They had disregarded the first law of Hooghly navigation and traveled through the night from Mayurmani. By a miracle they avoided submerged sandbars and floating crocodiles and eluded the Nawab's spies.

But this was a different Ajoy.

His long crinkly hair was adorned with an ochre turban and a bushy beard covered his normally clean-shaven visage. He wore a short rust-colored shirt over a knee-length yellow *dhoti*. A bulging cloth bag was slung on his shoulder and in one hand he carried a single-stringed wooden musical instrument. Prince Ajoy was disguised as a *baul*, a nomadic folk singer that singly or in small groups was a familiar sight in the towns and villages of Bengal.

The sun was just spotlighting the snarling tiger crest of Rai Mansion when Aruna, looking down from the verandah after her sleepless night, saw the three men walk up the path to the house. She recognized Ananta at once and hurried down as they reached the wide front porch and laid down their loads. Ananta bent and touched both her feet in the traditional gesture of respect.

"Live long, Ananta-*kaka,*" Aruna responded. "You look very weary. Where have you come from and who are these men with you? How is my brother?"

Ananta, whom Aruna and Ajoy knew from their youngest days and called *kaka* or uncle, was in his late-forties. His relationship with the Prince and Princess of Rajmahal had evolved from chaperon to companion to guide to retainer.

"Your brother is well, Princess," Ananta replied. "We have traveled through the night with news."

Once inside the central courtyard of Rai Mansion, Aruna asked again, "Ananta-*kaka,* who are these men with you? And where is my brother?"

"I am here, Little Sister."

Aruna whirled around.

"Dada! You are here!"

Aruna recovered and smiled with genuine pleasure. Then she wrinkled her nose and studied his costume.

"Why this attire? And why no announcement of your arrival? No, no, let me guess. The reason is still the same, isn't it?" She sighed. "Intrigue! How much longer will you play hide-and-seek with the Nawab, Dada?"

A steely glint played in Ajoy's eyes.

"Not much longer, Little Sister, not much longer. There is change in the air."

Aruna was not impressed.

Ajoy introduced the old man.

"Little Sister, this is Harihar-*dada,* headman of Mayurmani village. He has sheltered me for the past two months. I owe him much."

Harihar Mullick came forward to touch her feet and looked up at her with watery eyes.

"If your illustrious brother succeeds, Princess, we shall be saved from the Nawab's depredations for all time."

Aruna shook her head in disapproval. This village elder was obviously a simpleton and yet another who was taken in by Ajoy's grand designs.

"Where is Maharaj?" asked Ajoy.

As if on cue came the heavy tread and tap of walking stick.

"Mother! What is the noise? Who are these people? Ananta? Is that you?"

He was interrupted by the sound of running feet. Niamat burst in breathing in labored gasps, his eyes wide with fear.

"Maharaj! Maharaj!" Niamat said excitedly. "The Nawab is coming! Maharaj, the Nawab is coming!"

Everyone stared at him in alarm.

"The Nawab?" the Raja spluttered. "Have you taken leave of your senses, Niamat? Why on earth would the Nawab come here?"

During this exchange Aruna had put two and two together and glared at the scruffy musician.

Niamat hastened to elaborate.

"Yes, Maharaj! It is true. My youngest son, he saw them from the pier. He saw the Nawab's boats approaching and ran to tell me."

There was silence while everyone looked at him in dismay.

Finally Ajoy asked, "Did the boy actually see the Nawab, Niamat?"

The Raja and Niamat started violently and gaped at the *baul*.

"Oh Father, it *is* Dada," Aruna explained shortly, tiring of the dramatics. "On another of his wild schemes. He was telling me about it when you came."

The Raja fixed a baleful frown on Ajoy.

"So! It fits together. You arrive and the Nawab is at our doorstep."

Ignoring the accusation Ajoy repeated his question to Niamat, who was still goggling at him.

"Did your son actually see the Nawab, Niamat?"

Some of Niamat's excitement deflated.

"No, *huzoor*. The boy said he only saw the boats." He

revived and asked with some aspersion, "But who would come on the Nawab's boat if not the Nawab?"

Ajoy was about to reply roughly when he got the biggest shock of his life.

A figure appeared on the upstairs gallery that ran along the inside perimeter of the courtyard. The early morning sun, streaming through the open roof, cast a halo around a head of golden hair. In utter disbelief Ajoy saw the face he last remembered gazing at him ardently with bright moonlight pouring sweetness upon it.

The others followed his expression and looked up too. Harihar Mullick and Ananta were surprised to see a foreign woman in Rai Mansion.

Aruna came close, nudged Ajoy and whispered, "Yes, Dada. It *is* your admirer!"

Ajoy swung around.

"My *what?*"

"Your admirer, Dada. I will tell you everything later." She rolled her eyes, indicating the Raja's presence. "Unless you want her to witness your being dragged away to Murshidabad in chains!"

This brought Ajoy's mind back to business. Disoriented by Pauline's presence and the usually undemonstrative Aruna's inexplicable animation, Ajoy forced himself to address the Raja.

"Maharaj, it is not the Nawab who is coming. I have invited his minister, Minister Badri Narayan, who is my confidant, to discuss an important matter. Publicly, the Minister is arriving in state to meet with you on important administrative matters. He will see me later in private. I did not expect him to arrive so early. Needless to say, our meeting is a secret. Only those of us here must know who I am."

Aruna raised her eyebrows and her bright eyes indicated the figure above. *What about her?* her expression asked. Ajoy scowled. What was the matter with his sister? Then he looked at Pauline again. She appeared serious and a little tired but no less dazzlingly lovely with the sunlight now on her.

"Little Sister," Aruna called and turned her back on her brother when he incredulously mouthed *little sister?* "There is nothing to worry about. It is only a poor musician of no consequence who has come with his cronies. And the Nawab's minister is coming later. Dilip's Mother will prepare your tea and I will be up shortly to braid your hair."

All this was said in Bengali which, Ajoy noted, Pauline obviously understood. She nodded and disappeared. Ajoy stared with his mouth open at the space where she had been. Then he turned and saw Aruna looking intently at him with a queer expression. His curiosity got the better of his annoyance and he was about to demand she explain everything on pain of death, when he was again distracted by the reason for his coming to Neeladri.

The Minister was coming.

***

It was just after noon.

Raja Ranjit Rai and Minister Badri Narayan had completed their 'official' transactions and had come out into the courtyard to wash before sitting down for lunch. The Raja beckoned to the waiting *baul* to come forward.

"This, *Diwan-ji,*" he announced, "is Rosho Pundit. I know him well and can vouchsafe that he fulfills the promise of his name: 'Master of Arts'. I have heard that you require a musical troupe for performances at Hazarduari Palace. I recommend Rosho Pundit and his group highly."

Ajoy put his palms together and bowed to Badri Narayan.

"Ah yes," said the Minister. "How kind of you, Maharaj. So, Rosho Pundit, will you sing while we have lunch?"

After a moment of fright, Ajoy was equal to this.

"What on earth are you saying, *Diwan-ji?* Sing at the height of a Thursday afternoon? God alone knows what disaster we shall invite into Maharaj's palace!"

Ajoy's outrage was only partly feigned. Badri Narayan, who knew of his disguise, was carrying the charade too far with guards around. Ajoy could not sing a note!

After lunch, in the seclusion of the Raja's book-lined study, Badri Narayan 'interviewed' Rosho Pundit while the guards went to have their own lunch. They had an hour of privacy.

Without pleasantries the Minister launched into the subject.

"Prince Ajoy, I came as fast as I could. Events have accelerated since our exchange of messages. The Nawab and the French have already taken Cossim Bazaar and, true to his word, Shiraj will march on Calcutta in three weeks."

The Raja had a coughing fit.

He was overwhelmed by the appalling news of the annexation of Cossim Bazaar, a small English warehouse close to Murshidabad. As he stared in wordless dismay Badri Narayan briefed them rapidly of impending war. The Raja's expression began to show new respect for Ajoy as he grasped the gravity of the situation.

"Being used to the methodical Alivardi Khan," said the Minister, "I am amazed at how quickly his grandson acts. We must move quickly ourselves. There is no time to be lost."

"I agree, *Diwan-ji*," said Ajoy. "Surprise is the key."

"But we must be prepared to move as soon as the Nawab and his forces leave the city. Is this possible? How can we bring the armies of Bihar, Orissa and eastern Bengal to surround Murshidabad without the Nawab's spies being aware? Where is the time for preparations of this magnitude?"

The ragged *baul* began to pace the room.

"I have a plan," said Ajoy. "There shall be no armies. There will be a bloodless coup."

"How?"

"Listen to me carefully. We will dispense with the English and the Marathas and soldiers from Bihar. Wazir Ali and I shall assemble only a hundred trained and trusted men at the village of Lalgola, a few miles upriver of Murshidabad. As soon as the Nawab and his forces move south you will send a messenger on a fast horse. We shall then enter the city by the north gate."

"There will be resistance," the Minister objected.

"I don't think so. No one will expect an attack. With preparations for war with the English in full swing, people of Lalgola and those that remain in Murshidabad will think we are part of Shiraj's own forces. In fact, we shall wear the Nawab's own insignia."

"And then?"

"And then you will send another trusted messenger to the Nawab with news that his pregnant wife is in premature labor and in danger of dying. Shiraj is devoted to his *begum* and will return with only his bodyguards for he cannot turn the army around. When he returns we shall move swiftly, capture and execute him. With you, Wazir Ali and I standing together, the city will be ours. The army will be encamped in the wilderness. And then we shall send out a proclamation that all of Bengal, Bihar and Orissa are united in a popular revolution that has brought centuries of Moghul oppression to an end."

The two older men thought through all this.

"I see," said the Minister. "A good plan. But, Prince Ajoy, you have forgotten one crucial item."

"What is that, *Diwan-ji?*"

"The Nawab has a general. Rahamat Khan. He is a loyal and powerful man. He will stay beside Shiraj and, surprise or not, he will lead a strong defense against your hundred men."

"I have not forgotten him," Ajoy said quietly. "Rahamat Khan will not attack us."

"Why not?"

"He will be on our side."

"A miracle! How can you be so confident?"

"Because by then you, *Diwan-ji*, will have bought him. He, and therefore you, hold the key to our success."

"Rahamat Khan is totally devoted to the Nawab."

"Every man has his price, *Diwan-ji*. I have thought this through. There is no other way."

There was a very long silence.

The three men let their minds wander over the situation.

Minister Badri Narayan's thoughts were not pleasant. Why, he asked himself, was he placing himself at greater and greater risk as the years went by? What was in it for him? All the other conspirators stood to gain power and riches. They would have fiefdoms with the breakup of the united province of Bengal. He would get nothing. He wanted Shiraj Doula removed simply because he hated the Moghuls with a passionate loathing that spanned generations.

As a young man, Badri Narayan, a devout Hindu and a Brahmin, had watched his grandfather and father, extensive landowners in their own rights, humiliated by Alivardi Khan. The former Nawab had defiled their religion by forcing them to eat the meat of cows at a public function fifteen years ago. The Nawab had stopped short of the next step of forcible conversion to Islam when his advisers, gauging the mood of the mainly Hindu subjects and fearing open revolt, advised him to desist. Since that time the king and his minister had danced a dangerous waltz. Badri Narayan knew that the music would one day stop for him. His hereditary position was becoming terribly tenuous under Shiraj Doula. While his grandfather was at least amenable to advice, the new Nawab was completely unpredictable. So it was to be either him or Shiraj and the quicker it ended the better. Badri Narayan sighed and wiped his forehead with his shoulder cloth.

"I shall do my best," he told Ajoy. "The rest is in God's hands. With so much trust involved among the parties something will go wrong. Someone will betray us."

"It is possible, *Diwan-ji,* and I urge you to make sure your messengers are entirely trustworthy and you have complete control over their lives. Remember, every man has his price."

"We must stop now, Prince Ajoy. The guards will be here in a moment. Will you return to Mayurmani?"

"Tonight. I will send a courier to Wazir Ali as soon as I return. We shall assemble at Lalgola in exactly two weeks from now."

Reverting to his role, Rosho Pundit touched the Minister's feet and left the room.

Raja Ranjit had not said a single word throughout the entire dialog and had sat with his face crushed with worry. He had looked anxiously from one to the other as they talked. When Ajoy departed he closed his eyes in despair.

Badri Narayan sighed heavily.

"I keep getting drawn into this insidious danger and violence," said the Minister. "When will it end? When will it all end?"

"When will it indeed. With dear Mohendra's death my own life has ceased to have meaning. You however hold the balance in this game of survival, *Diwan-ji*. How will you buy Rahamat Khan?"

The two statesmen talked some more and then sat silently thinking.

Through Raja Ranjit's mind marched unpleasant images. Visions of protracted civil war. Hindus against Muslims, Indians against foreigners, French against English. A return of the dreaded Maratha bandits. Man-made famine, epidemic, fallow fields, hordes of hungry refugees, diseased bodies. Wraith-like millions starving on account of war. His only son was dead and there was no one to continue administrative reforms. His estate would decay when he passed on. Who would protect his beloved daughter-in-law after his death? Could Ajoy really succeed in dethroning Shiraj and ending Moghul rule? Had the fierce boy really matured? He ruminated on Ajoy. In the last three months he had built a relationship with the English. He had kept his freedom. He had united right-thinking Indian leaders against the Nawab. Would he, *could he*, become Bengal's overlord? The only way he would know was if the *coup* succeeded. And it all depended on whether Rahamat Khan, the key to the puzzle, could be bought. The Raja ran his hand through his iron-gray hair, thought long and hard and finally spoke.

"*Diwan-ji.*"

"Yes, Maharaj?" Badri Narayan stirred out of his own reverie.

"What do you need to bring Rahamat Khan to heel?"

"Money, Maharaj...and land. And status. Rahamat Khan is a man born in poverty in the distant hills of Afghanistan. He has risen in the Nawab's esteem through courage and fidelity. He is an ambitious man."

The Raja thought some more and then sat up straight indicating he had made a decision.

"I have a proposal."

"You, Maharaj? A proposal?"

"Yes, my friend. If the alternative is civil war, which in any event will destroy my dominion, I shall offer half my kingdom, all of northern Neeladri, six villages and the market town of Motirhaat, as a settlement to Rahamat Khan. It is a small price for amity in Bengal. With Ajoy in power through the support of Wazir Ali, the Biharis, the English and the Marathas, we shall be at peace. And poor Mother will have protection after I am no more."

Badri Narayan stared at the Raja, too overcome to speak

***

In the Minister's entourage was a guard whose name was Mujtaba.

Perhaps he was more intelligent than the other five guards. Perhaps he was better trained or more ambitious. Whatever the reason, unlike his indolent colleagues Mujtaba believed that to succeed as an enforcer of rules, he needed to *really* keep his eyes open and look beyond the obvious. He had recognized Prince Ajoy's servant when Ananta crossed the courtyard. He wondered why Ananta was here. He contemplated whether Ananta's presence indicated his fugitive master's proximity. Mujtaba was very aware that the

Nawab had placed a fabulous sum on the prince's head. He decided to keep his eyes *wide* open.

***

Pauline awoke from her afternoon siesta feeling groggy.

Her restless mind was buffeted by unsettled dreams. The events of the previous night had kept the heightened activity at Rai Mansion and Aruna's sparkle from impressing themselves on her. Once Pauline had caught Aruna looking at her with suppressed excitement. But she said nothing and Pauline had fallen back into the placid pace of existence at Neeladri.

She washed her face and brushed out her hair and changed into a fresh yellow cotton dress. Dilip's Mother brought her tea and sweets that dripped heavy syrup and which she found irresistible. Pauline put aside her problems and smiled at the friendly maid. Dilip's Mother was still shy in her presence but no longer scared. Then Aruna came in carrying her own cup of tea. There was no doubt about it now. Excitement shone in her eyes.

"Didi!" exclaimed Pauline. "What is the matter? You have looked happy all day."

"Oh, it is nothing. But I do have had some news."

"Then you must tell me. Don't I share everything with you?"

For a moment Aruna's strange expression of the night returned but was at once replaced by one of anticipation.

"Of course, Little Sister, I shall tell you while we go for our walk."

The sun had lost its fire. Like every evening after she had come to Neeladri, the two women strolled arm-in-arm into the pleasant-smelling orchards and gardens of the estate, with a protective Niamat following behind. They went out of the back entrance, past quarters that housed overseers, tax collectors, barbers, gardeners, footmen, servants and tradesmen with their families, and then a series of stables and cowsheds, all of which affirmed that Rai Mansion was a community unto itself. They walked companionably along a well-tended path between rose beds and hibiscus vines and jasmine bushes. The evening was full of color and fragrance. A woodpecker drummed busily while cooing wood-pigeons provided a pleasing backdrop.

"Tell me, Didi, what is your good news?"

"It is not mine, Little Sister. Someone has come to see *you*."

"To see me? Who? From the fort?"

"You will find out for yourself in a moment. There he is."

They had come to an ancient gatehouse. A figure stood leaning on the doorpost.

"The musician?" asked Pauline, perplexed. "He wants to meet me?"

"Yes."

"Why? I don't understand."

"Then you will have to ask him."

They reached the gatehouse. Pauline saw the rough-looking musician stand up straight and look at her. His gaze seemed so piercing that Pauline was taken aback. Who was he?

Aruna said "I will take Niamat and go on to the house the usual way. You can come after you finish with your musician."

"*My* musi... Didi, what *is* all this?"

But Aruna had already started to walk away.

Pauline studied Rosho Pundit.

"Who are you?" Pauline asked him in Bengali.

But before the man could reply Pauline turned from him in consternation. Aruna was disappearing!

"Didi! Come back!"

Aruna walked around a bend in the path and vanished. Niamat hesitated and looked back uncertainly. Then Aruna must have called him *sotto voce* for he suddenly speeded up and disappeared behind her.

Pauline turned back to the musician doubtfully. He looked positively mangy and unkempt. Why did he want to see her? What was in the dirty bag? And what was that funny instrument he was holding?.

Meanwhile Ajoy was gaping at her like a mouse transfixed by a cobra. Wainwright-memsahib! In Neeladri. Friends with his sister. How could it be possible? Whenever he thought of her, which was often, he thought of her as a foreigner—beautiful, courageous, forthright—but still a foreigner. And a married woman with whom he could have no connection. But here she was, speaking *his* language, at one with *his* world. She still had golden hair and wore a foreign dress, yet she blended easily into the household and the garden. The eyes that had gazed at him with bright points of moonlight now looked at him quizzically and with annoyance. Why didn't she smile or say something nice? She had spent a few intimate moments with him, hadn't she? Could it possibly be she had forgotten him? Then with a shock he remembered he was in disguise. Oh, that insufferable Aruna! She was actually having fun at his expense, a thing that had never happened before. How much had the memsahib told her? He wondered how he should break the pretence and face Pauline's wrath. And anyway, what was he coming to? He, Prince Ajoy Sena, made up like a fool, scared of being discovered as a fraud, hypnotized by a woman. Yes, but what a woman. And why was she looking at him so narrowly?

Suddenly Pauline's hand flew to her throat.

"Your Highness!"

Ruefully Ajoy put his palms together and bowed. So much for his masquerade. He fervently hoped that the Nawab's men would not have eyes as sharp as Pauline's.

"Namaskar, Memsahib. You have found me out. Believe me, I was sure my foolish sister had told you who I was. Do not be angry."

But even as Ajoy braced himself for thunder, the frown on Pauline's face was replaced by a blinding smile which set him back on his heels.

"*Ooooh!* The scheming creature! No wonder she looked like the cat that's swallowed the canary. I'll get her for this." As Ajoy did not follow this she asked, "How did you know I was here?"

"I did not, Memsahib. I could not believe my eyes when I saw you this morning."

"'Poor musician' Didi said! Is that a musical instrument?"

"Yes, Memsahib. I am a *baul*. A *baul* sings to the accompaniment of his *ektara*. See? This is an *ektara*, with just one string." He twanged the string and made a dull tinny sound. "But I do not sing!" he added hastily.

The trauma of the night dissolved in Pauline's happiness at seeing Ajoy. And just as before she felt an absence of inhibition in his company. His vibrant well-remembered voice and his theatrical English were delightfully reassuring and brought to her a blessed sense of contentment. As she studied his untidy appearance and the lines of worry on his forehead her expression softened.

"You have grown thinner, your Highness," she said "and careworn." Then Ajoy smiled and she saw a new light in his eyes. "Oh, and you look determined too. Is your mission progressing well?"

Ajoy explained the reason for his costume and before he knew it he was telling her about the unfolding chain of events and the thrusting and parrying that accompanied his plans for overthrowing the Nawab. He stopped once and considered the fact that this was a secret conspiracy. Then he plunged on heedless. What was it that made him confide in her? Have absolute faith in her?

She believed him.

That what the answer. She believed him. No, believed *in* him. And because of this she had brought him within striking distance of his goal.

Pauline never took her eyes off his face as she listened. Then Ajoy told her about the fall of Cossim Bazaar and of Shiraj Doula's intention to sack Fort William.

Pauline gasped in shock.

"Attack Fort William? Great Heavens! *You* must stop him, your Highness. The Governor at the fort is a spineless twit. The garrison commander argues with him all day. The soldiers lie about. Discipline is terrible. Everyone complains about the heat while they stuff their own pockets."

Ajoy worriedly digested this new perspective on his allies.

"What should I do?" she asked suddenly.

"You, Memsahib?"

"Should I stay here or should I go back to the fort?"

Ajoy considered. He knew that her husband was going to China soon. So why was she here? His mind dwelt for a moment on this fact and its ramifications. But be that as it may, shouldn't she be with her own people if there was danger? He said as much and Pauline's reply came in a rush.

"I don't like the people at Fort William. That's why I've come here. They are a selfish, short-sighted, prejudiced, power-hungry, greedy, narrow-minded lot. Here to plunder your country."

Ajoy listened with interest. Until now he had considered the hatmen only as allies in his quest for the throne. But what she said made sense when he thought about it. And when reduced to basics, which power *bloc* on the checkerboard of Bengali politics was different? How was *he* different?

Putting those thoughts aside he tried to decide what he should do with her. And why should *he* be concerned? What was she to him?

"...there are exceptions," Pauline was saying. "Mr. Morley and..."

"Ah yes, Morley-sahib. What a memorable day that was!"

At once their thoughts returned to the night when the moon poured calm over the pandemonium caused by the angry elephant and lighted their way along the sleeping village. Suddenly their eyes met and they knew they were thinking of the same thing and the magic came back. Neither felt brave enough to speak or take their eyes away as minute after minute passed. A hummingbird flitted among the hibiscus unnoticed, flying backwards and forwards on a blur of iridescent wings.

In and out of the big blooms went the tiny hummingbird. Still Ajoy and Pauline stood silently.

"*Mia-oww....mia-oww!*"

A nearby peacock called discordantly startling them.

The hummingbird flew away into the setting sun.

Ajoy sighed and broke the spell.

"It is late, Memsahib. They will be wondering. And I have a journey ahead."

"Your Highness, please don't call me Memsahib. It is so formal. Aruna calls me Little Sister. And she is younger than you are. Will you call me Little Sister?"

To her surprise Ajoy laughed out loud.

"No, I shall *not* call you Little Sister. You can be my little sister's Little Sister. But you are not *my* Little Sister. You are more to me. Much much more. You are my hope." His smile conveyed complete empathy but the timbre of his voice had sobered and he spoke with sincerity. "Whenever I am sad, whenever I am disillusioned I think of you. And I feel stronger. Until you came I was wont to give up in frustration and defeat. No longer. You are my inspiration."

Pauline drew closer. Breathless. Her eyes bright.

Ajoy's smile was warm.

"We have a simple Bengali word. A word that means all good things. Inspiration. Hope. Faith. Conviction. It means everything there is to look forward to in this world. That word is *asha*, Memsahib. From now you shall be my Asha."

"How lovely. Asha and her prince. Will you slay a dragon for me?"

They could never tell how it happened. But it did. Somehow she found her head resting on his shoulder and he found in his arms something incredibly soft and fragile, incredibly pliant and warm. Instinctively he held her close and Pauline buried her face in the rough earth-smelling material of the *baul's* costume. Ajoy felt a heart-stopping tenderness and a consummate responsibility for this person who had come halfway around the world to be his *asha.* Then he discovered that she was weeping in his embrace. He gently caressed her back and smoothened her hair. Then he held her at arm's length and looked down at the tear-lightened sky-blue eyes, the pert little nose, the disarrayed golden ringlets, and the eager face that looked at him with an ardor that frightened him with its intensity.

"Asha!" he breathed with a quiver in his voice and Pauline trembled in his grip. At last he dared to speak. "Please don't cry, Asha. I cannot bear to see you cry."

"No, no, I am not crying," said Pauline through a veil of tears. "Well, I *am* crying, but I'm happy. See? Here, I am laughing." And she laughed. Through her tears she laughed her joyous girlish laugh for the very first time since her wedding of many lifetimes ago. "Why am I so happy, your Highness?"

"I can tell you," he answered without hesitation. "It is because you *are* happiness and shall always be. And I am happy because you are!"

They did not talk any more as the unkempt Bengali musician and the pretty English girl started the walk back to Rai Mansion.

***

Later that evening Aruna dragged her brother unceremoniously into an unused room and shut the door.

"Little Sister, what *is* this?" Ajoy complained peevishly. "I have never seen you so."

"Never mind me. Do you love her?"

"*What?*"

"Do you love the English woman?"

"Are you completely and totally mad? *Love* her? How *can* I love her? She is married and she is a foreigner!"

"Answer me, Dada. Do you love her? She loves you."

Ajoy stared at Aruna. He was being overwhelmed by the rapidity and unfamiliarity with which events were unfolding around him. *Love!* What was love? Did he love Asha? What *did* he feel for her? The individual states of mind came to him distinctly. Inspiration. Contentment. Tenderness. Admiration. And the new one. Responsibility. He wanted to be with her. He wanted to take care of her. Was that love?

He saw Aruna was waiting pointedly for a reply.

"What do you mean, 'she loves me'?" he tried to bluster.

"She loves you, Dada," Aruna said flatly. "Do you love her?"

"She is…" began Ajoy and stopped. "She is a brave and wonderful person. She makes me believe I can do much. She gives me inspiration. I feel happy with her."

Aruna grabbed his arm and dug her nails into his skin.

"Dada! Do you love her?"

"Yes."

As the word left his mouth Ajoy felt the walls of the room spin and he was certain he was going to faint. But Aruna was shaking him urgently.

"Then you must save her!"

Brushing aside his dithering incredulity she plunged on.

"She is in a terrible hopeless situation. Her husband is the devil incarnate. Her father has been reduced to poverty and dependant on her husband's charity. She is alone in a foreign land. There is about to be war. And she is with child. And she loves you. She has no one else."

Ajoy stared at her blankly. All he could stutter was "Asha?"

"Save her, Dada. Save Little Sister. You must!"

*** *** ***

Still later that evening, clouds were filling the evening sky when Ajoy and Ananta retraced their steps in the direction of the pier. Harihar Mullick had gone on ahead to prepare the boat for the return journey to Mayurmani. Ajoy walked along in a trance. His brain was overloaded with the events and revelations of the day. He could not even begin to think of a plan for 'saving' Pauline. He knew that his bid for the throne was imminent. If he succeeded he could prevent civil war and bloodshed. But even this receded to the background as he walked along thinking of everything Aruna had said.

They were walking slowly in the gloom under gnarled *chhatim* trees of the cremation ground when there was an unexpected patter of running footsteps. In a moment Ajoy and Ananta were surrounded. There was only a brief scuffle. The attackers had the advantage of numbers and surprise. A sharp point of a knife pressed against Ajoy's throat and he relaxed.

A torch flared.

"You!" Mujtaba said to Ananta. "Who is this with you?"

"He is a *baul, huzoor.* Rosho Pundit."

"Why are you with him?"

"Maharaj asked me to see him to his boat."

"Lies! Where is Prince Ajoy?"

"My master is in hiding, *huzoor.* I know not where."

Mujtaba looked grimly at Ananta. Then he brought the torch close to Ajoy's face. Ajoy tried to hold up his hands against the light and the heat but Mujtaba roughly brushed them aside and looked long and hard.

"You *are* Prince Ajoy!"

The point of the knife pressed harder. Weakly Ajoy shook his head indicating denial. His mouth was dry. His head rang with the sound of his plans for the throne crashing around him.

"We shall see," said Mujtaba. "Take them to the boat. *Diwan-ji* must be told at once."

At the lamp lit pier two longboats with their distinctively carved peacock prows bobbed on the wavelets. Off to the side there was a small country craft from which Harihar Mullick peeped timorously as the procession came down the riverbank.

"Diwan-ji!" Mujtaba called out.

As Ajoy and Ananta were being marched down the steps, Badri Narayan, rubbing his eyes, sleepily emerged from the thatched cabin of the larger of the Nawab's boats.

"What is it? What is the disturbance? I was trying to..."

He saw the prisoners and stopped dead and swallowed. He tried to cover his dismay, thankful for the darkness. Then he recovered, cleared his throat and said as authoritatively as he could, "Who are these people? Why have you made them captive?"

"We have captured Prince Ajoy Sena, *Diwan-ji*."

Badri Narayan tried to look astounded.

"What absolute nonsense! You have captured a *baul*. Have you taken leave of your senses? I know this man. He will sing at the Nawab's music conference next month."

"He is a fraud, *Diwan-ji*. He looks just like the prince. And he has been seen with this other man, the prince's servant, many times today. I shall shave his beard in the morning and look at him closely. Then we shall take him to the Nawab."

Badri Narayan unhappily debated whether to pull rank and command Mujtaba to release the captives but, for the moment, decided against it. Mujtaba would probably obey a direct order, although there was a chance he may not for he seemed an exceptionally assertive person. But such an order would bring attention to himself. What should he do? He decided he would think about it and make a final decision in the morning before they sailed.

***

Still later that evening, Niamat who slept by the main entrance of Rai Mansion, was woken by the urgent rattling on the front door. He sleepily lit a lamp and wondered who the late visitor could be as he stumbled over and unbolted the door.

Harihar Mullick stood outside.

Chapter 16

To the hundreds of English men, women and children of Calcutta, to the thousands of Europeans and Armenians, and the countless Indians of Black Town, Fort William symbolized solidity. It was their fortress and their castle. Its imposing edifice crouched grimly over the river and dominated the landscape of Calcutta. Since its 1696 construction, Fort William had been the pivot for England's forays into the mysterious Orient. Large warehouses, built at its base, gave it height. The western frontage that faced the Hooghly was fourteen hundred feet long. Its north and south faces were six hundred feet long. The enormous east gate below high ramparts opened onto The Park. Fort William had four massive eighteen-pounder cannon mounted on bastions, one at each corner. As a last resort in the unthinkable possibility of abandonment, there was a direct line of retreat to the river and to waiting English ships.

On the floor above the warehouses was the large parade-ground into which Ajoy had brought Pauline to escape Lali the bull. Richard Armstrong's resplendent living quarters, his offices, his ballroom and conference rooms, collectively called the Governor's Residence, overlooked the western end of the parade-ground. On the north was Writers Building where Company apprentices, called writers, lived in monkish austerity. At the northern end and beyond Writers Building where Ajoy had once stayed, was the center of all business. Benjamin had his offices there. Here was the treasury which housed the Company's bullion and was guarded night and day. Beside it was the garrison's armory and stores.

Under the gallery that ran along the walls of the fort was the *kala agar,* the dark room, where elite prisoners were incarcerated. The main jailhouse on The Avenue outside was reserved for common criminals.

Those who lived and worked at Fort William took its solidity for granted and believed it to be completely impregnable.

***

Around the time Pauline was talking to the ochre-clad musician on the grounds of Rai Mansion, Benjamin Morley had come for tea at the Clarksons' and had sunk into a couch with a great sigh. Maggie fussed over him while her husband puffed quietly on his pipe. After a while Benjamin sat up.

"Sir, the Executive Council meets tomorrow."

"Yes, Morley. I know."

Benjamin shook his head, laughed mirthlessly and stretched with a groan.

"What a sorry state of affairs," he said in a tired voice.

"Laddie, you're exhausted," Maggie said. "You need a nice cup of hot tea and lots of sleep." She looked toward the inner door and called "Bearer! Tea!"

Gratefully sipping from his steaming cup, Benjamin started to talk.

"The news isn't good."

They waited.

"Cossim Bazaar has fallen."

"*What?*"

The effect of this statement on Benjamin's audience was electric.

"Yes sir, a runner has just arrived with the news. The Nawab left his capital yesterday with a small force and annexed our factory."

Clarkson's face was a picture of disbelief.

"Oh my God! The fellow really means business. What happened to Duncliffe, the station chief?"

"I don't know, sir. I tried to obtain information from the Jagat Seth but he couldn't add anything else. Governor Armstrong has the official letter. We'll hear about it in Council. I urged him to hold the meeting today. But several members are out of station and Armstrong wants to round them up. However, in passing I heard mention of ivory and McIver's ship, so there is probably some unfinished syndicate business to complete before the Council gets down to business." He broke off. "I'm sorry, Mrs. Clarkson. I don't bring cheerful news."

"Benjamin! Is there danger?" Maggie asked. "I mean real danger?"

Benjamin looked at the elderly woman who had treated him like a son ever since his arrival as a junior writer. He felt afraid. Afraid for her. Afraid for the men, women and children for whom Calcutta was home. He thought unhappily of Pauline. How was she doing in the interior where he had rashly dispatched her? Should he get her back from Neeladri? A thought struck him and he groaned again. Neeladri was in direct line of troop movements between Murshidabad and Calcutta! What a fool he was.

"I wish I knew, Mrs. Clarkson," he replied at last. "We have never been put to the test. We have our fort, our bastions, our cannon, our armory. The Colonel has his soldiers. We have *Europa* and other ships with guns on them. We are forewarned. Whether the warning is heeded is another matter. On the face of it we should be able to repel anything the Nawab throws at us. It's the changed environment that worries me, Mrs. Clarkson. We've lived in peace all these decades. We've become soft. Lethargic."

Clarkson thumped his armrest and stood up.

"Now look here, Morley, don't create demons. You know how Clive has put up with regular disturbances in the south. I'm sure you're aware our people in Canton have weathered many Chinese upheavals. Things will turn out fine once we have a plan for our defense. Let's go and see what Armstrong and Linnington have to say. I say, Maggie old girl, why don't you get the women together tomorrow night and we'll discuss the outcome of the Council meeting?"

Later Clarkson and Benjamin walked out to The Park for a breath of fresh air and a smoke. The air was heavy and humid. The sky was overcast. But no lightning flashed. Nor did it feel like rain. An unusual oppressive heaviness hung in the air.

***

In Neeladri heavy clouds covered the sky and shrouded the stone steps of the little pier in darkness. The two peacock-boats rolled gently on little wavelets that lapped at the steps. The nondescript country boat was still present, invisible in the shadows. All three craft were tied to iron rings embedded in the stone.

Ajoy and Ananta lay on the floor of the covered section of one of the peacock-boats. A kerosene lantern lit the interior of the tiny cabin. Lengths of rope were looped around their limbs and tied so that they were unable to move their arms and legs. Next to them Mujtaba and another guard dozed propped against the thatch wall. Both guards wore sheathed swords. On the deck of the same boat two other guards and a boatman were asleep. A turned-down lantern on the deck was the only source of light on the river. One of the guards outside snored. The other stirred and sporadically slapped at mosquitoes. The sound caused a sharp noise in the otherwise tranquil scene.

The second royal boat was completely dark. An anguished Badri Narayan had finally fallen asleep. His two clerks, the last guard and a boatman slept shrouded in sheets on deck.

It was two hours past midnight.

On the first boat, the guard who was bothered by mosquitoes slapped his face and then covered his head in his sheet. Better to suffocate than be eaten alive, he muttered to himself, his mind woolly with sleep.

A sudden bump made his boat rock.

The guard wondered groggily what it might be. Did the boat hit the side of the pier? Or was it a floating log? He began to drift back to unconsciousness. Suddenly the boat rocked violently and he sat up with a jerk. The other guard stirred. The rocking slowed. The first guard was now awake and reached for his sword.

"*Kay?*" he called loudly into the darkness. Who is it?

And then the most awful apparition burst upon him from nowhere.

Its face was white. It was clad in white from head to toe. Its flying hair was long and white too. It was huge and flew at him with fearsome talons.

The guard screamed in terror and half-crawled half-stumbled to the opposite side of the boat, his legs tangling in his sheet in his hurry, and leaned over the edge in a desperate attempt to get away. Then something clutched at his clothing from behind and heaved.

With a loud splash the man went into the river.

Rudely awakened by the noise the other guard and the boatman goggled at the apparition as it rushed at their colleague and made him disappear. Then it turned and advanced on them.

"*Bhoot! Bhoot!*" they shrieked. *Ghost!*

In panic they retreated to the prow of the boat, getting in each others' way. Suddenly the *bhoot* charged at them with a horrible screech. With a wild yell they backed away and tripped over the gunwale. The boatman fell on his back on the stone pier hitting his head with a sickening crunch. Then the *bhoot* was upon the other guard who arched his body away in a frantic bid to escape. At the same moment a powerful arm rose up from the river and dragged him out of the boat and into the water.

As soon as they heard the tumult, Mujtaba and the guard who were inside Ajoy's cabin hastened to get out and only managed to jam the narrow opening. Wild cries of '*bhoot!*' coming from the outside chilled their blood. Mujtaba pushed the other man roughly aside and crawled out. Before his eyes could adjust something white and shimmering in the lamplight ran at him and hit him sharply in the face and sent him spinning to the bottom of the boat. As he flailed his arms blindly in the dark, his shoulders were grasped on each side and he was bodily lifted and thrown overboard. The remaining guard inside the little cabin cowered back and his eyes opened wider and wider and his hair rose up as a white face with long white ragged hair and a white-sheeted body entered the cabin through the small entrance. It was followed by a man with a greasy coal-black face and black body. The air of the crowded cabin filled with a horrible slimy smell. The guard backed away as the black man pulled a knife and gestured threateningly.

"Out!" ordered the black man in a guttural voice.

The guard crawled out as fast as he could. As he emerged into the dark he felt a jab from the knife on his posterior and, simultaneously, a strong pair of arms grabbed his shoulders and propelled him forward. He crashed against the thwarts and was immediately rolled into the swath of water that had opened up between the pier and the boat.

The white and black intruders turned on Ajoy and Ananta. The two men stared back in terror. Then the black man raised his knife and, while they flinched in panic, he started to saw on the ropes on Ajoy's legs.

"Go outside. Quickly!" said the *bhoot.*

Ajoy squeaked in astonishment.

"*Asha!*"

"Listen to me!" Pauline's voice was breathless and urgent. "Go outside with Murali. There is no time to lose. There is a man waiting."

The ropes fell away and Ajoy followed the black man out

like a robot, grimacing at the pain of returning circulation. In the flickering lamplight he made out a strapping young man who dripped rivulets of water and whom he recognized as Badshah, Niamat's eldest son.

Pauline came out after him and finally Ananta.

"Quickly, *huzoor*," said Murali rubbing river ooze from himself. "Go to that boat. There is no time to lose,"

Ajoy saw the country boat that had pulled up alongside and carefully crossed over. A waiting Harihar Mullick helped him in. Murali followed. Pauline tripped on a thwart as she came to the edge. Ajoy put out a hand to steady her and then she was in his arms. A feeling of sheer joy swept through them and they held each other for a moment. When he released her, Pauline found her heart thumping wildly.

Meanwhile Ananta had crossed. Finally Badshah held the lamp aloft, jumped over and extinguished the light. The boats separated in total darkness. In the ensuing silence Pauline looked back in the direction of the pier. Her blood was racing with excitement. There were agitated cries from shoreward. They must be the men who had been pulled overboard. Then she heard a shout from the midstream. *Good!* The headman had been successful in cutting the hawser that held the Minister's boat to the pier. It must be floundering somewhere with its occupants. Yes, there it was, a light far downstream. Someone aboard had lighted a lamp. The Nawab's other boat, from which they had rescued Ajoy and which they had left devoid of people, was nowhere to be seen. She turned to survey their own boat. Harihar Mullick and their boatman were walking up and down the gunwale on either side, poling them away from shore. Murali went to the old village headman and took the pole from him.

Sometime afterward they went ashore to offload Badshah and wait for the first light of dawn. It was too dangerous to navigate downstream without a moon.

While the others lay on the deck in exhausted slumber, inside their miniscule reed-covered 'cabin', encircled by darkness and the arms of her prince, Pauline told her story.

"We faced our first problem when your headman—isn't he a darling old man?—when the headman brought news of your capture. There were no men at the Raja's mansion capable of decisive action."

"I *know!*" assented Ajoy feelingly.

"Now don't get me wrong. They're clever. They dislike the Nawab. But they're afraid of doing anything to anger him."

Ajoy nodded with his nose buried in her white-painted hair, his senses filled by her closeness.

"I am proud of you, Asha," he said and held her closer.

"Mmmmm... That's nice. But listen before you start anything, or what's the fun?"

"Fun?"

"*Listen!* So I took charge. We guessed you would be lightly guarded since their numbers were small and they would not expect a rescue attempt. But once they took you to the Nawab's capital there would be no chance. We *had* to get you away tonight. And to spare the Raja trouble, we had to do it without any of his people involved. The only way was through surprise. So I asked the men what the locals fear most in the night. They told me at once it was not tigers, not robbers, but ghosts." Pauline turned and made a scary face at him which he missed in the dark. "Did I frighten you?"

"*Shiva! Shiva!* You did then. But how can you now? You have the loveliest and happiest face in the world."

Ajoy reached around and tried to wipe the chalk off her face. She took his hand and lay back against him with a sigh and continued.

"You should have seen the Raja's and Didi's faces when I said I would lead the rescue. They were thunderstruck. Convincing them was the second problem. Then the third problem came along. We had to have physically strong men in case there was resistance. Murali alone could not handle five armed guards. The headman, Ananta and I would be no good in a fight. Not that there'd be any fight if our surprise failed. We'd all be run through with swords." She felt him recoil and held his hand tightly. "But we weren't! In the end we decided to enlist Badshah, who was visiting his father. He is young and sturdy. He doesn't live in Neeladri. And he will have long gone to his home when the Nawab's interrogators come. After we finalized the raiding party Didi helped me chalk my face and hair. You know, it wasn't a completely new idea. I've done this sort of thing in Burnham. In England I mean. But don't ask me why! At first Murali was reluctant to join us. But Badshah promptly agreed and planned our attack and convinced Murali to take part. On the way to the pier your headman kept my spirits up by whispering the names of all the different ghosts—heavens, it's an unending list!—that live in the big cremation ground we passed through. Oh dear, it was so dark and frightening and...and scary. Then we arrived at the pier and we had to decide which boat you were on. The fact that there was a lamp lit both inside and outside one of them indicated that prisoners were aboard. We could have been wrong, but it was a chance we had to take. We first went quietly to the small boat that brought you from Mayurmani. Mullick managed to get to the boatman before he made a noise. Then, while I set about the guards, Badshah pulled them overboard with Murali's help. Mullick cut the rope that held the Minister's boat to the pier. And you know the rest."

Ajoy listened mesmerized.

"I was shaking like a jelly when I came aboard. If it wasn't for Badshah, I wouldn't have been able to do it. He's a regular daredevil, that one! He kept urging me on, whispering encouraging words I didn't understand. I finally took a deep breath and plunged into the lamplight and did my banshee act. After I saw the fright I gave the first guard I knew I could do it. But we had to be quick before they saw through the ruse. *Ooooooh!* You should have seen Badshah propel those guards into the river like sacks of coal."

Pauline sobered.

"The Nawab will suspect the Neeladri household. But he

will have no one on whom to place the blame on. I suppose his guards will search the place inside out…"

She stopped.

Ajoy's shoulders were shaking. She laughed and peered at him but could not make out his face.

"Yes, wasn't it funny to see those big armed guards terrified by a ghost?"

A warm drop fell on her neck.

Pauline tensed and reached out to touch Ajoy's face. It was wet.

"What's wrong?" Her heart melted. "Oh, come to me." She turned and pulled his head into her arms. "It's all right. Don't worry. You're all right now."

Held tightly by her, Ajoy Sena gave himself up to utter desolation. He wept because of the frustration of one more failed grand plan. He wept because of his loneliness and transience. But mostly he wept because a slip of a girl in an alien hostile land was brave enough to risk her life against impossible odds to save him. And she had succeeded in her endeavor while he had failed in every one of his. She had rescued him, unworthy, useless, unloved, derelict prince only in name that we was. That night, under cover of darkness, in the tiny tunnel of a cockle-shell on the banks of an unfeeling river, his face buried in the soft breast of an English girl, Prince Ajoy Sena of Rajmahal cried his heart out while she rocked him like a baby and whispered soft words in his ear. After a long time he straightened and she tenderly wiped his eyes with the end of her white dress.

"Why?" he asked finally. "Why did you do it?"

"Why did I do what? Rescue you? Oh, it was fun!" Then the humor left her voice and she held his hand. "Because I love you."

He stared at her in amazement. Aruna's words, *'She loves you, Dada,'* came crashing down around him.

"You are my prince." Her voice was soft. "Do you remember the moonlit forest?"

Yes of course Ajoy remembered the moonlit forest. Tears formed behind his eyes again and a lump filled his throat.

"But why do you love me?" he asked when he could speak. "What is there in me to love? Why do you love a shadow?"

"Why? Crikey! I haven't thought about that. And you're not a shadow. You are good and you struggle against injustice and try to make wrong things right and you are the best and noblest person I have met...and...and...because I love you," she ended lamely.

"And I love you too, Asha." He had said it at last. The words sounded artificial and hollow, so he said it again. "I love you, Asha."

Pauline brought her face close and kissed the salty tears away.

"Asha, you are too good to me," Ajoy muttered.

"Shush, what drivel! And you a prince too."

She stayed in his arms as the night wore on, not talking, happy simply to be with each other. After a while he felt her breathing grow deeper and her muscles relax in slumber. But Ajoy did not relax. For the rest of the night he supported the sleeping girl while plan after plan chased one another through his mind.

Chapter 17

A cold wind blew through Fort William heralding the first rain of the season and flapping the window curtains of the Clarksons' home.

The magistrate was pacing his living room. After a while he stopped, ran his hand through his shock of white hair, and looked worriedly at his wife.

"Richard must be mad," Maggie said. "He's inviting disaster, he is."

Her husband resumed his pacing.

"The egotistical dolt!" Clarkson burst out. Coming from the mild-mannered magistrate this was severe incrimination. "Do you know, old girl, because his appointment hasn't been confirmed from London for a year, Armstrong's been trying to assert his authority at any cost? He will not reason, he will not listen to reason, and he will do nothing to placate the Nabob. Says its because he was treated discourteously in the capital. While that may well be true, he simply cannot act arrogantly toward a local ruler and not expect repercussions. Morley and I have been trying to convince him to bend a bit before the Executive Council meets, but will he listen? *Hah!*"

"Clarence, what shall we *do?*"

The undertone of fear brought her husband up short. He came and put his arms around his wife of thirty years.

"Don't worry, my dear. We will muddle through this one too. Haven't we been through worse times? And if we have to go back to England the boys will be there for us."

They stood thus, holding each other and drawing strength from each other. Their thoughts were on the their grown-up children and the happy years they had all spent together as a pioneering family in India. Footfalls in the hallway made them draw apart. Khurshid entered and salaamed.

"Memsahib come, *huzoor*."

Husband and wife looked at the bearer in surprise.

"Memsahib? Which memsahib?"

In their small community visitors usually walked straight into one another's homes. Who was it that Khurshid needed to announce? They did not have to wait long to find out. Pauline stepped daintily around the bearer and came into the room. A big smile decorated her face.

"Hello, Maggie dear. Good evening, Mr. Clarkson. It's me. I'm back."

"Pauline!" yelped Maggie and ran to envelop the girl to her bosom. "Sweet Jesus child, but it's absolutely wonderful to see you back. We've been so worried…"

Maggie's voice broke. Pauline hugged the motherly woman back with equal vigor. At last, when she was sure she would suffocate, Maggie loosened her embrace and held Pauline at arm's length.

"Lord in heaven, lass, *look* at you! You're soaking wet. What shall we *do* with you!"

They looked at her.

Pauline still wore the dress that had been improvised from one of Aruna's *saris* for her *bhoot* act of two nights ago. It was no longer white but drenched and stained and torn. Her scratched feet were bare and muddy. Her sandals had been left behind on the stone steps of Neeladri pier. Traces of chalk mixed with droplets of rainwater still smudged her face. Her hair was loose, white-streaked, and dramatically windblown. All of this together with a strange smoky expression gave her the appearance of a wild animal. Clarence Clarkson was struck by her heightened color and the uninhibited look of excitement in her eyes, by the absence of corset which made her appear rounded and sensual, and by her impish gypsy-like aspect. She reminded him of a beautiful caged panther. The old magistrate suddenly felt warm and happy just to be near her.

For a moment Armstrong and his transgressions were forgotten. Then Maggie began to fuss over Pauline.

"Lordy girl, just *look at you!* You need a hot bath and fresh clothes before you catch pneumonia. Oh, and your poor feet! They're bruised. Where *have* you been? Who's brought you? Have you had supper? Where is…"

"Steady!" broke in her husband. "The girl's just arrived. Give her air, will you? She'll tell us of her own accord. Bearer! Oh, you're still here, Bearer. Bring her luggage in."

"I don't have any, Mr. Clarkson."

The magistrate started to say something but changed his mind.

"Murali and Price Ajoy brought me back. They've gone on to Mr. Morley's. We left Neeladri in a hurry, you know. Actually quite a hurry. I was in a bit of a scrape."

"Oh, Pauline, you'll be the death of us!" wailed Maggie. "When are you *not* in a scrape? What are we to *do* with you?"

Pauline grinned mischievously. Then her expression sobered.

"Mr. Clarkson, Maggie, I have very serious news. It's a long story and there is little time. Mr. Morley will be arriving in a moment to hear it. Before we start can I get something to wear?"

***

A half-hour later Pauline, wearing a dress of Maggie's that fit her like a tent, sat at the dining table and dipped pieces of bread in hot broth. Benjamin, intercepted by Murali on his way to Council, had arrived at a run and was now sitting opposite her and staring in amazement.

Pauline looked unhappily at the anxious faces of her friends.

"Prince Ajoy's rebellion has failed," she began. "And the Nawab's army is about to march on Calcutta…"

***

While Pauline told her story in the Clarkson's dim drawing room, scores of lamps burned brightly in the reception chamber of Hazarduari Palace. Minister Badri Narayan stood before the Nawab with his head bowed.

Is this the end? he wondered.

Mujtaba and five guards who were at Neeladri stood beside him wearing hang-dog looks.

"What have you found?" Shiraj Doula rapped out the question.

Nobody volunteered an answer. The Nawab's temper, as always, began to boil.

"Which one of you is Mujtaba?"

"I am, my Lord."

"You were the leader of the guards. What did you find?"

"My Lord, we searched up and down the river for the prisoners. We searched the Rai Raja's entire property. We interrogated every member of his household on pain of death. All his family and staff are accounted for…"

He was interrupted.

"Minister!"

"My Lord?"

"Was it the dog Sena, Minister?"

"No, my Lord, it was a musician whose name is Rosho Pundit. I had just engaged him to sing at your palace. For some reason this guard thought it was Prince Ajoy."

"It *was* Prince Ajoy!" countered Mujtaba mutinously. "I am certain of it."

"Silence! If he was a simple *baul,* why was he rescued?"

"I do not know, my Lord," replied Badri Narayan. "I awoke when the guards on the captives' boat shouted *'bhoot!'* and fell into the river one after another. The next thing I found was our own boat floating in mid-river."

"You saw a ghost, guard?"

The Nawab's voice had a dangerous edge. Mujtaba, careful now, suppressed his own frustration.

"No, my Lord, I did not. These superstitious swine did. A ghost would not hold knife at my throat and ask me to leave."

The story that unfolded sickened the Nawab. It was apparent that there had been a rescue. But in trying to save their skins the guards exaggerated shamelessly. There were frequent cries to Allah to attest they spoke the truth. The white ghost had blood on its fangs. The hands that propelled them overboard belonged to armored soldiers with superhuman strength. After a few minutes Shiraj Doula was disgusted.

"Enough! You will clean my elephant stables while the Nawab's army marches to Calcutta. Now get out of my sight." Then he added, "You, Mujtaba! Stay."

The other guards left.

Badri Narayan made a motion to follow them but the Nawab rapped out, "The Minister shall remain."

***

In the Council Room of the Governor's Residence, the Executive Council of Fort William began its emergency meeting at six o'clock on the evening June 12th, 1756.

The Council members in attendance that day in addition to Armstrong, Clarkson, Linnington and Morley, were Angus McIver, supervisor of shipping, Captain Muldoon, supervisor of the armory, Stanislaus Kyle, engineer, and Matthew Broderick, paymaster.

John Wolfe, warehouse keeper, was missing once more.

It was universally known that he was enamored of a local mistress and spent most of his waking hours, and it was rumored, his sleeping hours, in her company somewhere deep in Black Town.

Also attending the meeting today by special invitation were the master of *Europa,* Captain Frederick Wainwright, and Prince Ajoy Sena.

Council members and Freddie regarded Ajoy with open hostility. It was the first time ever that a native was present at a Council meeting.

Richard Armstrong opened the proceedings.

"Gentlemen, we are meeting today in emergency session to address a perceived threat of attack by the Nabob of Bengal."

He got no further.

Angus McIver glared at Ajoy through beetling brows. He cleared his throat and spoke in his rasping voice.

"Hol' on a tick, Guv'nor. Can we be advised of the reason for the native visitor? Aren't we about defending ourselves from his ilk?"

The sarcasm was typical of McIver, a cantankerous consumptive man, who controlled the unofficial syndicates that channeled personal trade of the officers in parallel with that of the Company. He was becoming a source of discomfiture for Armstrong because of his growing misuse of preferential trade discounts that were meant for the Company. The Governor wanted to talk to McIver about the protests the Nawab had lodged. But he kept putting it off. He was wary of the acerbic nature and sharp tongue of the feisty Scotsman. But that was not the primary reason for his procrastination. Armstrong was waiting for his confirmation as Governor of Fort William which he expected to come through any day from London. As soon as this happened he would apply for a senior posting in the Home Office. Why, he rationalized, should one create unnecessary enemies? Also, he had an investment in the syndicates himself.

"Right," he said. "Native visitor! Now then, Morley. Why is the man here?"

Looking at Benjamin one would have difficulty finding the tiredness and anxiety that was evident in the Clarksons' home a little while ago. He wore a loose cotton shirt gathered at the sleeves and crisp cotton breeches. The recent rain had reduced the heat but had increased the humidity. The other men's tight silk clothing was stained with perspiration. Armstrong constantly mopped his forehead with his handkerchief.

"Sir, I have told you the reasons for Prince Ajoy's attendance."

"So you have, Morley, so you have. But why don't you tell the others, there's a good fellow."

Benjamin fumed inwardly. *Mother-fucking rabbit!* Doesn't want to take the heat even though he's given the permission. *Lily-bellied cad!*

"Prince Ajoy is a sworn enemy of the hostile Nawab," he explained to the Council. "He commands an alliance of local powers that includes us and is arrayed against Shiraj Doula and wants his downfall. He has insight into the Nawab's planning through spies at his court. Therefore Prince Ajoy is a valuable ally and a potential friendly ruler of Bengal if the alliance is successful in toppling the present one."

"Isn't this prince the very reason for the Nawab's displeasure?" interjected Broderick.

"That's right, by thunder!" exclaimed McIver. "Why dinna we turn the blackguard over to the Nabob and get on with our own business?"

There were grunts of approval.

Clarkson held up his hand.

"Gentlemen, that is an extremely short-sighted view."

McIver guffawed loudly.

"Not as short-sighted as some, mon!"

Clarkson glared angrily at the Scotsman. The irreverent dig at his thick glasses was in extremely poor taste and was typical of the people who came to the Company's field stations and moved into positions of responsibility.

"Governor, sir!" Clarkson protested. "Mr. McIver is out of order! If you will not then I shall remind him of his responsibilities as a Council member since they seem to have escaped him. This is not the forum for asinine jollity. We are discussing a grave predicament."

"Clarkson's right, Mac," Armstrong said. "Draw it mild, will you?"

The reprimand did not satisfy Clarkson but he let it go.

"And I would like to remind the Council," he continued, "that the cause of the Nabob's wrath is *not* the presence of Prince Ajoy at Fort William, but our insistence in defying him with our fortifications."

"Our fortifications are impressive though," said Broderick.

"Are they?" Benjamin looked fixedly at the stout paymaster, whose layers of fat had earned him the nickname 'Humpty'.

"Well," Broderick blustered. "Why shouldn't they be, eh? We have our cannon and our guns and…"

"Are they, sir?" Benjamin interrupted and directed the question to the Governor.

Armstrong cleared his throat.

"Of course they are. Morley. Do you have reason to believe otherwise?"

"I am the Company's Trade Councilor, unfamiliar with military matters. Sir, I hereby request a status of our preparedness in the event of a siege."

"*Siege!*" McIver, Linnington and Muldoon burst out together.

"Poppycock!" cried Broderick.

"Gentlemen, Cossim Bazaar has fallen."

It was a mild matter-of-fact statement made by Benjamin but it had the effect of a thunderclap. The members gawked at him and then at the Governor.

"Er, yes," assented Armstrong. "Fallen. It has indeed. Pity."

"Why the devil weren't we told?" exploded Colonel Linnington, livid with fury. "When did it happen? What abomination!"

Armstrong's face became red.

"I'll trouble you to keep a civil tongue in your head, Colonel."

Linnington made a rude noise.

"Gentlemen! Gentlemen!" Clarkson was disgusted. Here was the making of one more of the interminable altercations that earned Armstrong and Linnington the collective title of 'Punch and Judy'. "This simply won't do. Will you explain what happened at Cossim Bazaar, Governor?"

Armstrong mopped his face and adjusted his collar.

"Yesterday a runner brought a letter from Duncliffe written the day before. It appears that the Nabob's army surrounded the factory and asked Duncliffe to come out to negotiate. As soon as he did so he was imprisoned and the Nabob's guards entered the factory."

There was stunned silence which lasted many minutes as it finally dawned on the listeners that a native ruler had actually violated the sanctity of European property. There had been decades of threats but it had never actually happened before.

"Where is Duncliffe now, sir?" Benjamin asked.

"The runner could only say that Duncliffe and his men were imprisoned somewhere in the Nabob's camp. Oh yes, the women were allowed to leave and have apparently gone to nearby Fort d'Orleans under protection of the French."

Another long silence followed while they visualized the scene in their minds and put themselves and their families in it and wondered how they would have reacted.

"May I speak?"

The unexpected tentative request made everyone swing around to face Ajoy.

"Bloody Hindoo!" roared McIver. "You'rn the cause of it all."

"On the contrary, Mr. McIver," Benjamin countered. "Your adversary, the Nawab, is a Mohammedan."

"Rats! They're all kin. Damned heathens."

"Does it occur to you that Prince Ajoy wishes to help?"

"Stow it, Morley. We dinna need his help."

Everyone began to talk at once. They raged about the audacity of natives to dare intimidate white men in general and their garrison in particular and the pros and cons of Ajoy's value. Armstrong tried to bring the meeting to order without success. Clarkson and Benjamin exchanged glances.

"Silence!"

A new peremptory voice quelled the babble and everyone looked at the speaker in surprise. It was Stanislaus Kyle, a man of very few words.

"Gentlemen," said the rugged dun-haired engineer. "We have been waltzing around the most important question since this meeting began. Are the defenses adequate? Who should answer that question? Is it a military matter? The gun emplacements are. Is it a civilian matter? The walls and palisades are. I believe it is an *English* matter. The entire Council must undertake an official inspection of cannon in the bastions and powder and ball in the armory. I propose we survey the approaches to the fort for construction of fresh palisades. I..."

But Punch and Judy were at his throat.

How dare an engineer make military recommendations? A battle raged about whether the defense of the fort was a civilian or a military matter.

Kyle kept quiet through the din. He was a conscientious but disillusioned man. It was his job to look after public works. This was the area most neglected by the Council unless it directly affected its members' personal lives. There was apparently never money for his projects. Approvals were requested of Leadenhall Street but never arrived. Each new officer, on arrival from England, wanted his street to be the widest and his perimeter wall the highest, and his house the tallest. Yet the town's roads and battlements languished for want of budgets. The cells of writers got damper and ran with rats. The defensive Maratha Ditch degenerated into a public lavatory after the menace of bandits faded. And so it went on.

The time had come for the Council to rue their apathy.

Stanislaus Kyle stood up, adjusted his spectacles, and raised his hand like a middle-aged Caesar.

There was silence.

"Mr. Morley," Kyle said. "Is it true the Nabob's army numbers in the thousands?"

"Yes, Mr. Kyle, it does."

Kyle turned to Armstrong and spoke slowly enunciating every word.

"I *hope* you find that the defenses of your fort robust, Governor. Civilian or military notwithstanding. Because I *know* that the Towne of Calcutta *cannot* be defended against an army of thousands."

Chapter 18

The irregular rhythm of drums floated faintly on the air and gradually registered on Aruna's consciousness. At first she thought the *charak* festival had begun. Then she remembered it was only June and that festival took place at the end of the rainy season which had not even begun.

"Dilip's Mother!"

The plump maid appeared through an inside door.

"Yes, Mother?"

"Where is the music playing?"

"Music? What music?"

"Listen."

Dilip's Mother cocked her head and listened. The sound grew louder. First it was the sound of drums and then they heard strains of music. The sound came closer. Aruna and Dilip's Mother hurried out to the verandah which overlooked the road and the river. In another moment Raja Ranjit joined them. They stood at the parapet and looked in the direction of the noise. The music and drumbeats were now quite loud. The musicians were clearly moving fast in their direction. A crowd gathered below—gardeners, footmen, washermen and servants of the Raja's household. Women peered around the garden wall. Children ran back and forth on the path to the river, chattering shrilly.

Suddenly they heard an unearthly sound.

It was a high-pitched, long-drawn scream. Everyone recoiled and gibbered in fright.

At the same moment Niamat's youngest son, ten-year-old Afzal, ran into the verandah.

"Elephant! It's an elephant!" squealed Dilip's Mother.

"Maharaj! Maharaj!" Afzal clamored for attention.

"Have you seen the elephant, little one?" the Raja asked Afzal.

"Maharaj! The Nawab is coming. The Nawab's army is coming. Many elephants are coming."

They all stared at Afzal open-mouthed.

The music was now very loud. Aruna tried to see if anything was visible on the road. Niamat appeared and they turned to him for news.

"*Huzoor,*" said Niamat. "The Nawab is on his way to conquer Calcutta. His soldiers will pass by very soon."

The Raja looked worriedly into the distance. He had never met Nawab Shiraj Doula. When Shiraj ascended to the throne he should have visited the royal court to pay obeisance. But Mohendra's death, Aruna's sorrow, Ajoy's problems, and Pauline's visit had made him delay the journey. The Nawab's unsavory reputation had also subconsciously contributed to his putting off the decision to go to Murshidabad. And now the Nawab was in Neeladri! What should he do? Shiraj Doula, almost by definition, would be belligerent. Ajoy was his enemy. Ajoy had magically slipped through his fingers here at Neeladri. Did Shiraj know about the foreign woman who had stayed at Rai Mansion? If so he would surely consider the Raja his enemy.

The Raja came to a decision. Instead of waiting to find out he would anticipate the worst.

"Dilip's Mother!" he called and then noticed that the maid was on the verandah. In consternation Dilip's Mother covered her face with her *sari* and half-turned away from him. It was a rare occasion when the master addressed a female employee directly.

"Dilip's Mother, take Mother immediately to the rear gatehouse. At once, do you hear?"

Aruna looked at her father-in-law in surprise.

"Why should I go to the gatehouse, Father?"

"Listen to what I say. There could be trouble from the Nawab. It is best that you are not seen. Who knows what we can expect."

"But, Father! I shall remain indoors but near at hand in case you need assistance."

"The Nawab is a dangerous person. It is best if I know you are safe from him."

"Father, I will not run away."

While they talked a dust cloud formed on the horizon and grew larger. The cacophonous music was very loud and the low scraping sound of many feet could be heard. Another elephant trumpeted, an incredibly unnerving sound. The Raja looked toward the approaching multitude, his brow wrinkled with worry. A marching army of undisciplined ruffians led by an erratic leader would wreak havoc on the countryside and on his tenant farmers. How many *were* there in the army?

With a clattering of hooves the first of the cavalry appeared around the bend in the river path. The cavalry was made up of hundreds upon hundreds of plumed horsemen. They came on and on and on. The men rode twenty abreast, strung out inland from the riverbank. The width of the road was quite inadequate. The horsemen trotted over rice fields, around trees and vaulted over ditches. They wore red turbans and red-and-green tunics and trousers. The horses blew and pranced. The afternoon sun was reflected on swords, on golden thread of costumes, and on matchlocks slung crosswise across saddles.

What a sight it was!

Aruna had never seen, never imagined, never dreamt of a spectacle such as this.

Then a rider turned onto the path to Rai Mansion. Behind him three others followed. One bore aloft a peacock-blue-and-gold flag, the standard of the King of Bengal. They were an impressive lot. Their uniforms had the same colors as the flag indicating their elite rank of palace guard.

As one man, the crowd on the ground floor of the mansion vanished. Children were scooped up or dragged away.

The cavalry continued to pass outside.

From the balcony Aruna studied the leader of the horsemen. He was an alert, fiercely-bearded and well-built man, seated on an enormous black horse. He came to the portico and dismounted. As though moved by the same spring the Raja and the women on the verandah withdrew into the house. Niamat and little Afzal were left at the railing.

The leader called up to Niamat in a loud and deep voice.

"You there! Where is the Rai Raja?"

"Who wants to know, *huzoor?*"

Niamat had a quaver in his voice.

"You there! Listen carefully. I am the Nawab's *Sipah-sala.* I demand to see the Raja immediately. The Nawab will arrive in a moment."

"As you command, *huzoor.*"

The Raja had listened to the exchange and walked back to the parapet and looked over.

"Father, take care!" Aruna called anxiously from behind.

"What do you desire, *Sipah-sala?*" asked the Raja.

"Are you Raja Ranjit Rai?"

"I am."

Rahamat Khan bowed.

"*Salaam Aleikum,* Maharaj. I am the commander of the Bengal Army. The Nawab desires you to meet him. His war pavilion shall be set up this night in your garden." Without waiting for the Raja to agree he turned to his men. "Azeem-ul-Zaman! Arrange to set the standard over there."

Rahamat Khan's manner was respectful but there was no mistaking that his wishes were to be obeyed. Soon the Nawab's flag waved from the portico of Rai Mansion. The cavalry passed in a continuous stream. When everything was to his satisfaction Rahamat Khan bowed again, vaulted onto his horse and rode away. The three palace guards remained on guard beside the flag.

Aruna kept watch from a window. She had long ago lost count of the horsemen. What an immense army! And then the infantry began to pass. It was made up of innumerable soldiers who marched untidily to separate bands beating irregular rhythms. It was more of a loose shuffle than a march. With the drums were horns that played in complete discord.

The day wore on.

Nobody in the house thought of preparing the evening meal. The dust raised by the horses' hooves and soldiers' feet settled on everything and everyone in a thickening layer. The smell of droppings, the clank of steel, and sound of men's voices filled the air.

Aruna looked at the faces of the soldiers and shivered. They were cruel faces suffused with an unholy zeal. They were on a *jihad!* A holy war. She wondered whether they had looted houses and molested women on their way. Occasionally they made tentative movements toward Rai Mansion, but the sight of the Nawab's standard flanked by palace guards made them change their intention.

The sun was setting when another curious noise came to be heard. A struggling, bellowing, grunting, grinding noise. For the life of her Aruna could not think of what could be causing it. Then she heard many men shouting and cursing. Unable to contain her curiosity, she had started to cross the verandah to where the Raja still stood, when the air was split by the trumpeting of an elephant from very close. The watchers cowered back at the monstrous shriek. Had Dicky Glynnis been there he would have recognized the 'last peal of doom'. Aruna reached the parapet with her heart beating fast.

The sight that met her eyes was inconceivable.

Strung out in front of Rai Mansion were lines of cannon. Aruna knew they were cannon, not because she had seen cannon before, but because Ajoy had described them to her. Each cannon was made of a dull golden metal, probably brass, and mounted on a pair of big iron wheels. They looked extremely heavy. Each cannon was yoked to a team of ten oxen that pulled it jerkily forward on the urging of men with whips. Behind each cannon walked a war-elephant with its forehead decorated with elaborate painted markings. Bright drapery hung down the elephants' sides. The top of their backs were higher than the second story verandah where she stood. As soon as a cannon slowed or faltered, its attendant elephant pushed it forward with its trunk.

Aruna watched fascinated.

Behind the cannon, of which there were over a hundred, rode a company of white men. They wore no uniforms and their western clothes and hats were frayed and dirty. Mercenaries! Ajoy had told her that French artillery would support the Nawab in his attack on Fort William. So these must be Frenchmen.

The clamor and the dust were hellish.

Then the last of the army began to pass and hundreds of camels carrying bulky loads came into view. Aruna had never seen camels before. They were horrible scruffy creatures with villainous eyes and made disgusting belching sounds.

It began to grow dark.

Little Afzal was a constant source of information. The excited child would run out among the soldiers and return with news. He informed them that the army had camped on the field south of the palace. The cremation ground had become a sea of cooking fires. In the open area before Rai Mansion, lines of tents were set up. The smell of smoke was strong.

Then a line of camels turned into the path to Rai Mansion and came to a stop below the portico and mutinously sank down to their knees, coughing and grumbling. Men started to unload packages, unroll bales of cloth and struggle with furniture. Soon a very large tent with a canopied entrance took shape in the garden. Flags fluttered from its poles. Torches flared everywhere. Liveried matchlockmen took up positions beside the royal tent. An unmistakable air of expectancy built up. Aruna held her breath when suddenly all activity ceased and there was a hush.

A group of horsemen rode up the path to the mansion. At their head, sitting erect on a white stallion without any doubt, was Shiraj Doula, Nawab of Bengal.

For a moment only did Aruna look at the Nawab's prominent eyes and hooked nose under his jeweled turban. It was enough to fill her with a nameless fear. With a suppressed cry she ran into the house and bolted the door behind her.

Later that night Rahamat Khan came to summon the Raja. Uncertain of what to expect, the old man asked him to wait and went to say a last word to his daughter-in-law. Aruna controlled her dread and held back her tears and bent to touch his feet. Raja Ranjit Rai stood for another moment then walked back to the waiting *Sipah-sala*. In spite of his anxiety the Raja was awed by the splendor of the Nawab's camp as they passed scores of guards and servants and officials on the way to the tunnel-like entrance of the big tent. He had never thought such luxury could be possible and that too in a temporary structure. The inside walls of the war pavilion were hung with muslin. The floor was covered with Persian carpets. Multi-colored lanterns hung from hooks set in the cloth ceiling. The tent was hot and uncomfortable. Fumes of incense made the interior murky. As he was shepherded into the Nawab's presence the Raja was momentarily distracted by a bright green parrot that was perched on a hoop that hung from the ceiling. It held a chili pepper in one of its claws and looked ridiculously inappropriate in the martial setting.

A grey nondescript official rose from a low cushion at the entrance.

"My Lord," intoned the official. "Raja Ranjit Rai!"

Shiraj Doula, recumbent on muslin cushions on a teak divan, looked up from a scroll. The Raja saw before him a young man. But young only in age. In the set of face and arrogance of bearing there was an indisputable manhood and mastery over forces that surrounded him. The late Alivardi Khan that he knew had governed through perseverance. It was plain to the Raja that Alivardi's grandson was born to rule. He trembled as he bent and touched the Nawab's looped gold-threaded slippers.

"A hundred thousand salutations, my Lord!" said Raja Ranjit. "I beg forgiveness for failing to come earlier and pay homage." The Nawab said nothing and he added, "I am Raja Ranjit Rai of Neeladri. My humble abode is yours, my Lord."

Still Shiraj said nothing. The Raja felt increasingly nervous and extremely worried about Aruna's safety. Then came the abrupt question.

"*Where is the traitor Sena?*"

The Raja flinched.

"Sena? Oh, Prince Ajoy? I do not know, my Lord."

"He is in Calcutta!"

The Raja was uncertain of what to say. If Shiraj knew the whereabouts of Ajoy, why did he ask?

"*Sipah-sala!*"

Rahamat Khan stepped forward.

"My Lord?"

"This prisoner shall be confined with the hatmen from the Cossim Bazaar factory."

"My Lord!" The Raja was shocked. "Why am I to be imprisoned? What crime have I committed?"

"Captive!" an official admonished from the background. "You dare to question the Nawab?"

Shiraj Doula raised an imperious hand and addressed the Raja.

"A traitor was harbored by you. His escape was abetted by you. The Nawab shall *not* be aggravated by you further. You are fortunate the Nawab is not wiping you out. *Sipah-sala!* The prisoner shall be released only after Sena is in the Nawab's hands."

"My Lord!" implored Raja Ranjit. "My poor daughter-in-law cannot hurt a soul. Take my life but do not harm her."

Shiraj Doula looked at him with withering disdain.

"Infidel! Know you not the *Koran* forbids ill-treatment of women? And of captives? It is written in the Holy Book. Your women are safe. *Sipah-sala!* Guards shall be posted after the Nawab departs. Take him away!"

Shiraj Doula returned to his scroll.

Chapter 19

Just after the official inspection of the fort, Murali brought a folded paper with the embossed crest of the Rai Rajas to a despondent Benjamin. Benjamin could speak Bengali but he could not read it. Murali was in the same situation. Benjamin sent him to call Ajoy while he changed into a fresh set of clothes.

Ajoy arrived, unfolded the letter and read it out loud:

Praise be to Lord Narayan

Exalted Morley-sahib,
I beseech God to ensure this letter reaches your hand quickly and safely as I write with the saddest of news.

My heart worries for Miss Pauline who came to live with us and who became my dearest Little Sister. I pray she has returned safely to Fort William. Dada knows her story. Help her find peace.

It is now late on Monday.

The Nawab is presently encamped in our garden on his march to Calcutta. His army fills the fields of Neeladri. I have seen the full extent of the his force. It is colossal.

Today the Nawab has imprisoned honored Father for no

offense of his. The Nawab desires Dada in exchange for Father.
I am but a simple woman. I implore God we are spared such
a choice.
    Your humble well-wisher,
    Aruna.

The two friends looked at each other, overcome by the sadness in the letter and the momentum of unfolding events. Benjamin raised his eyebrows about the part regarding Pauline and Ajoy quickly told him of her pregnancy and that she was unaware of it. They naturally assumed she was carrying the captain's child.

"Oh my God, the poor thing!" exclaimed Benjamin. "What a terrible time she's had since leaving England. You'd never know it from her performance today at the Clarksons. She seems so content and full of strength."

Ajoy looked away afraid his expression might show something. But Benjamin was too deep in thought.

"We have to let Mrs. Clarkson into this and let her take charge of Pauline. This is beyond the capabilities of mere men."

***

Before long Benjamin and Ajoy arrived at the Clarkson's home but the environment into which they walked was hardly conducive to delicate feminine matters.

"Madness!" the magistrate was fuming. "Madness! Utter and complete insanity!"

In the cluttered living room Benjamin, Ajoy, Maggie and Pauline looked at him while it grew dark.

"Bloated through prosperity, merry men are we!" Clarkson said with a hollow laugh.

"Yes, sir, but Robin Hoods we ain't!" Benjamin smiled ruefully. "The Sheriff of Nottingham has the whip-hand."

Ajoy looked from one to the other in bewilderment.

"I'm glad you find humor in this," observed Maggie. "Clarence, will you *please* tell us what happened?"

"Madness!" Clarkson's voice was weary.

"Sahib! Please explain?"

"Sorry, old chap," said Benjamin. "Don't mind us. Stoic British humor you know. It's only part of the general insanity."

Benjamin stood up and moved around the large room and began to speak in stuttering disjointed sentences.

"We are exposed. Naked before the Nawab. Two gun bastions useless. Out of four. Look what I brought." He showed them a piece of brittle wood. "We went on a grand tour. Tour of the fortifications. Inspection! Hah! I tore this out. Without effort. From a platform that's supposed to support a cannon." He ripped the wood apart. "Rotten. Moth-eaten. Like us. Twenty-four of the seventy gun-carriages have rusted beyond use. And what does Linnington say? About our reserves of powder? 'Stocks have never been so ample,' he says. And Armstrong preens as though the battle's over. Won by him alone. Punch and Judy!"

Benjamin paused.

"Then we went to the armory."

Another pause.

"Imagine the scene. Captain Muldoon. Supervisor of the armory. Crumpled uniform. Alcohol fumes wafting. Only slightly tipsy for a change. Salutes. Linnington begins, 'Aha, Muldoon. Stout fellow! Ready to take on the heathens, what?' 'Heathens, sir?' says Muldoon. 'The Nabob's forces,' explains Linnington. More such drivel. I can see what's coming. But Linnington? Linnington wouldn't know a problem if it bit him in the leg. He rambles about how he'll blow the Nabob to shreds till I can't stand it any longer. 'Captain, what's the state of the armory?' I ask. Mind you, it's the first sensible question of the day."

Benjamin took a deep breath.

"Dead silence. Then Muldoon says, 'Powder's damp, Morley. Rain, you know. Roof leaked last monsoon.' *Last monsoon!*"

"Lunacy!" exploded Clarkson. "Last monsoon! A full year ago. The armory just forgot about the powder. Then Muldoon told us about grape."

"Grape, Sahib?"

Benjamin explained.

"Grape. Grapeshot. Small balls used as scatter charge for cannon. And the funniest part is that it doesn't matter that the powder's damp. Our grape's been lying around for so long it's full of worm holes. It's useless. So what need is there for powder?"

"Lord have mercy on us!" exclaimed Maggie.

"Well said, old girl," agreed Clarkson. "We may have to fall back on His mercy in the end. I'll describe the rest quickly. Most shells don't fit the guns. No fuses have been laid out. Bores of cannon have never been trimmed."

"No plan," Benjamin concluded. "No strategy for a coordinated defense of fort and town has ever been formulated. No, that's too generous. No plan has ever been *felt necessary!"*

There was a long silence.

"Why?"

It was Pauline in a small voice.

"Why? Why you ask, Mrs. Wainwright? Why indeed!" Benjamin laughed without humor. "I'll tell you why. It's actually quite simple. Nobody in Council has taken their responsibility seriously. Kyle and I've been trying to reform for ages. Kyle's given up. I'm overruled as a matter of principle because I'm supposed to stick to trade. That's unless Armstrong gets into trouble, whereupon he dumps the problem on me. Damn those desk-riders in London! Totally removed from reality. They have sat on my protest over Armstrong's elevation. My father, a senior Director of the Company, has recommended Mr. Clarkson's candidature for Governor. Even so nothing has happened for a year. In the meantime McIver runs the syndicates. Humpty filters payoffs from the treasury. Muldoon wallows in liquor. Wolfe romps in debauchery. Punch and Judy bicker. Why, indeed!"

"And I thought the women of the fort were insufferable," said Pauline. "I'm glad I went to Neeladri."

She turned to Ajoy. Her eyes were full of tenderness. Ajoy looked back with a troubled expression. The others were too preoccupied to take note of the exchange.

"Clarence," said Maggie. "What are you going to do? Princess Aruna's letter says the Nabob's army has begun its march. Do you know where they are?"

Ajoy answered.

"Memsahib, my sister's runner came from Neeladri. The army will take about ten more days to reach Calcutta. They are probably near the town of Nadia now. I expect the advance guard to arrive in a week or less. Magistrate-sahib, are plans for defense being laid now?"

"We are still in shock," replied Clarkson. "Here's a question for you, Morley. How many soldiers are there in the garrison?"

"Three hundred and fifty is the full complement, sir. Linnington said so today."

"Absolutely correct, except Linnington doesn't know this: *the complement isn't full!* Surgeon Warwick told me seventy—*seventy!*—men are in hospital with ailments ranging from fever and injury to over-indulgence and an affliction that he calls work avoidance. And as I was walking back young Glynnis told me thirty-five men have been sent by the syndicate on various personal missions upriver, mostly without knowledge of their officers. So the soldiers available for our defense number about two hundred and fifty. Of these only forty-five are English. Add the companies of *Europa* and McIver's *Beowulf* and we have a hundred sailors who can fight."

"And how big is the Nawab's army, your Highness?" Pauline asked.

Ajoy looked at her trusting turquoise eyes and felt his stomach knot. He turned and walked to the window without saying anything.

"Five or six thousand at least I'd wager," hazarded Clarkson when Ajoy did not answer. "With cavalry and cannon under that French rebel Villeaux."

Benjamin disagreed.

"I'd say more like ten thousand, sir. However we have time to set up new gun emplacements and we have *Europa*. All is still not lost if we get a plan..."

He was interrupted.

"What is the matter?" Pauline cried out. "What is it?"

Everyone swung around in her direction. She had not taken her eyes off Ajoy when he turned away from her. Alone at the window, he was shaking his head slowly from side to side.

"What is the matter, Prince Ajoy?," Benjamin asked. "You don't like something?"

Ajoy still shook his head with his back to them. Everyone stared in growing alarm.

"What's going on?" said Clarkson. "Have we missed something? Speak up, man."

At last Ajoy turned. His taciturn face was exceptionally drawn and somber.

"Perhaps the memsahibs should leave."

"Likely!" Pauline made an unladylike sound. "From the state of things the women should take *charge* around here. You can tell us the worst."

"Magistrate-sahib, the Nawab's cavalry *alone* numbers eighteen thousand."

"Sweet Jesus!"

"He has thirty thousand foot-soldiers. Ragged, untrained, barefoot, armed with swords, bows, arrows, matchlocks and even clubs. But thirty thousand nonetheless. Led by the great general, Rahamat Khan, who has several hundred competent lieutenants. And, contrary to what you think, sahibs, the Bengal Army is not inexperienced. It has fought Marathas for ten years and brought peace to Bengal. It has turned back wave upon wave of invaders from Central India."

He paused as he studied the horrific effect on his listeners.

"I am desolate for bringing such news, my friends. My information is direct from the Nawab's own Minister so it is true. And there is the artillery. Over a hundred cannon with French officers in command who will not scatter under fire. The Nawab is an accomplished rider and swordsman himself. In contrast, from what I have learnt, the English have possibly three hundred soldiers, another three hundred conscripts, a few ships on the water, questionable firepower and weak leadership. They face an army of fifty thousand under a fanatical leader that had declared a *jihad* against them and has taken an oath to remove them from his land."

They looked at him in stunned silence.

"Prince Ajoy," Maggie asked, her voice shaking. "If you knew all this, why didn't you tell the Council when you were present today at the meeting?"

For almost a minute Ajoy looked sadly at the gentle Englishwoman he had grown to respect.

"I am sorry I did not tell them, Memsahib. They would not let me speak."

***

"Ridiculous! Fifty thousand men! Hundreds of cannon? Don't believe a word of it."

Standing at the entrance chamber of the Residence, Armstrong scratched his ample stomach under the violent purple of his dressing gown. The late night awakening, in conjunction with the bottle of claret that he had finished before retiring to calm his nerves, had brought him out in the vilest of tempers.

Decisions!

He had make all these decisions!

"Sir," Benjamin was saying, "Prince Ajoy has no reason to exaggerate."

"Oh, is that so?" Armstrong brought his face close to Benjamin who tried not to recoil from the reek of stale wine. "Well, *I* think that we've had only trouble ever since the bounder's been around."

"I say, that's jolly unfair, sir. We can't blame the Nawab's depredations on the prince."

"Oh yes, we can. The two had a fallout. The Nabob won. He's been at us ever since for harboring Sena."

Benjamin couldn't believe his ears.

"Sir, Prince Ajoy is our ally. A likely ruler of Bengal. You've heard the ambassador recount the reasons for the Nawab's displeasure often enough."

"And he's always mentioned Sena."

"That's not true, sir. The Nawab's much more upset at our fortifications and trade practices."

Tiring of the familiar argument Armstrong glanced hopefully toward the interior of his house. And as though on cue came Martha's voice.

"Richard! Is everything all right?"

"Yes my dear. It's only Morley about his wild-eyed prince. We'll be done sorting this out in a second."

"Sir, the Nawab's marching on Calcutta."

"I know that, dammit."

Benjamin tried to control his own temper.

"Sir, I know the prince well enough to believe his estimates."

"Poppycock! Fifty thousand men? Herds of elephants? Genghis Khan's cavalry? Cannon? Does your Nabob have a monster magic carpet to whisk his mammoth army here? Will the waters of that river, the Hooghly, part for his legions as they did for Moses? Get a hold of yourself, man. Do you think we can't blow them to Kingdom Come with eighteen-pounders on our ramparts and the guns of *Europa* and *Beowulf*? Act your age, Morley!"

When Benjamin replied his voice was flat and toneless.

"We must set up better defenses around the fort."

Armstrong threw up his hands.

"Nonsense! Waste of time."

"Sir, we should set up better defenses."

This time there was a sharp edge to Benjamin's voice.

Armstrong looked closely and realized Morley was set on his idea with the usual mulish stubbornness. The Governor seethed. A pox on the insolent young scalawag! If it wasn't for his toff of a father he'd have him packing for insubordination months ago. All of a sudden the Governor felt old and tired. He wanted desperately to get back home to Huddersfield. The memory of his favorite Yorkshire pub with its aroma of ale and comfortable leather beckoned.

"Sir?"

Oh, how he hated this accursed country and its insufferable people!

"Sir?"

Armstrong gave up. If only his sanctimonious subordinate would shut up and go away.

"Oh, go on," he said rudely. "Do what you want. I've had enough."

To his amazement Benjamin still held his ground.

"Sir, the Council must listen *and agree* to Mr. Kyle's plans for construction tomorrow morning. Will you call the meeting? Can I count on your support for Mr. Kyle's suggestions?"

Richard Armstrong was completely fed up. The claret and the sleepiness and Morley's eternal twaddle was making his head hurt. He was ready to agree to anything his deputy said. In another minute Benjamin had extracted his promise and the truculent Governor was finally allowed to return to his wife.

Chapter 20

A land breeze proclaimed the imminence of the morning sun. Here and there a crow cawed drowsily to wake its fellows. A slow symphonic wave crested as thousands of sparrows began their twitter in the bushes and trees that bordered The Avenue. Flights of emerald parrots swept screeching over The Park. *"Kuk-kuk-kuk-kuk'm"* crowed competitive roosters as they vied for aural dominance. Brightening sunbeams turned fragile dewdrops into diamonds on brilliant hibiscus blooms.

The earliest peddlers were already abroad. Vegetable sellers, knife-sharpeners, fishmongers and barbers. The streets of Calcutta resonated with their drawn-out cries. Ascending domestic baritones of conch-shells and aroma of cooking-fires welcomed the new day.

But everything cannot be perfect.

That morning, oblivious to the sunrise sonata, Bahadur was annoyed. The watchman of one of the most luxurious homes of White Town wondered who had the audacity to rattle the chains of his main gate so imperiously. Vegetable- and flower-sellers had express instructions to enter through the back gate. It was probably a newly-arrived-in-town vendor, decided Bahadur, one who did not know the ropes. The tough slightly-built *Gurkha* from the Himalayan foothills shook his keys in anticipation of bawling out his victim.

But Bahadur was not destined to have his sport.

Through the bars of the gate Bahadur saw that a palanquin had drawn up. Four muscled bearers and an elderly nondescript man were waiting on the street. The man was about to rattle the chain again when he saw the watchman.

"Yes? Who has come?" Bahadur spoke in Nepali-accented Bengali.

"Open the gates," said Ananta.

"Who do you want?"

"There is a visitor for the Seth-*ji*."

"Who is the visitor?"

"Prince Ajoy Sena of Rajmahal."

A chastened Bahadur unlocked and quickly opened the gates. The bearers lifted the palanquin poles onto their shiny shoulders, two in front and two in the rear, and loped up the sweeping drive of the Jagat Seth's house. They lowered the palanquin under the stately portico. Ajoy pushed aside the curtain and clambered out. Ananta announced his master at the big wooden doors and Ajoy was shown into a waiting-room. A servant informed them that Seth-*ji* was at prayers.

Ajoy settled himself to wait. He had not slept the previous night, having spent it discussing with Benjamin and Clarkson every possible way to avoid the impending conflagration. While he waited trays of food arrived – a steaming container of tea, fresh-roasted strips of unleavened bread, curried vegetables, newly cut mangoes. He wondered for a moment how such fresh, hot and delicious food could be made available at the crack of dawn. Then he tucked in with relish. As he ate, women's voices and children's laughter floated from the interior. The Jagat Seth had a large family. Ajoy finished his breakfast and idly studied the vivid paintings of Jagat Seths past. Through the open window, the lowing of cows and cooing of wood pigeons made a soothing refrain. He caught himself dozing but his eyes refused to stay open.

"*Namaskar,* Prince Ajoy!"

Ajoy awoke with a start. The stout banker, dressed as always in crisp white, his moustache freshly groomed, shuffled forward on loose leather slippers and took both Ajoy's hands in his as he tried to get to his feet.

"No no, Prince Ajoy, don't get up, don't get up. You are very tired. Have you eaten?"

Ajoy sat back wearily.

"*Namaskar,* Seth-*ji.* Yes, I have eaten your excellent food." He sighed. "But life! Life has been hard."

The banker sat and faced him.

"I have heard of your experiences since we last met. *Narayan! Narayan!* Troubled times have returned."

"Seth-*ji,* much has happened and little of it is good. The Nawab is a formidable opponent."

"And we have made a habit of underestimating him. When he contended for the throne we dismissed him as a child. When he came to power we thought he was a puppet. When he railed against foreigners we thought it was bluster."

"And now, Seth-*ji,* he marches on Calcutta while the hatmen squabble among themselves. Meanwhile Cossim Bazaar has been captured."

"And soon he will be at the gates of Fort William."

"We must prevent it, Seth-*ji.* War helps no one."

They thought about the consequences without speaking. From the interior of the house came the cascading chant of a hymn accompanied by steady ringing of a hand-held bell. The eternal tranquility of the Vedic ritual made the talk of war unreal.

"War would be a disaster," the Jagat Seth said. "I am a friend of both sides." He lowered his voice. "Since we cannot bring down the Nawab, can't we placate him somehow?"

Ajoy did not answer. The banker looked at him questioningly and went on.

"The English Governor has incessantly provoked the Nawab. Can't he be made to desist?"

Again Ajoy did not answer.

The Jagat Seth sat back and crossed his arms.

"Prince Ajoy, I will listen when you are ready."

Ajoy looked out of the window at riotous blooms on flame-of-the-forest trees. The Sanskrit chanting from millennia-old Hindu *Vedas* was approaching its crescendo. The deep clang of a gong started up to accompany the bell. The tempo increased and the booming cadence of a conch joined the symphony. After some minutes the climax came and passed. Silence descended. The Jagat Seth closed his eyes devoutly, joined his palms together at his forehead, and offered up a prayer to a statue of Lakshmi, the goddess of prosperity. Ajoy did the same. Then he got to his feet.

"The time for compromise is past, Seth-*ji*. There *will* be a confrontation. Morley-sahib is at least making the hatmen take the Nawab's threat seriously. In the face of unbelievable skepticism he is getting them to set up gun batteries and build palisades around the fort."

"So it is to be war?"

Ajoy did not appear to hear the question.

"Seth-*ji*, you know the situation better than others. You have seen nawabs and sultans come and go. I value your advice more than anyone else's. That is why I am here."

The Jagat Seth nodded encouragingly.

"Shiraj Doula has taken prisoner the Rai Raja, my sister's father-in-law."

"My heart cries for Princess Aruna."

"Do you know why?"

The banker did not reply.

"Seth-*ji*, you know me too well. Why do I temporize?" Then Ajoy spoke in a rush. "I shall offer myself up to the Nawab."

The Jagat Seth sat back with a gasp but did not say anything. Ajoy looked at him, anxious for a response. Any response.

"Seth-*ji*, my imprisonment will solve all problems."

"Perhaps," was the Jagat Seth's only comment.

"You are right," continued Ajoy. "Who can guess how Shiraj Doula will react? He will be delighted to get his hands on me. That is for certain. And then, if nothing else, I will have departed from the scene. I who have caused many people much trouble. They will be glad to be rid of me. A dreamer. Dreamer of glories past and future. I live in a world of dreams. Each of my plans, ill-wrought, ill-executed, have collapsed. I have been a trouble-maker. A blight on society..."

The older man looked at him compassionately but let him run on.

"Do you remember, Seth-*ji,* my great and glorious observation on the night of the hatmen's gathering? *'Throw the Nawab some bones,'* said I grandly. *'And extract concessions.'* Do you know what that pronouncement was, Seth-*ji?* My own death-knell. The bones are here. In your house. This bag of bones. Throw them to Shiraj, Seth-*ji,* so others may live. The ultimate concession. Who needs me?"

"Many do, Prince Ajoy."

As soon as the Jagat Seth said this the night on the peacock-boat flashed through Ajoy's mind with absolute clarity. Tenderly he thought of the brave and beautiful English girl. Did she need him? He had called her his *asha,* his inspiration. His mood changed abruptly and a black pessimism came over him. Inspiration? Never! Inspiration was wasted on him. Was he, miserable wretch, the man into whose eyes this pure person had gazed and had said *"my prince!"* with complete conviction? He had done little to be worthy of that confidence while scheme after grandiose scheme disintegrated. Wasn't it abundantly clear to anyone who would face it that Shiraj Doula's forces would overrun Fort William? And that its foreign residents would be massacred?

Ajoy sighed bitterly, the sound ending in a hollow groan.

"Yes, I know, Seth-*ji.* I understand. And that is the tragedy. I fail those who put their faith in me."

"You do not!"

The Jagat Seth spoke forcefully at last.

"You do not fail them, Prince Ajoy Sena of Rajmahal. You are their lodestone. You are their destiny in a world gone mad. When you rise from failure and try again you are their hope and their inspiration." Ajoy recoiled at the banker's use of the Bengali word *asha*. "You unite opposing forces. You are the harbinger of peace and stability. Nawab Shiraj Doula will exhaust himself like a dust-devil in the desert sands of my Rajputana. The Senas of Bengal will outlast the Moghuls and rise anew."

The Jagat Seth nodded with complete conviction.

"Your day will come, Prince Ajoy."

***

While Ajoy's palanquin transported him back to Fort William, a bombshell, more severe than the Nawab's threat, was dropped on the Executive Council. Its members roiled with incoherent outrage against an unperturbed Stanislaus Kyle.

"Blow up our homes, will ye?" roared McIver. "Begorrah! Over my dead body ye will. Are thee out of thy mind?"

"What on earth do you mean, Kyle?" bellowed Linnington. "Blow up our own houses! What an extraordinary idea."

Kyle, enjoying their discomfiture, waited for the hubbub to subside. At last he had them in his grip.

"Listen carefully, you...," with a suggestive pause, "... gentlemen. Have you noticed how high your houses are? When this fort was built the guns on the corner bastions had free field of fire on approaching enemy. Since then every new house built tries to be taller. Now your homes block the range of the guns. They've got to go."

"Now listen, you!" John Wolfe's pointed beard bristled in anger. "Enough's enough. I will personally slay anyone who comes near my house."

Wolfe, the warehouse supervisor, had finally been found. He was one of the latest arrivals to Calcutta and in keeping with local rivalry had build the first three-storied house. It was an well-known that he first populated it with a harem of mistresses and had later thrown them all out in preference to his present lover, a pretty dancer named Kajal Lata. In the past Wolfe had been perpetually exhausted trying to keep his harem from each others' throats. When Kajal Lata arrived his exertions were confined to one woman but were apparently no less strenuous for he was rarely seen.

"Is that your plan to defend Calcutta?" was Kyle's rejoinder.

"We'll run the Nabob out so fast he'll leave his balls behind."

Captain Muldoon was nursing a severe hangover but was quite clear on this point.

"Governor?" said Benjamin.

"Oh! Yes. Right. Uh, what was that again, Morley?"

"May Mr. Kyle proceed with the demolitions?"

"Stow it, ye young idjit!" burst out McIver.

Benjamin turned his back on the Scotsman and looked at steadily at the squirming Armstrong.

"Right. Now then, let's see. Well, the Council feels rather strongly about all this, Morley."

"Sir, Mr. Kyle has stated he would like to raze the houses around the fort for our safety. Is that clear?"

There was another clamor of protest. Clarkson was the only one silent even though his home was a candidate for destruction. It held a quarter-century of his and Maggie's dearest memories.

"Well," Armstrong procrastinated. "It *is* causing deuced unpleasantness y'know."

Benjamin kept on looking at him. Armstrong writhed as he remembered his promise under duress last night. Decisions! Damned decisions. Always decisions. Why were the most difficult ones always *his* decisions? He tried a compromise approach.

"Gentlemen, we've got to defend our fort."

"Not by destroying our houses, we won't," replied

Linnington at once. "There're other ways. Aren't there, Kyle?"

The engineer looked at him with a mocking smile.

"In the event of attack the enemy will take house after house and get within cannon range of the fort while your big guns, Colonel, assuming they fire, remain useless."

"What utter rot!" said Linnington furiously. "Kindly concentrate on defense and leave strategy to the army."

"You contradict yourself, sir!" shot back Kyle. "Defense *is* a strategy!"

The meeting spun out of control and disintegrated into a rabble. Benjamin watched helplessly. Finally Armstrong said to him, "Sorry, old chap. Looks like the houses have to stay. Don't take it too hard, now. What else can we do, Kyle?"

While Kyle talked of barricades and palisades, of filling ditches and digging others, of strengthening platforms and walls and gates, of labor, materials and money, Benjamin listened stupefied. Armstrong had broken his most solemn promise of the night before. The leadership of the fort was willing to sell out those who depended on them. What in the world was going to happen? Horrific images of Calcutta put to the sword came back to him again.

But this time was different.

The enemy was at the gates.

Chapter 21

Far from the uproar of war preparations the midsummer sun rose on the only sizeable town between Murshidabad and Calcutta, ancient and picturesque Nadia.

Somnolent beside the River Hooghly, surrounded by soft fields, broken by tracts of characteristic vermilion soil, Nadia had relinquished its role as capital of early Bengal half a millennium ago. That had happened when the Afghan chieftain Muhammad-bin-Khalji defeated the poet-king, Laxman Sena, Ajoy's ancient forebear in an epic battle. Scattered sandstone ruins still bore testimony to its past grandeur. But Nadia did not fade with the Senas. Another of its sons, the great Chaitanya, founded a popular religious movement based on music and on tolerance, and Nadia became a pilgrimage center. A magnificent sandstone temple arose out of its red dust, to be visited through the centuries by worshippers from far and near.

***

On June 13th, 1756, a small group of horsemen clattered into the sleepy ecclesiastical town. People on the road stopped and stared at them. More eyes watched from houses along Nadia's dusty pathways. Ignoring the attention, the horsemen rode on down to the riverbank where their mounts' hooves made squashy sounds in the mud. At water's edge the tired horses refused the urging of their riders and stopped to drink. The men dismounted and walked the remaining distance to the big pier. Several boats were tied alongside. Bare-chested boatmen eyed the uniformed strangers warily. From the swords and knives and matchlocks they carried it was clear that they were soldiers.

"Ho there!" called the leader of the horsemen in a stern voice. "Who is the head boatman?"

No one replied.

"What? Why do you not answer? Speak! You are doing yourselves no good, you know."

"What do you want, *janab?*" ventured one man.

"Boats. We want boats. Many, many boats. We want barges. We want them tonight."

The boatmen clambered onto the pier and clustered around him.

"Why, *janab?* Tonight? Really? Who is going to cross the river in the dark, *janab?*"

"Who do you think? My maternal uncle? The Nawab of course! The Nawab's army will cross the river tomorrow morning."

"The Nawab's army! How many boats will he need? Where is he going?"

"Where do you think, you oaf? To Mecca? The Nawab is going to drive the hatmen out of Calcutta. That's where he is going. Now listen carefully. I am Chief of the Nawab's advance guard. Tell me your names. Then go up and down the river. Go across to the other side. Go wherever you wish. But remember. The Nawab wants five hundred boats and twenty barges by nightfall. Otherwise your lives and that of your families are forfeit. If you succeed you shall be rewarded. The army will cross tomorrow. Do you understand?"

The Hooghly is a mile wide at Nadia, but at this time of the year, at the end of a dry summer and before the rains, most of its width was dry or knee-deep. The main course flowed through a channel no more than a hundred yards across and the only section of any depth.

Next morning the Persian cavalry was the first to cross.

The proud horsemen disdained the hastily assembled flotilla and guided their mounts into the water while holding their weapons jauntily aloft. The horses carefully negotiated the reed-choked bank and upon entering deep water, began to swim. The current tried to push them downstream but in fifteen minutes the first horses were climbing safely onto the sandbar on the far side. Their riders triumphantly brandished their muskets. A cheer went up from watchers on the Nadia bank.

More cavalrymen entered the river.

Infantrymen began to board country-boats for the crossing. Most of the boats could take only twenty and there was much cursing and pushing as limits were reached. There was little discipline. Some soldiers lost their footing during the jostling and fell into the water. Muddied and bedraggled, they scrambled back to jeers of their comrades.

Suddenly a piercing scream was clearly heard over the tumult. Everyone turned to look in the direction from which it came. Horrified, they discerned what appeared to be a dead tree-trunk swimming away with a still-shrieking soldier in its jaws. The crocodile submerged and the screams were cut off abruptly. Then a soldier pointed, shouting hysterically. More 'logs' that had been sunning themselves on sandbars were moving into the water. A cavalryman howled from mid-river as a long snout topped with big knobby eyes rose up beside him. The bright sunlight reflected on wicked lines of teeth as the reptile opened its jaws wide. The horse squealed in terror and thrashed in the water unseating its rider. Luckily the man fell on the far side of the horse and kept a hold on the reins as his mount desperately tried to get away. In a few minutes frightened horse and rider dragged themselves out of the water on the opposite bank.

With several crocodiles now visible in the river the men refused to board the boats. Their position on the waterfront became precarious as more soldiers, unaware of the situation ahead, pushed toward the river. And soon the inevitable happened. The foremost terror-stricken soldiers were driven into the water. Those that could swam downstream and back to the bank. Those that could not floundered and shouted for help. After a few minutes they began to drown or fall victim to crocodiles.

More men fell into the water.

Wild confusion reigned on the riverbank.

Into this *melee* plunged an immense black horse. Men and animals scattered from its path. The black horse continued into the river, wheeled around and reared on its hind legs. Its rider faced the crowd from atop his plunging mount and raised his hand for silence. The din decreased but only slightly.

"Khamosh!"

Rahamat Khan roared out the Persian command for silence in such a penetrating voice that the jostling and noise died away. Men in shallow water began to pull others ashore. Fifteen horsemen in royal blue uniform of the Nawab's personal bodyguard went deeper and started to pull drowning men to safety. More elite guardsman marshaled the bunched infantrymen away from the riverbank and eased the strain on those in front.

Then, while everyone watched, Rahamat Khan and the horsemen in the river leveled their muskets and fired at crocodiles as they showed themselves.

With the first salvo flocks of frenzied birds flew into the air crying wildly. The riverside rang with the sound of musketry. The immense saurians jerked and thrashed spasmodically as the rain of fire poured into them. Soon the water was stained red with blood. Within ten minutes all the crocodiles had disappeared.

The firing stopped but only for a moment.

An infantryman cheered lustily and let loose a round with his matchlock. Others immediately joined in and bullets whistled around everywhere.

"*Khamosh!*" roared Rahamat Khan again, frantically raising his own weapon in the air and holding it up with both hands.

The firing stopped, permanently this time.

Rahamat Khan was livid with anger. For a full fifteen minutes the Commander of the Bengal Army unleashed a virulent harangue. Using the most colorful language he unfavorably compared the soldiers' ancestors to swine, their bravery to rabbits, their discipline to cattle, and their libido to eunuchs. He ended by making the flat statement that the crossing would occur now, and the crossing would occur in a disciplined manner. Anyone breaking ranks he would personally shoot.

The army continued to cross the Hooghly. There were no more crocodile attacks. Perhaps Rahamat Khan's very presence daunted those that remained. Perhaps the presence of such large numbers of men, beasts and *materiel* frightened them off. During the crossing some boats sank. A few more men drowned.

From a safe distance fascinated residents of Nadia, augmented by brethren from surrounding villages and visiting pilgrims, witnessed the monumental operation and the decimation of the crocodiles. At the same time they were very watchful. A move by a soldier in their direction would evoke hurried retreat.

By late afternoon, when most of the infantry had crossed over, the first of the cannon appeared. The onlookers' eyes grew large at the sight of grunting and straining oxen teams that pulled and the huge elephants that pushed the cannon. They fell back in fright when several pachyderms trumpeted in anticipation of the water which they loved and came down the steep riverbank to drink. One walked ponderously right into the stream and, livery and all, rolled over on its side squealing in delight. Another joined it and blew a fountain onto its back. Meanwhile the sweating oxen drank from the bank. The large animals milled around and bellowed and squealed and raised clouds of dust and plumes of water. The air was ripe with the smell of their droppings.

The cannon began their journey on barges.

The crossing of the river itself was relatively easy but the unloading of the guns and their transport up the sand on the far side was strenuous and fraught with disaster. The guns were then hitched back to oxen teams and bodily pulled ashore. With its trunk around a gun muzzle and its pillar-like feet planted firmly in the sand, each elephant helped in the process of hauling a gun across the sandbar. Thanks to the animals every one of the one hundred and fifty cannon crossed the river safely.

From the Nadia side, Jacques Villeaux, a swarthy Breton with thick sideburns and twirled moustache, watched the proceedings. He was enthralled. What a story to write home to Rennes!

And then the event that everyone was waiting for happened.

A gaudy peacock-boat which had been tied to the bank all day was poled to the pier. Followed by guards and servants, a gaudy palanquin was carried down to the riverside. When it reached the water's edge the palanquin was lowered and the Nawab emerged, drew up his robes and carefully boarded his flagship. The few moments he was visible were enough for villagers and soldiers alike to remember and relate to their children and grandchildren. They had actually seen the great Nawab on his way to wage war on intruders in their land.

The peacock-boat took barely fifteen minutes to cross the channel. The palanquin overtook it on a humbler craft and stood ready to receive its royal occupant the moment he stepped ashore.

That night the Bengal Army camped on sandbanks and fields on the eastern bank of the Hooghly. They were not very far from where a man-eating tiger had carried away Prince Mohendra Rai, Aruna's husband, three months ago. But on this occasion no tiger came near the huge assemblage and the field of flaring torches.

Shiraj Doula and his army were on the same side of the river as Calcutta and just five days from their goal.

Chapter 22

During those last days of peace an extraordinary transformation occurred at Fort William.

Every Briton, man and woman, responded enthusiastically to Stanislaus Kyle's call to arms. While the military paraded in a reassuring semblance of normalcy, a strange excitement filled the air. Writers cast off dreary routines and enlisted in droves. Women took up the task of stitching sandbags. The fort buzzed with activity. The sound of hammering and sawing came from all sides. In his finest hour Kyle became a superman. In the face of desertions he recruited thousands of *coolies* who barricaded the approach to the fort from The Avenue. Teams of horses dragged cannon to the barricades and workers formed them into batteries. Bullock carts stockpiled ball and powder. Small streets of White Town were closed off with six-foot high palisades. More *coolies* dug trenches across the main streets. A wide defensive ditch stretched across The Park. An alien energy permeated the town of Calcutta in striking contrast to its past lethargy.

On Colonel Linnington's orders, officers, soldiers and volunteers were formed into six divisions.

The three largest, numbering sixty men each, were ordered to man the batteries.

The fourth division of fifty men was stationed inside the fort to maintain discipline and guard against infiltration of spies.

The fifth, commanded by Lieutenant Dicky Glynnis and numbering thirty men, marched off to the northern extremity of Calcutta to defend a small blockhouse called Perrins Redoubt. This structure overlooked the point where the arc of the Maratha Ditch met the Hooghly and was crossed by a small bridge. The Council members were convinced that the Nawab's army, approaching from the north, would negotiate the ditch here to approach within firing distance of the fort. Captain Wainwright was directed to move *Europa* upriver in support of Dicky's company at Perrins Redoubt.

The sixth group of forty men under Lieutenant O'Malley was held at large, ready to provide assistance where necessary.

***

When the truth of Kyle's assessment that White Town was indefensible finally sank home to members of the Executive Council, Governor Armstrong reluctantly ordered English families to evacuate their homes and take refuge in the fort. Over the next two days, three hundred men, women and children left their comfortable homes and straggled in through gates with only their most precious belongings. They camped along the galleries bordering the parade-ground. It was Benjamin's theory that the sight of their loved ones huddled in abject misery in the open had at last spurred the Council into desperate action. Clarkson cynically disagreed. He believed that the sudden loss of their servants and of their pampered lifestyle had convinced Council members that the Nawab would and *could* attack them and thus there was cause for genuine concern.

And then runners brought news that the Bengal Army had crossed the river at Nadia. There was no longer time to destroy the tall houses to defend the town. Kyle was ordered to prepare defenses for only the fort.

The Towne of Calcutta was thus abandoned without a single shot being fired.

***

On the next day, June 16th, when the bedraggled European refugees were complaining bitterly about their privations of the night, the battle for Fort William had already begun.

The 'fortress' at Perrins Redoubt was a small round windowless building made of stone slabs, with several loopholes to see and fire through. Dicky and his thirty men had taken up their positions inside the day before and slept the night on its floor of hardened earth. In addition to their muskets and ammunition, they had seven cannon installed in wall embrasures. It was planned that two musketeers would operate from each loophole. After the first one fired he would withdraw to reload and prime his musket while the second musketeer would take his place. Each gun crew would fire its cannon every fifteen minutes, the time taken to reload powder and ball.

As they settled in Dicky was struck by the tranquility of the surroundings.

The redoubt was close to the river. A pleasant evening breeze blew in through the open doorway. Westward, in the direction of the river and over the tops of palms, Dicky had a heartening view of the mastheads of *Europa*. In front of the redoubt, beyond one hundred yards or so of open space, he could discern the dark outline of the Maratha Ditch. In past decades before The Park in front of the fort had been created, this open space had been the regular promenade for early settlers. Dicky tried to imagine well-dressed English men and women, attended by servants, emerging from palanquins and carriages and walking the dusty stretch. Or was it green and tended with flowers in those days? Behind the redoubt the rough road along which they had come stretched back southward to the fort. Eastward, about half a mile away and in Black Town, was the great Bagh Bazaar or

Garden Market. It was no longer a garden but a rabbit warren of narrow crowded lanes. In front of them, on the opposite side of the Maratha Ditch, was another open space. Then began a continuous line of jungle.

Out of this jungle they expected the enemy to materialize.

As darkness fell Dicky relaxed and his thoughts turned to Bessie Armstrong. Dicky and Bessie were rapidly approaching a decision point. Through risky clandestine meetings they had determined that if her father weathered this onslaught he would get his promotion and land the cherished desk job in London. But Bessie could not bear the thought of leaving her handsome and many-talented beau. What should they do? As the line of the Maratha Ditch faded into the night Dicky thought long and hard. His share in the ivory syndicate under the stewardship of Angus McIver had already built his family a home in Wales. More importantly, he had amassed savings that could support them for several years. Should he ask Bessie to marry him? Her father, who had visions of nobility through his only child's marriage, would hang him from the ramparts of Fort William before giving his permission. Should they run away on a ship going to England? He looked again at *Europa,* this time speculatively, and an interesting thought began to take shape. The *Beowulf* would be returning to England soon. She belonged to McIver, his mentor. Now McIver didn't overly like Armstrong...

Dicky's thought processes began to hum.

He must have dozed off with his back to the wall when a yell woke him. He got to his feet hurriedly and looked around. It was pitch black outside. The men were all clustered in front of the blockhouse and were looking toward the jungle. Rubbing his eyes Dicky joined them. Tiny points of light danced in the distance and faint sounds floated eerily across the intervening space. Presently the lights resolved themselves into flickering flames of a multitude of torches and soon afterwards they heard the voices of many men on the night air: curses, orders and bursts of dialog. The noise grew louder and closer while Dicky's company listened, too fascinated to sleep. Crashes and rumblings from the foliage foretold of cannon arriving. The men tried to envision the scenario that had been described to them: elephants pushing guns through trees while matchlockmen took up positions along the ditch.

One by one the tired men went back inside Perrins Redoubt and tried to sleep.

After an eternity the cocks from Black Town heralded the new day. It was still dark inside the redoubt. The usual sparrows and mynahs began to call. The sun rose in glorious crimson splendor over silhouetted roofs of Bagh Bazaar. But the bleary eyes of Dicky's company found not a soul in the space between the jungle in the distance and the ditch in front. Other than the clamor of birds there was an uncanny silence.

Eastern wars *always* began at dawn, thought Dicky. Why didn't the attack come?

Suddenly there was movement on their own side of the ditch. The men tensed, then relaxed and laughed. A troop of large silver-furred black-faced monkeys with long tails appeared out of the ditch and loped resolutely in the direction of the market. Langurs were a common sight in India. In the clear light Dicky could see tiny baby monkeys hanging upside down under their mothers' bellies.

The morning wore on.

Various animals and birds continued to entertain the men. But the attack still did not come. Dicky thought this was really strange. It was the time-honored code of Indian warfare that battles begin at dawn, break off at noon for afternoon siesta, re-engage and conclude at dusk. Benjamin Morley, who Dicky admired for his fund of knowledge about the country, had once told him a story from the great Hindu epic, *Mahabharata*. In the story Krishna, as prince Arjun's charioteer, had miraculously darkened the sky so that the enemy would leave the safety of its battle formation thinking it was dusk. And then Krishna made the sky bright and Arjun slaughtered the enemy.

Dicky wondered whether Rahamat Khan was employing the reverse process by waiting for the midday sun to relax their vigilance. It was now oppressively hot in the redoubt. There was no breeze. Even with the door wide open the June heat baked the stone blockhouse. The strain on the nerves of the idle men mounted. Most had not slept the night because of the tension. To compound their misery they had had nothing to eat or drink since they had arrived. In their hurried departure from the fort nobody had remembered to allocate supplies. The grumbling and oaths in the fortress increased. Dicky looked for the hundredth time at his father's big watch. The Nawab's men *had* to be inside the shimmering jungle. It was ominously quiet. Why weren't they attacking? Where was the famous French-commanded artillery? Where were the elephants they had heard the night before? Dicky's throat felt dry and gritty. Was something wrong? Terribly wrong? Had the enemy discovered their position and moved to another point for a Ditch crossing and were already approaching Fort William? On reflecting he did not think this likely. How could Rahamat Khan organize this in such silence? What kind of a man was he anyway? He fell to pondering what it would be like to command thousands, even tens of thousands of soldiers.

"Thunder and lightning!" burst out Corporal Wellman from one of the gun embrasures. "We've come to fight, man, not to bake like loaves of bread."

A couple of Dutch conscripts concurred with vitriol in their language.

"Let's go back, sir." It was Wellman again. "This ain't right."

There was a chorus of assent.

"Wellman's right, sir," someone agreed. "There ain't no Moors in that there jungle. They're probably gone attacking us somewhere else."

Dicky looked at his men unhappily. This was his first active command and it was disintegrating. What was he to do? He looked at his watch again.

"Ease off, men," he said, trying to placate them. "It's close nigh ten o'clock. If they don't attack by noontime, we'll send a body to the fort."

"Blimey, it's hot!" rumbled a huge Irishman. "Stupid major don' know 'nuff wot to send water nor food. No enemy, no supplies. This ain't war, man, jus' plain punishment. Hell's bells! I'm for returning at noon. D'ye hear, me mates?"

There was enthusiastic agreement. Master-gunner Bracken was a colorful character, popular with enlisted men but disliked by officers as a chronic trouble-maker.

Dicky began to argue with his men and a bitter dispute ensued.

While this was going on Corporal Wellman walked out of the open door and went behind the redoubt to empty his bladder. He stood comfortably in the shade of the blockhouse, making a neat rivulet in the dust, and ruminated on how wonderful it would be if he had a mug of cold ale.

That was when he heard it.

It was a single voice from the direction of the jungle that was now hidden from Wellman by the blockhouse. It began as an eerie wail and went up higher and higher in pitch right up to its top note. Then it held this note for a very long moment, almost forever.

"Al...lahhhh.....ho.....Ak...barrrrrr.....!"

Frozen, Wellman listened to the centuries old call to arms, and as he listened the hairs on the nape of his neck slowly stood up. Goose pimples fled up and down his arms. Then the wailing call died away and was lost in the babble still going on inside the redoubt. Wellman stood for just another moment and then frantically hitched his breeches and ran around the perimeter of the building and burst in on the company. It took a full minute to get the attention of the men who were on the verge of mutiny. But when they saw the look on the corporal's face, as a man they rushed to the door and to loopholes and embrasures.

"Great glorious Jesus!" cried Dicky.

Out of the tangle of trees and vines hundreds upon hundreds of men were pouring onto the open space. They came in a line that stretched for over two hundred yards. The air filled with war cries. The running men brandished swords and muskets and staves and waved pennants as they approached. More men appeared behind them.

A metamorphosis took place inside the redoubt. Gone were thoughts of mutiny. The thirty men ran to their positions. Even before Dicky could give the order a rattle of musketry rang out as every soldier who was assigned a loophole fired at the enemy. They could not have missed even if they tried. The Indian soldiers were bunched tightly together in open ground just over a hundred yards away. Reserve musketeers moved to the loopholes as others stepped back to reload. Another crackle of musket fire rang out. The Indians who were hit fell backwards like toy soldiers.

Dicky heard enemy bullets harmlessly hitting the outside walls of the redoubt with little thumps.

Then there was a colossal roar as Bracken's cannon opened up. The aim was high and the ball landed somewhere in the trees of the jungle. Bracken cursed while his men pulled back the gun and began the complicated process of swabbing, drying, priming and loading. Dicky swore at him angrily. Bracken's gun, their number one cannon, or any other, should not have been fired without his order. Meanwhile his men loosed off another volley of withering musket fire. Dicky watched as the first of the enemy reached the bridge. There were twelve of British muskets firing in each volley. Every bullet was finding his mark. But the sheer number of Indian soldiers made their impact negligible. More Indians entered the ditch. The sagging bridge they had to cross was only fifty feet long and in a moment the enemy would be on their side.

Dicky was about to give the command for the other six

cannon to fire when he heard a loud explosion followed by a strange whistling sound. He swung round just in time to see a geyser of dust rise directly in the middle of the multitude of Indians on the far side of the ditch. He heard screams and saw bodies flying in the air.

The ship!

They had forgotten *Europa!* A cheer went up from the blockhouse. A direct hit from a shipboard twelve-pounder had smashed a major hole in the enemy.

There was an orange flash from the riverside and then a roar and another long-drawn whistle. A second cannonball landed among the massed soldiers, this time closer to the ditch. Renewed screams testified to the number of enemy had been killed or maimed.

Dicky's men fired another enthusiastic volley into the crowd.

Then the first heads appeared on their own side of the ditch Enemy soldiers began to stream toward Perrins Redoubt.

Dicky gave the command they were all waiting for.

"Fire Two!"

The blockhouse shook as their number two seven-pounder fired through its embrasure. It made a direct hit on the enemy barely seventy yards away with catastrophic effect.

"Fire Three!"

There was another explosion as number three cannon fired. It was aimed at the near side of the bridge, but went high. The ball plowed into the enemy in the open space beyond the bridge. Dicky wondered how many this killed or wounded.

"Fire distant!"

Three of their big guns, including Bracken's, which was still being reloaded, were trained on the near side of the bridge, and four on the further side. The earth shook as the several cannon roared out simultaneously. Wellman cursed mightily as the fourth, under his command, misfired.

The effect on the enemy was horrendous. But it failed to stop the Indians. More and more of them crossed the bridge to their side.

Suddenly Perrins Redoubt shook to its foundations and Dicky staggered back from flying debris. There were tormented shrieks. The interior filled with dust and loose plaster. A French cannon had scored a hit on the blockhouse. Sun streamed in through a gap blown in the wall. Dicky rushed to help the three men who had been hit. One, a Dutchman, was dead.

"Sir! Sir! They are attacking, sir!" Wellman cried.

Dicky turned and ran to a loophole. He saw a number of Indians running toward them. He turned and shouted to his musketeers at the top of his voice.

"*Form!*"

The men went to their positions.

"*Load!*"

Some men loaded powder. Others had already done so.

"*Fire One!*"

Bracken's number one cannon, ready and trained on their own side of the bridge fired. There were squeals of pain as it poured shot into enemy from point black range.

"*Fire muskets!*"

Twelve muskets fired in concert. Each found a mark.

And still the enemy came on.

"*Rod!*"

Musketeers jammed in their ramrods.

"*Return! Cap!*"

The musketeers capped their charges.

"*Aim!*"

Each man pointed his weapon from a loophole.

"*Fire muskets!*"

Ten muskets fired together. Each felled an enemy soldier.

"*Fire Two!*"

Number two cannon roared. Its ball cut a swath through the Indian soldiers. A terrible carnage was occurring on the promenade before them.

"Load!..."

The men reloaded, sweating, cursing, exulting.

A second enemy cannonball crashed into the redoubt destroying a gun embrasure and killing both its gunners. A pot of boiling oil used to heat shot rocked precariously then settled back. The men were black with smoke and grime. Dicky orchestrated musket fusillade and cannon fire like an automaton. Two more cannon shots from *Europa* made direct hits. A ball from the French cannon landed harmlessly on their roof.

And then the first Indians reached the redoubt.

They brandished swords and staves and muskets. In a moment of complete clarity Dicky saw that one of them carried a bow and had a quiver of arrows on his back. They tried to force their way through the broken gun embrasure but were driven back in hand-to-hand combat. The attackers pounded on the iron door.

Dicky had a sudden brainwave.

"Pot fires, men!"

Putting action to word he grabbed up one of the ramrods with its swab of flaming cotton and thrust it into the face of a wild-eyed man who had half entered through the damaged embrasure. With a yell the man fell back. Several of the company followed Dicky's lead.

Dicky turned to command another two rounds of cannon fire into the enemy across the ditch. These were almost simultaneous with three twelve-pounder shots from the ship on the river.

The massive roar of synchronized artillery died away and the earth seemed to stand still for a moment.

Then one Indian soldier on the far side—Dicky would always remember the man wearing a green tunic and turban and a white shirt and *dhoti*—turned and ran back in the direction of the jungle. Then another. More men turned to run and in another instant the entire army panicked. It was as though the same message had magically entered the head of every Indian soldier. Those at the Englishmen's door dropped their weapons and rushed for the bridge. They tripped and fell over their fallen comrades, picked themselves up and continued to run.

For only a brief moment Dicky's company watched the scene in amazement. Then with a frenzied cheer they pulled open the door, ran outside and fired, ran back, reloaded, went out and fired again at the retreating enemy. Cannonade from the ship completed the rout. Within minutes all that was left on the battlefield were strewn bodies and squirming crawling wounded.

Finally there was silence.

Dicky looked at his watch. It was ten-forty. The engagement that seemed an eternity had been less than an hour. Three of their company had been killed, three wounded, one seriously. Their fortress had suffered severe damage.

No one spoke. There was nothing to say. Thirsty and hungry, they sat along the wall, dazed and exhausted, overcome by the heat and dust and blood and smell and noise. Somebody passed around a packet of cigarettes.

One by one the men fell asleep.

Rahamat Khan's second attack came thirty minutes later.

***

It was midday when Colonel Peter Linnington finally put his plan into action.

The second and half-hearted attack on the fortress had been repulsed without further loss of life and the Bengal Army had disengaged for afternoon siesta. The men in Perrins Redoubt, starving and utterly exhausted, had dropped where they stood and were instantly asleep.

In the battleground decrepit long-necked vultures were wheeling down in their hundreds from the brassy sky on the dead.

Presently there there a sound of horse's hooves and someone rapped on door of the redoubt. A voice called in

English. Getting no response, it called louder. Dicky awoke in great excitement and tore open the door with a wild hope of reinforcements. But to his astonishment only one man stood outside, a plump, red-haired, pink-cheeked young man in civilian clothes and a blue sash that indicated his status as a conscripted writer. Dicky looked past him but there was nobody and nothing except a thin horse tethered to a palm. His face fell.

"Lionel Smith, sir," the roly-poly man said, making a clumsy attempt at a salute. "I bring an urgent message from the Colonel."

He handed over a note which read:

> *Fort William*
> *Calcutta*
> *June 16, 1756*
>
> *To: Lieutenant Richard Glynnis*
> *His Majesty's 1st Bengal Fusiliers*
> *Perrins Redoubt*
> *North Calcutta*
>
> *I am confident that by the grace of God, the support of your company and with British resolve, you have withstood the onslaught of native forces.*
> *In view of the importance of your position, I have decided to assign our most precious resource, an eighteen pounder cannon, entirely at your service. By the time this letter reaches you, Lieutenant O'Malley will, with horses and oxen, have installed this cannon in the native market to your east. He has been ordered to commence fire upon the enemy encampment at exactly fifteen minutes past two o'clock when native forces are expected to remain at the height of torpor. I have sent a messenger by boat to instruct Captain Wainwright to align Europa's guns on the enemy and commence fire at that same instant. You are hereby ordered to do the same. I am convinced the combined fire will break the enemy.*

May God be with you in your endeavor for the King.
Col. Peter Linnington
Commander, HM 1st Bengal Fusiliers

Dicky was about to whoop with joy but stopped himself just in time. Silence was essential to the plan. He was struck by its ingenuity and his heart warmed with respect for his superior officer. If had known the truth, it was wasted emotion, for the plan was not the colonel's, but had originated from the only mind that understood the psyche of the Indian soldier, the mind of Benjamin Morley. The execution of the plan had been a difficult achievement. Benjamin knew that if he proposed his plan to the Council it would die in debate. Linnington, to whom he suggested the idea early that morning, would initially have none of it. It took two hours of coaxing before Benjamin convinced the colonel to execute the plan.

Dicky looked at his watch. It was just after one o'clock. He began to wake his men, a difficult task for they were close to collapse. But the news galvanized them into action.

Ex-writer Lionel Smith was drafted into a gun-crew as replacement for a dead Dutchman. Master-gunner Bracken fixed a baleful glare on the chubby recruit and asked if he had brought food and water. Smith shook his head.

"Sod-soaking English officers," growled the big Irishman. "Don' feed ye none wot 'spect ye to fight his fucking wars. Great balls of fire!" he said over his shoulder. "Ye ain't heard the last of this, Lieutenant, ye mark me words."

"Let's cap this show, men," urged Dicky. "You have me promise of roast pork and beer after, if'n I have to pay for it meself."

That thought cheered the company and they ran the three cannon that were still serviceable into their embrasures and moved debris to one side along with the dead men. A Dutchman who was critically wounded was breathing in labored gasps and was desperately in need of water. Dicky looked down at him worriedly and had an idea. Turning, he asked a surprised young ensign to climb one of the palm trees that grew just outside and cut a green coconut. When the ensign returned, Dicky used his sword to chop the top of the coconut as he had seen natives do. Then he poured water from it into the wounded man's mouth. The man first gagged, then drank eagerly. Some of the liquid ran down the sides of his mouth but his breathing eased. The others watched with interest. They had all seen locals drink water from coconuts but had never deigned to try it themselves. But times were different. Within moments twenty more of the plentiful coconuts were brought down and their liquid drunk with gusto. The men were surprised by how tasty and satisfying it was. They wiped their lips and felt much better.

Suddenly the stillness was torn apart by a loud roar from the direction of the river. They heard the sound of ball whistling through the air and the crash as it landed among the trees of the jungle.

It was 2:15!

The men ran to the guns which had been primed and kept ready. Before Dicky could give the order to fire there was another roar from the ship and a second ball landed in the trees.

"Fire!" shouted Dicky exultantly.

Lionel Smith put his hands to his ears as Bracken lit a pot fire and applied it to his cannon. The gun roared and ran backwards in the embrasure. Smith jumped and jumped again as another cannon fired from just behind him. Then another.

One more cannon roared out from the ship.

There was a moment's lull.

Then from the jungle came shouts and wails and a new and electrifying sound. The maddened screaming of an elephant in pain.

There was a deep echoing boom as O'Malley's mammoth eighteen-pounder opened up from Bagh Bazaar. This was followed by the sharper rattle of field-pieces firing from the same direction. *Europa's* guns began to fire monotonously, one every two minutes. Dicky understood Captain Wainwright's tactic and synchronized his own cannonade so that he was firing every six minutes. O'Malley's big gun boomed again. A hail of fire poured unremittingly into the jungle.

Some trees started to blaze.

And then, as the small group of soldiers watched from Perrins Redoubt, a wall of humanity broke out of the trees and into the open. Terrified enemy soldiers fled helter-skelter, their sense of direction confused by panic. Some ran into the ditch but most bolted toward the presumed safety of Bagh Bazaar.

Dicky's and O'Malley's men continued staggered musket fire on the hapless exposed Indians while O'Malley's field-pieces in the bazaar were turned low on them. The running Indians came to a stop in amazement when they realized at last they were being fired upon from a third direction.

While everyone's attention was on the panicked Indians, without warning three elephants appeared out of the trees trumpeting shrilly. Their massive fear-stricken shapes were clearly visible from the redoubt and the market and the masthead of *Europa*. All firing stopped and everyone, including the Indians, watched the massive gray creatures, all painted gaudily and covered with colorful livery. The sight of the uncontrolled energy of enormous stampeding animals in full flight was awe-inspiring. Dicky could see on the side of one of the elephants a gaping wound from which blood poured. It was rapidly staining the blue-and-gold silk a bright red. The three big animals shuffled along unbelievably fast with trunks were curled high against their foreheads. Their screams were especially unnerving to Dicky who had seen one of these creatures at close hand.

Everyone watched spellbound as the maddened elephants scattered people in their path and approached the Maratha Ditch. As the animals approached the trench something he had heard from Benjamin Morley kept repeating itself in Dicky's mind.

'*Elephants always test their ground*', Benjamin had said.

"Oh my sweet Jesus! They won't do it!" breathed Dicky. "Elephants always test their ground. They won't do it. Please God, they won't! No! No! They won't! *Don't! No, don't!*"

But they did.

In slow motion, and before the transfixed watchers, one by one the three massive beasts, trailing pennant and banner, ran over the edge of the ditch without seeming to notice, hung in the air for a very long moment and then vanished over the brink and out of sight.

Demoniac squeals came from the trench.

This was all that was required for the Nawab's soldiers to break and bolt back into the jungle.

The English did not fire again. There was no need to. The battle for the little blockhouse called Perrins Redoubt was over.

Chapter 23

While the battle raged for Perrins Redoubt, men and women of Fort William, six miles away, could hear the booming of guns and faint crackle of musketry. Wild rumors swept the garrison. But apart from Lionel Smith, nobody traveled the dusty path between the blockhouse and the fort.

With a major engagement now a foregone conclusion, Catherine McIver, the Shipping Councilor's wife, accelerated the task of marshaling European women to fill more bags of sand and cotton waste that would be used to raise the level of parapet walls and fill gun embrasures that had rotted away.

Pauline was given charge of the children.

Contrary to what she had told Aruna in Neeladri, there were a large number of European children, many quite small, who used to live in and around the fort. Pauline counted seventy-one in her brood. While their mothers stuffed sandbags, Pauline organized games and recruited impromptu musicians and jesters from fort personnel. Little more than a girl herself, she went from one bewildered child to another to take their minds off the unusual and frightening situation they were in.

Strange people these, Pauline thought. Mr. Morley warns

them. Prince Ajoy and Didi warn them. Mr. Clarkson and Mr. Kyle warn them. They take no heed. Yet the moment their servants and nursemaids and cooks leave they recognize adversity and leap into action.

Late in the afternoon the guns in the distance fell silent. Soon afterwards, a flurry of hoof beats proclaimed the return of Conscript Smith. Covered in grime, his hands blistered by hot brass, the jubilant Lionel told and retold the story of victory at Perrins Redoubt to eager listeners.

Later, a large crowd gathered at the north gate to welcome Dicky's company. Their appearance, dirty, weary, bruised, ragged, supporting their wounded comrades, was a shocking foreshadowing of what could come. Several women, Leonora Linnington and Catherine McIver among them, hurried to tend to the heroes.

After he had eaten and bathed, Dicky was taken to the Residence by the Colonel for an audience with the Governor. Armstrong appeared almost immediately.

"Governor, may I present the leader of the valiant company that held Perrins Redoubt against an immense native force?"

"Right," said Armstrong. "Pleased to meet you, m'boy." He looked closer. "I know you. You're young Glynnis. You sing."

"Yes, sir," Dicky said. "That I do. By the by, sir, we won thanks to the Colonel here's plan we did, sir."

Linnington almost crowed with delight, completely unabashed by the fact he had been talked out of squashing the scheme. The military arm of Fort William had just scored a major success. He pointed this out in some detail to civilian Armstrong who for once could not contest his assertion. Dicky concluded that Judy had put one across Punch proper.

"Well, there can be no question that Glynnis here fights as well as he sings, Governor. And, Governor, I have had the pleasure of promoting him to the rank of captain."

"Jolly good. Jolly good. Well deserved, young man, well deserved."

Dicky glowed, his exhaustion forgotten, especially since

behind the stout Governor he had just noticed two bright eyes peering around a curtain and drinking all this in.

Then Bessie came into the room.

"Hem!" said Armstrong. "Captain Glynnis, please meet my daughter, Elizabeth. Bessie my dear, did you hear this young fellow and his men held Perrins Redoubt against thousands of natives today?"

"Hundreds, sir," corrected Dicky while Bessie made her eyes innocent and huge.

Armstrong brows came together in a frown. He hated being corrected. Then he relaxed. Let the boy have his day, he decided magnanimously. Fellow's been through a lot.

"Right. As you say, young man. Hundreds. Oh, Colonel, may I have a word with you about the south battery? Yes? Capital! Bess, d'you mind seeing young...uh...Captain Glynnis out? Jolly good show, soldier!" he repeated over his shoulder as they went into the drawing room.

Bessie did not show Captain Glynnis out.

Within moments she dragged him into her room and fell upon him. They kissed madly and made passionate love. Afterwards Bessie lay on the bed on her stomach with not a stitch on and looked at him with worshipping eyes.

"You're a hero, Dicky darling. And Daddy likes you. Fancy that!"

"Yes and deuced lucky too," observed Dicky while his eyes roved appreciatively over her. "We don't have to sail away on *Beowulf* no more."

Bessie stared at him blankly.

***

Pauline was taking a moment's rest after distributing an early supper of carrot curry and bread to the children when Maggie came over. Maggie frowned as she saw the tiredness etched on Pauline's face and the way in which she held her side and leaned against a column. The usually jubilant girl looked ten years older. Benjamin had finally managed to tell her about Pauline's pregnancy. Now that she knew, Maggie could make out a definite swelling of Pauline's stomach. It would show very soon. She decided she would have a long talk with the girl as soon as her little charges went to sleep.

"How are you bearing up, child?" she asked laying a gentle hand on Pauline's arm.

"Oh, hello Maggie."

Pauline straightened with a tired sigh, smiled and brushed the hair from her face with the back of her hand. Her cheeks were red from heat and exertion.

"I'm doing fine." Some of her old warmth came back. "These are good children. You look all in, Maggie dear. Would you like a drink?"

She gave the older woman a brass pitcher of water. Maggie drank gratefully and wiped her face with her sleeve.

"Isn't it absolutely wonderful how Dicky held that redoubt place?" Pauline asked.

"Yes, indeed. He's a good boy. I've always liked young Glynnis."

They talked about the encounter at Perrins Redoubt. Then Maggie looked around at people sitting on boxes of their belongings or on the stone floor. There was clutter everywhere.

"What have we come to?" she exclaimed. "Herded into this creaking old structure with the enemy at the door. Too spoilt to help ourselves. I hope we never forget this lesson."

"I want me Mummy!" announced a little girl in rompers.

Pauline gave the child a hug.

"Yes, Jenny dear. Mummy'll be here before you know it. Would you like a nice toffee while you wait?" Jenny's face broke out in a smile. "Why, you're a big girl, Jenny. You can help me by giving toffee to the other children."

Jenny went importantly to distribute candy. A brawl erupted as a big boy tried to snatch a little boy's share. The little boy held on to his toffee in his fists and closed his eyes and screamed while the bigger one pummeled his chest. Maggie and Pauline hurried to separate them.

Suddenly Maggie remembered why she had come.

"Looky here, child, can you guess who wants to talk to you?"

"To me? A man, I hope!"

Maggie once again marveled at Pauline's ability to submerge her own unhappiness.

"Well, yes dear, it *is* a man. And a prince to boot. Prince Ajoy found me and said he wishes to speak to you. Something about his sister…" She looked toward the women filing sacks and the men waiting to take them away. "Oh, my God, Sarah Hunter looks poorly! She's expecting her baby any day." Maggie turned back to Pauline. "I told the prince you'd meet him near the river-gate in an hour."

Maggie hurried off muttering something about inconsiderate babies and did not notice the sun break out on Pauline's face. But Jenny, who had returned for a fresh supply of toffee, did.

"Why, you're smiling, Mum!" said little Jenny. "Are we going home now?"

***

While Maggie and Pauline were talking, young Ensign Shipling, sentry at the river-gate, was suspiciously observing a well-dressed native who was loitering around his preserve. The man carried a straw basket and paced forward and back with a grim expression. Periodically he shook his head violently and berated himself. When he spat loudly and thumped his chest, Shipling decided the fellow must have had too much sun and that it was time to take action.

Shipling walked up to the Indian.

"Here! Who are you?" he rapped out.

Prince Ajoy Sena, lost in thought, did not hear and started to pace away while Shipling hurried after him.

"*Hie! Stop!*"

This time Ajoy heard and turned.

"What's bitin' ye, man?"

Ajoy stared at Shipling blankly then began to turn away.

Ensign Shipling was only sixteen. He had flaming red hair and a strong Midlands accent. "Hie!" he cried. "Wait! Strange business this I'll wager. What's the matter with ye?"

Ajoy was trying to decide how to handle this situation when he saw the sentry look past him and his eyes pop. He turned to see what it was.

Pauline had appeared on to the landing above and was walking down the long flight of stone steps. Her golden hair contrasted dramatically with her long loose dark-green dress. The wisps that escaped from the bun above her slender neck formed a halo in the slanting sun. The tiredness that Maggie had seen in her face was replaced by excitement and anticipation. She hurried down the steps and filled the narrow lane that led to the river-gate with her presence. Shipling had never in his whole life seen anything so beautiful. Neither had Ajoy. Side by side, the young English ensign and tall Indian prince watched as she came toward them.

Pauline tried her best but simply couldn't prevent it. She stopped on the last step and burst into helpless peals of laughter. Shipling and Ajoy gaped at her as she wiped her eyes and tried to regain control.

"Oh dear, I'm so sorry. You both look so funny. You have your mouths wide open!"

Ajoy looked away and cleared his throat but Shipling continued to gawk at her. Pauline felt very happy. It had been a long time since anyone had so openly admired her. And the soldier was so young. She was positive he had not started shaving. She went to the boy and put a hand on his cheek.

"At ease, soldier," she said softly. "I like you too."

Ensign Shipling came to earth with a bump. With his ears flaming he went to his post at the gate and kept his eyes glued to the ground.

Pauline and Ajoy faced each other.

After a long while Shipling screwed up courage to look out of the corner of his eye. To his surprise the mad Indian and the pretty girl in the green dress were still exactly where he had left them. They were looking at each other, motionless and silent.

***

Later, Pauline and Ajoy walked across to the river-gate.

Pauline gave Shipling a radiant smile while the young ensign tripped over his feet in his hurry to unlock the gate for her. As she passed him Pauline said, "Don't worry, soldier. Captain Glynnis said it was all right for us to go out." After all, she rationalized, it wasn't right to sweep him off his feet when he had duties to perform.

Another series of steep steps led from the gate down to the river's edge. Pauline remembered this place. A very long time ago she had come here with Maggie and picked flowers for the fateful bouquet that had attracted the bull and driven her into the arms of the man beside her. She wondered for a moment what would happen to Lali if there was a battle for the town. She reminisced about her first meeting with Ajoy and then told him about the state of affairs in the fort. Ajoy listened without comment as they stood beside the muddy river and watched the ships. The unmistakable profile of *Europa* was absent and the scene was dominated by a somewhat smaller ship, the *Beowulf*. Three other English ships were anchored in midstream. From a distance it did not look as though there was a great deal of activity aboard although they all had their gun ports open. There was some Indian shipping in the river and small country craft plied between ships and shore. Sundry small boats, like the one that brought her from Neeladri to Calcutta, were tied up at the Governor's Wharf. On their deck fires smoked in little clay grates as boatmen prepared their evening meal. Oil lamps were beginning to twinkle on the water. After a while Ajoy asked her to wait where she was and walked down to the pier. As she watched him go fatigue caught up with her and she felt heavy and slow. She looked around to see where she could sit. But between the walls of the fort and the river there was nowhere to sit. Pauline felt dizzy and the old nausea came back. Then Ajoy returned still carrying his basket and uncaring of who was watching she leaned tiredly against him. With concern on his face Ajoy put his free arm firmly around her. Pauline closed her eyes and gave in to the feeling of security that always came when she was with him.

There was a sudden squelching sound.

"Come Asha. The boat is here."

"Oh!" Pauline's eye flew open. "Boat? Where are we going?"

"Out on the river. Come."

He helped her to the water's edge and onto the boat's narrow prow. Pauline was getting adept at managing herself on these small Hooghly boats. Ajoy climbed in after her and spoke briefly to the lone boatman who pushed back and poled them toward midstream. Ajoy and Pauline sat quietly next to each other and watched the lights of the fort recede. After the grueling hot day the evening coolness on the river was a blessing. Then in the light of a lantern Pauline watched as Ajoy produced a pair of green coconuts from his straw basket. The boatman came over and with an enormous crescent-shaped knife sliced the top off each coconut. At Neeladri Pauline had grown to like the nourishing fluid of coconuts. Digging into his basket Ajoy unwrapped food tied in banana leaves and spread it beside the lantern on a thwart. Pauline surveyed the tall stack of *loochis* and spiced potato curry that she had once relished at Rai Mansion and found she was ravenous. They ate with their fingers, Indian-style, without speaking while the boat bobbed comfortingly.

Pauline studied Ajoy as she ate. What was he thinking? He seemed more serious and preoccupied than usual and had hardly said a word that evening. Was it the desperation of their situation? Couldn't they always get away from the fighting in their ships? They finished their meal and washed their hands over the side with water from a brass gourd.

"You can tell Asha," she said matter-of-factly.

He looked up at her.

"Look. I am still your Asha. You can tell me everything."

But still Ajoy did not speak and seemed suddenly very distant. Pauline began to get worried. What *was* the matter?

Ultimately Ajoy spoke.

"Everything I do fails. Everything I touch breaks. Everyone I come close to suffers."

Completely taken aback, Pauline tried to protest, but Ajoy continued in a flat and very uncharacteristic tone.

"No Asha, listen to me. My attempt to claim the throne when Alivardi Khan died led to the exile of my good friend Wazir Ali. My involvement with the English and friendship with Morley-sahib has brought the Nawab's army down upon them. My plot to capture Murshidabad was hopeless failure and led to Minister Badri Narayan's arrest. Who knows whether *Diwan-ji* is alive or dead. And now Maharaj is imprisoned and his life is forfeit on my account."

Pauline moved closer placed a hand on his mouth.

"You and Didi are my true friends. I have opened my heart to you. You two alone know what a monster my husband is. The irony is that I can never speak of his misdeeds to anyone from my own country. Even to Maggie."

Ajoy drew her to him then and Pauline relaxed and closed her eyes.

"Asha, you have suffered greatly. My only happiness is I have brought you some cheer. I pray every night I can be of support to you in the troubled time ahead."

Pauline snuggled closer. The stars were bright in the clear night sky. The lap of water against the boat was a peaceful refrain. She loved him and that was all.

"Will you listen to me?" he asked.

Pauline nodded.

"I love you, Asha."

A lump filled Pauline's throat. They were thinking of the same thing together!

Ajoy held both her hands.

"I love you more than anything in the world. You are my only inspiration. More than anything else I want to take you away from the problems around us..."

"Oh, good!"

"...but that is not possible..."

"Nonsense! Why not?"

"Asha, listen. While everyone has been busy I have been languishing and thinking. Where is the world for us? My property and wealth in Rajmahal have been taken away. I am a hunted fugitive. An Indian. You are a married English woman. Where can we go?"

"We are together," Pauline protested. "We *love* each other, don't we? We can go anywhere."

Ajoy studied her. He instinctively knew she was still unaware of the person forming within her. Should *he* give her the devastating news. Benjamin had told him today that Clarkson-memsahib would tell her about the baby. How could he make lighter the distress she would face on hearing the news?

Ajoy sighed. Nothing! There was nothing he could do to relieve her pain, except what he was about to tell her. He would give himself up and perhaps the Nawab might spare some of his enemy in return.

"Asha, there will be war."

Pauline was silent.

"Have you been in a war?"

She shook her head. What *did* happen in a war? Freddie had gone away to war with Russia. Pauline's idea of war was a big noisy event far away from everyday life where big red-faced clumpy men legitimately killed one another. Officers like Freddie came back from war and had honors heaped on them. The immediacy of events—Ajoy's rescue, Armstrong's truculence, preparations for defense, Dicky's heroics—had kept her from thinking about what could happen in the future. Suddenly she felt very frightened and lonely. Ajoy sensed her unease and caressed her hair. Pauline hid her face in his chest and tried to become as small as she could. They stayed thus for a long time.

Ajoy looked over the water to the lights of Fort William. His mind was unsettled and unsure. War was imminent. People were going to die. Many people. His friends. And all because of him.

As if to symbolize his mood a cloud began to dim the stars on the eastern horizon.

Ajoy wished the delayed rains would arrive. That could be their salvation. No guns could fire and nobody could fight a war in muddy downpours that lasted for days. But what if it did not rain? The Bengal Army was already on the outskirts of Calcutta. Even so, he could still take Asha away from here. But where to? To Aruna in Neeladri? For how long? The baby had changed everything. Asha needed peace while her child grew inside her. He remembered the grief and fear in his sister's letter describing the Raja's imprisonment. Without the Raja's protection, there was no longer a haven in Neeladri. To Rajmahal? There was nothing in Rajmahal. He had a price on his head in Rajmahal. And in Calcutta, in Neeladri and everywhere else in Bengal. There was nowhere he would be safe with Pauline. Perhaps they could go to Orissa in the south and live under Maratha sanctuary. Perhaps being close to Wazir Ali there would renew his desire to fight. That might be true for him, but what about Asha? It was unthinkable to transport her to unknown Orissa in her present condition. He felt her move against him. What would happen to her if Shiraj's army overran the fort? He could not have her face that terrifying experience. Ajoy made up his mind at last. He *had* to get her away from Calcutta.

Pauline's face was still buried in his chest.

"Asha!" he said into her hair. "Listen. Look at me. Asha, you must go with the boatman to my house in Mayurmani village. You will be safe there until this war is over."

Pauline did not want to think. It was too difficult. Didn't anyone realize they could *lose* this fight?

"Oh, can't somebody stop the Nawab?"

With that outburst Pauline drooped tiredly as she remembered Ajoy had tried. God knows how he had tried! But he was one and the Nawab had legions. She wanted no more of this. All she wanted was for the boat to take the two of them to a peaceful place where she could rest. A place peaceful like tranquil Neeladri. Peaceful like the carefree days at Burnham. She wanted Father. And she wanted Ajoy. Oh, how she wanted him.

"Come with me," she pleaded.

When he did not reply she raised her face to his.

"Please come?"

The thought of spending days together, however few, just the two of them alone, was bewitching.

But Ajoy was not listening.

Pauline's anguished words, *Can't somebody stop the Nawab?* had hit him with the force of a lightning bolt. His head rang with the words. The girlish petulance was explosive in its simplicity. The Nawab must be stopped! They were all so worried about his cavalry, his infantry, his artillery and his elephants, they had forgotten it was Shiraj who was the cause of their problems and his varied army merely the effect. He had realized in Neeladri that if they could remove Shiraj and buy Rahamat Khan, the entire army would become impotent. A lowly guard's vigilance had thwarted that plan. But here in Calcutta no one had thought of it. A thought seared through his brain and he involuntarily reached for the knife he always carried inside his shirt. But Pauline was in the way and he tightened his hold on the girl instead. She felt the urgency of his grip and tried to squirm around to look at him but could see nothing in the darkness. Ajoy held on to her and stared fixedly into the night. An idea formed in Ajoy's mind, grew and took shape. A faint beacon of hope beckoned in the blackness. Could he do it? He could try. Was it worth the risk? Yes, yes, many times over, yes, it was worth the risk! The pliant body in his arms was answer enough. He held her closer. He *had* to do it. There was no other way. He *would* do it.

Meanwhile, ensconced in his firm embrace, Pauline wanted him to kiss her.

"I must go," said Ajoy.

"What?" Pauline was thrown into confusion. "Where? With me to the village?"

She turned to him with wild hope.

"I cannot."

His inflection was unwavering. And urgent.

"Please come?" insisted Pauline in a small voice even though she knew it was hopeless. When he replied Ajoy's voice was strange.

"Asha, I have something to do. I have to rid the world of a monster. Lives are in my hands. My country. My sister. The Raja. The Europeans. And you. Most of all, you. I must get you away from here quickly. The boat will take you to Harihar-*dada* in Mayurmani."

The picture of heaven was dissolving.

"Can't we be together now? Just for a little while more?"

Ajoy was silent.

Slowly Pauline resigned herself to reality, extricated herself and sat up. A black depression settled on her. Of course she was not going to Mayurmani. The fable of Cinderella and the handsome prince was just that. A fable. She had an equal duty to her own people as Ajoy had to his. To her children. To Maggie. To the people of the fort. Dejectedly she turned to look at the fort.

The cloud had grown bigger and had covered all the stars in the eastern part of the sky. Was it going to rain at last? A soft glow was visible on the eastern horizon. Pauline stared at it in astonishment. They had talked all through the night! How time flew when she was with her prince. She wondered what Benjamin and the Clarksons were thinking about her absence.

"Let's go back to the fort," she said dully. "It will be morning soon."

"No Asha, we still have much of the night. Please let me send you to safety. You can be in Mayurmani by afternoon."

Pauline shook her head. So he also had not realized how long they had talked. "It's too late, your Highness. We must go back now. Dawn is breaking."

She was startled by a cry from the shadows. It was the forgotten boatman.

"What do you want?" answered Ajoy irritably and kept on speaking to her. "Asha, why don't you..."

The invisible boatman said something in a querulous voice. Ajoy gasped and looked fixedly at the fort.

Following his gaze Pauline also looked east and her heart stood still. *"Oh no!"* she cried out when she realized what was happening. *"Oh my God, no!"*

The dark cloud, she realized now, was not a rain cloud at all. It was smoke. A smoke cloud. The cloud that obliterated the stars was smoke. And the pink glow she had thought was the rising sun was fire. She could even smell it faintly now. Ajoy and Pauline stared eastward and as they watched, the pink began to metastasize into separate orange glows that flickered in the distance. A morning land breeze started up and immediately tongues of flame shot up behind the silhouette of the fort and the smell of burning grew stronger.

It was a riveting sight from their vantage point on the river.

Huge and frightening.

Pauline stared at the spectacle, her hand at her throat.

Calcutta was burning!

Chapter 24

Benjamin had been standing alone for hours on the ramparts of Fort William before the fire impressed itself on his mind. His thoughts had not been pleasant. Most of all he was crushed by the stupidity of their situation and its possible aftermath. Two leaders, a petulant Englishman and a bellicose Indian, were at each others' throats. Neither could see the damage he was doing to the long-term interest of their respective countries.

Damn you to hell, Armstrong!

What an unfeeling short-sighted self-centered cretin was he whose duty was to lead the Company in Bengal. The man was not just destroying the hopes and homes of hardy pioneers whose lives depended on his wisdom, he was dismantling the work of generations. The work that had begun two hundred and fifty years ago with Vasco da Gama's discovery of the sea route around Africa and, and a hundred years after that, the formation of the East India Company by visionaries, among them Queen Elizabeth herself. In the final analysis Richard Armstrong was jeopardizing the potential for England's future greatness. Benjamin's mind dwelt on the days of his apprenticeship in the Company's offices in London and he recalled the magnificent heroes of his youth. Prince Henry the Navigator, Vasco da Gama, Ferdinand Magellan, and all the other seafaring giants of Portugal, who had broken the shackles of the Old World. Close in their wake, Francis Drake and Richard Hawkins, awe-inspiring seafarers who launched England toward maritime supremacy. Who were their heirs? Who today symbolized the greatness of Josiah Child, founding father of the Company, the one who wrought England's economic miracle? What had these men in common? Courage! And conviction. And vision. And leadership. And competence. How miserably ant-like were their successors! The Armstrongs, Linningtons, McIvers, and all the petty bureaucrats of Leadenhall Street. They lived for today. They lived to milk the brilliant accomplishments of their predecessors.

Benjamin's mind moved to the future.

With Bengal lost, three tremendous economic platforms would evaporate: an established source of silk and indigo for English textile mills; an alternate source of tea from the Himalayas that could stem the outflow of English capital to China; and an English beachhead for dominance of the rest of Asia. Spice-laden Siam and Sumatra, enigmatic Japan, and the huge brooding Middle Kingdom, China, with its untold riches would never be England's.

Would Calcutta really fall to a minor regional despot? *It could not!* If it did, it would take with it England's hopes for the Orient. It could not fall! They would fight. Just as Dicky and his men had showed them today. As Robert Clive had showed the world in the battle of Arcot! A handful of determined and disciplined Englishmen could prevail against a multitude of rabble. *Europa* and its guns would buttress Fort William as it had done Perrins Redoubt. They would not give up! Perrins Redoubt would be the rallying call.

Benjamin looked defiantly over the ramparts in the direction where the Nawab's troops were encamped and something caught his eye.

It was a dull pink glow in the eastern sky.

***

Deep inside Black Town, an eleven-year-old boy was trying his hardest to wake his ailing mother.

After his memorable encounter with the memsahib of the fort, Ashraf had returned to work as odd-job boy in the opium den that was one of Master's many business interests. While busy filling the pipes of recumbent customers he heard a disturbance in the road outside. Ashraf ran out and found groups of men talking excitedly. He sidled up to one such group and heard them talking about the Nawab's army. It appeared that the soldiers were very close and were bent on pillage. Forgetting Master, Ashraf quickly ran along the dark alleys of Black Town and pushed aside a gunnysack that served as a door to a cardboard-and-cloth hovel, one of many in the narrow lanes of Bagh Bazaar. He waited a moment for his eyes to adjust and then squatted down beside an inert figure on the ground.

"*Maaa!*" Ashraf called in his high voice. "Ma, wake up!"

Ashraf's mother, fevered with recurrence of malaria and weak from malnutrition, did not move from her dirty cane mat. Master, to whom the family was bonded, had come to take his pleasure from her today. But because she was ill she had not pleased him. He had beaten her in anger and left. Now as Ashraf prodded her, she turned away listlessly and refused to respond. Ashraf gave up and shook his sister Rubia who was sleeping on another mat.

There was a sudden uproar outside.

Men's voices raised in anger.

Ashraf shook Rubia again.

"Wake up, Ruby!"

Eight-year-old Rubia sat up and rubbed her eyes. She was tiny and skeletal and wore a dirty one-piece shift, her one and only dress. Her hair was matted and fell forward onto her smudged face.

Ashraf made one more attempt to arouse his mother but it was no use. She groaned miserably and it was obvious she was going nowhere tonight.

"Let's go, Ruby. Now!"

Ashraf pulled his sister to her feet. Rubia grabbed up the rag doll that the memsahib of the fort had sent through her brother and which was her treasured possession. They went out into the lane. They took nothing else. They *had* nothing else. Master had discovered and confiscated the money Ashraf had brought back from the fort.

Brother and sister melted into the street.

It was a vile thoroughfare, used both as a garbage dump and public latrine. Ashraf and Rubia did not notice the stench. It was the only home they knew and they were used to it. The two children walked warily through the smokiness that typified nights in Black Town.

"Are we going to steal some food again, Dada?" asked little Rubia. "Can we? Please?"

Ashraf had not thought about where they would go, but Rubia's suggestion seemed a sensible thing to do in passing. So he led the way to the town's main market where food-sellers and merchants gathered. They had almost reached, and could see the oil lamps and smell the tantalizing aroma of food cooking and peanuts roasting, when they heard hoof beats approaching from behind. The sound grew louder rapidly and within seconds the horses were on them.

Ashraf frantically pulled his sister out of the way of flying hooves.

Then the horsemen fell upon the peddlers in the square.

It was difficult to see how many riders there were. Perhaps a hundred. But within moments the town square was a scene of chaos. People screamed as they fell under the horses' hooves or were sliced by swords. Their merchandise stands disintegrated under the onslaught. Their wares, meat, vegetables, sweets, cooked food, pots and pans, were scooped up by the raiders. A large cabbage, kicked by a horse, rolled in Ashraf's direction and he instinctively gathered it up under his arm.

The horsemen dismounted. In twos and threes they

entered the well-to-do houses that surrounded the square. Within minutes they had pulled their occupants into the street. More looters appeared, now mostly afoot. They began a systematic torture of residents and shopkeepers. The petrified children watched the scene from behind the trunk of a large tree. They were very close to the mayhem and could see that the eyes of the marauders were glazed. They moved about in small groups, vicious and determined, like packs of hunting dogs. Their attention flitted from one target to another. They fell upon a woman and left her when someone shouted another find. They descended on their prey with incredible ferocity. They first beat and kicked their victim if he was male. Then two of them held him upside down. If that did not elicit the required information, water was poured into his nostrils. When the victim told them where his savings were hoarded, his torturers re-entered his house or shop and emerged with booty, usually pitiful brass, perhaps copper, rarely silver and once gold. The victim was then beaten to death or tossed back into his doorway. The women that were found, unmindful of age, were stripped off jewelry and clothing and carried screaming back indoors or into alleys. Mercifully, this northern part Black Town, far from the fort, was full of transients who were overwhelmingly male, and so rape was a rare bonus for the greed-crazed mob. Groans, oaths, shrieks and maniacal laughter filled the scene of devastation in front of Ashraf and Rubia. More looters appeared and spread into the tentacle-like lanes of Black Town. These new arrivals were not dressed like soldiers. No one seemed to be in charge. It was a rabid mob, greedy and undisciplined and vicious. The two children slowly moved south staying hidden. Ashraf wondered why people had said these were the Nawab's men. Their actions reminded him of stories he had heard of the old Maratha bandits, men called *borgis,* who had plundered the country before he was born. Had the dreaded Marathas returned?

The pillage lessened as the plunderers devastated the square and wandered away in the direction of the fort.

Then Rubia cried, "Dada! Something is burning!"

Ashraf smelt smoke. It came from behind them. They tore their eyes from the carnage in the square and saw flames rising from Bagh Bazaar, now a half mile to the north. A breeze blew in their direction and the acrid smell of burning became overpowering. One of the huts on the lane they had come along abruptly burst into flames.

"*Maaa!*" shrieked Rubia and tried to run back but Ashraf held her tightly.

Out of the smoke strange figures appeared at the head of the lane. They looked and acted quite differently from the horsemen and looters they had seen before. These men had dark-chocolate, almost black skin. They wore yellow *dhotis* and had red bands in their tangled hair and sported red hibiscus blooms behind their ears. They had long streaks of ash on their faces and chests. They carried torches and brandished swords and gourds of country liquor. And they sang in unison. The chorus was fierce and melodious and hauntingly beautiful. As they reached a house, they stopped before it and swayed to the rhythm of their song, forcing back with their torches any resident that tried to flee. They did this until the song reached its climax. Then they set fire to the house and slaughtered the inhabitants. A blazing inferno followed their progress.

As they came closer, Ashraf made out words of a song:

> *Oh Mother Kali!*
> *Gardner of skulls,*
> *Of dripping tongue*
> *And lightning eyes.*
> *Dance your death waltz*
> *On your foes' blood…*

Frozen by the macabre scene, Ashraf listened to the mesmerizing melody of the Kali-worshippers, until Rubia said in a shaking voice, "Oh, Dada, they're coming this way!"

Ashraf was galvanized into action. He grabbed her hand and they ran down a lane.

Finally Ashraf began to think.

Where could they go? The town would soon be reduced to ashes. If they were caught they would be killed. Safety lay to the south in the open area in front of the fort where the fire would not reach. Thinking about the fort, he remembered the yellow-haired memsahib he had pulled out of the river and who had been kind to him for taking her home. Ashraf, in spite of the poverty and starvation he had suffered, had a quick mind. He and Rubia could go to the memsahib's house or to the fort and seek shelter from her. With the innocence of youth and the optimism of the street urchin Ashraf decided at once to put plan into action. He took his sister through the streets of Calcutta, along short cuts and detours to get ahead of the plunderers who were now approaching the part of Black Town close to the fort. The homes here were predominantly occupied by families of Indians who worked inside the fort. These people were mainly laborers who had either fled the area or were conscripted as *coolies* to reinforce the defenses. There were also a large number of native soldiers of the English garrison who lived here with their families. Consequently this part of Black Town was more family oriented and had significantly more women and children than the northern and seamier section. Word of sacking and rape had flashed ahead of the pillagers. And so as Ashraf and Rubia finally overtook the looters they found around them a growing throng of hurrying women, many carrying small children or leading them by the hand. They kept looking over their shoulders all the time. The sight of a burning house, a roar from the mob, or the climax of an arsonists' song, spurred them forward. Aged grandmothers dragged themselves along. The sick and weak fell to their knees and were pushed over and trampled. The trickle at the head of the procession, where Ashraf and Rubia were, became a stream of humanity behind them, and further back, a torrent. When brother and sister finally emerged from the confines of Black Town onto The Avenue, they were borne along by a swarm of many hundreds of women and children making for the safety of the fort. Ashraf and Rubia were among the first to traverse The Park. They skirted the trench freshly dug across it and came to a stop at the massive east gate of Fort William.

The gate was closed and barred.

Dozens of fists hammered on the gate and a multitude of female voiced called upon God and Allah and the *Laat Sahib* to witness their predicament and their impending dishonor and death and open the gates.

The gate remained closed.

Rubia and Ashraf felt pressure building on them. It was becoming difficult to stand upright and even breathe. Prudently Ashraf maneuvered his sister and himself in front of an exceptionally fat lady who provided a cushion.

On the opposite side of the gate another chaotic situation prevailed. The large crowd of women had been seen approaching from the ramparts of the fort. Husbands and fathers clamored for the gates to be opened. Laborers threatened to strike. Indian soldiers threatened to lay down arms.

A riot was imminent.

And then, before anyone could control the situation, the sentries in the tunnel behind the gate found themselves pinned to the wall by a human mass and the doors were pulled open.

Ashraf and Rubia and the fat lady were at the head of a surging tide of three thousand men, women and children, refugees from the fire, that flowed through the east gate. Within minutes the broad parade-ground was a sea of humanity.

The Governor of Fort William, his face purple, watched helplessly from a balcony with his wife beside him. He shouted words which Martha could not make out in the din. Armstrong's prized parade-ground was in shambles.

***

Pauline returned to shore filled with foreboding.

She had clung to Ajoy as he helped her up the steps from the river-gate while a bewildered Shipling looked on. Once inside the fort, she left Ajoy and went to look for her children. She found that Maggie and Mrs. McIver had put them to sleep in the drawing room of the Residence. When she came back Ajoy was gone. She walked back and forth along the gallery above the river, shutting out the fire from her mind, wanting him, unsure of what to do.

Then came the uproar at the east gate and simultaneously she saw Ajoy walking across the parade-ground and hurried in his direction. Hearing the noise he started to run the remaining distance up to the ramparts above the gate. Pauline arrived a few minutes later gasping for breath. Benjamin saw them both and rushed over. In horror the three stood together and watched the blaze grow stronger, the sky brighter, the stream of refugees sweep to the fort, the standoff at the gate, and the flood of fugitives pour onto the parade-ground.

Suddenly Pauline felt a tug at her skirt and looked down in surprise. Ajoy and Benjamin turned at the sound of her gasp and all three stared blankly at two dirty little ragamuffins. One carried a doll. The other carried a cabbage.

"*Eshechi*, Memsahib," Ashraf said. *We have come.*

Then Pauline was on her knees hugging the two little bodies to herself.

Chapter 25

The terrible night ended but the coming of dawn saw no parrots in the sky. Nor did the sun appear with its usual freshness. In the still oppressive air smoke from Black Town rose in thick columns and cast a gray pall on the fort. Even in the first sunlight flames were visible in Bagh Bazaar. Scavengers descended in their thousands. Dogs, hyenas, jackals, rats, wildcats, mongoose, insects, mynahs, crows, hawks, vultures, even a few bears were visible, squabbling over corpses that littered the blackened lanes and the sides of the Maratha Ditch. The smell of decay grew overpowering. Flies droned everywhere.

Inside Fort William conditions were abysmal.

European and Indian soldiers sagged at their posts after the traumatic fire-ravaged night. Refugees from Black Town lay in fetid misery on what was once manicured grass. On the galleries that bordered the parade-ground, European evacuees awoke in marginally better conditions. Accustomed hitherto to being served breakfast in bed they morosely contemplated a ration of hard biscuit. There was no tea to wash it down because pots and pans had been left behind in the scramble to evacuate. With the filth and grime and their tattered clothes it was increasingly difficult to distinguish Europeans from Indians.

After another sleepless night Benjamin Morley climbed to the top of the gallery and surveyed the chaos in all directions below him. His senses were numbed by the devastation around him. The worst was the smell. Depending on the wind direction, the odor of decomposing corpses, human excreta or charred structures prevailed. The next worst was the suffering. Wherever he looked people were in pain. Pain of loss of loved ones, pain of hunger, pain of diarrhea resulting from unsanitary conditions, pain of revulsion caused by swarms of flies and hordes of rats. And, most acute of all, the pain of lost hope. All of these added to the physical pain of those hurt in the battle for Perrins Redoubt and the sack of Black Town.

Benjamin noticed a skirmish in the tightly packed mass of refugees below. His jaw dropped in amazement as he made out a fat well-dressed Indian sitting on an iron box in the middle of the crowd and eating cold rice and fish curry from a tin plate. Three servants held containers of food, water, sweets and pickles for the man. The same number of bodyguards held at bay a wall of women and children who watched fixedly while the fat man ate with unconcern. One young woman, with a baby on her hip, tried to get past a bodyguard and was shoved back roughly. The baby wailed.

Something broke inside Benjamin.

He stormed into the crowd and sent the bodyguards spinning. The next moment he found himself looking straight into the goggling eyes of the fat man whose jaws still worked on pieces of fish and rice. Benjamin knocked the plate from his hand and swiped at the food held by the servants sending it flying in all directions.

In an instant the crowd fell on the food, fighting and snarling. Horrified, Benjamin watched for a minute, then walked away feeling sick. When he looked back the upheaval had subsided. The fat man still sat on his box looking reproachfully in his direction. Benjamin felt a ludicrous pang of guilt for having spoilt the man's breakfast.

He stalked back to his rooms and tried to shut out the disintegrating world outside. To bring himself under control he tried to think of a way out of their situation. What could they do? It was now clear there was a battle on their hands. They had to fight with their meager force because as far as reinforcements were concerned they might as well be on the moon. London, and even Madras in southern India, the nearest British military presence, were weeks and months away. It was too late to effect a rapprochement between Armstrong and Shiraj. The wolf was at the door. Events had followed each other in a terrifying avalanche and had resulted in the desolation that now lay everywhere. And this was only the beginning. Prince Ajoy had said there were fifty thousand enemy troops. In their sights were five hundred Europeans, including over a hundred and fifty women and children who looked to the Council for safety. The odds in favor of an English victory were ridiculous even if the Council had been a competent body. But the Council still clung to the delusion that primacy of the European was absolute. Dicky's valiant stand yesterday had appeared to vindicate that belief. But that had been a minor engagement. It was apparent to any clear-thinking individual that the main body of the enemy would ultimately smash through.

Benjamin stopped pacing, lay down on his bed and descended into total despair.

From outside came the forlorn sound of children crying in hunger. Time passed. The sun rose higher.

There was a knock on the door. Benjamin ignored it. The door was pushed open and Ajoy entered quietly. He looked around the darkened room and did not seem surprised to see the English sahib, usually brimming with vitality, lying on his bed with his eyes closed. Ajoy sat on a chair and waited. Different noises filtered in through the windows. Children crying. Women calling to each other. An officer giving an order. The buzz of flies and cawing of crows were a continuum in the background.

After a while Benjamin stirred and looked up at his visitor. A subdued light cast Ajoy's face in shadow.

Ajoy spoke almost casually.

"I am going to stop the monster. Will you hear me, my friend?"

***

While Ajoy and Benjamin talked, the opposing force was not faring well either. Stretching outward from the Maratha Ditch, a sea of tents and fenced enclosures marked the Nawab's camp.

At the outermost periphery were offal.

Soldiers wounded in the previous day's encounter at Perrins Redoubt, unwanted, unsung and left to die. They had limped back to face a tirade from Rahamat Khan about their failure in the *jihad*. Now in their paddock they wretchedly moaned in pain and hunger and begged succor from passing soldiers. They were ignored. Several had died of their wounds in the night. The growing heat of the day was already killing others by dehydration.

Moving inward, there were extensive corrals of animals. Here were housed thousands of horses, hundreds of elephants, donkeys, oxen and camels. As the day wore on, streams of animals were led down to the river past the outcasts.

"Water!" cried one whose broken leg was already suffused with gangrene. "Give us water please. If the animals can drink, why can't we?"

The animal tenders averted their eyes and walked on.

A vast uncovered area where infantry and cavalrymen slept came next. Then, increasing in quality of accoutrements and retainers, were the tents of Indian officers and French gunners, followed by those of generals and noblemen, the suites of Jacques Villeaux and Rahamat Khan, and finally, in the very center of the encampment, the resplendent pavilion of the Nawab of Bengal.

The Nawab's pennanted, carpeted and muslin-walled war palace was a circular structure of canvas, over eighty feet in diameter and raised around a massive central pole of beaten gold. Among its mahogany furniture was a bed of gold that had been borne along on backs of camels.

Shiraj Doula was still asleep on his golden bed.

A gray-eyed, gray-bearded, cadaverous man sat on the floor beside his master. His name was Gaffar.

Gaffar had served the young ruler since the day of his birth. He was the only person allowed to remain alone in the Nawab's presence when he traveled outside Murshidabad. Everyone knew that this gray man did not have a life of his own, that he never slept, that he always watched over his young master with a drawn dagger, that he would sacrifice his own life for the Nawab's, that he always tasted the Nawab's food before the Nawab, that he searched the Nawab's visitors for weapons and sat within striking distance when the Nawab held court.

All through that night Gaffar had husbanded the incense samovar whose wraithlike fumes kept odious smells away from the his sleeping overlord. The instant Shiraj Doula stirred, Gaffar went to the curtained doorway and motioned to the retinue that was waiting since daybreak for this moment. It was well known that the Nawab's notorious temper was at its vilest when he awoke. Many a servant who had the misfortune of disturbing Shiraj when he was asleep or half-awake, had had their ears or noses separated from their faces for their trouble. The same could happen if the Nawab's wants were not addressed the moment he awoke.

Gaffar was a master at gauging the somnolence of his master.

Today, even before the Nawab sat up on his huge bed, his washer, barber, valet and cook were at his side. They waited while he yawned, stretched, scratched his armpits and shuffled across to the royal privy curtained from common view. When he returned his washer washed his face, his barber shaved carefully around his narrow beard, his valet helped him into robes of lightest silk, and his cook offered his repast. Gaffar tasted the food and the tea. The tea was a recent fad copied from the English by Shiraj's grandfather.

Finally Shiraj Doula issued his first command of the day.

"*Sipah-sala* shall be summoned!"

Rahamat Khan was waiting at the door and did not have to be summoned. He cleared his throat, entered before the Nawab had finished speaking and greeted Shiraj in the traditional Muslim way, heel of the cupped right hand touching the bowed forehead.

"*Salaam Aleikum,* my Lord."

"*Aleikum salaam, Sipah-sala.*"

Rahamat Khan looked up surprised. The Nawab must be in rare good humor to actually return his greeting. It was a relief that his confidence in ultimate victory over the hatmen was strong after yesterday's reverse.

"What news, *Sipah-sala?*"

"My Lord, Bagh Bazaar has been razed at your command."

"Good. Conniving devils! That should teach them about harboring guns in the market. Tell me more."

The two men spoke in Persian.

"My Lord, our soldiers entered Black Town after midnight, destroyed all businesses and set fire to many houses."

"Yes, I saw the fire. What happened to the people?"

Rahamat Khan was silent.

The Nawab looked at him keenly. He knew his general well.

"There is bad news?"

"Yes, my Lord."

"The Nawab shall be told at once!"

"The foul plunderers ran amok, my Lord."

"What? You could not control the vermin?"

"No, my Lord, the blood lust was in them, those infidel Kali-worshippers. They had drunk vats of hashish-laced *sharbat* and had made human sacrifice to their evil goddess. There was nothing we could do to control the carnage."

"What happened?"

"They took the torching of the town into their own hands. They went about in bands from house to house, singing savage chants in praise of their deity. They tortured inhabitants, they raped some women, speared a few children, looted and destroyed all they could lay their hands on." Rahamat Khan bowed his head. "I am ashamed, my Lord."

Shiraj Doula seethed with frustration.

His southward march, broadcast with great fanfare, had had a noxious side effect. It had attracted every bandit, every highwayman and every thief in the country. A growing mob of desperados, mostly ardent worshipers of the black robber-goddess, Kali, had followed in the army's wake toward Calcutta, reveling in the confusion caused by its passage. They laid waste to the countryside after the army passed. Rahamat Khan had twice turned his forces around on them, but, without the overhead of armaments, the thieves easily scattered and melted into jungle and fields. Rahamat Khan could not fight on two fronts. And so, while Shiraj Doula's disciplined regiments respected mandates of the *Koran,* abstained from liquor, treated prisoners and civilians honorably, the pursuing rabble made a mockery of his ideals.

"As a result of their depredations, my Lord, thousands of women and children from the town have taken shelter in the fort."

The Nawab deliberated moodily. This was very bad news. How could he attack Fort William and get at the hatmen when the fort was full of women and children? He decided he would worry about it when they got closer to the fort. Perhaps he could make them flee again. At this point they were interrupted.

"My Lord!"

While the Nawab was pondering someone had attracted

Gaffar's attention from the outside. Gaffar now came forward. Shiraj glanced at him indicating he should speak.

"Hazrat Sayyid Naseer wishes audience, my Lord."

"Hazrat Sayyid has leave to enter."

The orange-bearded ambassador came in and performed the customary salutation.

"My Lord, I have good news," he said in his gravelly voice.

"At least someone has good news. The Nawab had begun to lose hope. Speak, Hazrat Sayyid."

"My Lord, I have learned that our impression of the Maratha Ditch has been wrong all along."

"What?" exploded the Nawab. "What do you mean by impression? What impression? Whose impression?"

"My Lord, our army can easily cross the trench."

"*What?*"

"Yes, my Lord, it is true. The Raja of Rangamati has a house on the outskirts of Calcutta. After he heard of the Nawab's travails of yesterday at the Perrin bridge he came to see me." The Nawab and the general had his full attention. "We thought that the ditch was wide and deep and fortified all around the town of Calcutta. Did we not, my Lord? The infidel hatmen have always maintained they needed the fortifications against the French and we assumed they were at least rudimentarily fortified. Is that not so, my Lord?" When the Nawab flared at the second unnecessary question Naseer hurriedly plunged on. "As a result of that impression, my Lord, we decided to concentrate our first attack on that bridge near the river. It is amazing how the hatmen defended that point from three fronts. My Lord, it appears we lost three hundred men at a place which was defended by a handful of hatmen."

The Nawab's foot tapped. The volcano simmered close to the surface.

"Hazrat Sayyid, you are speaking to the Nawab and his *Sipah-sala*. We *know* what happened in the battle. Make your point."

"Yes, my Lord, of course," said Naseer hastily. "The hatmen have managed to delude us. There are points along the ditch where our army can cross easily, especially the place where the road the hatmen call The Avenue meets the ditch."

Rahamat Khan's face lit up. Shiraj's foot stopped tapping.

"We need not need attempt crossing the bridge again?" asked Rahamat Khan. "How do we know it is not a trap engineered by the hatmen?"

"*Sipah-sala,*" Naseer addressed Rahamat Khan. "Listen to me. There is a small building at this place I speak of. I have been advised that villagers, who supply the fort and who display their wares to the servants of the hatmen, have in the past insisted they would have trouble crossing with their goods if the trench was dug. So the hatmen argued the need for a patrolled bridge at this point. Meanwhile the trench was not dug. A trap, my Lord? *Sipah-sala* can send his men to reconnoiter…"

***

All through the rest of that day reports of the Nawab's troop movements poured in to the Executive Council. It was clear that Perrins Redoubt was not to be the point of entry and that the enemy had discovered the large gap in the ditch where it met The Avenue. The attack would now come along the wide main road of Calcutta, directly aimed at the east battery and Fort William itself.

Captain Muldoon, commander of the armory, was placed in charge of the east battery. Benjamin volunteered to serve under him.

Standing at his defensive position Benjamin understood why Kyle had wanted so desperately to have the largest buildings of White Town demolished. The Playhouse and St. John's Church rose above the east battery. The Company House dominated the south battery. The north battery stood below Angus McIver's palatial home. If the enemy took these structures the batteries would immediately be rendered ineffectual. If the east battery fell the enemy would be at the main gates of the fort. If either the north or south battery fell the path of retreat to the river and to the ships would be cut off. The Council members understood all this now but it was too late. So they argued about who had made the decision *not* to have the buildings pulled down. In any event the Council no longer held much authority. Sporadic orders from Armstrong or Linnington had things happening at cross purposes.

That evening, as Benjamin walked along The Avenue to the guns stationed behind the palisade of the east battery his hope that the garrison would prevail in spite of incompetent leadership and hasty defenses faded. There was now left only one possible course of averting a disaster of unimaginable proportions.

The final plan of Prince Ajoy Sena.

Chapter 26

The next day was the 18th of June, a Friday. Friday is the most auspicious day of the week in the Islamic calendar. And it was the day that Rahamat Khan launched his final offensive. For the Bengal Army's *jihad* it was a good omen.

Rain clouds were a lost hope. The sun rose strong and bright directly before the east battery. It found Benjamin sitting on a pile of bricks and shading his eyes as he kept vigil through a gun embrasure.

The east battery where Benjamin served was positioned at the junction of The Avenue and Rope Walk at the very place where Maggie Clarkson, a lifetime ago, had pointed the way to the Kali-temple to a newly-arrived Pauline. Fifty yards ahead and to Benjamin's left and right were two large buildings. These were the Old Courthouse and the Playhouse. Further ahead and to the right was the Company Jail. Thereafter The Avenue entered Black Town and demarcated the section of the town that had burnt and that which escaped the holocaust.

Presently Benjamin heard a soft rustle as though dry leaves were being blown along by a breeze.

He turned to look back at the British flag that had just been raised on the ramparts of the fort to the accompaniment of *God Save the King.* The flag drooped limply. There was no breeze.

He soft rustle came again.

Benjamin shaded his eyes against the low sun and squinted along The Avenue that stretched broad and dusty to the horizon. All he could make out was an ugly gray-brown haze that still hovered from the inferno.

What *was* the sound?

He looked around at the cold determination in the faces of the small handpicked group of soldiers around him and was reassured. These men would not break under fire.

Soon they all heard the rustling sound, louder this time. It was coming from the direction of Black Town. Benjamin looked east again and saw a dark line shimmer and move as it resolved itself out of the smoky haze.   Benjamin recognized the sound at last.

It was the shuffling of many feet. A horse neighed faintly in the distance. A cloud of dust rose up and quickly discolored the rising sun. After twenty more minutes he could distinguish marching soldiers, strung out fifty abreast, approaching in their direction. As they came closer he discerned their green and red uniforms. The jingle and clank of swords and muskets could now be heard.

So *this* was the enemy!

Since the day Shiraj Doula foreshadowed events at Hazarduari Palace, Benjamin had visualized two scenes over and over in his mind. One was of Calcutta being 'put to the sword'. This had already occurred, except that White Town and the fort had been spared. The second scene was the attack by the Nawab's army. That too was about to come true, except that in Benjamin's scenario, the enemy wore royal blue of the Nawab's elite guard and made a sweeping cavalry charge. In the reality he was now witnessing, the approaching infantry wore red and green.

Benjamin felt a constriction in his throat. His hands were cold as ice. He looked around again at his men. There were fifty of them, all standing at some vantage point, watching the oncoming enemy. Their faces mirrored their emotions. Captain Muldoon stood on a cannon and looked out over the top of the earthworks.

Benjamin studied Muldoon. The commander of the east battery was the odd man out in the otherwise resolute group. An alcoholic, he predated Benjamin's arrival in Calcutta. Ever since Benjamin had known him the man had been in a state of numbness. His words and actions always held an infuriating vacancy. The sorry state of the garrison's armory had been direct evidence of the laxity of his command. And now, the lives and safety of the people of the fort were in his unsteady hands. Having realized this, Benjamin had volunteered to serve in the east battery in an effort to counterbalance Muldoon's incompetence. God only knew how the captain would react when enemy cannon opened up. At least they would not have to wait long to find out.

Benjamin returned his attention to the advancing enemy. He could make them out individually now. The infantrymen all looked alike. They carried ancient matchlocks or long spears. A few carried bows and had quivers of arrows on their backs. The men had dark pinched faces and long moustaches and wore loose shirts with crossed belts for their sword-scabbards and sashes that held ammunition. Their bare feet scuffed the dust into a cloud. Their number must be in the thousands.

Benjamin began a silent prayer. But before he finished the quiet was shattered by a sudden rattle of musket fire and the coincident roar of a cannon and a cheer went up from the men of the battery.

"Huzzah for Marston!"

Under cover of the previous night Sergeant Peter Marston had taken a company of fifteen men and set up an advance post at the Company Jail. With him were two twelve-pounders. And so, while the attention of the Indian troops was concentrated on the formidable east battery, Marston delivered the first surprise blow. As the exultant men ran to their battery positions Benjamin remembered the difficulty he had encountered in convincing Muldoon to allow Marston to take up the advance guard.

There were two reasons for this.

First, the captain was insulted by the rank of honorary major that had been conferred on Benjamin by the Executive Council which made him technically outrank Muldoon. Anticipating this Benjamin had made it clear to the Council that he would server *under* Muldoon at the battery. But the incident still rankled heavily in Muldoon's mind.

Second, Muldoon had strenuously objected that the colonel had not approved the move of placing a force at the jailhouse and that transportation of the two cannon would weaken the battery itself. He had stuck to his position against every explanation. Benjamin knew that to take the matter to Linnington would be futile. In the end he had had to reluctantly pull his rank and threaten to expose a couple of dark secrets before the Captain capitulated. In the process Benjamin knew he had made a bitter enemy. And now as Marston's forces kept up sustained fire and the initial astonishment and confusion among the Indians became chaotic, Benjamin could not help stealing a glance of triumph in Muldoon's direction.

He got a black look in return.

Benjamin put aside the past and concentrated on the enemy. Marston's first cannon sally had taken a big toll and was followed up by several rounds of musket fire. Then both cannon of the east battery fired at once. The havoc they wrought was appalling. At least a hundred Indians were down and the first line began to falter. But the army advanced again and, although horribly exposed and mercilessly cut down, their sheer numbers assured their progress. Returning fire began to be concentrated on the jailhouse.

And then, with a crashing boom, one of Jacques Villeaux's big eighteen-pounders opened up from behind the enemy line.

From the protection of the brick and mortar jailhouse, supported by flanking fire from the east battery, Peter Marston, a likeable man in his mid-twenties, fought the battle of his life.

It was a repetition of Perrins Redoubt.

A disciplined nucleus of determined soldiers, reinforced by a strategy of divided offense, held a much larger enemy at bay. Marston and Muldoon's coordinated musket and cannon fire mowed down hundreds of enemy soldiers until a cannon ball from Villeaux made a direct hit on the jailhouse. A big gap opened up in the wall, killed one and injured four of Marston's men, and showered the company with bricks and dust. The men hastened to reposition their guns and close the gap with sandbags. Benjamin watched this performance with admiration. It was evident they could not last much longer but they had accomplished their objective. They had wrested the initiative from Rahamat Khan and delayed his attack on the battery and on the fort.

Benjamin's evaluation of the Indian soldier, which had been reinforced by the outcome at Perrins Redoubt, was that morale of the poorly armed and mostly untrained fighter was a very tenuous thing. The only chance of the English against overwhelming numbers was to strike first and strike hard and hold out obdurately.

Rahamat Khan had set strategy to storm the fort directly. Instead he discovered that he first had to eliminate the jailhouse and then the east battery to get at the fort. And by drawing fire to themselves, Muldoon and Marston had, for the moment at least, diverted Rahamat Khan's attention from the less impregnable north and south batteries.

The second round belonged to the British. The first had been Perrins Redoubt.

Astonishingly, impossibly, the intrepid band at the jailhouse held on for two more hours. In the overpowering heat they took tremendous punishment and checked the enemy at the Cross Roads until a cannonball flew in squarely through a gap in the wall and exploded on the far side of the interior. Its effect was horrific. Shrapnel from ball flew in all directions. Marston died instantaneously, his body mutilated beyond recognition. Five soldiers were also killed. Two men were injured and lay on the ground with blood pouring from their wounds.

The jailhouse was silent at last.

The men who were whole spiked their cannon to prevent their use by the enemy and, supporting their wounded comrades, began the arduous journey to the east battery. While Muldoon watched, Benjamin, with the energy of a madman, coordinated a hail of fire to cover their retreat. Eight men from the jailhouse reached the battery safely and collapsed into the arms of their friends.

It was almost noon.

***

It was unfortunate for the British that the fall of the jailhouse came just before the customary afternoon disengagement. It spurred the enemy to greater glory and for the first time Rahamat Khan abandoned the period of siesta. As afternoon wore on, Muldoon's force exchanged cannon fire with Villeaux but slowly the inevitable happened. Under covering fire, one at a time, the houses of White Town were occupied by men of the Bengal Army. The Nawab's blue-and-white colors began to appear on one rooftop after another. Enemy firepower concentrated on the battery in increasing intensity.

It was around three o'clock when Benjamin came to a decision.

The formidable breastworks of the battery were still holding. If they could last until dusk they may be able to retake the houses in darkness when Indians were notoriously lethargic. In this way the battery might fight on another day. But it did not seem likely that this would happen. Their ammunition was dangerously low and at least fifteen men from the position had been killed or seriously wounded.

"We must have reinforcements, Captain," Benjamin told Muldoon.

"Why?"

Benjamin controlled an urge to lash out with his fists. Instead he explained his reasoning while gunfire crackled.

"That's impossible, Morley."

"Oh? And why?"

"We can't weaken our position."

Benjamin stared at Muldoon.

Had the man lost his sanity in the bedlam?

"By thunder, Captain, reinforcements strengthen, not weaken."

"Damn your heart, Morley, I know that! I meant if we send for reinforcements now, we lose the men who can defend our position."

"I see. Well, but we'll not hold much longer anyway without reinforcements."

"I know that too. I was about to order our evacuation to the fort."

Benjamin was aghast.

"But that'll mean victory for the natives. We can hold out another day if we have reinforcements. We've got to delay their progress."

Muldoon's jaw set.

The habitual squabble was about to begin.

Benjamin turned away, sickened to the core. *Short term, short term, short term!* That's how they all thought. With the world disintegrating around their ears, couldn't the leaders display *some* fortitude, some planning, some originality? And just a tiny bit of resolve? What *were* they coming to?

"I'll go!"

And before Muldoon could remonstrate Benjamin vaulted onto a horse and rode back to the fort.

***

A familiar scene of confusion and misery greeted

Benjamin as he trotted in through a doorway in the east gate. The refugees had suffered through another day of abject misery that was compounded by the sound of guns booming around them. An occasional shell hit the fort itself. One had just landed in the open parade-ground and killed or injured several women and children. The crowd was surging around in panic.

It took Benjamin some time to find Linnington. He finally tracked the colonel down in a corner of the officers' mess.

Linnington listened to his report while Benjamin drank a welcome cup of tea.

"Sir, we've got to move Lieutenant O'Malley's men into the battery immediately."

"Oh?"

Benjamin went through his hypothesis. When he finished Linnington thought awhile and, surprisingly, agreed.

"All right, Morley, we'll do it. Resnick!"

"Sir?"

Linnington directed his orderly to find Lieutenant O'Malley and fetch him at once. A half-hour passed and Benjamin was about to go looking for O'Malley himself when the lieutenant arrived.

"Sorry, sir. I'd a-gone to the privy when Resnick came by. Somethin' I ate."

Linnington gave him his orders while Benjamin fretted. It took yet another half-hour before O'Malley's company of forty men with Benjamin at its head marched out of the gate.

Halfway to the battery they met Captain Muldoon limping back. Behind him his shell-shocked soldiers were mechanically dragging themselves along. Their faces were gray with tiredness.

Benjamin was livid. He begged, he coaxed, he swore, but try as he might, he could not get the men to return to the battery.

"Well, Lieutenant," he told the O'Malley as Muldoon's men continued on to the fort. "You and your company have to take over the position."

"Sorry, Morley," Muldoon shouted over his shoulder. "That's won't be possible."

Benjamin stared at him.

"Why?" he asked fearing the worst.

His fear was justified.

"We've spiked all cannon there, *Major!*" Muldoon said, almost in triumph.

Chapter 27

Catherine McIver held Jenny in her lap and rocked her to sleep. Pauline, Maggie and Bessie sat silently while Jenny's mother cried softly. Maggie held her hand and fought back her own tears.

Sergeant Peter Marston had been little Jenny's father.

Night cast its gentle covering on another terrible day.

Pauline stared into the distance with unseeing eyes and listened as Mrs. McIver sang a Scottish lullaby for Jenny:

> *"Wearie is the mother that has a storie wean,*
> *A wee stumpie stoussie, that canna rin his lane,*
> *That has a battle aye wi' sleep, before he'll close an eye;*
> *But a kiss frae off his rosy lips gives strength anew to me.*
>
> *Oh, Wee Willie Winkie, he rins through the town,*
> *Upstairs and downstairs in his night-gown,*
> *Tirlin' at the window, cryin' at the lock,*
> *`Are the weans in their bed?—for it's now ten o'clock."*

Pauline got to her feet and began to walk aimlessly through the clutter around her that were human beings. Everywhere debilitated, dehydrated and hungry refugees sat dispiritedly or lay awake holding on to the uncertain safety of Fort William.

She marveled at the strange transformation of Catherine, wife of Angus McIver. Heretofore Mrs. McIver had been a frightening figure, big, rawboned, red-faced, outspoken, prejudiced. With the onset of hostilities she had metamorphosed into a tower of strength for the traumatized women of the garrison. She berated the Governor until he turned his cherished ballroom into a hospital and his drawing room into a nursery. She enlisted and trained helpers, among them Pauline and Bessie Armstrong. She did everything to make patients comfortable while Stanislaus Kyle, who did double duty as the fort's doctor, and Surgeon Fellowsmith from *Europa* dispensed medicines, applied salve, treated wounds and set broken bones. One-third of the wounded, in spite of the efforts of Mrs. McIver and her ministering angels, did not last through the day. The survivors suffered through the heat and dust, lying on sheets and mats laid on the floor of the ballroom.

And amid the clangor of the day's battle, Mrs. McIver wrought a miracle. In the spare bedroom of the Residence she delivered to Abraham and Sarah Hunter a healthy baby girl.

Bessie Armstrong was another person transformed.

Gone was the pampered darling of the chief of station. Gone was the shy violet shielded from the world by powerful parents. Nothing, absolutely nothing could faze her. She hit out at snarling rats and made them retreat. She cleansed the most grievous of the patients' wounds and dressed them. She comforted the children. She scrubbed the hospital floor and did the work of ten men. Before news of Sergeant Marston's death reached them, Bessie had told Pauline that she and Dicky were going to marry as soon as 'this business' was over. Pauline was ecstatic. She hugged her friend and wished her a lifetime of happiness with her dauntless lover and felt a personal pride because her role of Cupid had been successful.

All day while the battle raged outside Pauline had divided her attention between the children in her care and the wounded in the hospital. Ashraf and Rubia, confirmed orphans now, became her helpers. They brought water. They ran errands. They fanned and cleaned the children by turn and forgot in their attempts to please that they were children themselves.

Ajoy was never far from Pauline's thoughts.

Always when she thought of him she became two people: one despairing of a future, another hopeful of a life together. She mused on his strange behavior on the boat before the Black Town fire. When he had said he must rid the world of a monster he was obviously talking about the Nawab. Had he thought of another last ditch scheme to topple Shiraj? She speculated about what it could be. She was terrified he would be careless and fall into the Nawab's clutches once more. Would Shiraj win the war? If so, what would happen to him? To her?

She had been walking for an hour in the darkness and had come near the solitude of Writers' Building. After the day's pandemonium, lulled by the quiet, she sat on a low wall and let her mind wander.

She thought of Father, of her brother, and of Robert. Darling Robert who had loved her so completely. Would she see him again? What was it he had said at their first meeting at the glade? She remembered the words, *'Oh, Pauly! Ye be so pretty, I could die!'* The memory brought tears to her eyes. How uncomplicated life had been with Robert in Burnham by the gentle river Orwell—now just a beautiful dream a million miles away. How much had happened since the day Father first told her about Captain Frederick Wainwright...

Pauline heard a shuffling sound behind her. As she turned to find out what it was she was seized violently around the waist. A rough and dirty hand clamped on her mouth cutting off her scream.

***

The soldiers of Fort William had legitimate complaints.

Their only ration since the outbreak of hostilities had been hardened ships' biscuits. They knew that even though rice and vegetables were available in plenty, they could not be cooked because there were no utensils and no cooks. They roundly cursed the officers, the Governor, the Army, the Company for their uncaring attitude and near-sightedness.

Master-gunner Bracken, the massive Irishman who had fought at Perrins Redoubt, was a natural center of discontent. He was chronically intolerant of authority. As matter of course he considered his superior officers lazy and self-serving. To a large extent he was right. Tonight Bracken told a group of his cronies, some English and some Dutch, that if they couldn't eat properly, they would bloody well drink to their hearts' content. They scoured the kitchens for liquor and unearthed several barrels of ale. After putting away numerous pints accompanied by ribaldry they began to look for ways to get even with the despicable natives who were causing such grief.

"Wimmen!" said Bracken.

He did an incongruous bump-and-grind as the group emerged, wiping their mouths, from the kitchens.

"Aye! Women!"

His friends rambunctiously appreciated Bracken's performance.

They did not have far to look. The parade-ground was full of women.

Bracken's gang was drunk enough to be both vicious and cunning. Aware that their actions could lead them to jail, they watched the crowd of Indians from a dark alcove. When a young mother separated herself from her family and came in their direction, three soldiers pounced on her. Before she could scream they carried her with a hand covering her mouth to the abandoned rooms of Writers' Building.

The other soldiers waited in ambush and before long they had secured their own victims.

The men took great care not to attract attention. They did not worry about whether their prey was young or old and took turns raping a victim. They beat her unmercifully if she resisted or attempted to scream. At one point there were four women being violated at once in a horrible fetid room. When victims were finally cast aside they were either dead or horribly mutilated.

But like most hate crimes, this did not satisfy the perpetrators. They began to look for newer and more innovative avenues to vent their passion.

***

To the grieving eleven-year-old Ashraf, his white memsahib, pretty, kind and gentle, had assumed a goddess-like stature. All he and Rubia wished was to remain close to her and help her with her tasks. When she walked away from the group of other memsahibs, Ashraf left the sleeping Rubia and followed her. When Pauline sat down on the wall and stared into the distance, unknown to her, Ashraf was hunkered down in the shadows and trying to keep awake.

Also unknown to her, pig-like eyes of Master-gunner Bracken were watching greedily.

When Bracken grabbed Pauline and began to carry her away struggling and kicking toward Writers' Building, Ashraf's first reaction was to run to her aid. But the retreating back of the sahib, who was built like the trunk of a banyan tree, quickly dispelled that idea. He turned and ran for help. With his sharp eyes Ashraf soon located Benjamin and Ajoy and breathlessly told them what had happened. Then he ran back to Writers' Building with the men at his heels. But there was nobody to be seen at the spot where Pauline had sat.

Ashraf pointed out the direction he had last seen Bracken going.

Beside themselves with anxiety, the two men dashed toward Writers' Building. This was a two-story structure with fourteen rooms on each floor, seven in front and seven at the back.

They pulled open the first door.

Only blackness greeted them.

The same happened with the second and third rooms. The fourth door would not open. Ajoy desperately rattled the door knob before he realized it was bolted from the outside. The fifth door was open. They burst in and were stopped in their tracks by the hideous smell and the scene.

A candle that flickered madly in the gust caused by their entrance threw weaving shadows on the walls. The room reeked of rum and body odor. Two uniformed men in front of Ajoy and Benjamin were looking down at something on the floor. That something made grunting animal sounds. While Benjamin held back, dreading what he might see, Ajoy pushed forward. The standing men did not even notice his presence. Ajoy shoved them aside and cried out in horror when he saw the woman held down by her neck by one man while another leaned over her body and grunted and groaned as he raped her. In the light and shade Ajoy saw the woman's tightly-shut eyes and her teeth bared in pain. Black patches of blood glimmered on her face and chest. In a welter of anxiety he made out that the woman's hair was black.

The man violating the woman squealed in agony. Benjamin had viciously pulled him backwards by his long hair.

Ajoy gripped him friend's arm and spoke urgently in his ear.

"Leave them. Come with me. Quickly!"

Benjamin took a moment to comprehend what Ajoy was saying. He still thought the woman on the floor was Pauline.

Without waiting for him Ajoy ran out of the room.

***

Bracken had thrown Pauline down on a narrow rope-and-wood frame cot set against the wall. Her freshness and the fact she was English and young had driven him wild with lust. He bent over and pinned her arms with one hand and held her face covered with the other. Pauline writhed and kicked and scratched to no avail against his apelike strength. Bracken growled and roughly hoisted her skirts up around her waist with his elbow. Then he took away the hand that covered her mouth to push down his breeches. At that instant Pauline twisted her face close to his, clamped her teeth on his jaw, and simultaneously brought up her knees and dug them savagely into his genitals. The gunner bellowed like a wounded bull into her face and involuntarily moved his other hand to protect his groin. Releasing his jaw, Pauline swung one hand and hit him in the face with her fist with all her strength and in the same motion rolled away off the cot and got on her feet.

With surprising agility Bracken recovered and blocked the exit. There was blood flowing down his chin. His eyes gleamed murder as he held his arms wide apart and came toward her.

At that moment Bracken was seized by his collar. The next instant he felt the sharp point of a knife in his spine. He struggled to turn and see his assailant. The knife pressed deeper and pain shot up and down his body. Someone snarled something to him from behind. Bracken moaned and relaxed. Then he was pushed into the middle of the room.

Pauline stood shakily with her back to the opposite wall and prepared to face the new intruder.

"Asha!"

"Oh dear God, it's you!" she cried and was about to rush to Ajoy when he shouted, *"No!* Stay away from him." When he saw she was out of Bracken's reach he asked, "Are you all right?"

"Y-yes, darling. You came just in time."

"Shiva! Shiva! Go out through the door quickly, Asha. I have him."

"And you?"

"Go out, Asha!

"Take care, darling! He is an animal."

"And he will die like one. Go out!"

Pauline went out.

Ajoy suddenly pressed the knifepoint in slightly and pulled it out. Simultaneously he pushed Bracken forward as hard as he could. The gunner lost his balance and collapsed onto the bed with a wild cry as it gave way with a crash under his weight. Ajoy backed out and pulled the door shut and bolted it from the outside.

Meanwhile Benjamin had come out of the adjacent room with a pistol in his hand.

"Pauline!" he exclaimed as he saw her. "There you are, thank God. Are you hurt?"

Ajoy joined them.

Pauline was trembling and swaying on her feet. Benjamin put out his arm to steady her and looked questioningly at Ajoy. Ajoy did not respond and looked at the girl in concern. After a minute Pauline stood up straight and smoothed her clothes. The two men watched her anxiously. Other than rips in her green dress and a bruised and throbbing hand with which she had hit her attacker, Pauline found she was unscathed. Her mouth and teeth felt vile more with the memory than with the taste of her aggressor. But she was getting over her experience and longed for Ajoy, not Benjamin, to hold her. She took a deep breath and smiled at her men.

"I'm fine," she said.

Their relief was palpable.

"Thank God," repeated Benjamin as the tension abated. "But this is no place for you, Mrs. Wainwright. Prince Ajoy, I shall deal with these men. Will you take her to Mrs. Clarkson?"

"Yes, Sahib. But do you not need me with this scum?"

Benjamin looked around grimly.

"No, my friend, thank you. I was made honorary major yesterday. I intend to use my rank."

He stood for a minute and watched Ajoy lead Pauline away. He saw her take his arm and lean her head on his shoulder. After a few steps Ajoy put his arm around her. Poor thing!

What a gruesome experience. Then Ashraf came up to them from the shadows. They stopped and Ajoy spoke to Pauline who went down on her knees and clasped the small boy to her and kissed him on his eyes and cheek. Benjamin felt a lump form in his throat. If it hadn't been for that destitute ragamuffin who had already saved her life once...God, he couldn't bear to think of what could have happened. With a grim resolve he returned to the room where Bracken was imprisoned.

"This is Major Morley. Come out when I unbolt the door. I am armed."

Bracken emerged warily, one hand behind his back where the knifepoint had cut through his skin. The two men who had been watching the rape of the Indian woman in the other room had fled when Benjamin roared a command and pulled out his pistol. The other two, both Dutch, were still inside. Benjamin ordered them out after Bracken. With the gun in his hand he faced the three offenders.

"You dirty swine! You will face a firing squad in the morning."

"It was only a native we had," a Dutchman said in an accented whine.

Benjamin raised his pistol with a jerk and the Dutchman shrank back.

"You bastards! Put your identity papers on the ground."

The Dutchmen complied but Bracken did not move. He brought the hand from behind his back and looked at it. It was covered with his own blood. He looked at Benjamin with eyes filled with venom.

"Ye cock-sucking officers got it coming, me dandy major who's never done no duty. Any day now. Jus' ye wait!"

"Drop your papers or I'll shoot you like a rabid dog. Now!"

The steel in Benjamin's voice and the intent in his eyes were unmistakable. Bracken took his time but obeyed.

"Move!"

Benjamin picked up the papers and herded his prisoners toward the parade-ground. He found Corporal Wellman, head of the evening watch, and handed the prisoners over with a brief account of what had happened.

"Jes' ye wait!" said Bracken again, leering at Benjamin over his shoulder.

"Get out of my sight, you worm!"

"Worm, eh? We'll see who'll worm nigh soon. I've yer number, ye hear?"

Wellman led the prisoners away.

Drained and frustrated, Benjamin walked slowly back to the room where the rape had occurred. The woman still lay on the ground inert. At first he thought she was dead. But when he bent down to feel her pulse she came to life, screamed hysterically and shrank back from him. Benjamin tried to say a soothing word but she shrieked again and fainted.

There was a dull rattle from a far corner of the room.

Benjamin looked up startled, his hand going to his gun. The sound came again. Because of the darkness he could see nothing. Benjamin rose, picked up the candle and gingerly approached the sound and cried out in horror as he saw another woman on the ground. She lay on her back. Her broken body was clothed with blood. A rattling wheeze came from her throat.

And then he saw the two other forms beside her.

He barely made it outside before his knees gave way and he leaned against the wall of Writers Building and retched uncontrollably.

***

"Asha, if that big devil was Indian, I would have killed him instantly."

Pauline put her hand on his mouth.

"No your Highness, don't speak of devils and more killing. We've seen enough death and cruelty to last a lifetime. I was lucky to escape the way I did. But you know? That brute was more hurt than I was." She held up her bruised hand for him to see and smiled her 'brave' smile. "I got him good in the balls and then, blimey, I came near breaking my wrist on his face!" She quickly sobered. "Of course, if you hadn't come when you did..."

Pauline shivered violently.

Ajoy, once again marveling at the magnificent resilience of the girl, drew her close. "Asha, are you tired? Shall I take you to the memsahibs? Or can we talk for a few moments?"

"Let's talk. I want to be with you. I'm just a little tired." She turned to Ashraf. "Water, Ashraf dear?"

The boy scuttled away happily.

They went up to the ramparts where two sentries looked at them suspiciously. Ajoy turned his back. For a while they stood silent looking out over the walls of the fort. The houses which had been fought over today with such ferocity, were invisible in the darkness. The smell of cordite was heavy in the night air. It was quiet. Most people were asleep after the tumult of the day. Ashraf came back with a green coconut and Pauline drank thankfully. A scuffle broke out some distance away and a man shouted in pain. The shout was abruptly cut off. The sentries went to investigate.

"Asha, my love."

"You are going then?"

"Going? Where am I going?"

"You are going to stop the Nawab."

Ajoy regarded her somberly.

"You always surprise me, Asha. How do you know? But yes, I do have to stop him as you put it. For you. For Maharaj. For Aruna. For *Diwan-ji*. Hundreds of lives have already been lost. If I cannot stop the killing, why should I exist?"

"What will you do?"

Ajoy took both her hands in his.

"I have decided, Asha. I will do what I have to do."

Pauline's eyes were luminous.

"Remember, my love. I need you. Always."

Then she was in his arms and her tears were wet on his lips. He caressed her hair in the way she had grown to love. After a while she stopped crying and they stood close together, each trying to black out the reality of their predicament.

Then he was gone into the shadows of the night.

***

The sentries who had left Ajoy and Pauline to investigate the fracas came across the inert body of a man on the parade-ground. The attackers had fled. As they reached to turn him over, they were shocked to see the uniform of an English soldier. They drew in their breath simultaneously as they saw the knife protruding from the chest of the dead man. Then they looked at his face and cried out in horror.

It was Corporal Wellman.

***

A little later the chain rattled once more at the gate of the ornate residence at the Cross Roads.

On this occasion the Jagat Seth's serene household was in uproar. All through the previous nights everyone had watched fearfully as the fire spread. They had listened to reports of looting and killing in the town and of fleeing refugees, and heard the terrifying sounds of battle. The Bengal Army had passed by extremely close that day but because of the Nawab's specific directive, the Jagat Seth's house had not been harmed. Still the banker's bodyguards were primed to defend his citadel-like home and everyone stood ready to evacuate to boats that waited at Surman's Garden, a mile south of Fort William. Even though the Jagat Seth was an ally of both warring factions, he had decided that the battleground of Calcutta was getting too hot for civilians.

Watchman Bahadur, armed now with a matchlock, opened the gate and looked with questioning eyes at two drawn-up palanquins. A liveried servant stood beside them. Bahadur did not recognize the man. The servant said he wanted to see the banker on a very important matter. When Bahadur sputtered and protested, horrified that a common servant would want to meet the great Banker of Bengal, the servant interrupted and asked him to convey a message to his master. The message was 'Bag of bones'.

Something in the man's demeanor made Bahadur obey. He reluctantly went in and delivered the insane message, quite convinced he would receive a severe tongue-lashing from the Jagat Seth. To his surprise the banker at once came to the gate and began an earnest discussion with the servant in rapid-fire Bengali. Bahadur had difficulty following the conversation, but as he looked on his master's expressions and gestures depicted several emotions. Astonishment. Apprehension. Disbelief. The banker looked back several times at his house. After ten minutes the servant abruptly entered the first palanquin and, to the watchman's amazement, the Jagat Seth, without a word to anyone, clambered into the second. Soon Bahadur was standing alone on the Cross Roads and staring after the departing bearers.

Chapter 28

During that same night there were flashes of cannon fire out of the sea of torches burning beyond the walls of the Fort William. Now and then a shell landed in an open space of the fort in a shower of sparks. The Indian refugees had moved away from the parade ground and taken shelter near the walls, packed in close to the Europeans. Fights broke out over rights of space and sentries were hard pressed to maintain order.

The tone of the Executive Council meeting late that night was of desperation. It had been a difficult meeting to convene. The members were scattered around the fort and it took a long time for orderlies to round them up. But, miraculously, at one in the morning, when the Governor called his meeting to order in the still-inviolate Council chamber of the Residency, all members were present.

Armstrong, Linnington, Clarkson, Morley, McIver, Muldoon, Kyle, Wolfe and Broderick took their seats around the familiar conference table, a rock of solidity amid the torrents lashing the garrison.

"Gentlemen," opened Richard Armstrong. "The situation is precarious."

He got no further.

Linnington immediately slapped the table. "'The situation is precarious!' Hah! The situation has been precarious for days. Morning will bring a major onslaught."

"Aye!" affirmed McIver.

There was a silence. Benjamin, exhausted by his experiences, looked on disinterestedly.

"What should we do?" asked the Governor in a shaky voice.

Proposals were voiced.

Captain Muldoon suggested strengthening the eastern gun embrasures.

"With what?" Kyle wanted to know.

Linnington stated that the riverside batteries to the south and north be reinforced now that the east battery had surrendered.

"Why not simply open the east gate to the Nabob?" Wolfe responded, his voice heavy with sarcasm.

The colonel gave him a glare, but let it pass, something indicative of the distress of the Council. He then informed the meeting that Captain Muldoon would assume command of the north battery. That's the end of *that* position, thought Benjamin. Linnington continued troop deployment updates. Lieutenant O'Malley was to take command of the south battery. Captain Glynnis would hold the Company House at the southern end of the wharf with twenty men.

It was Clarkson who finally articulated the issue that was on everyone's mind.

"What about evacuation?"

"No!" said Linnington emphatically. "We *can* hold the fort."

"What's the point?" asked Wolfe. "The enemy's all around us."

McIver fixed him with a baleful eye.

"Ye want to sail away to England? Aye, Wolfe?"

"Aye, Mac!" retorted Wolfe with his best McIver imitation.

The two men glowered at each other. John Wolfe was in an

unusually nasty mood today. In the plunder of Black Town he had lost his Indian mistress. When inquiries failed to reveal her whereabouts, he concluded she was dead and suddenly lost all interest in his posting and his adopted country.

McIver had hit upon a raw nerve.

Ironically Kajal Lata had escaped the raiders of Black Town and was at that very moment a refugee inside the fort. But she was too awestruck by her surroundings to send word for Wolfe.

"What about the treasury?" asked paymaster Broderick.

No one heeded Humpty's attempt to divert the discussion from the topic of evacuation which they discussed for a long time. In the end it was resolved they would defend the fort for at least another day.

"For God's sake, Governor, let's at least get the women and children to the ships under cover of night," urged Clarkson. "The men can hold the garrison."

"Aye," concurred McIver. "That would be wise." He thought for a moment and added, "Me wife and I'll chivvy the women and bairns. And, aye, we must fight on."

It was the first time Clarkson and McIver had agreed on anything.

"All the women and children?" Kyle asked incredulously and gestured toward the window. "There are thousands."

"The Europeans, ye dimwit!" burst out McIver. "The Europeans! I dinna ken taking dirty natives on *Beowulf,* mark me words."

"How many are there? European women and children, I mean?" asked Broderick.

Nobody seemed to know exactly. They agreed on a rough figure of a hundred and fifty and worked through the logistics of their removal. After that there was another awkward silence. Nobody wanted to bring up the eventuality of a surrender.

In the end Linnington summed up the Council's position.

"We must keep access to the wharf intact. Let us pray that Muldoon's and O'Malley's batteries hold through the day."

No one had anything further to say and the meeting broke up. As he passed behind the colonel, McIver was heard to mutter, "Let's do more'n pray, mon, or we be dead men!"

Benjamin had been silent through the entire proceeding. He got to his feet and went across to the Colonel.

"Colonel, a word with you?"

"Certainly, Morley. You've been a quiet one. Rough day out, eh?"

"I have a grave situation to report, sir."

"I already have status of our engagement with the Nabob, Morley. Something graver? Now *that* should be difficult."

"This is serious, Colonel. There have been assaults on women by our soldiers."

Linnington turned his full attention on Benjamin.

"Really?"

"Yes, sir. Rape."

Linnington flinched.

"And how can you confirm this? Which women? Are there witnesses?"

"Yes, Colonel. Myself among them."

While Linnington stared at him Benjamin went on.

"I have intercepted the rape of several native woman by four soldiers. There may have been more miscreants. I have seen the victims of the violence. Some are dead. Some *should* be dead. All attacked by the same culprits."

"Sweet Christ, Morley, are you sure?"

"Yes, Colonel. But there is worse. Little more than an hour ago I have prevented the attempted rape of an English woman *and* have apprehended the culprits."

"Oh my God! What are we coming to? Why didn't you mention this at the meeting instead sitting like a bloody stuffed owl?"

"It'd have become a righteous debate leading us nowhere. We've got to stop this business at once."

"Just a minute, Morley. Oh, Governor!" the colonel called across the room.

Armstrong was sitting slumped, deep in thought, and did not hear. Benjamin and Linnington went over to him.

"Governor," said Linnington. "We have a situation here. A band of rogue soldiers have violated women. Native and European. Morley has been policing this abomination and has just reported to me."

"It's true, sir," added Benjamin. "These men are vicious and dangerous and I've had some of them incarcerated. God only knows what else is happening around us. We need to take harsh…"

Benjamin stopped abruptly. With a shock he realized that Armstrong had not heard a word but was goggling at him with wild hunted eyes in his puffy face.

"Sir," urged Benjamin, resisting an urge to shake the man. "For the morale of the fort we must take immediate action. Harsh and punitive action."

At that point the Governor of Fort William went to pieces.

No! He could not handle it. He simply could not handle it. His world was falling apart all around him and they wanted him to do something. All of them. All the time. *Do something! Do something! Decide!* He had to make these infernal decisions. *Action! Immediate action! Harsh action! Punitive action!* He did not want to take immediate action. He did not want to take harsh or punitive action. He did not want to take *any* action. He wanted everyone to leave him alone. He wanted the world to return to its unfettered rhythm of the past. He wanted to shut out from his mind the noise and the pain and the smell and the dirt and the natives and the danger and the actions and the decisions. He wanted no part of this. In front of Benjamin's astounded eyes Armstrong's face crumpled like a crushed paper bag. Suddenly the Governor jumped to his feet and hurried, almost ran out of the Council chamber while everyone stared after him.

Linnington shook his head sadly.

"Man wasn't meant for the job. Now look Morley, you've done a great service curbing the wretches. I'll send a detail to scout the area. We'll hold the miscreants in the lockup. Just give me the details."

"One moment, Colonel."

Benjamin had been watching the Governor walk away and started after him.

"Governor! Sir!"

Armstrong heard Benjamin's call and accelerated. He went down the colonnade stairs as fast as he could, almost tripping in his hurry. Benjamin followed for a few steps, then stopped, uncertain what to do. And while he did so Armstrong disappeared into the night.

***

Two hours later the evacuation of the women and children began under the supervision of Angus McIver.

The seventy children were divided into two groups under Pauline and Bessie. Pauline wondered at McIver's about-face. The Scotsman had built a reputation as a pugnacious penny-pinching self-serving individual. Why then was he so anxious to help women and children evacuate? She got her answer soon.

"How are you, child?" asked Maggie, who was getting the sixty-odd women together. She eyed Pauline with concern. "Is the effort to much?"

"I'm all right. But this must be awfully hard on you."

Maggie sighed deeply and her hand tightened on Pauline's arm.

"I pray to the good Lord we survive tomorrow. *What* we have to contend with! It drives me to distraction when brave young men are fighting with their lives, their leaders are such craven lily-bellies."

This was very strong language from Maggie. Pauline was surprised out of her worries about Ajoy.

"Why, Maggie, you're angry! What is it?"

"Should you ask! I just heard that Richard left a Council meeting without making a vital decision. And, true to form, we're going on old Angus's prize boat, the *Beowulf.* Isn't he ever the gallant now, helping lassies to the pier!" Maggie snorted. "You can even see the gold reflected in his eyes. He'll collect later from the Company for evacuating us. And *will* he collect! The turncoat!"

While Maggie heaped abuse on McIver, Martha Armstrong appeared looking worried. Her husband was nowhere to be found. When Maggie had come to get her from the Residency, Martha had half a mind to stay behind until Richard was found, even though her senses were constantly assailed by the nearness of the horrid natives, by their never-ending sounds of misery, their stench, by the flies, and by the thunder of artillery that made her heart leap. She wanted to find Richard and ask him what she should do. But the opportunity to leave this hell was too enticing. And so, guilty and ashamed, Martha followed behind Maggie and joined the mass of European women assembled below the colonnade.

At three-thirty in the morning, the surprised and rebellious children were woken up and shepherded, sleepy and protesting, down the steps to the river gate. The women came after them in a straggling line. Torches in wall sconces threw pools of light on the procession. Everyone had been admonished to remain perfectly quiet. The word had been passed around that Indian refugees should not be made aware that an evacuation was taking place. Otherwise a general panic could ensue. Nonetheless many small children wept in their wretchedness. But that was all right as the sound of crying children was commonplace in the fort. The women carried nothing and stumbled along bemusedly.

Catherine McIver stood at the top of the steps.

"Wary, now!" she cautioned to the stupefied crowd as it moved along in fits and starts. "Watch them steps! Carefully there!"

Ensign Shipling was still on duty at the river gate. No one had thought to relieve him. He had fallen asleep sitting propped against the gate when someone shook him by the shoulders. He awoke with a start and stared with popping eyes into the face of the pretty woman who had caressed his cheek and who had occupied a large part of his subsequent thoughts. Strands of Pauline's golden hair now brushed his face as she looked at him closely to see if he was awake. Half-asleep, Shipling reached out to touch her face.

McIver's loud voice shattered the beautiful picture in Shipling's mind.

"On your feet, soldier! Open the damn gate!"

Startled into reality Shipling got to his feet and looked around in amazement at the large number of people in his narrow alley. Why, it was full of children! Many of them were crying. What was happening?

"Damnation! Open yon gate, man. D'ye hear?"

"Yes, sir, Mr. McIver."

Shipling fumbled with his keys. The gate squealed open on rusty hinges. Shipling tried to catch Pauline's eye but she didn't look at him again.

"Mrs. Wainwright," ordered McIver, "ye take yer group down first, if ye please. Then the women go. And last go Bessie's bairns."

"Come children," Pauline said mechanically. "It'll be over soon and you'll be safe on a big ship."

She took Jenny Marston's hand and led her group to the Governor's Wharf near the northeast corner of the fort. She found that it was still just as crowded with country shipping as when Ajoy had hired the boat the night before. Memory of the unhappy parting after their closeness brought tears to her eyes. And then he had come back and saved her from the monstrous soldier. Where was he now? She brushed tears away with the back of her hand while Jenny looked up at her with concern. The steps leading to the pier were slimy and treacherous and several children stumbled. One little boy shrieked and fell flat on his back. Shipling and another soldier came down unbidden and helped him back on his feet and carried the smaller ones to the waiting boats. It took four boats to load all the children.

McIver stood above everyone, an irritable frowning presence. Pauline wished he would go away.

"Get in, lass!"

From the top of the steps McIver called down to Pauline when the last child was aboard. She turned and looked at him blankly. Maggie and her crowd of women had arrived on the bank. Everyone seemed to be waiting for her to get in with the children.

After Ajoy's farewell Pauline's mind had stopped working. When Mrs. McIver had given her directions for the evacuation, she had moved about like a robot and herded her children down to the pier. She had not even thought about leaving the fort herself.

"Get in, woman, and clear the way!" McIver's voice had risen in irritation. "Canna ye hear?"

His wife had come up next to him to see what the holdup was. When Pauline lingered undecided, McIver lost his patience and walked down the steps.

"Get in the boat, Mrs. Wainwright," called down Catherine McIver. "We be waiting."

"*No!*"

That word 'Wainwright' galvanized Pauline into action. With a scream she retreated from the edge of the pier where Jenny stood at the prow of the boat.

McIver came closer.

"Come on, lassie! All the women be goin'."

Pauline backed away from him, getting perilously close to the edge of the wharf.

"Easy now, all'll be fine. Jus' get in."

"No!" cried Pauline again. "I'm not going to the ship. Any ship. Never!"

"Aye, that ye will!"

"No!"

McIver grabbed her arm and tried to drag her to the boat.

"Let her go!" shouted Jenny and made an attempt to come to her aid. A boatman held her back.

Pauline twisted around to face her second attacker of the night. Bracken's hideous visage floated back before her eyes. The awful taste of sweaty stubble and rum-soaked breath choked her senses.

With teeth clamped tightly and lips drawn back in a snarl, Pauline jerked her arm free and slashed viciously at the Scotsman with her nails. She drew blood from his face and almost gouged out an eye. Too astonished to defend himself, McIver stepped back.

"Angie!"

Catherine's frantic warning was too late. McIver took a step into space and with a wild yell disappeared from sight and fell into the slush of the riverbank with a huge splash. The children screamed in unison while the women watched in horror. Pauline blindly brushed past Mrs. McIver and, as the mass of women parted, stumbled up the steps and into the fort.

Ensign Shipling bent over the edge of the pier and found McIver foundering in knee-deep water.

"Here, sir!"

Shipling and the other soldier reached down, grabbed a hand each and pulled McIver, dripping mud and water, back onto the pier. The Scotsman sat on the stone wharf and blew like a beached whale. Every eye was on him.

Nobody moved.

Suddenly, with a terrifying whistle and a crash a cannonball landed on the bank a short distance away. It caused no harm but effectively broke the tableau.

"Look here, Catherine," said Maggie. "I'll take the children. You get the women on board."

Maggie climbed in beside Jenny and their boat poled away

into the gloom. A swinging lantern in the mid-river indicated where *Beowulf* was anchored. More boats came alongside and, struggling and slipping, the women with help of the soldiers went aboard. Weary Sarah Hunter and her newborn baby were helped aboard by Shipling and Leonora Linnington. At last only the McIvers and the soldiers remained on the pier.

"Leonora," called Catherine. "I'll stay for Bessie and them other bairns. Can ye manage the gairls?"

Mrs. Linnington responded with an affirmation and the boats with the women floated away.

"Hurry, hurry! Day's a-breaking!"

Mrs. McIver bustled Bessie and her children down the steps from the river-gate. Her irate husband furiously shoved them toward the boats making them slip in the slime. Bessie made a move to stop him but Mrs. McIver shook her head warningly. The soldiers helped with the loading. The last children were aboard and Catherine McIver had also embarked when Bessie turned around and started to walk back up the pier steps.

"And where do *ye* think yer going, Bessie lass?" asked McIver.

"Back to the fort, of course. You know, you're proper muddy don'tcha, Uncle Angus? Did you trip then?"

"Never ye mind, lassie. Yer a-going aboard with Auntie there."

"No, that I ain't."

Bessie had made up her mind long ago she would not leave the fort without Dicky and had even planned her strategy for remaining.

"Someone's got to look after Daddy and Pauline and you and Uncle Peter, right Uncle Angus?"

McIver looked at her with a strange expression.

"Look after me?"

"Yes, Uncle Angus," Bessie said brightly. "You and all the men that defend the fort."

"Oh, all right, lassie, go on up. I'll finish things here."

Bessie continued up the steps to the river path. When she reached the gate she turned and looked back. The boats with the last children had disappeared into the darkness. The two young soldiers still stood on the pier holding lanterns. She squinted into the darkness for McIver.

But Uncle Angus was gone.

Chapter 29

The next morning broke with a vengeance.

With the first light of dawn, Jacques Villeaux's cannon opened up from the captured east battery and every ten minutes a cannonball thundered onto the fort. The Residency was severely damaged. Gaping holes appeared in the garrison walls. The parade-ground, which bore the brunt of the firing, began to resemble the surface of the moon. Rahamat Khan's forces moved up The Avenue to attempt to force the east gate and scale the walls. Major Morley, now in charge of all troops inside the fort, lined the ramparts with soldiers who showered the exposed Indians with musket fire and inflicted heavy casualties. Yet the enemy came on. Then the Bengal Army deployed an ancient form of attack to force soldiers from castle walls, fire arrows. A phalanx of archers stood behind smoking cauldrons, lit oil-soaked wads on their arrowheads, and launched them toward the fort. Benjamin reacted hurriedly. Teams of fire-fighters were drawn from ships' companies and pressed into action with buckets and swabs. Even though they were mostly successful in defusing the threat of fire, some structures, including the guest quarters, where Prince Ajoy Sena had once brought Pauline, began to burn. The din of musketry and cannon fire was continuous.

In the middle of the tumult, several people looked for Richard Armstrong. But the Governor of Fort William could not be found.

***

The Governor of Fort William had tottered out of the late-night Council meeting a completely broken man. His only wish was to find a hole in the ground, disappear rabbit-like down it, and be insulated and safe. He blundered out of the chamber desperately looking for a way to run and looked with horror upon the mass of refugees in every direction. Then he heard Morley, that insufferable busybody, coming after him with yet another problem. Armstrong quickly retreated down the colonnade steps. He wanted a cool quiet dark soothing place to rest his overworked mind, his aching body and his embattled soul.

The wine cellar!

That was it!

Actually, it wasn't really a wine cellar but a section of the underground passages of the warehouse below the parade-ground that had been specially set aside for his precious supply of Madeira and Bordeaux. Like a thirsty horse scenting water he quickly went down the steps to the landing that led to the river-gate behind the fort, and then followed another set of steps to the passageway below. Reveling in its cool peacefulness, he entered the dark tunnel-like entrance and felt his way along one of the walls in the direction that he knew would lead to his cellar. Suddenly he tripped and fell over something soft. A woman's squeal of pain startled him and then a child's protesting cry. Even here, he thought, they're even here! In his very own cellar. How dare they? He lashed out in blind rage and his fist landed by chance in the woman's yielding stomach. She cried out once more in agony and fled. Armstrong sat on the floor trying to catch his breath and his eyes gradually adjusted to the darkness. A torch that flared at the entrance of the passageway cast a very dim light but he made out the bent-over form of the woman he had struck going deeper into the tunnel. And then more *sari*-wrapped corpse-like forms began to appear out of the gloom. The ones close to him had sat up and were watching him warily. Several had children clutched to their breasts. The distant torchlight was reflected in their eyes giving them a ghostly look. Frantic with aversion, Armstrong shouted all the obscenities he knew. Then he got up and walked to his cellar while the refugees in his path retreated.

Armstrong suddenly lost his temper.

Swearing, he rushed forward and hit out at those that were within his reach, raising howls of pain. Then he half-walked half-ran the last fifty feet until he came to a locked cage-like alcove in the wall of the passage. He flailed at the women who were around the alcove. They scattered, catching blows from a fist or a boot.

By now the refugees were all awake but instead of fleeing they regrouped and watched him from a safe distance. Standing in front of his alcove the Governor railed at them and made short ineffectual darts. Finally resigning himself to their presence and grumbling and complaining, he unlocked his cellar and went in. Then he locked it from the inside and brandished the key at the onlookers who had now approached almost to the barred door.

"Vermin! Bitches! Cows! Get away! It's mine. Shoo!"

But the women came closer and watched him with interest. Their shadowy faces were covered by folds of *saris*. Curiosity was evident in their hollow eyes. The older children came all the way to the bars and gazed in wonderment at the fat hatman whom many had now recognized as the great *Laat-sahib*. No one made a sound. After a while, Armstrong shrugged and sat down on a stone ledge and pulled a bottle out of the wooden rack. He found a corkscrew and popped the cork. The massed humanity jumped back at the sound.

Armstrong sniggered at his audience. Then he tilted the bottle to his lips and the tart red liquid poured down his throat and brought heavenly relief. He turned his back to the crowd and drank another draught and the ugly world receded. He finished the bottle in three more gulps and put it down with a deep sigh. Bliss! He popped another bottle and leaned back against a supporting column and put his feet up. He felt comfortable and drank the second bottle more slowly and put it down on the stone floor. Then he drank a third. And before long Richard Armstrong was fast asleep, his breathing settling into in a resonant snore. The throng of dirty ragged women and children watched the *Laat-sahib* for a little longer and then they too settled outside the cellar door, as though on guard, and joined him in slumber.

Among the women at the door to the cellar was Kajal Lata, John Wolfe's missing dancer-mistress.

***

While the Governor of Fort William and his entourage slept contentedly, a tremendous battle was raging above them. Attack after Indian attack was repulsed from the eastern walls of the garrison. To shoot down at the Indian troops trying to scale the walls, the European soldiers had to stand up and expose themselves to enemy fire. As a result losses to both sides during this phase of the battle were severe. Villeaux's cannon would sometimes land a ball in a crowded section of the ramparts with horrendous results. The occasions when this happened were rare because the same buildings that prevented the big guns of the fort from being trained on the enemy had the same adverse effect on the French artillery. By this time most of the houses of White Town were burning or in enemy hands. On the southern side of the fort the Nawab's colors flew above the house where the Clarksons had lived. Other Company houses were either shells or had flames pouring out of their windows.

Rahamat Khan at last decided that the fight for the east

gate was not worth the losses and so, while keeping up a barrage on that front, he shifted the emphasis of his attack onto the southern side and closer to the river. Under relentless fire, the south battery, which had heretofore seen minimal action, was abandoned. Lieutenant O'Malley withdrew to the Company House and joined forces once more with Captain Glynnis. The two young officers knew it was to be a life-and-death battle for the vital structure. If it fell, the narrow strip of land that separated the fort from the river would be in enemy sights and retreat for the remaining Europeans from garrison to ships would be cut off.

Two twelve-pounders had been hauled back from the south battery to the ground floor of the Company House. One was manned by Master-gunner Bracken and the two Dutchmen who had been with him the previous night, and who had overpowered and murdered Corporal Wellman. During a lull in the battle Bracken looked malevolently at Dicky. Captain Glynnis represented authority, and after his knife injury last night which he mistakenly assumed was inflicted by Benjamin, Irish Bracken was determined to stamp out all British authority in the fort.

Inside his jacket pocket, Bracken fingered a piece of paper that a secret messenger had just brought him. It was a reply to a note he had sent to an aide of the Nawab earlier that morning by the same messenger.

"Jest ye wait, me Welshy popinjay," Bracken whispered and grinned diabolically at Dicky's back. "We'll see who's in charge here."

***

Like Bracken, Corporal Riley was also an Irishman. He was barely twenty years old and attached to the Fort William armory. The complete opposite of Bracken, Corporal Riley was conscientious and hard-working. But right now he had a serious problem. He needed to deliver an important message to a senior member of the Executive Council. He went looking for one but to his surprise they all seemed to have suddenly disappeared. This was very strange. His own chief, Captain Muldoon, was outside the fort at the north battery. He looked for Colonel Linnington, but could not find him. He looked for McIver and Armstrong, and could not find them either. Where *were* all the important people when you needed them, he asked a squad of soldiers on patrol. He received several different answers, many jocular, but none were useful. With a frown on his face Riley continued his search. He had no time to waste on pointless humor.

At last he came across Benjamin Morley near the *kala agar,* a concrete vault by the side the parade-ground. Benjamin had come to check whether Bracken and the other miscreants had been placed there under arrest. To his disgust there was no one inside.

"Sir!"

Benjamin turned.

"Yes, Corporal?"

"Sir, I'm looking for the Colonel."

"As a matter of fact, Riley, I am too. By the way, do you know where Corporal Wellman is?"

Riley shook his head.

In the surrounding chaos, the discovery of Wellman's corpse had not been publicized. Riley looked at Benjamin speculatively. Mr. Morley was a Council member. Should he describe the problem to him? He decided not to. Mr. Morley was a major, but not a real one. And he was not a very senior Company officer either and only a trade councilor, whereas his was a military matter.

"Sir, do you know where the Guv'nor's at?"

"No, I don't. No one's seen him all of today."

Riley again debated whether to tell Benjamin.

"What is it, Corporal?"

Riley decided to try once more to find Armstrong. If he was unsuccessful Morley would have to do.

"Sir, do you know where the Guv'nor could possibly be?"

Benjamin's mind was on the rapists of the night and he did not want to prolong this conversation. He told Riley that Armstrong was last seen going down the colonnade steps.

Riley turned on his heel and walked across the parade-ground and into the galleries and threaded his way between native women and children silently suffering the midday heat. He reached the steps above the colonnade and went down to the river-gate.

"Have you seen the Guv'nor?" he asked Shipling.

"Aye, sir, that I have," replied Shipling helpfully, "but not today."

Riley bit back an oath. The pressure of battle appeared to have made everyone idiotically witty all of a sudden.

"He was seen coming down those steps before the evacuation. Good God, Shipling! Did he leave with the women?"

"No, sir, he dinna. I was there. But Mr. McIver, he did."

"Oh, Old Mac did, did he?"

Riley's long-held opinion of the scheming Scotsman was confirmed.

"Where could the Guv'nor be?" he said more to himself.

Shipling knew the area around the narrow alleyway very well. "Sir," he said. "It ain't likely, but if he came down here, he may've a-gone into yon passage."

Riley and Shipling together went down the steps and into the dark tunnel below the parade-ground. They waited a minute for their eyes to adjust. It was still gloomy inside but the sunshine at the entrance made the tunnel much brighter than the night before. Its vile vermin-infested smell mingled with the rank odor of human urine. They passed refugees lying along the sides and presently came to the cluster outside Armstrong's cellar. Some of the women there awoke at their footsteps and called out to each other and moved away. The two soldiers came up to the bars of the cellar and recognized the recumbent figure of their chief-of-station. One each of Armstrong's legs and arms hung down from the ledge atop which he was sprawled. His chin was buried in his chest and he snored loudly. Three opened wine bottles stood on the floor beside him.

For a moment Riley and Shipling studied the sleeping man thoughtfully. Then Shipling tried to open the gate. It was locked from inside.

"Sir!" called Riley, his voice echoing eerily.

Armstrong did not stir.

"Sir! Open the gate!"

No response.

The two men looked at each other and nodded.

"*Sir!*" they shouted in unison.

A few children around them giggled.

Armstrong stirred and settled more comfortably on the ledge. They tried calling him twice more. The only effect was the increased merriment of the watchers. Riley asked Shipling to wait and went outside. He returned with a long stick and poked the Governor in the chest with it. Armstrong swatted at the spot without awakening. The women and children doubled over with laughter. Riley set his jaws grimly. This sort of undignified behavior could not continue. He yelled at the refugees and they withdrew a short distance, regrouped, and came back, unwilling to miss the entertainment. This time Riley poked the Governor hard in the stomach. Armstrong muttered angrily but still did not open his eyes.

"*Wake up, sir!*"

The soldiers shouted together and applied the stick at the same time.

Richard Armstrong awoke.

"Huh?" he said groggily as he struggled to sit up.

"Open the gate, sir!"

Armstrong blinked at them.

"What's happening? What?"

"Where's the key, sir? We must get you out."

"Key?"

Riley swore in frustration.

Shipling spotted a big brass key lying on the ledge. Armstrong had been sleeping on it. With the stick he dragged it forward and it clattered on the floor. While Armstrong rubbed his eyes, they pulled the key toward the gate.

"Sir, there's the key. Please open the gate."

Armstrong bent and groped for the key, picked it up and unlocked the gate.

The crowd came closer.

"Are you all right, sir?"

"Yes, yes! Who're you? Where am I?"

"Connor Riley, corporal, garrison armory, sir. This is Ensign Shipling. You're in the passage below the parade-ground, sir. I have urgent news for you."

"Where is everyone?" Armstrong peered at the crowd of women. "Where's Martha? Is she here?"

"These are refugees, sir. The English women and children have been evacuated."

"Good God! Really? Are we in trouble? Women, children, evacuated?"

"Yes sir. We *are* in serious trouble. We're out of powder, sir."

Shipling gasped in horror. But the impact of the words had not registered on Armstrong.

"Where is everybody?" he asked.

"We're out of powder, sir," Riley raised his voice. "We've no more ammunition."

Armstrong stared at him blankly.

"All's lost, sir!" Riley said dramatically.

At last Richard Armstrong understood and just for a moment everything remained frozen.

Then from behind the soldiers there was a loud wailing cry in a female voice that raised goose pimples on Benjamin's arm.

"*Shesh! Shesh! Shob shesh!*"

The cry came from a single refugee woman. Everyone's head snapped around at her.

Armstrong and Shipling did not understand the Bengali words, but Riley did. They meant, `The end! The end! Everything's finished!'

It was an unfortunate co-incidence that in the crowd of watchers outside the cellar there was the only Indian woman in the fort who understood English. She was Kajal Lata, Councilman Wolfe's lover. Before Riley could stop her she screamed out the words again and again at the top of her voice and ran for the exit. Riley made a desperate attempt to grab her but Kajal Lata eluded him and ran shrieking out of the passage. The other refugees, panic-stricken, ran wildly after her taking up her wailing cry.

The three men were left alone in the passage.

Chapter 30

Meanwhile Captain Glynnis was embroiled in one more battle against impossible odds. With him was Lieutenant O'Malley, his partner in victory at Perrins Redoubt. The building they were defending, the Company House, was a two-storied brick structure used for housing visiting dignitaries and their staff. Robert Clive had stayed there, as had the Wainwrights. It rose above the south bastion of the fort. On its northern side it overlooked the river, the Governor's Wharf, and the steps down from the colonnade and the alley leading to the river-gate that Ensign Shipling patrolled. To its immediate south was a palisade of tall staves erected by Kyle's *coolies* as the second line of defense from the south. The fall of the south battery had now made this palisade and the Company House the first line of defense.

The battle for the Company House, however, did not follow the pattern of Perrins Redoubt. Realizing its strategic significance, Rahamat Khan threw all his might into its capture. Firing, reloading, retreating, regrouping, firing and reloading again, Dicky and his men fought like lunatics to hold their position for three hours against intense sustained fire. Their original strength of fifty was reduced by twelve. Just before midday, in a frantic attempt to capture the building before the afternoon disengagement, Rahamat Khan redoubled his offensive. A hail of cannon and musket fire from The Park and from rooftops of the still-unburnt houses around it fell on the Company House. Three more European soldiers were killed and ten wounded. Realizing that at this rate they would soon be decimated, Dicky unwillingly decided the Company House had to be abandoned. He sent two men to the fort to request covering fire. A half-hour later enemy fire slackened indicating the afternoon siesta. Simultaneously, a message arrived from Colonel Linnington giving them permission to retreat.

And so, with the Company House abandoned, their escape route to the river was now under enemy control.

Wearily Dicky's men made their way to Shipling's gate and were just beginning the laborious climb to the parade-ground when there were shouts and screams from above and before they could react a flying wall of humanity cascaded down the steps toward them. The confused and shell-shocked soldiers were swept aside by the flood of running women. Two soldiers tripped and fell on the steps and were trampled to death by hundreds of bare feet. Dicky flattened himself against the wall to let the mass of refugees flow past him and out of the open river-gate. All the women ululated *"shesh, shesh, shob shesh"* in unison like a sad refrain. Dicky was awed by the expression in their eyes, wild, dilated, filled with the headlong fixation of animals trying to escape a predator, prepared to wipe aside anything that stood in the way.

It was a repeat of the panic-stricken night of the great fire. Only now there was a irresistible urge to flee the very edifice they had so convulsively sought as a haven.

Shiraj Doula's wish of three days past was coming true.

The narrow river-gate momentarily checked the rush and there was some frantic pushing and shoving. Several children were crushed in the frenzy. And then the crowd poured onto the river-path. It checked again, looking for a way to escape. The Governor's Wharf and its cluster of boats was the obvious choice and the women swarmed toward the pier. But the boatmen, taking one look at the huge fear-maddened crowd, untied their boats as fast as they could and poled away. In spite of this, the first of the women, some still clutching smothered babies, reached the pier before the last boats had managed to cast off and threw themselves aboard before the boats drew away. Those behind tried to jump the widening gap and screamed as they fell into the river. Still others were forced off the edge of the wharf by the press of arrivals and foundered helplessly in the mud. Then the main body of the crowd realized that the wharf was of no further use and the pressure slackened. Some women in the water scrambled out while others were drawn away by the current and drowned.

The mob re-focused its attention on a large unattended barge that was tied to a tree root upstream from the pier.

It was a long barge used for transporting cargo up and down the river. The women reached it and began to climb over the high lip. Having lived all their lives in their homes they were unaccustomed to this activity, but in their desperation most managed to pull themselves aboard and hurry over to the opposite end. Those unsuccessful were brushed aside and used as stepping stones. As a result it became easier for the later women to get onto the barge. Within minutes the barge was full.

There was no way to count the number its passengers, but Benjamin, who had joined with Armstrong and Riley on the landing in the wake of the exodus, estimated it to be around four hundred. The shallow barge was dangerously low in the water and in imminent danger of either being swamped or running aground. No one had thought of cutting the hawser that tied it to shore. With the deck jammed women on the side facing the bank fought tooth and nail to prevent others from boarding. It was nightmarish scene of complete pandemonium. More women and children were losing their footing on the bank and falling into the water.

Benjamin could stand it no longer. A catastrophe was

unfolding right before his eyes. Telling Riley and Shipling to come with him, he dashed down the steps and into the crowd.

"*Shoro!*" he yelled at the women on the bank. *Move!*

Nobody heard him in the pandemonium. Benjamin pointed at Shipling's sword and then at the hawser. Shipling unsheathed his sword, brandished it to scatter the women in his way, and cut the rope. The barge immediately drifted away and evoked a wail of despair the hundreds left behind. Benjamin took Shipling by the arm and quickly led him back to the river-gate before they drew the wrath of the remaining refugees. Riley followed. They re-joined the Governor who was watching the scene bemusedly from the top step. Below them the rudderless barge, crammed with people who knew nothing about navigation, drifted downriver while turning in slow circles. It was now sixty feet from the bank and beginning to pick up speed.

Benjamin heaved a sigh of relief.

But he relaxed too soon.

When the barge was just upstream of the surrendered Company House, there was a shout. A row of heads appeared on the roof of the building and Benjamin saw Indian soldiers gesticulating and pointing at the barge. Then a fire arrow was loosed off. Then another and another. Most missed and fell harmlessly into the river but a lucky one landed on the barge. Benjamin saw the women shrink back from the smoking flaming arrow. The barge heeled over precariously.

"*Hey!* Get back to the other side!" Benjamin shouted even though the barge was two hundred yards away. "They can't harm you!"

It took only another fire arrow to complete the calamity.

The gunwale on the side opposite the riverbank went under and the barge took on a large amount of water. Screaming in fear, the women scrambled away. The barge rocked back menacingly. And then, heavily overloaded to begin with, the additional weight of the water made it sink like a stone. One moment there was a craft in the river laden with frightened passengers, in the next there was a medley of thrashing figures were being pulled under the mud-colored water.

Most of the victims did not know how to swim or to fight the undertow caused by the sinking barge.

Benjamin shut his eyes and then his ears as the cries of the helpless victims reached him. Then with helpless fascination he watched the bodies in the water sink or drift out of sight.

The refugees who had not made it onto the ill-fated barge or had not been trampled in the rush to board, slunk past him, around the broken bodies on the steps, and back into the fort. The eyes that looked at him momentarily from the faces hidden as ever by the ends of *saris* were wild and glazed.

Five minutes later all that floated on the river were a few clumps of brightly-colored cloth and extinguished arrows.

***

The events of that horrific afternoon were far from over.

Benjamin's attention was still riveted to the tragedy when he heard a shout from above. He looked up and saw a crowd of assembled soldiers that had been watching the spectacle from the ramparts above. The men were pointing urgently at something upriver.

Benjamin looked along the riverbank and tried to see what had attracted their attention. At first he could see nothing unusual.

"Sir, there!" cried Shipling. "By the main wharf!"

The main pier of Calcutta on the Hooghly River was the Governor's Wharf, recently vacated by the stampede. It was three hundred yards upstream of the fort. Squinting against the sun, Benjamin made out a boat being dragged from a large building just beyond the wharf. This was the home of Colonel Linnington and, since it was inside the second line of defense to the north, it had not succumbed to the enemy.

Not really knowing why, but instinctively feeling that something vitally important was about to happen, Benjamin ran down the steps and out of the river-gate and half-walked half-ran up the path in the direction of the boat. As he neared he saw that an uniformed soldier and the Colonel had almost succeeded in dragging the small boat to the water's edge.

"Hie!" Benjamin exclaimed breathlessly. "Colonel, what are you doing? Where are you going?"

The two men looked at him in surprise. Then they increased their efforts to launch the boat.

Benjamin reached the pier and realized what was happening. The garrison commander was trying to desert to the ships even in full view his men. If he succeeded, the effect on the morale of the garrison would be devastating. It became clear to Benjamin that he *had* to be stopped.

"Sir," he shouted as he ran the last steps along the big pier. "You can't leave us."

"Get away, you meddling fool," snarled the colonel, his face red and sweating with exertion. *"Pull, damn you!"* he bellowed at the soldier.

The boat landed in the water with a splash.

"Sir! Listen to me. Stop! Please."

Benjamin grabbed Linnington's sleeve. The colonel hit out and Benjamin stumbled backwards but miraculously kept his footing. The soldier was now in the boat. Linnington was about to jump in when Benjamin grabbed his arm and holding on like a leech, pulled him backwards and away from his boat, impervious to the blows that the colonel rained on him.

"Help me, you fool!" Linnington bawled at his aide.

At that moment there were running footsteps on the pier and a pair of hands gripped Benjamin by his neck and coat collar and pulled him backwards. Startled, Benjamin let go of Linnington and turned to defend himself from the new threat. With surprise on his side, his attacker pushed Benjamin violently away. Benjamin lost his footing and fell sideways on the pier. Instinctively he protected his head, but banged his shoulder painfully on the unyielding stone. The sky and trees spun before his eyes.

When at last he shook off the mist, rolled over and looked toward the river, he saw three men in the boat that was fast pulling away from shore. The soldier was rowing. Colonel Linnington sat in the bows. Beside him sat Governor Armstrong.

"Come back!" Benjamin's yell came out as a croak. Punch and Judy stared stonily back. Benjamin reeled back in defeat.

Then he was being lifted to his feet by Ensign Shipling and surrounded by soldiers who carried him back to the fort, stopping periodically to hurl obscenities at the rowboat as it converged on *Beowulf.*

Chapter 31

What happened next was a complete paradox, but perhaps no more illogical than the long and erratic sequence of events that had led to the current state of affairs. The ascension of a volatile despot who replaced a progressive monarch, and whose immediate clash of temperament with a pompous and self-serving foreign chief was not improbable. Their standoff had been heightened by the absence of the only man, when Benjamin was out big game hunting, who might have prevented Armstrong's original truculent letter to the Nawab. But how could one explain the simultaneous arrival on the scene of Prince Ajoy, an enemy of the despot, which caused the standoff to escalate further? And what about the failure of the *coup* because of rare vigilance of an ordinary palace guard? And then there were the depredations of the unconnected Kali-worshippers which led up to the calamity of the panic-stricken refugees, which in turn allowed the top leaders of the fort to desert?

None of these events were premeditated.

Benjamin sat dejectedly on the top step above the river-gate with his eyes closed. He was drained of every emotion and held his throbbing head in his hands. His shoulder and ankle hurt abominably. A complete emptiness filled him. The emptiness of defeat.

Around him soldiers still screamed incoherently at their chiefs who were now aboard *Beowulf*. And then, horror of horrors, in front of their eyes, the ship began to move. Her slow but definite downriver progress was emulated by the other European ships. The soldiers' shouts took on a note of hysteria.

In another moment there would be mutiny.

It was young Dicky Glynnis who saved the day. He, alone among those present in the crowd, was able to grasp the significance of Benjamin's frantic attempt to stop the desertion, an event that had been witnessed by the entire garrison. Dicky held a hurried conversation with Clarkson and O'Malley, and hurried over to Benjamin. What he told him made Benjamin forget his desolation.

Captain Glynnis jumped on the parapet in front of the assembly.

"Men!" roared Dicky in his best parade-ground voice.

The soldiers turned their attention to him.

"We been betrayed!"

The soldiers on the rampart replied as one man.

"Aye!"

"Men! Punch and Judy done fled!"

"Aye! Fled!"

"They be traitors!"

"Aye! Traitors! Aye!"

"They be cowards!"

"Aye! Cowards!"

"British soldiers! We ain't cowards. We shall fight!"

"Aye! Fight! Fight!"

"We don't need no turncoats! We need leaders!"

"Aye! Leaders!"

"We *have* a leader! Major Morley. Our new Guv'nor!"

There was a moment of astonished silence.

"He has my trust, men!" Dicky proclaimed.

"And mine!"

O'Malley joined Dicky on the parapet.

"And mine!"

The elderly magistrate heaved himself up beside them.

"Men! Does he have your trust?" bellowed Dicky.

"*Aye!*"

There was tumultuous approval.

***

At that crucial moment of transition the only thing the unhappy Benjamin could do to revitalize himself was pour warm river water on his head from the nearby fire-fighting buckets. It had a miraculous effect! The accumulated grime and exhaustion were swept away. The throbbing in his head disappeared and even the pain in his shoulder lessened. Benjamin wondered for a brief moment whether there was truth in the healing power of the waters of Mother Ganges. But he had no time to dwell on this before he was bodily lifted onto the vacated parapet.

The new Governor stared dumbly at the crowd while droplets of water ran down his face and neck and mingled with the perspiration under his shirt. His hair stuck wetly to his forehead. The upraised faces of the men were expectant. They were waiting for a speech. Beyond the crowd he saw several huddled Indian survivors devastated by the loss of the barge. And then, to his dismay, he noticed English women. So all their womenfolk had not been evacuated! Squinting against the sun, he recognized Bessie and a downcast Pauline. Two others he recognized as wives of English soldiers. Were there more?

Benjamin took a deep breath.

Before him stood people, men and women, who depended on him at the most vulnerable moment in their lives. They had just been brutally betrayed by those they had trusted. Their garrison could fall at any moment. Further evacuation was impossible as the Governor's Wharf was in musket range of the enemy-held Company House.

What could *he* do?

Benjamin looked around uncertainly. The guns were silent. Where was the enemy? Then he remembered that it was the time of the siesta. He pulled out his watch. They had two precious hours before the siege would resume. What miracle could he perform in two hours? He looked back at the river. *Beowulf* and four other ships were still visible. He looked again carefully. *Wait!* Was it true? Had they stopped moving? *Yes!* It was true. The ships had stopped. Perhaps they had been scared by the fire arrows and had decided to wait out of range and send boats at night to evacuate them. But why didn't the ships help more actively? Why didn't...

A thought hit him like a bolt of lightning.

Europa!

They had all completely forgotten *Europa.*

Benjamin swung around.

"Men!" he roared exultantly. *"We can do it!"*

Instantly he had their rapt attention.

"Look! The ships have stopped moving."

The assembly turned to look and there were exclamations of hope.

"We shall board at night. We must hold firm now."

He waited a moment.

"Men! *Europa's* not there. I need a volunteer to summon *Europa.*"

There was moment of stunned silence and then a burst of cheering as the import of his words sank in. Hats flew in the air. Men danced and whooped. Benjamin looked at the women. Pauline's face was still a picture of despair but the other three were smiling. Then his eyes fell on a hulking figure on the sidelines and he gasped in shock. Hate and a strange gloating that was evident in Bracken's visage was in direct contrast to the excitement around him. The outlaw was still at large. Damn! More trouble. Benjamin cursed the worthless Linnington for not jailing the man. Then he was distracted by a clamor from the crowd. All of them wanted to volunteer! Finally two men, a lance corporal and Lionel Smith, the heroic messenger of Perrins Redoubt, were dispatched to fetch *Europa*. The crowd cheered from above as they were poled away on a country boat.

There remained the question of powder. In their euphoria the crowd had forgotten about that crisis.

"Corporal Riley!"

The young soldier stepped forward nervously. He was overwhelmed by the cataclysmic effect of his dutiful message to the Governor. The crowd had stopped cheering. Connor Riley hoped he was not about to be lynched.

"Corporal," said Benjamin loud enough for everyone to hear. "We cannot be *completely* out of powder. Check the stores once more. See if there are caches in special places. We *must* hold until nightfall."

Corporal Riley departed on the double.

Benjamin and Dicky began to issue instructions.

The men were told they had to defend the south gate at all costs, all the while conserving ammunition that had already been distributed. Somebody pointed out that the Company House, being at a higher vantage-point, prevented the defense of the gate, and that they had been lucky that the building had been surrendered just at the noon siesta hour. Even to Benjamin, unused to military matters, the course of action was obvious. To survive the day they *had* to hold the south gate. And to hold the south gate the Company House *had* to be neutralized. He said as much to Dicky. There was a hurried conference and as a result two nine pounder cannon were dragged across from the north battery. Captain Muldoon, in command of that post and removed from the events of the afternoon, had protested but was ignored. His position had seen little action and he had to surrender his guns.

Things happened very quickly thereafter.

Corporal Riley came sprinting back from the armory accompanied by a fresh-faced soldier.

"Sir," cried the jubilant Irishman. "I'm terribly sorry, sir. We have powder! We have powder! Young Ogilvey here found a week's stock in the ante-room."

"Hooray for Ogilvey!" applauded everyone.

And as if to mark the magnitude of the news there was a tremendous thunderclap and the reinforced English guns at the south gate simultaneously opened up on the Company House at point blank range. There were startled shouts from the enemy. A cannonball landed on the roof of the building and started a fire. Two balls smashed through second story walls. A fourth demolished the balcony overlooking the river.

Within moments the Company House was crumbling in flames.

Chapter 32

"My Lord!"

Shiraj Doula looked up irritably.

In his royal tent the Nawab was busy reading Rahamat Khan's latest report from the front. The scroll in his hand contained stirring news. The Company House had fallen and the end of the siege was imminent. The message also contained infuriating news. The soldiers had fired upon and sunk a barge carrying hundreds of women.

He was debating how to censure his men when Gaffar spoke.

"My Lord, the Jagat Seth requests audience."

Shiraj Doula was surprised. What could the banker want just as he was poised on the brink of a historic victory? The last things Shiraj wanted to discuss were money and commerce. His first impulse was to order the Jagat Seth to go away.

"My Lord," Gaffar added. "Seth-*ji* has critical news."

Shiraj Doula stroked his thin beard. The banker was the confidant of both warring sides. Could he be carrying a message of surrender from the hatmen? Maybe an offer of gold in exchange for safety of hatmen?

The Nawab made up his mind.

"The Jagat Seth shall be summoned."

The Banker of Bengal entered the decorated tent and stood for a moment before his overlord, then he bent down ponderously and touched his forehead to the ground. The Nawab was treated to a pleasant aroma of rose and betel nut. The banker's servant remained at the entrance and offered the same obeisance.

Gaffar took up his usual station by his overlord.

"Praise be to Lord Rama," opened the Jagat Seth.

Shiraj Doula grunted.

"By God's grace you are winning, my Lord. I am happy."

"Oh?" Shiraj said sarcastically. "Does it matter to the Jagat Seth who prevails? He shall be equally happy if the accursed foreigners win."

The Jagat Seth was mortified.

"*Narayan! Narayan!* What are you saying, my Lord? The Jagat Seths shall prosper only as long as Murshid Quli Khan and his illustrious descendants grace the throne of Bengal. I cannot think of Bengal without a Moghul Nawab."

When Shiraj Doula looked at him keenly the banker quaked. Had he gone too far in his flattery? He recalled the last time he had played a game involving the Nawab and the British. That was when he had taken the hatmen to Murshidabad to win cotton discounts. He clearly remembered the Nawab's piercing eyes drilling into his back. Would he be as lucky this time? Shiraj Doula looked away disinterestedly at last.

"Say what you want and leave me."

"I want nothing, my Lord. I come bearing a message."

The Nawab's interest returned.

"Ah, a message. From the hatmen? Are they prepared to surrender?"

"No, my Lord. I...I mean...the message is not from the hatmen. I have not mingled with the enemy. I hear they have been given a good beating."

The Nawab waved his hand brusquely. His men were dying! He certainly hoped the enemy had been being given more than a 'good beating'. He impatiently wondered why people always dithered in his presence.

"Seth-*ji shall* tell the Nawab why he is here and what 'important' message he brings. And then he shall be gone. The Nawab of Bengal has matters to attend to that are also important."

"At once, my Lord. I bring a message from Prince Ajoy Sena."

"The traitor!"

"Prince Ajoy is prepared to capitulate."

"Where is the turncoat?"

"My Lord, Prince Ajoy has said he will surrender once you grant him two requests."

The Nawab's temper flared.

"Never! A conspirator dares ask favors?"

"My Lord, the requests are reasonable."

Shiraj Doula's eyes blazed.

"The Nawab decides which requests are reasonable!"

In spite of the Nawab's fury the Jagat Seth rejoiced inwardly. It was going according to plan. He and Ajoy had rehearsed the possible approaches many times over.

"Should my Lord not hear the requests to decide?"

"All right, all right. Tell me. A dying man's wishes should be respected I suppose."

"The first request, my Lord, is that Raja Ranjit Rai, father-in-law of the prince's own sister, be released."

The Nawab did not hesitate a moment.

"Granted. What is the second request?"

This was the difficult part.

"My Lord, Prince Ajoy has asked me to ensure that the first request is executed before the second is stated."

The Nawab became livid once more.

"You have the nerve doubt the Nawab's word?"

"No, my Lord. Never. I would never think of such abomination. I am but a messenger."

"Messengers have been executed for less. Far less. Only

your status protects you, Seth-*ji*. But let us get on with it. Gaffar!"

"My Lord?" The gray man inclined his head.

"Gaffar, the chief of the guard will immediately escort the Rai Raja to the river. He will be placed on a boat with armed guards and transported to Neeladri with provisions for his journey."

Gaffar went out. The Jagat Seth was impressed. He had expected the Nawab to be far less tractable.

"Now what is the second request? Or does honorable Jagat Seth wish to witness the Raja boarding his boat?"

"No no, my Lord, I would not dream of it. Prince Ajoy's second request is that the Nawab spare the foreign women and children."

"*Bismillah!* When I have the traitor, the swine, in my hands, I *shall* tear him limb from limb! What does he think of the Nawab? Have I ever had women molested?"

The Jagat Seth said nothing and waited for the latest round of anger to subside. To his surprise the Nawab cooled down quickly. Was he so eager to get his hands on Ajoy that he was making a show of outrage? Or was there some weakness that he had touched? The news of the sunk barge and drowned women had not reached the Jagat Seth yet but the astute businessman filed away this information for future use.

"*Sipah-sala* has reported that all foreign women have left the fort last night," the Nawab said finally. "It was unnecessary. Nawab Shiraj Doula does not ill-treat women."

"The Nawab is most gracious."

"And the Nawab is most disgusted by this trivia. The Jagat Seth is quite aware the Raja was to be held hostage until the dog Sena surrendered. Islam decrees women be treated with dignity. This charade is unnecessary."

"I am but a messenger, my Lord."

"*By Allah!*" Shiraj Doula burst out violently. "You are wasting the Nawab's time! Where is the accursed traitor? If he is not delivered instantly, your life is forfeit."

"He is here, my Lord."

The soft voice came from the shadows.

The banker's liveried servant stepped forward and the lamplight flickered on his brocade waistcoat and silk turban. He looked directly for just a moment into the eyes of his enemy, the eyes that were dulled momentarily by surprise, then he lunged at Shiraj with his drawn knife. The Nawab put out his hands and shrank back with a wheezing sound.

Prince Ajoy Sena raised his knife for the kill.

In the next instant there was an exclamation from the banker and Ajoy felt a flash of intense pain in his side. Then he was violently pushed aside, tripped, and sent spinning to the carpet.

This was the moment for which the gray man lived his life. Before Ajoy could rise Gaffar's dagger was at his throat. Ajoy closed his eyes and waited for the spurt of pain that would signify the end. It was over.

But Gaffar did not kill him. Instead, he put his knee on Ajoy's chest and, keeping the knifepoint as his throat, looked up at his master.

The decision to kill belonged to the King of Bengal.

Shiraj Doula was breathing raggedly while he recovered from the shock. His face changed from the pallor of dread and darkened with anger. For a full minute the scene was frozen. Ajoy felt the pain growing. A warm liquid sensation spread near his stomach.

The Jagat Seth, forgotten, stood ashen-faced.

Shiraj Doula found his voice.

"Guards! Guards! At once! At once!"

Four armed bodyguards rushed into the tent with swords drawn and stopped dead when they saw the scene.

"Hold them!"

Two guards jerked Ajoy to his feet while the others pinned the Jagat Seth by his arms. More guards came in.

Ajoy's eyes were shut and he drooped like a wilted flower. It was the end. He had failed. It was over. His spirit left his body and went to a land far away. *Failure!* Asha admonished him in that land. *Failure! Couldn't do it! Failure! Failure!* Ajoy wanted to die. Why wasn't he dead? His eyes flew open.

"*Couldn't do it! Failure!*" Shiraj Doula stormed at him, his pupils narrowed into glittering points of rage. "You are useless. You have lost. *Again!* You are good for nothing. A failure!"

The guards hauled Ajoy erect and supported him as he sagged. The pain in his side was unbearable.

"What now?" jeered the Nawab. "Where is the bravado? Where is the skullduggery?"

Ajoy wanted to sink like a pool of water into sand.

"When your cohorts couldn't do it, you had to try yourself, didn't you? You're a failure. An abandoned useless failure."

The Nawab turned to the Jagat Seth.

"And Honorable Jagat Seth? You are the last person expected to plot against the Nawab. I am aghast."

Nobody spoke.

Shiraj Doula went into a paroxysm of rage.

"*Both of you will die!*"

Ajoy tried to speak but words would not come. His tongue and lips would not move. The pain in his side was a continuous miasma of agony.

"Your wealth is confiscated!"

The Jagat Seth stared at the ground.

Shiraj Doula spat disgustedly.

"Filthy schemers in positions of power. Remove them from my presence! They shall be held in chains until the Nawab decides on the method of their execution."

The guards began to drag the prisoners out.

"*No!*"

It was a wrenching croak from Ajoy. Everyone stopped.

"Me! My plan!" His words were almost inaudible.

"What does the dog say?" demanded the Nawab. "Hold him up."

"It was only I!" Ajoy mumbled. "Seth-*ji* had no idea."

"What is the villain saying?"

"He is trying to say Seth-*ji* is innocent," said one of the guards holding Ajoy.

"Is that true?" Shiraj rounded on the banker.

The Jagat Seth's sickly face covered a mass of conflicting emotions. Should he claim innocence? He had a wife and many children and many more grandchildren, all of whom depended on his wealth. Prince Ajoy was going to die anyway. He had courted retribution since Alivardi Khan's death. *He* had no dependents. But the desperate way in which Ajoy was trying to save him when they were both guilty filled him with shame. In the end the hereditary survival instinct of the Jagat Seths to side with the winner prevailed.

"My Lord, I agreed only to bring him to your presence."

"Why was he disguised?"

"Disguised? Oh...Prince Ajoy was afraid he would be captured as soon as he was seen. He wanted the Raja released before he surrendered."

The Nawab studied the banker's face dubiously. They were all schemers, these men. Shiraj was certain that the fat money-man was trying to save his own skin. Ordinarily he should be executed. But the Jagat Seth was no ordinary mortal. He was a grand personality. His license to bank and mint money came directly from the Sultan in Delhi. True, the Sultan's hold over his empire had well-nigh disappeared, yet executing the Banker of Bengal would generate ill-will from his subjects and detract from the soon-to-be-gleaned honor of victory over the British. Shiraj Doula thought this through while everyone waited and blood dripped from Ajoy's stomach wound and stained his livery.

"Do you swear you are innocent?"

The Jagat Seth nodded dumbly, his eyes on the flowery design of the Persian carpet.

The Nawab made his characteristic snap decision.

"Honorable Jagat Seth shall be released."

The guards stepped away from the banker.

"Go!"

The Jagat Seth stumbled out not daring to look at Ajoy.

"The prisoner shall be held until his execution is decided."

The guards went out with Ajoy. Only the Nawab and the gray man were left in the royal tent.

"Gaffar-*chacha!*"

Shiraj Doula had not used the uncle honorific since his childhood.

"Yes, my Lord?"

"Gaffar-*chacha,* my grandfather's trust in you is vindicated. I owe you a blood debt."

"I live only to serve, my Lord."

Shiraj nodded then thought for a while.

"The scribe will be summoned."

The Nawab's letter-writer arrived within minutes.

"Scribe! Ask the Chief of Guards to put forth the following proclamation:

> "*The villainous traitor, the last of the rebel Sena clan of Bengal, shall be stoned to death as a common criminal on the ramparts of the fort on the morning after the fall of Calcutta, in full view of his foreign cohorts. This shall be the culmination of our jihad.*'

Chapter 33

At Fort William the destruction of the Company House and discovery of fresh ammunition had breathed new life into the beleaguered troops. Attack after Indian attack was beaten off as the afternoon progressed. Musketeers and gunners picked targets carefully making every bullet and every ball count.

Governor Morley circulated among his new-found charges. He talked to them, encouraged them, and helped with the wounded. Returning to the eastern ramparts that overlooked The Park, he surveyed the Great Tank and the broad Avenue, now littered with putrefying corpses of the enemy. He tried to calculate the magnitude of the enemy's losses. The garrison itself had lost two hundred, perhaps two hundred and fifty men. The enemy had suffered much more grievously as they executed massed approaches over exposed ground. Ten-to-one in losses? More likely twenty-to-one, maybe even thirty-to-one. That would mean any number from two thousand to more than seven thousand enemy soldiers killed. Untold thousands more wounded. He cringed at the astronomical numbers.

But that was only one aspect. The military aspect. The trader in Benjamin considered the mercantile impact of the defeat. If Fort William fell, one day someone would sit down and estimate the enormous loss to British commerce...

***

Amid the monotony of battle the sun gradually faded into a smoky mist that hung over the river. It was still light but with sunset, enemy fire slackened and stopped. Perhaps Rahamat Khan concluded it was unnecessary to overtax himself when he could deliver the *coup de grace* at leisure tomorrow.

Tired, grimy and ragged, the defenders of Fort William wilted on their weaponry. With cessation of hostilities, Benjamin ordered a detail of refugee women to cook rice and lentils using *their* pots and pans. Enveloped in falling darkness and with a cool wind from the river wafting away the stench of death, Europeans and Indians sat down to enjoy their first hot meal in five days. After supper and upon the newly-elected Governor's orders, brandy was broken out for all hands. This was greeted with a loud round of *For he's a jolly good fellow* in Benjamin's honor.

"Oy, suh!" drawled a gunner in boisterous East End camaraderie. "Bully for yer, suh!"

"Good fight today, Guv'nor," a conscript said, respectfully touching his hat.

"We a-goin' to fuck 'em Moors good, ain't we Guv'nor?" crowed a big master-sergeant.

Benjamin shook his head in wonder. What had he done except to infuse his troops with a little resolve, a little foresight, and a genuine concern? And here it was being paid back by a determination and an optimism that had never been evident before. And then, wonder of wonders, as night fell and torches lit up the ramparts, a soldier produced a fiddle and there was a call for the entertainment services of Captain Glynnis. While Benjamin watched, cheers, wolf-whistles, hoots and leers greeted Dicky as he appeared arm-in-arm with Bessie Armstrong. The two other soldiers' wives, their eyes glistening in the torchlight, hung onto their men.

Did these men and women look like they were under siege by tens of thousands of whooping heathens and tomorrow could see them massacred by a rabble?

What a waste, Benjamin lamented. What a terrible, terrible waste! Oh Armstrong, you spineless bastard, what *couldn't* you have accomplished if you had demonstrated even a little mettle?

Then he noticed Pauline standing by herself in the background. He walked over to her and as he did so he made out that she was the one person who was not rejoicing. Her eyes were clouded and her face was seamed and aged by years. He stood beside her and gently put his arm around her shoulders. They stood together and watched as Dicky prepared to sing.

Pauline's body began to shake with suppressed sobs.

"It might be good news, old girl," murmured Benjamin. "We may still get out of this. Prince Ajoy might even now be delivering the fatal blow."

Pauline spun around.

"You...you know?"

Benjamin nodded.

"Yes, I was the first to hear his plan. It was his idea and he was determined to do it with the Indian banker's help." He paused and looked away. "He could be in the lion's den even as we speak."

"Oh, dear God!" Pauline's voice caught in her throat. "I can't stand the suspense. I can't. I can't. When can we get news?"

Benjamin was intrigued by her concern. But before he could phrase his question, Dicky launched into a wistful melody composed by his beloved songwriter, Robert Herrick. Pauline and Benjamin turned to witness the extraordinary spectacle unfolding before them.

Surrounded by desertion, benumbed by destruction, diminished by death, marooned in a hostile disease-ridden country, bereft in a land far away, Dicky Glynnis sang straight from his heart to the yearning faces before him that glowed in the flickering light and dreamed of home.

> *I sing of brooks, of blossoms, birds and bowers,*
> *Of April, May, of June and July flowers.*
> *I sing of May-poles, Hock cards, wassails, wakes,*
> *Of bridegrooms, brides and of their bridal cakes.*

Flooding memories of an England they may never see reduced strong men to tears. The women wept openly. Benjamin felt Pauline sobbing anew and his heart went out to her. A violin played softly and Dicky sang of hedgerows and green fields and the gentle river Avon.

Someone else took up a Macaulay ballad of battles long ago and others joined in with vigor.

> *"Attend, all ye, who list to hear*
> *Our noble England's praise;*
> *I'll tell ye of thrice famous deeds*
> *She wrought in ancient days!*
>
> *Night sank upon the dusky beach*
> *And all the purple sea,*
> *Such a night in England ne'er had been,*
> *Or e'er again shall be.*
>
> *The rugged miners poured to war*
> *From Mendip's sunless caves..."*

The singer went on to the stirring deeds of Belvoir and Lincoln, Skiddaw and Gaunt. Abruptly Pauline became rigid beside Benjamin. He held her tightly and gently pressed her shoulder.

"Look!" he reassured her. "I'm your friend. Remember?"

Pauline turned around and Benjamin was stunned by the haunting intensity of the lovely devastated face. Suffering, hope, tenacity, desolation pulsated across the gray tear-streaked visage and the impossibly huge eyes that were blue-black in the torchlight. Taken aback, Benjamin loosened his hold and stepped away in alarm. *What,* he was about to ask, *what is the matter?* And then he knew. At first he was astonished. Then his surprise passed. Yes, it had been there for some time but he had been too preoccupied to see it. Strangely, he was neither shocked nor jealous because of it. Of course! Ajoy and Pauline. Incurable romantics both. Made for each other! But the utterly impossible setting of their romance made Romeo and Juliet's celebrated tribulations trifling. How hopeless was their love. The yawning gulf of culture and race on opposite sides of an on-going war. Her heartless husband. The child of whom she was unaware. The likelihood of being annihilated at dawn. Her lover, driven to destroy an evil king, may have even now have sacrificed himself so she might live. Could there ever, Benjamin asked himself, could there ever in the history of mankind, could there ever have been a more tortured lover than the forlorn woman before him?

"You love him, don't you?"

It was said very gently but Pauline started violently and stared at him in shock and palpable fear. But when she saw no anger in his face, only a profound understanding and compassion, she cried out and threw herself into his arms, sobbing uncontrollably.

"Oh dear God. I do, Benjamin, I do! I *do* love him. More than anything else in the world. Oh God, please take care of him. Please bring him back!"

Benjamin held her tightly.

Around them the men sang one popular song after another, their voices uniting in rising crescendo. The hours passed. Finally the singing reached its climax and the ramparts of Fort William reverberated with Thomas's evergreen rallying song of English dominance:

"When Britain first, at Heaven's Command,
Arose from out of the azure Main,
This was the Charter of the land,
And guardian angels sang this strain:
`Rule Britannia, Britannia rule the waves,
Britons never will be slaves."

***

The crowd began to break up. Pauline drew apart and listlessly wiped her eyes on her sweat-stained sleeve. Where, wondered Benjamin, was Ajoy? How was he doing? When would the banker's coded message come? What would it be? A banyan leaf signifying success? Or a banana leaf indicating failure?

And most important of all, where, oh where, was *Europa?*

***

Europa was still exactly where she had been for the last five days, hove-to opposite Perrins Redoubt. Her crew were able to hear the sounds of warfare from the fort, but unable to come to its defense.

Europa had not engaged in combat because old Rufus van Holten was dying.

Van Holten was a sixty-year-old Dutchman. He was one of the many who had stayed behind after the French had overrun the Dutch settlement in Bengal several years ago. Van Holten, a riverine pilot, had begun his career guiding heavily loaded barges that traversed the Rhine and Maas river systems between the industrial Westfalen region of Germany and the North Sea port of Maastricht in Holland. He had come to India in the heydey of Dutch exploration in the East Indies and had become an expert on the twists and turns and shifting shoals that characterized the Hooghly River. Rufus van Holten had never failed to give selflessly even when beset by the bitterest gales off the North Sea or the ferocious cyclones that swept the Bay of Bengal. Yet, on this Saturday, the 19th of June 1756, when his services were needed more urgently than at any other time in his life, Van Holten was unable to deliver because he was dying of malaria.

Captain Freddie Wainwright was frantic with frustration. He had heard that malarial fatalities usually siphoned away *early* arrivals to India. The prevalent theory was that after surviving a year or two in the country a visitor developed immunity to the dreaded fever that was endemic to the swampy marshes. It had to be so, Freddie reasoned, or else how could one explain so many natives? Wouldn't they all have died of malaria?

When the Dutchman complained of fever on the day they inched upriver in support of Dicky's company, Freddie had not been overly worried. Van Holten, despite his ailment, had successfully guided the ship along the eight sinuous miles. Then, while cannon boomed on deck and the battle for Perrins Redoubt raged, Van Holten collapsed into his bunk. Four days later when the frantic summons came from the fort, Rufus van Holten was sunk in the last stages of the disease.

Without a pilot the big ship could not navigate the upper Hooghly shoals. In a drastic gamble to save the situation, Freddie ordered the shivering hallucinating van Holten to give directions to a native lascar who professed some knowledge of navigation. Freddie sat at Van Holten's bedside and tried to listen to his tortured description of the river terrain. The words, forced through chattering teeth, were occasionally drowned by explosions from the battle going on downstream. Freddie worried that his own understanding of the dying man's Dutch-accented English, when translated to Bengali for the lascar, might introduce inaccuracies.

When van Holten labored through his last instruction and fell back with his lifeblood ebbing, the sun had set. Even the most valiant or most foolish of captains would not risk moving a ship the size of *Europa* in the fast-gathering darkness. They would have to sail on the morrow and hope for the best.

Late that night Freddie went below having issued orders to weigh anchor at the first hint of dawn.

***

Downstream from *Europa* and aboard *Beowulf*, Maggie spent the night rooted to the for'ard gunwale and agonized for morning to come. Had the fort held out? What was Clarence doing? Was he safe? Or was he lying wounded and bravely suffering in silence and longing for her just as she was longing for him? Throughout the evening she had talked herself hoarse imploring Linnington, McIver and Armstrong to return and relieve the garrison. But having witnessed the tragedy of the women in the barge, the Council members were adamant that the undertaking was highly dangerous. Colonel Linnington opined that the safety of their own women and children were too important to risk a another calamity. Maggie was appalled! Wouldn't the defeat, imprisonment and execution—she could not bring herself to say massacre—of their own men be a calamity too? What about the guns on these very ships? Couldn't *they* join the battle? Linnington explained that their four ships were traders and their guns, unlike *Europa's*, were for defense and not to engage an army that had eighteen pounders and could pick them off like sitting ducks…

"*When?*" she implored as other frenzied wives clustered around. "*When?*"

A rage quite uncharacteristic of Maggie then came upon her and she furiously rounded on the colonel.

"Peter! What on earth has happened to you? And to Richard? And Angus? Clarence is out there. *Fighting!* My Clarence, who has never said an angry word to anyone in his life. Fighting! Dicky and Bessie are there. And Benjamin. And Pauline. They're all there. All those brave young men and women. *Help them, Peter!*"

No one, man or woman, had ever talked thus to Linnington. He flew into a rage and his face became red.

"Are you telling me what to do, Mrs. Clarkson?"

"*Their blood is on your hands!*"

A dam burst inside Maggie. She drew herself to her full four feet ten inches and looked a titan as the tall colonel fell back before her presence.

"You cowards! You have run like craven rats! Whatever happens, there will be a reckoning. The world will be told. What you and Richard and Angus have done will not be forgotten even if I have to go myself and tell the King."

Gentle lovable Maggie raged like a Moses on the mountain. Linnington began to bluster and argue. The women, inspired by Maggie's transformation, pressed their demand for the ships to go in for rescue.

Finally, Maggie with hands on her ample hips, cut through the babble.

"Are you going to get them out, Peter? Say yes or no."

In the silence that followed Linnington looked into the eyes of the angry women and felt shame. The rigid, resentful, unfeeling, upper-class army man in him saw in those eyes the pain and disgust. At last he felt remorse for his act of desertion. The feeling grew and stuck in his throat like a fishbone.

"All right, Mrs. Clarkson!" he capitulated. "We'll get them out if we can. Don't you fret, ladies. Let's see what the morning brings."

Even Maggie had to be satisfied with that.

Chapter 34

Four things happened in quick succession on Sunday morning.

First, the guns of the Bengal Army opened up with a murderous salvo and this time, ominously, the barrage was from the *northern* side of the fort. But to Maggie, aboard *Beowulf,* the gunfire brought a joyous message of salvation. *They've held out!* she rejoiced. *Thank God they're still fighting!* Then she went to find the colonel.

Second, one of the few remaining Indian *péons* inside the fort was given a note by Master-gunner Bracken. The *péon* took the note and went down the steps past the western colonnade and requested permission to leave the fort by the river-gate. Ensign Shipling saw no reason to stop him.

On the path outside, the *péon* passed another Indian hurrying in the opposite direction. The *péon* wondered what could be wrapped in the big folded leaf the man was carrying.

And as bright sunlight flooded the parade-ground a frenzied cry rang out from the northeast bastion and electrified the fort.

"*Ship ahoy!*"

Forgetting the enemy everyone crowded onto the northern

ramparts and watched the tall masts that had become visible around a bend in the Hooghly. *Europa* was still more than a mile away and moving very slowly with all sail except top-gallants furled.

The men cheered lustily.

Simultaneously the enemy fire slackened. The Indians had also seen the ship.

Then, before all eyes of the garrison there appeared an orange flash from *Europa's* side as her first cannon opened up. A moment later they heard its boom and a ball landed in the Hooghly and raised a tall fountain. There was a second flash. This time the shot cleared the river and landed just short of the Indian soldiers massed between the north battery and the fort and showered them with mud and rubble. Their cries mingled with the boom of the twelve-pounder.

There was wild jubilation inside the fort.

"Hooray!"

"Jolly good shot!"

"Not a moment too soon!"

Clarence Clarkson was exulting beside Benjamin.

"Good man, Wainwright! Good man! But he'd had better watch it. He's getting close. No point in landing a ball inside the fort!"

Europa came nearer. There was one more tight bend to negotiate and then she would be in the straight passage leading to Governor's Wharf. *Europa* loosened off another volley which landed short.

There was an answering boom as the French artillery aligned its sights on the ship. The ball flew high over her bows and landed in a big waterspout.

"Come on!" urged the soldiers. "Come on, *Europa!* Stick it to them!"

Two cannon of Muldoon's company in the north battery added to the fusillade pouring on the Nawab's army on the waterfront.

Something made Benjamin turn around and look south.

What he saw made him jump up and down and clutch Clarkson's arm in excitement.

"*Sir! Sir! They're moving in! Look!*"

Clarkson squinted into the sun.

Beowulf was indeed moving slowly upstream. It was difficult to tell because the flowing river could make it appear the ships were moving even if they were not. But it was no mistake. The four English ships *were* moving up to join *Europa*. And then, to cap it all, *Beowulf* fired an audacious cannon. The shot, with incredible luck, landed dead on the Indian soldiers near the south battery. There was a short period of chaos among the enemy and then renewed fire from the Bengal Army. There was cries of pain and consternation as bullets rained down on the British soldiers from housetops on the north of the fort. The garrison regrouped and fired back stoutly. It was now a race against time. Could Rahamat Khan deliver the deathblow before the united firepower of the ships could come to their aid?

And then there was utter and complete disaster.

***

Every eye aboard *Europa* was focused on the savage battle raging around the fort. Watching mesmerized, was the lascar who was the ship's stand-in pilot.

Suddenly there was a grinding tearing sound and *Europa* came to an abrupt halt throwing everyone onto the boards.

"*Hell's bells!*"

Captain Freddie Wainwright picked himself up from the quarterdeck, surveyed the situation and cursed mightily. *Europa* had run aground just as the Bengal Army was coming within range of her fore twelve-pounders. He hurried down to the maindeck and joined the crowd that had gathered at the bows.

Europa was stuck in the mud of the very last shoal they should have gone around.

"You godforsaken heathen dimwit!"

Freddie bellowed in frustration at the lascar who cringed like a beaten dog. His mind raced to find ways of getting the ship afloat.

"All hands to stern!" ordered the captain.

Sailors scuttled to the rear of the ship.

Freddie hoped the increased weight on the stern would raise the front of the hull high enough to free the ship so that the strong current could swing her around into deeper water.

It did not work. The ship remained stranded.

Freddie thought rapidly and decided to try another maneuver.

"Up mainsail!"

Freddie prayed that the shearing motion of the wind, added to the river current and the countervailing weight of the ship's company at the stern would pull them off the shoal. Hands swarmed up the rigging to yardarms. Snow-white canvas of the mainsail billowed out and filled with a crack like a cannon shot. The ship jerked backwards and heeled sickeningly. But still she was held fast by the ooze.

The captain looked around in desperation.

"The anchor, sir!"

It was Midshipman Roberts.

For a moment Freddie looked uncomprehendingly at the young officer.

"By Glory!" he exclaimed as he understood. "It might just work, Mr. Roberts. Good thinking, lad." He turned to the second mate. *"Lower aft anchor! Smartly now."*

The capstan squealed, the heavy chain roared out, and the massive aft anchor splashed into the muddy water behind *Europa*. Freddie gave it a few moments to settle while he ordered all sail on fore- and mizzen-masts raised to add the wind's force to the mainsail.

With all fore-, main-, and mizzen-sails unfurled, *Europa* was rigged as though she was in the high seas ahead of a strong following wind. She pitched and yawed horribly under the opposing forces that buffeted her, but still could not shake off the stubborn hold of the glutinous mud.

Once again enemy fire slackened as Indian attention centered on the unusual activity on the big English ship. From a distance soldiers of the garrison as well as sailors and women clustered on *Beowulf's* rail watched *Europa's* attempts to free herself. But few understood the horrifying implications of what had happened.

Captain Wainwright tried his last gamble.

"Up anchor! Shoulders to it, men!"

Could the pull of the anchor raise the stem just that last bit?

Four strong deckhands put their shoulders to the capstan. Everyone held their breath as the men gritted their teeth and their muscles stood out with the effort to turn the capstan that hauled the anchor chain. Would the keel come clear under push of the wind in her sails, the strong river current, and the counteracting pull of the anchor in the mud?

There was squelching sound from the front of the ship.

It was happening!

The stem rose a few inches.

Then a few more.

There were encouraging cheers.

Europa heeled back with an ominous rasping sound which indicated she had settled further into the shoal.

Cheers turned to groans.

"Belay there! Once more around."

They would try again. Four new hands were assigned to the capstan.

Then the first fire arrow landed on deck.

***

Most of *Europa's* company was clustered around the capstan at the stern or aloft in rigging and yardarms, watching the mud bank on which they were stuck. No one noticed the horde approaching from shoreward. It was yet another manifestation of the unfortunate set of coincidences that had plagued the defense of the fort that today, for the very first time in the battle, the Nawab's forces were concentrated on the northern perimeter of the fort, that is between the fort and *Europa*. As a result, when Rahamat Khan grasped that the dreaded ship had foundered, he immediately rallied his soldiers and ordered them along the riverbank and into the attack.

The tide in the Hooghly was ebbing. With every wave *Europa* settled deeper into the mud.

Ant-like, Indian soldiers swarmed toward the ship, employing the age-old but effective weapon against riverine craft, fire arrows. When the first cry of alarm was raised from the ship's forequarter, it was too late. Arrow after arrow landed on deck and on the sails.

Europa's mainsail started to smolder.

From below a rope was thrown up to the jib that overhung the bank and invaders began to ascend. A deckhand named Snead fearlessly crawled onto the jib boom with a knife in his teeth and cut the rope. With a wild yell the climbing soldiers fell back into the mud. Snead brandished his knife in triumph. Then a musket ball took the exposed sailor in the face and with a gurgling cry Snead plunged into the Indians below.

Another rope was launched and took hold.

This time climbers were covered by musket fire and within minutes there were Indian soldiers on *Europa's* deck.

The smoldering mainsail burst into flames.

The first of the boarders were mowed down by musket fire.

With musket, pistol and cutlass, English sailors were now fighting for their lives. For fifteen terrible minutes a pitched hand-to-hand combat raged on the deck. However it was a matter of time before the overwhelming number of the Indians began to prevail.

Freddie threw down his useless musket and fired both his

pistols. Each knocked down an enemy soldier. More soldiers advanced on him, red-and-green sequined uniforms shining in the sunlight, twirled moustaches smiling hideously. Freddie pitched his pistols at the crowd and retreated until his back was against the mainmast. Orange flames behind him made the captain look as though he were on fire. The crowd closed.

Freddie Wainwright brandished his blood-stained cutlass.

"Come ye blighters!" he roared and thrust and parried. "Benighted heathens! Taste English steel!" He thrust again and ran his cutlass through the chest of a soldier. The soldier screamed like a stuck pig.

Then a musket banged and a bullet lodged in the captain's chest and Freddie died instantaneously.

***

The battle for *Europa* was almost over. Flames from fires in her innards began to pour out of companionways. Sailors began to abandon ship by jumping over the side. Most were killed by the enemy as they landed in shallow water. Only those at the very rear of the ship, who landed in the deeper waters of the Hooghly, managed to evade the enemy and drift downstream with the current. Contrary to popular belief, most sailors did not know how to swim and drowned within minutes.

Midshipman Nathaniel Roberts was one of the few who could swim.

He had supervised the operations with the stern anchor and had thus jumped from the stern and survived. He made an attempt to save a drowning man and just managed to extricate himself from a convulsive grip on his throat.

The thrashing man floated away.

Roberts swam away from the ship. Then he turned and, treading the warm brown water, watched as the burning mainmast fell on the deck with a huge crash and a shower of sparks that were visible even in the bright sunlight. Roberts was a strong swimmer and, allowing for the current, made for landfall in front of the fort. Then he noticed other swimmers from the ship who were floating around him.

Several soldiers had rushed down from the fort to the Governor's Wharf. Some stripped off their boots and jackets and plunged in to rescue those in the water while others commandeered boats.

Five minutes later Roberts was lifted by his shoulders into a boat.

"Shipling, sir, Ensign. Are you a-right?"

Roberts saw a red-haired boy in uniform looking at him worriedly. He felt quite well and said so and the two of them began to pull other soldiers from the river. After they had rescued five men there were no others left to save.

Then they looked toward *Europa*.

Roberts cried out in horror at the sight of the ship that had been his home for the past two years. *Europa* was a spectacular sight, completely engulfed in flames. The clear morning sky was sullied by black smoke from the burning ship pluming over the river. There were loud cracks as deck beams split.

A large crowd of Indians on the riverbank stood and watched the spectacle.

There was an enormous flash followed a moment later by a thunderous report.

Europa's magazine had exploded and broke the tableau.

Indian soldiers, many of whom had been knocked over by the blast, raised a war cry and began to run back toward the fort.

The shattered *Europa* continued to burn.

***

Nathaniel Roberts landed at Governor's Wharf.

He was a taciturn young man and it had all happened too quickly for emotion to have got hold of him. It was only when he reached the top of the long flight of stone steps and Shipling presented him to the new Governor, that Roberts finally broke down. While Benjamin and Shipling supported him, with a heaving chest and in a voice breaking with sadness, Roberts described what had happened.

"She's gone, sir!" he ended. *"Europa's* dead. The cap'n fought to the end, sir. He died with his back to the mast. Snead's gone too. And Bos'n Kelsey, he..."

They were starting by a muffled scream and swung around and saw Pauline. Her face was a mask of horror, her mouth wide open, her eyes wide as saucers. Then the light died from her eyes and she began to fall sideways. Benjamin let go of Roberts, caught her and carried the unconscious girl to the shade of the passageway where Armstrong had his cellar. After a few minutes the three English women arrived, summoned by the faithful Ashraf, and Benjamin reluctantly left Pauline in their care.

Emerging from the passageway a distraught Benjamin found Roberts sitting on the steps where he had left him. To the north, *Europa* was still burning. The rapid succession of setbacks was making his mind reel. Everything seemed cloaked in unreality. Then Benjamin looked southward and could not believe his eyes. *Beowulf* and the other ships were falling back downstream. He ran to the parapet and cursed mightily. Those within earshot stared at their Governor and followed his gaze. Soon their own curses and cries of derision rent the air.

The French artillery began to fire.

Soldiers of the garrison wearily returned to their posts and a dreary exchange of fire continued for some time.

Then three junior officers who had been talking among themselves approached Benjamin.

"Sir," said Lieutenant O'Malley. "We've tried. But we thinks we're done in. The men've 'ad it. It's time we surrendered, sir."

Benjamin nodded. Then he helped Roberts to his feet and pulled out his watch. It was ten o'clock.

"A few minutes, if you please?"

The officers moved away and Benjamin considered his options. They were now about three hundred English, European, Eurasian and Indian men, and four English women left under his command. Their superiors had betrayed them. Their enemy had broken down defenses on all sides. Their retreat to the river was cut off. There were only two choices left. They could fight to the death. Or they could give up and be imprisoned or massacred. Try as he might, Benjamin could not accept either choice. There had to be another option. A way out. There *had* to be! He swore in frustration and looked around. The Governor's elevated Residence had taken several direct cannonball hits and was in shambles. The big ship in the river was becoming a hulk. Huge holes in the fort's masonry testified to the pummeling it had suffered. Dead and wounded were lined up in separate rows under the eastern gallery. Lines of anguish and tiredness marked the face of every man. They were almost out of ammunition and out of options. The world had abandoned them and the enemy was tearing down their doors. And here he was, Governor Morley, second-in-line to the distant earldom of Ashford, as good as on the surface of the moon, about to be overrun and decimated.

Which option should they choose? Which *could* they choose?

No, no, no! They would *not* die like rats in a trap. There *had* to be another way. He debated with himself for a full ten minutes. At last he thought of a third alternative and felt better. *They would surrender honorably!*

They knew, but the Nawab did not, that they were on their knees. Benjamin was aware of the strictness with which Shiraj Doula followed the formal rules of war. *Honor thy enemy,* preached the *Koran*. Fort William would not surrender under fire. Fort William would surrender voluntarily. Honorably. Then their lives would be spared and they would be freed to leave the land. Shiraj Doula would have achieved his objective of driving the *feringhi* away.

The timing of the surrender was vital.

Benjamin found O'Malley and gave him the order to fight on. O'Malley and the other officers glared at their new commander rebelliously, but Benjamin's confident bearing made them hesitate to speak out.

Exactly at noon, when the enemy salvos began to taper off, Benjamin asked O'Malley to attach a white flag to his musket and wave it in the air from the ramparts above the east gate.

Most of the garrison was gathered behind them.

For a long time nothing happened.

O'Malley waved his flag in big sweeping arcs. A few shots stuttered here and there and stopped. Benjamin and his men continued to look in the direction from which Shiraj's forces had first approached along The Avenue.

Finally Benjamin nodded to O'Malley and the lieutenant stopped waving.

More time passed. The men continued to stand and look eastward in the blazing noonday sun.

And then, from the damaged roof of the Company Jail, a white flag was hoisted at the end of a pole. There was no breeze and the flag drooped wearily. The pole was lifted and swung to and fro. Benjamin looked at it carefully and realized that it was not a flag at all, but a torn *dhoti*, pressed into service to acknowledge their offer of truce.

For another moment, a stillness filled the air, during which groans of the wounded from below and the cawing of crows could be heard with complete clarity.

The ragged *dhoti* continued to wave in the air.

Suddenly Benjamin began to laugh.

It was too much!

What better a fitting finale to the whole ludicrous progression of events than some unfortunate soldier having to be stripped to symbolize disengagement? And that broke the spell. The Englishmen cheered and danced in the noonday blaze.

The battle was over and they had survived.

But after the first uproarious excitement the men sobered and an uncanny quiet descended on the fort. Always, during the last week, there was noise: boom of cannon, crackle of musket, rattle of harness, rumble of many people talking, crying of children, yelping of dogs, staccato of orders. Now there was nothing. The people of the fort stumbled around in hushed silence.

Everyone wondered about the same thing.

When would the Nawab of Bengal appear?

And what would he do to them?

Clarkson took Benjamin by the elbow and the two men went down to the parade-ground.

"Great show, Morley. The men have their spirits up."

"Well, sir, it all depends now on the *Nawab's* spirits. I've been told that he treats prisoners honorably."

"What *do* you think will happen? And don't call me sir, young man. You outrank me now."

"Oh, that's just temporary, Mr. Clarkson. If anyone is to be Governor, it should be you. Getting back to the Nawab, I think he will release the women. I'm not sure what will happen to the rest of us."

Clarkson looked toward the river.

His wife must be anxiously waiting and worrying. From his location on the parade-ground Clarkson could not see the ships and tried to imagine Maggie's suspense because of absence of news. Couldn't McIver put out boats for them at night?

"It's terrible." Clarkson shook his head sadly. "It's appalling the way they deserted us after all these years of working together."

"I've been thinking about that," said Benjamin grimly. "When we get out of this ...or should I say `if'?... Anyway *some* of us are going to get out of this alive. And when we do, the message of their incompetence and desertion will be taken to London. They *will* pay! The harm done by weak-minded leaders in positions of authority..."

Chapter 35

To Pauline, time ceased to have meaning. The rise and fall of hopes and fortunes of Fort William swirled by her unnoticed.

The morning's messenger had delivered the folded banana leaf to Benjamin just after *Europa* had been sighted. The banana leaf indicated that Prince Ajoy's attempt on the Nawab's life had failed. The joy Benjamin had felt upon seeing *Europa's* majestic return at once turned to sorrow. Poor Ajoy. While *Europa* approached he stood alone thinking of their brief but eventful association. He had felt a camaraderie with the prince that he had not felt for anyone else in Calcutta, European or Indian. He remembered the moment vividly when they had simultaneously raised their muskets in the face of the charging elephant. Ajoy had been strong and brave but he had taken on impossible odds all his life and he had made the ultimate sacrifice in his final mission. Benjamin's heart quailed as he tried to think of how he would give the news to Pauline after what he had learned last night. But he had to and quickly, before coordination of garrison fire with *Europa's* required his attention. He could not keep the news from her when any minute could be their last.

Benjamin walked around trying to find Pauline and

stumbled over a box and dropped the banana leaf. The big green frond fell open. As he bent to pick it up Benjamin noticed something scrawled on it.

His heart leaped.

A message!

But it was written in Bengali script. In a welter of agitation he looked around for someone who could translate. He saw Ashraf nearby but Ashraf was illiterate. On Benjamin's urgent order, the boy scampered away and returned with an Indian conscript. Benjamin pointed out the lettering to the man.

"Jibito," said the conscript.

"What?"

"Bondi."

"What the devil is he saying?" Benjamin asked Ashraf in agonized impatience.

Ashraf looked back at him blankly.

"Jibito bondi," the man repeated, pointing at the leaf.

Benjamin did not know the meaning of the words. He couldn't stand the suspense any longer.

"Someone is alive, Sahib," explained the conscript in simpler Bengali. "And a captive! Who is alive, Sahib?"

***

That was the news Benjamin had given Pauline when he found her. Ajoy's mission had failed but he was alive and a prisoner of the Nawab.

Since that moment Pauline had been devising one scheme after another to free him as she had done once before. Nothing she could think of would work. But Pauline kept planning. The thunder of *Europa's* exploding magazine drew her to the northern rampart and she saw the familiar ship burning.

Freddie!

Her body first felt hot. Then a cold sweat broke out on her arms. Chills ran up and down her spine and the sweat felt freezing as she stood petrified and watched the mayhem on the sandbank. She recognized Midshipman Roberts as he was helped up the steps and her heart stopped. When Roberts was brought forward and introduced to Benjamin, she hesitantly, unwillingly, took one leaden step after another until she stood unnoticed behind the men and heard the terrifying words: "...Europa's *dead, sir. The cap'n fought to the end. He died with his back to the mast.*"

At this point a huge weight descended and suffocated her and Pauline found herself falling...falling into complete oblivion. When under Bessie's ministrations, her consciousness returned. She got up and silencing Bessie's protests, walked away.

Bessie, a hand at her throat, looked on miserably.

***

With cessation of hostilities, all members of the garrison congregated at the eastern side of Fort William.

The riverside to the west was almost deserted.

Midshipman Roberts still sat slumped under the shade of the colonnade where Benjamin had left him. He watched as *Europa* was reduced to a smoldering ruin partially submerged in the shallow water off the sandbank. His thoughts were not pleasant. *Europa* had been his home for the best part of his life. He remembered the time he had joined the navy as a raw officer recruit and the pains of initiation into naval life and the seasickness that he was too ashamed to admit. He thought of slave-driving Bos'n Kelsey and the his mind wandered away to memories of Mombasa and Malacca.

Ensign Shipling was still guarding the river-gate. His thoughts were not pleasant either. His young and impressionable mind was traumatized by the horrors and the suffering he had witnessed. To counteract the oppression he had begun to think compulsively of the lovely woman with golden hair who had caressed his cheek and pushed the domineering Scotsman into the river. Since that day when she had first appeared on the landing and Shipling watched her the steps with heart-stopping beauty, he had seen the warmth of her face gradually replaced by utter dejection. The climax came when she had fainted before his shocked eyes. Shipling spent his hours at the river-gate wondering what he could do to make her happy.

Some time after the clamor and revelry following the truce died down above, Shipling heard hurried footsteps coming down from the colonnade. He looked up and saw two men in uniform approaching. One was a thick-set hulking figure. The other was younger and fairer. They wore the insignia of artillerymen. Shipling recognized them as Bracken and Peterbilt, members of a gun crew.

"Open the gate, soldier!"

The thick-set man spoke in an unpleasant voice.

"You've orders, sir?"

The big man turned to his colleague and the look they exchanged made Shipling's blood run cold. He held his musket at the ready.

Bracken noticed this and paused.

"We've a need-a fetch things off yon burnt ship, soldier," he said finally. "Important things, ye know! Guns'n'all."

Shipling did not like Bracken. He knew him as a bully and a man to be avoided. But he had no reason to refuse a perfectly valid request. It was dangerous to go out to the ship with Indian soldiers around. Well, it wasn't *his* funeral! He took out his keys and undid the padlock and pulled the bolt on the gate and Bracken hauled it open. He was breathing hard, Shipling noticed, and his face was red. That was strange. The men had come *down* the stairs. What had made them so breathless?

The two gunners went out.

Shipling was about to close and lock the gate when it was violently pushed back from the outside.

"What the devil d'ye think ye be doing?" Bracken stormed.

"I've orders to keep the gate locked, Mr. Bracken."

"No ye won't that, damn ye!"

Shipling was about to argue when there was a shout from the outside and the sound of running feet. Shipling tried to push past Bracken to see who was coming but the big Irishman viciously shoved him backward. The next moment Shipling was sitting on the ground with his back against the wall and watching bare dusty feet, hairy legs and flapping blue *dhotis* fly past. Indian soldiers, summoned by Bracken's *peon,* were pouring through the open gate. He was so overwhelmed that he took a while to pull himself back to his feet and find the musket he had dropped. Dozens of soldiers were climbing the steps to the parade-ground. Shipling tried to push himself in front of the men streaming in. He slashed at them with his bayonet and shouted *"Stop! Stop!"*

His musket went off involuntarily.

Then they were on him.

Within seconds Shipling was hacked to death and thrown aside.

More men flooded in.

Bracken led the charge up the steps screaming like a maniac.

There were only five men on the landing at the top of the stairs. Two soldiers and a lance-corporal, Midshipman Roberts and a seaman from *Europa.* They heard the commotion and the sound of Shipling's musket firing. There were plenty of muskets on the parapet left by soldiers who had gone to witness the truce. They grabbed a bayoneted musket in each hand and rushed to the head of the stairs just as the first group of Indians reached it with Bracken in the front. There was no room or time to fire. With a moment's hesitation at seeing the uniformed Irish gunner leading the attack, Roberts swung his musket like a club. It moved in a arc and landed with a crunch on Bracken's head and the big Irishman went down with a split skull. Three invaders were run through by bayonets and fell back on those advancing behind them. With room now available, the Englishmen fired into the massed Indians.

There was a fearful tangle on the steps.

Then muskets cracked from below. The Englishmen fired over those sprawled immediately before them and into the next line of Indians.

There were shouts from behind. Help was on its way.

"Hold them, lads!" Roberts shouted.

The element of surprise the Indians had had in their favor was gone. If only they could hold the stairs for a few more minutes.

A musket banged from below and Roberts felt a pain in his chest as though a mule had kicked him. He fell backward. The Indians climbed the remaining steps and in minutes all five defenders on the landing were dead.

***

Benjamin and Clarkson were halfway across the parade-ground and deep in conversation about how to impeach Armstrong when they heard the sounds of the invasion. Benjamin shouted to attract the soldiers behind him on the eastern wall. Then he ran as fast as he could toward the western colonnade, leaving Clarkson behind.

He reached the top just in time to see the climax of the skirmish.

Benjamin stared horrified at the massed blue-and-white uniforms. Then he turned and with his mind working at top speed ran back the way he had come. His men were already down on the parade-ground and running to him. One sentence kept repeating itself over and over in his mind.

There will be a bloodbath! There will be a bloodbath!

As Benjamin ran he thought of ways to save them from slaughter. He reached Clarkson and tried to drag the old man along with him. But Clarkson was completely spent and crumpled to the ground.

An idea hit Benjamin.

He left Clarkson and raced toward the British soldiers frantically signaling them to stay where they were. He had another thirty yards to cover and they were the longest he had ever run in his life. He reached the men and grabbed O'Malley's musket with the white flag still attached to it.

"Hold your fire, men! Come what may!"

Benjamin shouted the order between gasps for breath and repeated it as loudly as he could. Then he turned and walked toward the enemy, waving the white flag aloft.

The first Indians came onto the western margin of the parade-ground as he reached the bent-over form of the magistrate.

In the burning sunshine, in the middle of the expanse of parade-ground, with the slumped form of his mentor beside him, Benjamin Morley, Governor of Fort William for less than a day, stood erect and waved the white flag as scores of Indians in regalia of the Bengal Army flowed into Fort William.

Was this the end?

Benjamin held the flag aloft, closed his eyes, and began to pray.

Chapter 36

Ironically—but what was ironic any longer?—what saved the fort from a massacre was the fact the invaders were the Nawab's crack bodyguards and not undisciplined infantrymen. They were Persians, selected from the best that Moghul India had to offer. They were uniformed in royal blue tunics with white shirts and sky-blue *dhotis*. They had been trained by Rahamat Khan himself. Upon pain of death they were required to follow the rules of war as laid down in the book of Islam. Among the rules was the edict to treat defeated enemy honorably and give him quarter. And so, when English soldiers on the ramparts miraculously held their fire and Benjamin's white flag waved in surrender, the Indian troops did not decimate them. In opting for honorable surrender Benjamin had strategized correctly. Within minutes the British soldiers were rounded up, relieved of their arms and packed into a tight group around the supine Clarkson. Benjamin, presented as the *Laat-Sahib,* was not touched and was allowed to retain his knife and sword.

The first minutes of defeat passed slowly.

The blazing sun shone down mercilessly on the captives who sat or lay tiredly on the grass with the four women at their center. There was no conversation. Sunk in private thoughts, overcome by thirst, benumbed by heat and hopelessness and the violence and treachery they had witnessed, nobody spoke. They looked on while the Bengal Army took control of their fort. The east gates were thrown open and a tide of green-and-red-clothed infantrymen streamed in and immediately set about ransacking the buildings and systematically setting them afire. Furniture and bundles of clothing were carried away. The sun became obscured by smoke rising from Writers' Building and the offices of the merchants and from the Governor's Residence. Infantrymen approached the captives and made threatening gestures but were firmly repelled by the Nawab's guard.

A group of horsemen swept through the gates and performed a splendid victory lap around the parade-ground and came to a stop in a cloud of dust before the prisoners.

The riders dismounted.

Benjamin, coughing from dust that billowed onto him, got to his feet. He recognized his old adversary in the big man leading the group.

Well, congratulations! Benjamin toasted him silently. *To you, the victor! The achievement of a lifetime, old chap. The very first defeat of an European overseas garrison to native forces. But then, I can't tell you that, can I?*

Rahamat Khan approached the prisoners.

Benjamin stepped forward and stood stiffly to attention. His eyes were fixed on a point on the wall high above the *Sipah-sala's* head. A guard grabbed him by the shoulder and tried to push him to his knees. Benjamin shook him off roughly. The guard drew his sword.

"*Sheath your weapon, Idris Beg!*"

The guard jumped back in fright as Rahamat Khan's famous voice roared out.

"The prisoner will kneel!"

Rahamat Khan's command was in Bengali. Benjamin took a deep breath before replying stiffly in the same language.

"*The English Governor kneels only to the English King!*"

There was a shocked silence. Before Rahamat Khan could react Benjamin continued, his voice papery from thirst but holding firm.

"The English Governor will surrender his sword to his captor. To his captor alone. English prisoners *shall* be treated with compassion."

Rahamat Khan stared at him in surprise. Then, perhaps to cover his confusion and petulance, the Indian general bellowed in the tone he had used to quell the riot at the Nadia river crossing.

"The prisoner's life hangs by a thread!"

Benjamin flinched but said nothing.

Rahamat Khan took a step forward.

"Behold! Thy captor stands before thee. Present thy sword. What do infidels know of rules of war that have already spared their lives?"

Benjamin looked Rahamat Khan in the eyes for the first time and inclined his head slightly, very slightly, acknowledging his mercy.

"The *Sipah-sala* is a brave and honorable man...," said Benjamin and looked away. The fierce mien of the general relaxed momentarily. "...yet he is but the *Sipah-sala*'. There was a gasp of astonishment from the guards. Rahamat Khan's teeth came together with an perceptible click as Benjamin finished. "The English Governor will surrender his sword only to the Nawab."

Involuntarily Rahamat Khan mouthed an oath and raised his hand to strike while Benjamin continued to stare stonily into space. From among the prisoners, Pauline, who had understood the exchange, made ready to spring to Benjamin's defense. But Rahamat Khan controlled himself at the very last moment. Simultaneously, he felt a pang of embarrassment. He had let the hatman get under his skin and almost goad him into a serious breach of battle etiquette: beating a captive enemy. An astute man, he admired Benjamin's ploy of drawing anger to himself and away from the other prisoners.

Breathing heavily, Rahamat Khan dropped his hand to his side and regarded Benjamin quizzically. Then he swung on his heels and walked back to his horse and remounted. His followers did the same.

From the commanding height of his black stallion the *Sipah-sala* issued orders to the bodyguards.

"Move the prisoners to the shade. Give them water. Water only."

Benjamin looked into Rahamat Khan's eyes again. A long moment passed as they regarded each other with mutual respect. Then at a signal from their leader, the horsemen wheeled their mounts, raised a billow of dust and swept out of the gates.

The guards barked out orders. The prisoners were moved into the welcome shade of the gallery. Water was brought for their parched throats.

During the rest of he day the number of captives decreased. Surviving refugees from the Black Town fire and Indians and Eurasians who had served under the English were allowed by guards to leave. Using the opportunity, several darker Europeans slipped away.

There remained a hundred and fifty men, mostly English, and the four Englishwomen.

***

Two hours later the King of Bengal entered Fort William at the head of a tumultuous victory procession.

The afternoon sun was lowering into the heat haze across the Hooghly River. Ramparts and galleries of Fort William were filled with a golden light. The parade-ground was festive with pennants and awash in blue-and-white and red-and-green uniforms.

A dull roar filled the air as of thousands upon thousands of voices together gave vent to the full-throated traditional salutation to a monarch.

"Shiraj Doula zindabad!"

On this momentous day the illustrious Nawab of Bengal, Bihar and Orissa sat resplendent on his handsomely plumed milk-white Afghan mount. For his triumphant entry into the vanquished citadel Shiraj Doula had preferred poetry of equine beauty to ponderous magnificence of a war-elephant. The Nawab rode side-saddle with his back erect. The malevolence of his hooked nose and hooded eyes was counter pointed by a jaunty peacock feather in his gaudy fez. Shiraj's silk robe had rich tones of shimmering green with blue and pink patterns and was laced heavily with gold thread. A curved scimitar, sheathed at his side in a tooled leather scabbard, bounced as he rode. On his feet the Nawab wore velvet *nagras*, purple moccasins that ended in long leather strips that made generous curves upwards and backwards.

Behind the Nawab came the architect of his victory, Rahamat Khan. They were followed by a hundred trusted officers and ministers. Among them was the grey Gaffar and the sagacious Mujtaba, now instated as the Nawab's chief of guards.

Shiraj Doula looked every inch a king.

Ignoring the prisoners, he inspected the fort. He studied its armory and the colonnade, spending much time at the corner bastions. He rode to the ramparts above the colonnade and looked out contemptuously at the carcass of *Europa,* and then at the European ships visible to the south. Figures standing at the ships' rails could be made out faintly from this distance. After regarding the shipboard English for a few moments Shiraj Doula dismounted and symbolically turned his back to them.

Then the Nawab faced west to Mecca and stretched both his arms, palm upwards, in supplication to Allah. And at the same moment the Union Jack fluttered down from Fort William's main flagpole and the Nawab of Bengal's royal-blue-and-white colors rose amid uproarious jubilation.

"Shiraj Doula zindabad!"

"Allah ho Akbar!"

"Feringhi murdabad!"

Five cannon fired in rapid succession to mark the occasion. This was followed by silence while a senior *mullah* sonorously intoned a prayer from the *Koran*.

Shiraj remounted, wheeled his horse, and rode down to the gallery and the motley crowd of English prisoners. He did not dismount but his bodyguards did. They formed a tight circle around his white horse.

Benjamin Morley stepped into the open.

The slanting sun was in his eyes as he bowed to the Nawab. When he straightened he kept his gaze no higher than the withers of the white horse.

The Nawab scrutinized him for a moment then turned away.

"Sipah-sala!"

"My Lord?"

Rahamat Khan stepped forward and inclined his head.

"The *Laat-sahib* shall be brought forward."

"The *Laat-sahib* is before my Lord."

Shiraj Doula looked back at Benjamin and his lip curled in disdain.

"I know this one. It is the schemer who came to the Nawab begging allowances for his worthless country. This one is not the *Laat-sahib*. The *Laat-sahib* is older and fatter."

"The fat *Laat-sahib* is on the ships over there, my Lord," supplied an aide. "This is the new one."

"So, the fearless leader has left his people and fled?" Shiraj scoffed. Without waiting for a reply he pulled a scroll from his robes and brandished it at Benjamin.

"See, *feringhi?* Here is the insolent message your fat cowardly *Laat-sahib* had the impudence to write defying the Nawab's wishes. And where is he now? I have kept it only to have it thrown in his accursed face." He tossed the scroll to the ground. "So you are the new *Laat-sahib?* What is your name?"

Benjamin waited a moment then drew himself up to his full height.

"Benjamin Morley of Ashford, my Lord, acting Governor of His Majesty's English East India Company at Fort William."

He spoke the words in ringing aristocratic English, all the while keeping his eyes fixed on the hooves of the Nawab's horse.

Shiraj Doula did not understand and waited expecting a translation. His aides had not understood either and began to squirm. When he judged he had allowed their discomfiture to reach breaking point Benjamin slowly spoke in Bengali, carefully selecting his words.

"My name is Benjamin Morley, my Lord. I am an English peer from Ashford. I represent before your Highness the Sultan of England, the second George. I act today as *Laat-sahib* of the English East India Company's Calcutta station in the unfortunate absence of the Honorable Richard Armstrong."

After waiting a few moments for this to sink in, Benjamin continued.

"As Commander of the Calcutta garrison, my Lord, I hereby surrender my sword to you..." He ceremoniously undid his belt, bent down and laid his sheathed sword on the ground before the horse and stepped back. "...with the entreaty that our soldiers, who have fought bravely, and our women, who are innocent, be treated with honor and compassion."

If Shiraj was impressed by Benjamin's speech or by his Bengali aptitude, he did not show it, for his next question came like a pistol shot.

"Where is the treasure, *feringhi?*"

Benjamin was not prepared for this question and was taken aback. Treasure? What treasure? Did Shiraj mean their treasury? Paymaster Broderick and Governor Armstrong were in charge of the garrison's treasury. He looked around at the uncomprehending prisoners who were watching him anxiously. Broderick was not there. What should he do? He decided that if it came to a choice it was his duty to protect his men first and the Company's capital later.

"My Lord, our treasury is situated beside the armory. If the Nawab desires, I shall…"

"Your treasury has been discovered and examined. It contains but a few thousand rupees. Where is the rest hidden?"

Benjamin was nonplussed. Had the treasure been looted by the Indians? Obviously he couldn't suggest that to the Nawab. Had McIver's syndicate, adding grand embezzlement to their many sins, decamped with coins and bullion? He couldn't suggest *that* either!

"I am desolate, my Lord, but I do not know. I was but a Trade Councilor until yesterday."

Shiraj Doula launched into a vitriolic attack on Armstrong and gave instructions to torch the tottering superstructure of the Residence, believing it belonged to Armstrong personally. He asked Benjamin about the treasure again and again. Benjamin kept silent, sick with anger that at this most vulnerable moment, the Council's misdeeds had once more been their undoing.

The boiling Nawab paused to catch his breath. As he was about to lash out again at Benjamin he looked at the setting sun and abruptly checked himself.

"*By Allah!* The *feringhi* has made the Nawab forget it is time for evening prayers. The prisoners shall be dealt with in the morning."

The Nawab swung his horse's head around and trotted away. His entourage mounted and followed.

Benjamin leaned weakly against a column. He felt empty and dizzy. His head and shoulder hurt. Dicky and Bessie helped him to a place where he could sit. When he had recovered somewhat, Pauline came close and whispered, "If the king hadn't suddenly gone off just then, I would have asked him to spare Prince Ajoy. I've been so worried…"

"*Oh my God!*"

Benjamin forgot his headache and stared at her aghast. He tried to imagine what the effect of that request would have been on Shiraj Doula. A captive woman, a *woman*, speaking, actually *speaking* to a Moghul Nawab? Making a demand of the Nawab! A *foreign* woman! Wanting him to release a prisoner! *A hated enemy!* Shiraj would have had an apoplectic fit.

But where *was* Prince Ajoy?

In his concern for the English survivors, Benjamin had forgotten about Ajoy. He recalled the banana leaf containing the intriguing message from the Jagat Seth. Had Ajoy confronted Shiraj or had he been captured before he could act? Was he still alive?

He laid a comforting hand on Pauline's arm.

"It's rather lucky you didn't ask, Mrs. Wainwright. It would have made it worse for the prince. Now look here. It's getting dark. You and the other women must leave."

"Leave?" Pauline looked around startled. "And go where?" Suddenly hysteria filled her voice. "Where *is* there for me to go? *Who* is there to go to? I *must* know where is. How he is. Help me, Benjamin. *Please!*"

Benjamin patted her arm.

"He is in God's hands, Mrs. Wainwright. And so are we all. There's nothing more we can do for Prince Ajoy. All I want is to get the rest of us out of here alive."

Their attention was drawn to the roaring inferno that had blazed up around the Residence. Other buildings were burning too. In the deepening darkness the flames came frighteningly close. Later still they heard drunken laughter. Fights broke out between Indians and freed Dutch soldiers. The Dutch were notorious for their rough behavior. There were musket shots. Benjamin became more worried. If there was a serious altercation between the Nawab's men and the Dutch, intoxicated Indians might wreak vengeance on them. He asked their guards what was going to happen but they refused to answer. He was told that they would be supplied water but no food.

It became dark.

One by one, in spite of the surrounding uncertainty and

menace, the prisoners, overcome by weariness and hunger, began to fall asleep.

***

As the day wore on Nawab Shiraj Doula became increasingly angry and frustrated, obsessed with the missing English treasure. The Jagat Seth, whom no one could find now, had assured him that there was at least a million rupees in gold and valuables in the fort's treasury. Shiraj was certain the new *Laat-sahib* was lying. In spite of his public ridicule Shiraj had recognized the young man to be a shrewd diplomat. He *had* to know where the treasure was. In the evening Shiraj led his army in *namaz* and gave thanks to Allah for the supreme victory in a holy war. Later he was contemplating his options for extracting the information when an armed man entered his royal tent. Gaffar rose from his position and went over to him.

"The Chief of Guards requests audience, my Lord," announced Gaffar.

Mujtaba came forward and made obeisance.

The Nawab grunted impatiently.

Mujtaba came directly to the point.

"My Lord, where should the prisoners be housed for the night?"

Shiraj looked up in extreme annoyance.

"Ridiculous! Why do you ask the Nawab? Has no one any sense? The prisoners shall be put in the prison."

"The prison is destroyed, my Lord."

Shiraj lost his temper.

"Does the Nawab have to make *all* the decisions? Is there not a place to secure prisoners in the fort?"

"There is, my Lord. The *kala agar* – the dark room. It is below the northern gallery near the treasury."

"Well then, the prisoners shall be kept in the *kala agar*. Perhaps spending the night near the treasury will help them remember where they have hidden the treasure. Now go! The Nawab shall not further be bothered with trivia."

Mujtaba hesitated.

"But, my Lord…"

Shiraj Doula stopped him with a look.

"Listen carefully, Guard. The traitor Sena shall be caged for the night with the dirty hatmen whom he befriended. The gallows shall be prepared for his execution in the morning. The traitor shall be hanged in full view of his spineless comrades on the ships and in the fort. Now the Nawab *shall* be left at peace. Go!"

Mujtaba said no more. Continuing to make obeisance, he walked backwards from the Nawab's presence.

Chapter 37

When it happened, it happened so fast that they did not have time even to think.

Benjamin had dozed off where he had been sitting with Clarkson and Pauline on the floor of the eastern gallery. Dicky and Bessie were nearby. They held hands and her head rested on his shoulder. Most of the other prisoners were stretched out on the hard ground in exhausted slumber. They had eaten nothing since their breakfast rations.

Suddenly there were loud shouts.

"Get up! Everybody, get up!"

The captives sat up and looked bemusedly at the guards.

"Feringhis! On your feet!" ordered Mujtaba. "Move! You are going to prison. Hurry!"

"On your feet!" urged the guards prodding everyone.

The prisoners struggled up and allowed themselves to be shepherded toward the northern side of the fort.

"Wait!" protested Benjamin. "Where are you taking us? There is no prison. The Company Jail has been destroyed."

Benjamin was one of the very few in the crowd who were alert. From the east battery he had witnessed the demolition of the Company Jail at close hand.

Mujtaba came close, took his arm in a firm grip, and propelled him forward.

"*O Laat-sahib,* you are on your way to your special quarters!" Mujtaba said as he hurried Benjamin along ahead of the others. "You are going to be placed in the *kala agar* for the night and then you will be afforded the luxury of witnessing the hanging of your princely friend."

Benjamin was distracted for a moment by the reference to Ajoy. Then a horrible thought hit him like a slap in the face.

In the *kala agar?*

All of them??

"*No!*" he cried out and tried to wrench his arm away. "It is too small!"

But by then the two of them had left the others behind and nobody heard his shout of protest. Benjamin struggled frantically but could not get away. Mujtaba was extremely strong. He held the exhausted Englishman easily and frog-marched him forward. In a few minutes Benjamin heard the squeal of hinges and was shoved violently through a doorway and into darkness.

Benjamin rushed back to the door, but Mujtaba was waiting for him. This time the chief of guards held him by both shoulders and sent him spinning back on to the prison floor.

Benjamin fell forward in the dark with his breath knocked out and tried to get up. Suddenly he heard a rustling sound nearby. Something moved on the floor beside him. What was it? The large shadowy form moved again. Was it a big rat, or a dog? Heavens, not a coiled snake! Then he noticed to his right, opposite the door, two high barred windows through which firelight glimmered. Through the windows he heard the main body of prisoners approaching. There were shouted orders and curses from the guards. Someone yelped from a blow. Benjamin forgot the thing in the room, jumped to his feet and rushed to the barred opening.

He *had* to stop the others from being forced into the room.

The first of the prisoners had begun to enter the *kala agar* when Benjamin went berserk.

"*No!*" he shrieked from the window. "Don't come in! *Run! It's too small!* Do you hear me? It's a trap. *Run! Scatter!*" He shook the bars. "*Run! Get away!*"

But if the others heard, in the confusion at the door they had no time to react. The guards worried them like sheepdogs. More and more captives were pushed into the prison. Benjamin kept on shouting at the guards to let them go. Soon the *kala agar* was packed. Yet full thirty prisoners remained outside. The guards began to beat and harry those outside and they, not realizing, pushed at those by the door just to be get away from their tormentors. As the pressure mounted some of those inside lost their footing and were trampled upon by others desperately seeking space to ease the pressure.

Most of the prisoners had now been forced in.

"*Fight!* Fight back!" shrieked Benjamin from his window, trying not to be flattened against the wall. "No, no, no! It is death! Watch out for the women. Bessie? Alice? Mrs. Wainwright? Where are you? Mr. Clarkson? *Oh God!*"

Benjamin's voice broke.

The last man was shoved in with crushing force and the iron door clanged shut. The prisoners were packed in so tightly that they found it impossible to breathe. In the darkness groans and cries of pain filled the air.

A primeval animal instinct for survival took over everyone's behavior almost immediately.

A miasma of panic replaced lifetimes of values. Single-minded aggression dictated everyone's act as, in a heartbeat, millennia of societal behavior lost their grip. A primitive feral fight to stay alive began. Men pounded one other for supremacy of breath. Those on the verge of losing their vertical stance perceived they were about to die and kicked and scratched ferociously at those around them simply to remain perpendicular.

"Oh sweet God!"

"Jesus help us!"

"I can't bear it!"

"Mother!"

All semblance of order disappeared in the *kala agar*.

For those who were away from the two small openings, breathing became a wrenching effort. They fought fiendishly for room to simply expand their lungs. In minutes the temperature in the chamber soared. Perspiration ran in streams down bodies. An awful stench began to pervade the atmosphere. Instinctively, like plants to sunlight, the stronger began to push toward the fresher air by the windows. Like lobsters they climbed over fellows in the way. Those close to the windows brutally pushed them back. The pressure became intolerable and the legs of those weaker began to give way.

Meanwhile the ones who had fallen in the headlong rush into the prison began to die of asphyxiation.

Benjamin held onto a window bar tenaciously. Their situation had descended into absolute anarchy. He *had* to bring order or they would all die.

"Quiet!"

Benjamin shouted as loudly as he could but his voice was hoarse and no one paid attention.

"Listen to me. We cannot panic. Please! Please! We mustn't panic. Silence! We'll all going to die."

Benjamin persisted until despair set in.

"Silence!" bellowed a stentorian voice from just beside him. It was Lieutenant O'Malley. *"Quiet!* Calm down, men! Panic'll finish us. *Silence!"*

It took a full ten minutes before the mass hysteria abated.

The room quieted and the pressure eased slightly, and incredibly, miraculously, civilization reasserted itself. Many in agony moaned uncontrollably. Others endured in grim silence.

Benjamin, from his slight elevation at the window-sill

looked at the horror of the chamber. It was a macabre scene of suffering. Of hopelessness and death. The flames of buildings burning outside lit the hunted pain-wracked faces and glistened on the beads of sweat on the traumatized people looking back at him.

Benjamin began to shiver violently. His every nerve was on edge.

He was in charge. In charge of what? They had truly believed he would work a miracle and save them. A malignant, black despair took hold of him. Was there any hope? How many were they? One hundred? Two hundred? In a cell meant for twenty. Fighting each other like rats in a cage. They would die. Most of them would die. They would be slowly suffocated and dehydrated. And they had thought they had survived the worst. He had an uncontrollable urge to relax his hold on the bar and sink into the morass. Into sweet oblivion.

Dear Lord, let me die now. I cannot carry the responsibility any more. I've done all I can. It's over. Let me go now.

From the back of the room came a woman's muffled cry.

Benjamin came back to reality with a jerk. He could not give up while women who depended on him.

"Listen to me," he shouted. "We cannot panic. We are men and we will die like men. Like Englishmen. Not like barbarians. Not like rats. Are you with me?"

There were a few muttered affirmations.

"Good! We will care for our women first. Even on the very point of death we *shall* care for our women. And then our oldest."

There was a half-hearted chorus of approval.

Benjamin raised his voice.

"Bessie!"

There was no answer.

"Bessie Armstrong!"

No answer.

"Bessie! Answer me!"

Still no reply.

"Wait a moment, sir!" It was Corporal Riley's voice from the far end of the room. "I think she's here. Half-fallen. I thought I heard a moan. Move ye sods! Let her up."

"Mrs. Wainwright!" called Benjamin.

"I'm here."

Pauline's voice came from the same area.

"Thank God!" Benjamin breathed.

"Help Bessie over to me," called out Pauline, her voice strong. "There's an iron bed here that I'm standing on."

Where was Dicky, wondered Benjamin. It was strange that he hadn't responded on news of Bessie.

At that moment somebody at the back made a dive to get under the iron bed to escape the crush. Several others followed at once.

"No!" screamed Pauline. "You won't get out!"

But it was too late.

Crazed to relieve the pressure on their chests, five or six men went under the bed before they realized their mistake. Recoiling at the closeness of the air at floor level they tried to get back out but the legs of the others blocked the way. One man tore at the offending ankles with his teeth. The victim screamed and kicked at him.

Pandemonium began to take over once again.

"Mrs. Plunkett! Mrs. Doyle!" Benjamin shouted frantically.

"I'm here. By the door," responded Alice Doyle. "Johnnie, where are you?"

There was no reply.

"Johnnie! Answer me!"

Everyone held their breath.

There was no reply.

Alice began to cry in heartrending sobs.

Tears came to Benjamin's eyes.

"Mrs. Plunkett!"

It was O'Malley who called out this time.

No answer.

O'Malley called twice more without result.

"No! Please God, no!" came a wild scream. *"Mary!* Where are you? Answer me!"

No reply.

"Mary!"

It was an abject cry of hopelessness that made Benjamin's blood run cold and raised goose pimples on his arms.

"Belay there!" called a voice. "There's someone here. Yes, it be a woman. Hurt bad too, I reckon."

Sergeant Matthew Plunkett charged like a bull through the massed bodies to his wife's side. He bent down and pulled her up.

Mary whimpered softly in his arms.

Benjamin remembered Dicky.

"Captain Glynnis!"

No answer.

"Dicky!"

Benjamin called twice more with no result. *Oh Bessie!* His heart bled for her. There was no sound from Bessie. He hoped she was unconscious, which was probably best.

"Mr. Clarkson!"

"He's here, beside me," Pauline responded.

Her voice sounded surprisingly steady amid the general hysteria.

"How is he?"

"He's alive, but very weak. We're keeping him on his feet. Bessie won't last very long. Mr. Morley, what on earth are you *doing? Do* something about us, can't you? Open the door. Call the guards and tell them about us. You're near the window."

There was an immediate roar of angry assent and Benjamin felt the rebuke like a blow to his stomach. God, he told himself, what an absolute tower of strength was Pauline! And what an absolute self-pitying idiot was he! Of course she was right. He turned to look through the window and saw three guards slumped against the wall of the gallery, apparently unaware of the chaos in the prison.

"Hie! Guards!" he called. *"Look here! Listen!"*

Those by the door banged on it.

Suddenly someone grabbed Benjamin's arm and pulled. Benjamin, concentrating on the guards, tried to shake the hand off. Other voices were calling the guards who were now sitting up and staring at the grate. The unseen hand pulled at Benjamin once more, distracting him. He shouted at the guards again and then turned to see who his tormentor was. His eyes had difficulty focusing back into the gloom so he bent down to look closer. He discerned a dark face with large terrified eyes with the whites very prominent. Behind it was a shock of long black, curly hair. A voice spoke in an urgent whisper.

"Morley-sahib!"

Benjamin went rigid with astonishment.

"Prince Ajoy! Are you all right?"

Ajoy spoke in a labored whisper.

"They have killed me. Listen to me. Asha? Please, can I...?

But before Ajoy could finish a desperate hairy hand brushed aside Benjamin's loosened hold on the window. Caught by surprise, Benjamin staggered, lost his footing and was inexorably borne down to the floor by the crush instinctively homing on the fresh air of the window. Fighting like a madman he slid between the bodies and the legs of the captives and into the quagmire of boots. He struggled, he fought, he clutched and he even bit, but the force pushing him down was relentless. Then a heavy boot planted itself squarely on his chest driving the breath out of his body in a primordial wail. Then another trod on his face and his cry was cut off. A foot stamped on his left leg and another landed heavily on his groin. He felt an excruciating pain. Bright stars swirled around his vision against a red background.

Sensing his situation, Lieutenant O'Malley had grasped his arm and tried to pull him up. Benjamin's shirt sleeve ripped, but O'Malley retained his grip and kept pulling. But the boots held Benjamin down. A second hand fastened on his shirt and then a third on his other arm. But the boots still held Benjamin fast. There was a loud squeal and the boot on Benjamin's face lifted and then the one on his chest. The hands pulled together. Benjamin, almost unconscious now, was pulled back to an upright position. He would have collapsed had not O'Malley and another soldier, both breathing heavily with their efforts, kept their hold on him.

Then his rescuers turned on the burly writer who had displaced Benjamin at the window. Keeping their hold on Benjamin, they forced the writer away and thrust Benjamin's face to the window. An ensign joined in their efforts and the three men formed a cordon around their tortured Governor.

From the other window Englishmen continued to shout at the guards but were studiously ignored.

Benjamin remained semi-consciousness for a very long time.

His whole body was a mass of bruises. His eyes would not open and his legs would not support him. He wanted only to die. O'Malley brought his face close to Benjamin's and his eyes grew round at what he saw. Panic-stricken, he tore up his shirt. Wetting a strip with the only liquid he could find, the sweat from his own arms, he wiped the blood caked over Benjamin's eyes and tried to stanch the nosebleed.

As time passed O'Malley and the soldiers continued to work on Benjamin. They wiped more blood and massaged him. They spoke to him encouragingly and somehow kept the lifeblood from ebbing away from his broken body.

Finally the Englishmen gave up the effort of trying to summon the guards. It had been discovered that the entry door to the *kala agar* opened inward and the large mass of bodies stacked against the door made it impossible to pull it open even assuming it was unlocked. Gradually the panic and hysteria faded to exhaustion and a dour battle for life ensued. An enormous thirst wracked everyone's throats. They stood or lay or died where they were, holding each other, breathing air that grew fouler with each minute. The temperature of the room rose higher and steam mixed with sweat filled the foul atmosphere. Someone suggested that by removing their shirts they would be better able to withstand the heat. Immediately people tore off their clothes. But almost at once they found this was another grievous error. Without their shirts hey could not hold onto each other and stay erect as their bodies were slippery with sweat.

The hours became trackless.

The efforts of people to stay upright became unendurable and one by one, they quietly slipped to the ground where the air had even less oxygen, and eventually died of asphyxiation. Bodies piled up on the floor in layers. Then, as more men fell, the pressure for space on survivors eased. And finally, at some divinely-ordained moment in that dreadful night, when demand for oxygen fell below a critical point, a fateful balance was passed. The air quality improved and the temperature come down.

Eventually, little by little, strength returned to Benjamin's limbs and to his mind. He found he could stand with O'Malley's support. His left leg hurt but nowhere near as much as the pulsating in his head and the pain in his face and groin. His vision was completely fogged.

In a voice that was barely audible, he asked his first question.

"Have the guards come?"

O'Malley heard him and brought his face close.

"No, sir. They ignored us."

"Why?"

O'Malley shrugged but Benjamin could not see this. He turned to the window, drawn to it by the freshness of the air, and tried to call the guards. His voice was an inaudible croak. He turned back to O'Malley.

"Did you tell them there are women here?"

"Yes sir. But they wouldn't listen."

Benjamin became agitated.

"We've got women. The Nawab said he'd spare the women. That *must* get their attention."

O'Malley shouted through the window but nothing happened.

"Can *you* make a last try, sir?" asked the ensign. "Try their language. None of us knows it."

Benjamin cleared his throat and took a deep breath. Both actions hurt immensely. He could see nothing. His eyesight was completely gone.

"Guards!"

Benjamin called in Bengali. His voice while not loud but audible in the quiet of the night outside.

"Guards!"

One of the guards looked up. The other two were sleeping.

"Listen, guards! We have women. If our women die your Nawab will kill you."

The guard sat up at once.

"The Nawab has promised in public on the *Koran*...the *Koran!*... that women will be spared. He will execute all of you if they die."

Benjamin stopped. The effort was too much. Benjamin could not see this but the guard had got to his feet and had come to the window.

"Who will die?" he asked.

"All of us will die if you do not let us out," Benjamin replied unseeing.

One of the soldiers in the *kala agar* understood this exchange.

"Many have died already, sir," he told Benjamin.

Benjamin went rigid with shock. How long had he been unconscious? He turned in O'Malley's direction and asked urgently, "Who is dead? How are the women? Mr. Clarkson?"

"I'm so sorry, sir. Mr. Kyle is dead, God rest his soul. Miss Armstrong and Mrs. Plunkett are dead." Benjamin sighed.

"Many men have died. Lord knows how many. Mrs. Doyle is alive, but she mourns her husband. Mrs. Wainwright tries to keep our hopes up."

A desperation came over Benjamin.

"We *must* get them out of here. We've *got* to save them."

He turned to the window.

"Guard! Are you there? There are many men dead here. Women too."

"Why are they dead?" asked the guard.

Benjamin could not believe his ears. The man had no idea of what was happening!

"Why? Do you know how many we are in this small room? Many have died of suffocation."

"Really?"

There was disbelief in the guard's voice.

"Come closer," Benjamin urged him. "Smell the air."

His feet scraped as the man came forward and smelt the odor emanating from the window. Benjamin followed up as he heard him reel back in revulsion.

"*You!* You are responsible for our deaths and for the death of women captives. You are in great trouble. Let us out now or the Nawab's anger will grow."

The guard hesitated for a moment. Then he went back and woke his colleagues. There was a hurried discussion and the other men came to smell the air. Then the first guard disappeared. After a few minutes Mujtaba appeared, rubbing his eyes.

"I am the Chief of Guards," he said, standing a short distance from the window. "What is this noise?"

"Chief of Guards!" Benjamin couldn't see Mujtaba, but tried to make his tone commanding and urgent. "We are all dying in here. Let us out."

"I cannot. You are to stay there. My Lord has commanded."

"But my Lord has not wished us to die. You were there, Chief of Guards, when he said so. Let us out at once."

"It is not my problem. I do what my Lord commands."

"Wait! You have heard that my Lord say he would spare the women because of what is written in the holy book. Two women have died already and the others will soon. You must release them at least."

Mujtaba looked at the small barred windows indecisively. On one hand the Nawab had expressly directed him to put the prisoners in the *kala agar*. He, Mujtaba, had known that the room was small, but the Nawab had not given him a chance to protest. So it was not *his* fault. On the other hand, he knew how deeply Shiraj Doula believed in honor and the *koranic* rules of war. The Nawab would be terribly upset if women died because of ill-treatment in his captivity. As implementer of the order Mujtaba should have remembered and kept the women separately or reminded the Nawab about them. Also, he had not realized that so many prisoners would die in his charge. But if he tried to take the women out now, he would be disobeying orders because the women were prisoners too.

What should he do?

Maybe the Englishman was lying.

He asked one of the guards to check if indeed many prisoners were dead. This man came to the window, screwing up his face against the odor, and tried to look inside. He could make nothing out in the interior darkness and reported back accordingly. Mujtaba wondered whether he should open the door and check but was afraid that if he did this the prisoners might try to break out and cause a commotion that would bring the Nawab down on his head.

He came to a decision.

"I cannot, Sahib. I must obey my Lord."

"Ask my Lord, Chief of Guards," implored Benjamin. "I am the English *Laat-sahib*. I shall reward you handsomely if you do."

Mujtaba weighed the dilemma. He had heard about the treasure of the fort and the Nawab's firm belief that the *Laat-sahib* knew of its whereabouts. The *Laat-sahib's* offer could be his one chance to make a fortune. For a wild moment he thought of freeing the hatmen and decamping with the loot. But he would have to wake the Nawab and ask for fresh orders, an extremely hazardous task, especially when the Nawab had clearly told him he would not bothered with trivia. What if the Nawab found out he had struck a deal with the hatmen? And anyway, where could he escape with a king's ransom? As a former palace guard he knew well that the Nawab's spies would make flight impossible. Mujtaba had worked very hard to reach his new position. He was too level-headed to throw away his success in a moment's fixation.

"My Lord sleeps," he told Benjamin. "We must wait until he wakens."

Mujtaba walked away. The other guards looked uncertainly at the little windows for a few moments before they too went back to their stations against the gallery walls. The prisoners at the window looked after them dumbfounded.

"What's happening?" asked Benjamin.

"They have gone back," said O'Malley with finality. "It is no use, sir."

Then Benjamin, his commanding tone thrown to the winds, shouted at the guards, pleaded with them, and tore at the bars in his desperation. The guards ignored him. Benjamin kept on alternately demanding and beseeching, not realizing that his voice had completely failed.

A soft hand touched his face. Then it took his shoulder and gently pulled him from the window. Benjamin turned and sensed rather than saw who it was. Her eyes, reflected in the dying flames of the burnt buildings, were pools of pity and understanding. But his own blinded eyes could not see this. In a fetid room in a devastated fort, surrounded by the corpses of his closest friends, enveloped by ghosts of lives lost or broken forever, all the hopes and dreams that shored up Benjamin's heart finally broke asunder. Tears from his sightless eyes coursed down his cheeks and made rivulets in the dried blood and grime on his cheeks. He shook his head and mouthed incoherent words and the tears continued in an unending stream.

"*No!*" Benjamin's voice was a strangled murmur. "*No, no, no, no, no...!*"

Pauline forced back her own tears and, supporting herself against the wall of the prison, pulled the blind, broken, grieving man to herself. She put her arms around him and laid his head on her shoulder. She comforted him thus as though he were a child and tried to draw away his terrible suffering to herself. Sobs racked Benjamin's frame. Defeat and frustrated anger at his own powerlessness drove him to the nadir of despair. Pauline buried her face in his grubby cheek and held on to him tightly, knowing she was his only hope of survival, and that he *must* survive at all costs so the world could know.

After a while she raised her head – and looked over Benjamin's shoulder into firelight reflected in the eyes of a ghost she loved. In the dancing flames she saw dilated pupils that offset a pain-ravaged face that was framed by long matted hair. She saw dark eyes that gazed at her with everlasting empathy that was theirs and theirs alone. Wonderingly, she freed a hand from Benjamin and felt the face and it was warm to her touch. The face came nearer and mouthed *Asha!* and Pauline found his arm and pulled him unresisting to herself.

The young woman stood thus, holding them both, her back to wall below the barred window, unmindful of her own fading strength, speaking soft endearing words, a final lifeline for her two mortally wounded men.

And then, slowly – ever so slowly – one of the men began to slip away. With her tears dropping sorrowfully, helplessly, on his upturned face from which life was inexorably ebbing, he slid down the length of her body, out of her weakened grip, and came to rest motionless at her feet.

As the last hours of the night dragged by, Pauline held on with stubborn tenacity to the one that remained.

Chapter 38

Early the next morning, under dark clouds in a lowering sky and the threat of rain, Mujtaba and his guards tried to open the door to the *kala agar*. They were surprised at the effort it took to do this for they were unaware of the bodies massed behind it. At last they got it open and stood back aghast as twenty-two men and one woman staggered out or were helped from the room, only to be overwhelmed by the abundant morning air and collapse on debris-strewn grass of the parade-ground.

They left one hundred and twenty-three dead behind.

***

Three hours later, Maggie Clarkson, a frenetic fixture at *Beowulf's* rail since the fort's Union Jack had been replaced by the Nawab's colors the previous evening, saw through a veil of rain, a large group of people come down from the fort to the Governor's Wharf. Before long several country boats drew away from the pier and headed in their direction. Maggie, her sense of dread growing every moment, leaned over the rail trying to make out the occupants of the boats as they came closer.

In the lead boat she made out several men, European, but

wearing Indian clothes and lying back against the gunwale. Then her heart leaped. Among the men was a woman. And then relief almost made her swoon as she made out the figure of a man that looked like her husband, lying in an attitude of total debility with his head resting on the woman's lap. Then in the overcast she saw the blond hair and knew the woman was Pauline. The boats came nearer and she recognized among the men Lieutenant O'Malley and Corporal Riley. Her face fell as she realized Bessie and Benjamin were absent as were the other wives and Council members.

Beowulf's captain lowered a platform for his men to carry the feeble survivors up the side of the ship. Pauline was first aboard and Maggie, on the point of rushing to her, stopped in horror.

The sensuous radiant golden-haired girl of seventeen was gone. In her place stood a wasted woman, her gray creased visage and wild hair eloquent of intense trauma, her thin dehydrated body accentuating the discernible bulge of her stomach. With a strangled sob Maggie folded her soiled and battered friend into her arms.

"It's all right, child," was all she could say. "It's all right. Maggie's here. Don't worry, love."

Then Clarence Clarkson was being helped over the gunwale. The visibly bruised magistrate had lost half his weight and could not stand by himself. He was clad in a sodden Indian shirt over torn breeches. His white hair was in disarray. His once-puffy cheeks were hollow. His spectacles were gone and his unfocussed eyes darted in all directions.

Pauline and Maggie tenderly helped Clarkson to a cabin bunk.

***

When the survivors were all aboard, dressed in clean clothes, and attended by the ship's surgeon, Pauline, who had spoken to no one and had ignored Armstrong and McIver when they attempted to question her, sat tiredly with Maggie at the magistrate's bedside while the old man jerked and twitched in sedated slumber.

Rain drummed steadily on the deck.

Finally Pauline spoke.

"You want to know what happened, Maggie?"

"Yes, dear. But only when you're ready. Just tell me who came through and who didn't. The rest can wait."

"Mr. Morley is alive, but only just." Pauline's voice came from a long distance. "He was elected Governor yesterday and was badly hurt in the jail last night. The Nawab would not let him go for he wants the treasure. He's also holding Captain Muldoon and a very hurt Mr. Wolfe until one of the Council Members tells him where the treasure is. Everyone else is either dead or is here. The Nawab was extremely upset because he had not kept his promise of our safety and ordered the release of everyone but the Council Members. Then he let Mr. Clarkson go because of his age."

Pauline stopped.

"I'm sorry, dear," Maggie said gently.

Pauline's face went white and rigid. Maggie tightened her grip on the girl's hand and leaned closer.

"He's gone," was all Maggie heard.

"Who's gone, child?"

But Pauline would not say. She only shook her head slowly from side to side and continued to do so for a long time.

EPILOGUE

Fort St. George
Madras
India
November 15th, 1756

Dearest Father,
Here is the letter for which you have waited months. Your loving daughter is safe and well. She has so much to tell you that her thoughts tumble in a waterfall and clamor for attention of her pen.
Where do I begin?
Every day around me, event after unbelievable event has unfolded at great speed. How terribly have I missed you and my dear brother Giles ever since I left Ipswich with Freddie. I wish I were in Burnham today in our little house, telling you my story, instead of writing from the other end of the world.
All of England will learn at the time that you get this letter, that Fort William fell to the army of the King of Bengal five months ago. All of England will learn that Captain Frederick Wainwright, my husband, died in battle with his back to the mast of his ship, outnumbered and overrun by the enemy. Later that fateful day after the garrison surrendered, the remaining

English and I among them, were packed into a tiny prison in Fort William. I do not know why, Father, but I survived.

The memory of physical pain of that ordeal has faded. But that day took away my love, he who meant everything to me, and a half of me died.

The other half stayed alive for those who remained. It stayed alive for our dying leader to live so the world outside our barred window would know. It stayed alive for the Nabob to awaken and release us from our hellhole. It stayed alive for dear Magistrate Clarkson to be delivered to his beloved wife.

These things happened and the world needed me no more.

Or so I thought.

When we were brought back to the ships from the destroyed Fort William, Maggie Clarkson told me of my coming baby. Yes, Father, I was with child and I did not know. Who but a silly village girl would remain ignorant for months? However, at the moment Maggie told me, that village girl vanished. Your daughter became determined her child would live and for that reason she would stay alive.

Mr. Benjamin Morley, our new Governor, was grievously wounded in the night in the dungeon. His condition worsened for want of medical attention and his confinement in the Nabob's stables. The injuries would have killed a weaker man. His inner strength and his will to fight saved Mr. Morley. While he has regained some of his strength he has suffered irreparable harm. He will never see with one eye. He will never walk erect. And he will never have children.

Or so I thought.

We remained for three months on ships on the Hooghly River. Uncertain of our course of action. Exposed to the elements. Exposed to unending monsoon rain. Exposed to visible and invisible vermin. Many died of chills, of fevers, of consumption, while the Executive Council argued about how the story of the fall of Calcutta should be broken to England and the King.

September came and the rains slackened.

It was decided at last that Mr. Clarkson and a frail Mr. Morley would carry the news to Colonel Clive in Fort St. George. Everyone urged me to go with them and have my baby born in the safety of a British garrison. I did not want to abandon my suffering friends on the muddy Hooghly, but I had to think about my child. Happily, dear Maggie Clarkson agreed to come and look after us.

We traveled south on a smelly Dutch freighter for hundreds of miles. In those three rain-sodden weeks Mr. Morley alternated between extreme anxiety to deliver the news and intense concern for my well-being. I had already witnessed his courage and his intelligence. I had heard about his sincerity and his idealism. Aboard the freighter Texel, *close-hauled to the Indian coastline, I witnessed all those qualities.*

As the sun was setting on September 16th, the evening before our arrival in Madras, Mr. Morley knocked on my cabin door, knelt before me, took my hand in his, and asked me to marry him.

Why is life so complex, Father?

Why are there such impossible decisions to make?

Imagine, Father dear! There sat your Pauly, a widow of four months, huge with child, with a handsome nobleman, a future earl, kneeling before her, holding her hand, looking into her eyes, waiting for her answer.

What should I have answered, Father?

My love had been pledged. But he who held the pledge had been harshly snatched away. Everything that I held precious had been cruelly destroyed. Could I ever find happiness again? How could I, a low-born nobody, be worthy of this magnificent person who held my hand? He was offering me his position, his honor, his friendship, his valor, and his trust. Above all, he was offering my unborn child parentage to be proud of.

What could I do, Father?

I looked at his eyes and I asked my heart.

And I said yes.

We were married on September 18th in the hundred-

year-old chapel of St. Mary's in the Towne of Madras. Little Robert Joy Morley arrived two weeks later. We called him Robert, a common name perhaps, yet Lord Morley of Ashford, Benjamin's father, is named Robert. I like the names very much. Is it because, true to his middle name, my tiny bundle has brought me happiness after the longest and most hopeless of trials? Or is it something else?

Colonel Clive, Governor of Fort St. George, is a powerful man. He sets sail tomorrow at the head of a large convoy to defeat the King of Bengal and retake Calcutta. Dear Benjamin, half-blind, still weak, but resolute, accompanies the Colonel as his right-hand man.

When my husband leaves my life will be reduced to waiting. Waiting for news from Bengal. Waiting for news from Burnham. Waiting to nurse my husband to health. Waiting for where my next home will be. Waiting for where life will take me.

Do not fret for me, Father. I have survived where those stronger have not. In the midst of calamity I have found comrades that will be mine to the last. Little Joy is my solace and he will keep me whole.

With love to Giles from his little sister, and to you, Father dearest, I remain

Your devoted daughter,
Pauline Morley.

***

Pauline sighed and melted a stick of red sealing-wax over a candle and secured the letter with the seal of the Governor of Fort St. George.

Then there was nothing left to do.

She slowly walked to an open window. A cool sea breeze blew in. She sighed again and watched large cotton-wool clouds sail across a laundered sky high above rows upon rows of coconut palm.

Joy cried from his cradle.

Pauline went across and picked up her son. Then she sat back on an armchair near the window and put Joy to her breast. The only sounds in the room were the swish of wind in the palms, the cadence of breakers and little gurgling noises from the contended baby.

Pauline closed her eyes and allowed herself to dream.

THE END

HISTORICAL NOTE

A Flight of Green Parrots is based on the true story of a bizarre chain of events that led to an avoidable tragedy at a critical moment in the history of colonial expansion. The chain of events did not end on the ill-fated night in a tiny dungeon below the ramparts of Fort William. After a vengeful Colonel (later Sir Robert) Clive returned to Bengal, the chain wove its way on through many twists and turns to ultimately affect the destiny of one-third of mankind that came to be known as the British Empire.

But that is another story. Perhaps several stories.

The history of the Company is interesting. Four hundred years ago, Queen Elizabeth I chartered the English East India Company to compete with the Dutch for the valuable spice trade of the East Indies. Ships of "John Company" appeared in western India in 1608 and immediately set out to establish their naval superiority over the Portuguese who had arrived another hundred years earlier. The Company moved to Bengal in 1651 with the establishment of a factory beside the river Hooghly. That same year it obtained an official order from the great Mughal Emperor Aurangzeb granting exemption from custom duties. This exemption offered the British traders a decided commercial advantage over other European nations and even over native traders. More importantly, it gave the British a cause to defend their base with military strength if needed.

In August 1690, under the leadership of the legendary Job Charnock, the Company erected a few huts on the Hooghly that were destined to grow into the second city of the British Empire. In 1696, the Calcutta settlement was buttressed by the building of Fort William. The first half of the eighteenth century saw restoration of firm rule in Bengal under a line of Nawabs from Murshid Quli Khan to Alivardi Khan. During this period, British expansion remained under check.

With the advent of Shiraj-ud-doula, everything changed.

In *A Flight of Green Parrots*, the character of this ill-starred King of Bengal is real. I have animated Shiraj through the many legends that celebrate his brief but explosive tenure astride the world's stage. The destroyed British citadel of Fort William, the Black and White Towns of early Calcutta, Bagh Bazaar, Perrins Redoubt, the historic town of Nadia, Shiraj's palace of a thousand doors, Colonel Robert Clive, all existed as described.

All other characters and places in this book are drawn from my imagination.

The character of Pauline requires a word of explanation.

A Flight of Green Parrots is set in the early days of exploration before the English became rulers. English women of the time either accompanied a husband to India or came there looking for one. In those days the uppermost strata of Indian men, kings, princes, ambassadors and bankers interacted on equal footing with the then-not-so-dominant foreigners. It was thus possible for an impressionable married woman who held her husband in revulsion, to have social dialog with an elite native, for this was before the repressive and prudish Victorian ways of colonial society.

Calcutta has grown into one of the largest cities of the world. It has a new name, Kolkata, which is how Bengalis have called it always. Kolkata has rapidly modernized with the rest of India. A new Fort William, built by Clive after his victory over Shiraj-ud-doula in 1757, dominates the Hooghly strand three miles downstream of the destroyed garrison in our story. In the business center of the metropolis, beset by turbulent traffic and massed pedestrians, the original St. John's Church remains an oasis of peace. Its steeple has been repaired. Across from St. John's, looking down on the Great Tank which no longer holds fish, is the monumental edifice of Calcutta's General Post Office. Just behind the frenetic GPO is a small parking area where mail delivery vans come and go. In a corner of this parking area still exists the dark room where, allegedly, 123 English prisoners died on the night in 1756, which earned it notoriety as the Black Hole of Calcutta.

Allegedly?

The Black Hole of Calcutta is a sensitive and highly controversial subject. British schoolchildren read of it in their history books. An authoritative historical treatment of the incident can be found in Noel Barber's excellent work, *Black Hole of Calcutta.*

Then why allegedly?

The original account of the event that attained infamy as the Black Hole was reported by James Holwell, magistrate of the defeated garrison. It was adopted by English historians after Clive vanquished Shiraj-ud-doula in the Battle of Plassey. On the other hand, not one Persian or Bengali historical work of the time - and there are many - mentions the event, and numerous Indian historians contend the incident was concocted to explain away the ignominy of first defeat of an overseas English garrison.

Is accepted history always written by the victorious?

The following translation by the author from Purnendu Patri's *Glimpses of Old Calcutta,* is illustrative of the on-going debate:

"The memorial column of the Black Hole was erected by Holwell himself, with his own money, and not out of enthusiasm or funds of the Company. During the governorship of [Warren] Hastings, in 1821, the column was broken to build the Customs House. In 1902, Lord Curzon, on the throne of [British] India, found the account of the Howell affair while digging through old papers. The ancient tragedy affected him deeply. At the junction of Clive Street and Dalhousie Square, at exactly the same spot, he rebuilt the column with pure marble. Then began the era of the freedom movement, and the attention of [nationalist leader] Subhas Chandra Bose was drawn to the ignominy. He had it dug out and thrown into the cemetery of St. John's."

Dipak Basu
November 2003